Pr...

# DEAD CANARIES DON'T SING

"Clever, fast-paced and well-plotted, *Dead Canaries Don't Sing* stars an appealing heroine and furry sidekicks sure to enchant pet lovers. Five paws up for Cynthia Baxter's first in the *Reigning Cats & Dogs* series."
—Carolyn Hart

"Dead canaries don't sing, but you will after reading this terrific mystery!"—Rita Mae Brown, *New York Times* bestselling author

"A little bird told me to read this mystery, which is awfully good. For the record, I would shred any canary who insulted me."—Sneaky Pie Brown, *New York Times* bestselling cat

"*Dead Canaries Don't Sing* is top dog, the cat's pajamas, and the paws that refresh all rolled into one un-fur-gettable mystery entertainment."
—Sarah Graves

"Loads of fun! Baxter's veterinary sleuth and her menagerie of animal companions are a great way to spend an afternoon. So pull up a chair and dive in."
—T. J. MacGregor, Edgar Award winner for *Out of Sight*

"An auspicious debut... Messages, murder and a menagerie of odd animals are along for the fun."
—*Mystery Scene*

"Charmingly humorous . . . [Baxter is] funny without being fussy. Along with lovable Jessica and her menagerie, the author has created a subtle yet creepy antagonist whose unmasking is as intense as it is surprising."—*Romantic Times*

"A truly refreshing read that moved the plot right along. I'm looking forward to more in this new series."
—*Rendezvous*

"A lighthearted mystery with a strong convincing plot. Recommended."—*I Love a Mystery* newsletter

"Baxter's lighthearted, enjoyable mystery is an entertaining debut featuring a likable menagerie of characters, a few surprising plot twists, and a touch of romance." —*Lansing State Journal*

# Putting On the Dog

## A *Reigning Cats & Dogs* Mystery

## Cynthia Baxter

BANTAM BOOKS

PUTTING ON THE DOG
A Bantam Book / August 2004

Published by
Bantam Dell
A division of Random House, Inc.
New York, New York

All rights reserved
Copyright © 2004 by Cynthia Baxter
Cover art by Bob Guisti

No part of this book may be reproduced or transmitted in any
form or by any means, electronic or mechanical, including
photocopying, recording, or by any information storage and
retrieval system, without the written permission of the
publisher, except where permitted by law. For information
address: Bantam Books, New York, New York.

If you purchased this book without a cover, you should be
aware that this book is stolen property. It was reported as
"unsold and destroyed" to the publisher, and neither the author
nor the publisher has received any payment for this "stripped
book."

Bantam Books and the rooster colophon are registered trademarks
of Random House, Inc.

ISBN 0-553-58642-4

Manufactured in the United States of America
Published simultaneously in Canada

OPM   10 9 8 7 6 5 4 3 2 1

To Jesse

# Acknowledgments

I would like to express my gratitude to the many people who assisted me in writing this book, overwhelming me with their generosity, their creativity, and above all, their patience:

Dawn Rella, Scott Rella, and Roy Curnuck of Ice Sculpture Designs, Inc. of Deer Park, Long Island, New York;

Martha S. Gearhart, D.V.M. and the staff of the Pleasant Valley Animal Hospital in Pleasant Valley, New York;

Dorothy Hayes, V.M.D., Judy Lombardi, V.M.D., and the staff of the Corner Animal Hospital in Setauket, Long Island, New York;

Dan and Amy Wagner, Lisa Pulitzer, and of course, my gem of an agent, Faith Hamlin, and my editor from heaven, Caitlin Alexander.

# A Note to Readers

*Putting On the Dog* is a work of fiction, and all names and characters are the product of the author's imagination. Any resemblance to actual events, organizations, or persons, living or dead, is coincidental. Although some real Long Island places are mentioned, all are used fictitiously.

# Putting On
# the Dog

# Chapter 1

"All men are intrinsically rascals, and I am only sorry that not being a dog, I can't bite them."

—Lord Byron

**D**amn you, Marcus Scruggs!" I grumbled, leaning closer to the windshield of my van and peering through the sheeting rain. "Be honest, guys: Am I totally nuts?"

Max and Lou, scrambling around on the seat beside me, offered no opinion about my sanity. They were too busy acting like unruly preschoolers, wrestling for the space nearest the window. It was a close contest. Lou, my one-eyed Dalmatian, had longer legs. But Max, being a terrier, was infinitely more determined.

I sighed. Somehow, this wasn't the way I'd pictured my arrival in the Bromptons, a cluster of posh seaside communities famous for their palatial summer estates, spectacular white-sanded beaches, and four-star restaurants featuring twelve-dollar desserts. Between the area's attributes and the fact that it was less than two hours from Manhattan, it wasn't surprising that the movers and shakers from New York City and Los Angeles had claimed Long Island's East End as their own. For decades, the Bromptons had been known as the summer playground of movie stars, rock legends, writers, and artists, as well as the agents, managers, and executives whose names weren't as well-known, but whose summer homes were at least as large.

So it hadn't been difficult for Marcus Scruggs, a fellow Long Island veterinarian, to sell me on the idea of spending the last week of June standing in for him at a charity dog show, answering pet owners' questions at the "Ask The Vet" booth. I could practically hear his voice, floating over the phone as low and smooth as an FM disc jockey's: "I'm telling you, Popper, I'm talking Glamour—with a capital G."

But in the pouring rain, the area's main east–west route, Sunset Highway, looked more like Main Street in a ghost town. Few cars crawled along the puddle-strewn thoroughfare, and fewer yet stood parked outside the pool-supply shops and imported-tile boutiques lining its edge. Even the scrubby trees and shrubs that dotted the two-lane highway looked pathetic.

Gritting my teeth, I veered around a body of water only slightly smaller than Lake Superior. I was no stranger to the Bromptons. As a vet who makes house calls in my clinic-on-wheels, I routinely travel all over Long Island. That includes visiting clients who live on what's popularly called the South Fork, the lower of the two fish tails that make up the Island's eastern end. And Marcus had given me detailed directions for getting to the estate of someone named Wiener, the man who'd volunteered to put me up during the weeklong event. I'd followed his directions to the letter, but I still couldn't find Darby Lane. Of course, not being able to make out the street signs through the pouring rain didn't help.

I clamped down on the brake when I spotted a yellow-and-white striped awning, a sure indication I was approaching a farm stand. *Somebody* around here had to know where the Wiener estate was, and it seemed as likely a place as any. I made a sharp turn, sending Max and Lou collapsing against each other in a heap.

"You guys okay?" I asked as my van rocked along a badly pitted parking lot that no one had ever bothered to pave—no doubt, a self-conscious attempt at capturing the rural charm of Tuscany or the South of France.

I didn't need an answer. By the time I pulled into a space, the two of them were already climbing all over each other again, making little yelping sounds and occasionally nipping each other playfully in the butt. I was glad somebody was having fun.

I stared out at the rain morosely, wondering why I hadn't brought along an umbrella, and with a loud sigh of resignation, I opened the door of my van.

"Stay!" I instructed my two canines. They paused in their shenanigans, both shooting me surprised looks that said they wouldn't even have *considered* venturing out in weather like this.

"You guys are much too smart," I muttered. "You make the humans do all the dirty work."

I picked my way across the dirt parking lot, noticing that it was quickly turning into a *mud* parking lot. I regretted dressing up. I'd made a few Sunday morning emergency calls in my usual work ensemble, khaki trousers and a polo shirt embroidered with "Jessica Popper, D.V.M." But before corralling Max and Lou into my twenty-six-foot van and embarking on the drive to the East End, a good hour-and-a-half trip from my hometown of Joshua's Hollow on Long Island's North Shore, I'd changed into an outfit I felt better suited my destination. I'd donned a pale blue silk blouse and black rayon trousers, the finest that Bloomingdale's "Clearance" rack had to offer. I only hoped the drops of rain that were turning them from solid colors into polka dots wouldn't have a lasting effect.

I scurried past the displays that ran along the front of the farm stand, mounds of vegetables and fruit so large and richly colored they looked like they were made of wax: bright orange-red tomatoes the size of baseballs, slick dark green cucumbers that could have doubled as baseball bats, and an impressive selection of exotic-looking fruits that had probably been flown in from so far away that they'd amassed more frequent flyer miles than I had.

"Excuse me!" I called to the clerk standing behind the displays, protected from the rain by the awning.

"Be with you in a minute," she returned coolly. She turned her attention back to her customer, a woman who'd had the good sense to bring an umbrella *and* wear a slicker.

I glanced around frantically, looking for some friendly local who might be willing to help. And then I let out a screech.

Before I knew what was happening, I was blasted with water. It was as if someone—someone not very nice—had suddenly turned a hose on me.

"Wha-a-a!..." I sputtered.

I stood frozen to the spot, gradually realizing that the front of my silk shirt was splotched with huge, grimy wet spots, while my stylishly loose pants clung damply to my thighs. I could feel cold rivulets dripping off my face and down my neck. My dark blonde hair was plastered around my head, no doubt giving me the distinctive look of a sea otter. When I ran my fingers through the soggy strands in an attempt at pushing them off my face, I actually encountered clumps of mud.

I blinked a few times, struggling to get the water out of my eyes. As soon as I did, I saw that a low-slung sports car the same color as the ripe tomatoes on display had just pulled into a parking space less than five feet in front of me. Because it was going ridiculously fast, its wheels had thrown up a tremendous spray of water.

I just stared as the door of the Ferrari opened. The driver was dressed in torn jeans and a T-shirt. A Dodgers baseball cap was pulled down low over his eyes, which were hidden behind a pair of sunglasses. With his shaggy hair and a sorry attempt at a beard, he looked like he'd stolen the car, not earned it.

I plunked myself right in front of him.

He peered up at me over his shades. "Gee, did I do that?"

"No, I'm on my way to a wet T-shirt contest," I shot back. "I thought accessorizing with mud would be a nice touch."

"Hey, I'm really sorry. I hope you'll let me pay the dry-cleaning bill."

"That's the least you can do. But if you don't mind, I'd rather not discuss this in the pouring rain."

He gestured toward the seat next to him. "Climb in."

"Thanks, but my mother taught me never to get into cars with strange men."

"Good advice. Unless you happen to be in the middle of a downpour."

I stood firm.

"Okay, have it your way." He climbed out of the car, grabbed my hand, and pulled me after him. I would have protested except for the fact that he actually seemed to know where he was going.

I was so busy following him that I didn't pay much attention to the Mercedes that had just driven up beside us. When a wiry man in tight jeans and a black silk shirt jumped out, I just assumed he'd come in search of vegetables big enough to stage a baseball game.

The Ferrari driver led me through the farm stand's side entrance, bringing us into a small room. It contained a few shelves lined with household basics like mango chutney and wasabi rice crackers.

He turned to me. "How much do you think is fair? To get your clothes cleaned, I mean."

"Isn't there something else I deserve?"

His expression tightened. "Don't tell me you're planning to hit me up for pain and suffering! Look, if you're one of those people who's going to start screaming about your lawyer—"

I tossed my head indignantly. "Actually, I was looking for an apology. Or is that too much to expect from somebody who drives like this was the Indy 500—"

Suddenly, the man I'd seen get out of the Mercedes appeared in the doorway, holding an impressively large, professional-looking camera. He immediately started snapping pictures, one after another.

I was so startled I didn't know what to think. But the Ferrari driver appeared to have figured it out immediately.

"Get the hell out of here!" he yelled. "You people are leeches—and you're the worst, Barnett! Can't I even go shopping for food without you harassing me?"

The more he screamed and waved his arms, the more the man with the camera snapped away.

The Ferrari driver finally turned his back on the photographer. "Look, I'm getting out of here," he told me. "Funny, but I've suddenly lost my appetite." He reached into his pocket, took out a wad of bills, and pulled off two twenties. "Here. This should take care of it. And I really am sorry."

He thrust the cash into my hand and dashed out. The man with the camera took off after him.

I was still trying to figure out what I'd just witnessed, when the clerk who'd blown me off earlier came over, snaking her way between the aisles.

"Did you get his autograph?" she asked, her eyes glittering excitedly.

"Who?"

"Shawn Elliot, of course!"

"That was him? In the Ferrari?"

She looked at me as if I'd just climbed out of a UFO. "You didn't recognize him?"

I shook my head. I knew who he was, of course. So did every other red-blooded woman between the ages of twelve and a hundred and twelve, at least if she'd been to the movies in the past five years. I stuck my head out the doorway, trying to get another look. But he'd already hightailed it out of the parking lot.

"He didn't look the way he does in the movies," I told the clerk with a sheepish shrug.

She nodded knowingly. "He does that on purpose. When he's out here, I mean. During the summer, he tries to throw off his star persona. You know, grow a beard, dress all grungy . . . act like he's a regular person."

"How do you know all this?"

"I read it in the *Stargazer*," she replied, looking smug. "Besides, that's exactly what I intend to do. After I get discovered, I mean." She leaned closer. "I'm not really a clerk, you know. I'm an actress, waiting for my big break."

I sighed. I'd been in the Bromptons for less than twenty minutes, and I already felt as if I'd made one of the biggest mistakes of my life. Famous actors who drove Ferraris and wore ratty jeans, photographers who leaped out from behind the cucumbers, cashiers who were really movie stars in disguise . . . it was more than I could handle.

I was beginning to wonder how I'd ever get through the next few days.

•  •  •

As I climbed back into my van, Max and Lou predictably acted as if I'd been away on a Himalayan trek instead of spending ten minutes getting directions and getting wet.

"Hey, Maxie-Max. Come here, Louie-Lou." I patiently

allowed my canines to slobber over me. As usual, Max got the best seat in the house, my lap. His four paws dug into my thighs like cleats. When you're a Westie—meaning you have the face of a teddy bear—you can get away with that kind of thing. Lou held back, nuzzling me questioningly and constantly glancing over at Max. My leggy, sixty-six-pound Dalmatian is in the habit of deferring to his twenty-pound stepbrother, even though Max is only the size of a large loaf of bread. Lou's scars from his original owner go far beyond his missing eye.

"Okay, guys," I finally said, shooing them over to their side of the front seat and shifting my van into gear. "Let's try this again."

I pulled out of the parking lot, then carefully followed the directions the clerk had scrawled on the back of a Ralph Lauren receipt. Left onto Sunset Highway, a sharp right at the Antiques Barn ...

"Yes!" I breathed, when a road sign reading "Darby Lane" suddenly emerged from the gray mist. After making another right, I drove to the end of the street. I had no idea if the clerk at the farm stand was any good at acting, but she'd turned out to be great at directions. Thanks to her, I'd finally found the Wiener estate.

Unfortunately, a wrought-iron fence that looked like a leftover from Leavenworth separated me from it.

"Damn!" I muttered.

Through the rain splashing across my windshield, I could see something white clinging to the big lock smack in the middle of the gate. I hoped it was a note.

By that point, even the prospect of standing in the unrelenting downpour no longer fazed me, so I got out and retrieved the soggy piece of paper. The ink was so badly smeared it was barely readable.

" 'Gate is locked.' " I read aloud. "Now *there's* a useful bit of information. 'Use side entrance. Come to the house for the guest house key. Thanks.' "

Sure enough, the side entrance was open. As I drove along the curving driveway, I spotted a small building nestled in the trees in the back corner of the sprawling grounds. The guesthouse, no doubt. It looked like a cottage out of a fairy tale, the kind of place the Seven Dwarfs had lived in.

The main house was an entirely different story. I hadn't seen anything that grand since my high school trip to Paris, which included a day at Versailles: white columns, dramatic marble steps, and enough square footage to spark a revolution.

I parked in the driveway, gave Max and Lou the usual warning about behaving themselves or else, and tromped across the lawn. As I neared the front door, I jumped, startled by a black cat who suddenly leaped out of the bushes. He snarled at me, then skittered across my path and disappeared into a clump of rhododendrons.

Not a good sign, I thought grimly, wondering what else could possibly go wrong.

I rang the bell, suddenly self-conscious. Glancing down, I saw that not only was I covered with muddy streaks; the see-through effect of my wet clothing really did make me look like a competitor in a wet T-shirt contest.

Given the formal look of the house, I didn't expect Mr. Wiener to have much of a sense of humor. As I heard someone inside unlock the front door, I prepared an apology.

I never got to use it.

"It's *you*!" I gasped.

Standing on the other side of the doorway was the man who was responsible for my appearance in the first place—the person the clerk had insisted was Shawn Elliot.

"I guess I could say the same." He didn't look

particularly happy to see me. "You haven't had second thoughts about calling your lawyer, have you?"

It took me a few seconds to figure out what he meant. "Oh, *that*. No, I don't even have a lawyer. You've got nothing to worry about."

"Good. You'd be surprised how many people think meeting up with somebody a little bit famous means their big payday."

*A little bit famous?* My eyes drifted past him to the huge movie posters that decorated the entryway. Each one advertised a different Shawn Elliot blockbuster, box-office hits that had made him the fantasy love object of a large percentage of the world's female population.

He just stood there, looking at me expectantly.

"I read the note," I said. "About the key to the guest-house?"

He frowned. "Are you associated with Dr. Scruggs?"

"Didn't anyone tell you?"

"Tell me what?"

"Marcus—Dr. Scruggs—isn't going to be the veterinarian at the dog show. I am."

He just blinked.

"I'm Jessica Popper. *Dr.* Jessica Popper."

"Oh, boy." Shawn shook his head. "Now I feel *completely* ridiculous. Not only did I zap you with mud back at that farm stand, but I'm leaving you standing in the rain because of some administrative glitch nobody bothered to tell me about."

"It's all right. If I could just have the key—"

"Please, come in. At this point, I'd consider it a personal favor."

I only hesitated for a moment before following him into the house. I figured that just getting inside would make me feel more like a human being and less like a water mammal. Instead, the air-conditioning, combined

with my sopping wet discount designer outfit, made me
so cold I started to shake.

Shawn noticed immediately. "We have to get you out
of those wet clothes."

"I'm fine. As soon as I get the key, I'll—"

"There's a guest room at the top of those stairs, with a
pool robe hanging behind the door. Why don't you put it
on? You must be so uncomfortable."

At that point, the chance to put on something dry was
hard to turn down. I climbed up to the second floor and,
just as he'd promised, found a bedroom at the top of the
stairs. It looked like something out of a design magazine,
a perfectly coordinated medley of soothing earth tones
and rich, textured fabrics that made me want to curl up
and go to sleep.

Instead, I closed the door and began unbuttoning
my blouse. But something felt wrong. Maybe I was
simply a little overwhelmed by all the bizarre events of
the day, but I had the distinct feeling I was being
watched.

*You're just paranoid,* I told myself.

But I kept glancing around the room nervously as I
slipped out of my shirt and pants, then pulled on the
white terry-cloth robe I found on a hook. It was as thick
as shag carpeting, monogrammed with a swirling "S. E."
on the pocket. As I did, I could have sworn I felt somebody's eyes on me. I was even convinced I could hear
breathing. But there was no one in sight.

It wasn't until I opened the door so I could go down-
stairs that I discovered I'd been right all along. The Peeping Tom who had watched the entire strip show slunk
out of his hiding place under the bed, then tried to slip
past me without getting caught.

But I was too smart for a bulldog.

"Oh, no, you don't." I grabbed him by his collar.
"Think you're pretty clever, do you?"

"Is that Rufus?" Shawn yelled up from the first floor. "Damn! I don't know how he does it, but every time a woman's getting undressed around here, he manages to get a front-row seat."

"Is that true, you rascal?" I demanded.

Rufus just looked at me, as innocent as could be. But I was certain I saw a twinkle in the jowly beast's deep brown eyes before he toddled off, lumbering down the stairs toward the safety of his master's side.

"Sorry about that," Shawn called out. "I swear I had no idea he was up there."

"Is anybody else lurking under beds and in dark corners?" I descended the staircase, carrying my wet clothes in a bundle so I wouldn't drip on the expensive-looking carpeting. "Like maybe Mr. Wiener?"

"I'm afraid you're looking at him."

"Excuse me?"

"Wiener is my real name. Shawn Elliot Wiener. When I started acting, I was advised to drop the last part." He grimaced. "Think about it. Can you imagine somebody named 'Wiener' doing a love scene in a movie? 'Mr. Wiener' sounds more like a high school math teacher— which is probably what I would have become if the acting thing hadn't worked out."

"I see your point," I said as I followed him into what looked like a den. "By the way, thanks for letting me use your guesthouse."

Shawn shrugged. "It's the least I can do for such a good cause. I've been a strong supporter of the SPCA for a long time.

"Besides," he added, "I figured it might help Rufus win a blue ribbon. Not that he couldn't do it on his own. Right, boy?"

He crouched down in front of the animal at his feet, as squat and sturdy as a footstool, and scratched his neck vigorously.

"*Wuzza, wuzza, wuzza,*" he said in a funny low voice that was almost a growl. "Who's the best boy in the world? Who's the *best boy*?"

I had to admit, it was pretty endearing—not only to me, but also to the fifty-pound lump of dog. Rufus lay with his four short legs splayed out on the Oriental carpet, grunting and wheezing and obviously in a state of ecstasy. Shawn looked pretty happy, too. I suspected this was a side of the Hollywood heartthrob that few people ever got to see.

"I guess you can tell I'm pretty crazy about this guy." Shawn glanced up at me, his cheeks flushed. "He's one of the few individuals I know who likes me for myself."

"Or else because you fill his food bowl every night."

He laughed. "At least I know he's not just kissing up to me because he wants to impress his friends with the fact that he knows a real live Hollywood actor. And he never nags me about introducing him to some casting director."

"Maybe he should. He's got real star quality."

"You think?" He beamed proudly. "I guess I don't have it in me to be a pushy stage father. I'd rather protect my loved ones from the heartbreaks of this business. So for now, Rufus is destined to remain just another ordinary house pet."

"Except when it comes to the dog show."

"Hey, every parent has to show off some time. Maybe I don't want Rufus's name in lights, but that doesn't mean I don't want him to be appreciated for the glorious creature he truly is."

Much to the bulldog's dismay, Shawn stopped scratching and stood up. "I don't suppose you have any pull, do you?"

"Me? Naw. I'm just the hired help."

"Too bad. It'd be fun trying to get you on my good side."

Now *my* cheeks were flushed. I was sure of it. How could I not be, when Shawn Elliot was flashing me the boyish grin that, along with his startlingly blue eyes, had gotten him voted "America's Sexiest Man" three years running in *T.V. Guide*'s annual poll?

I quickly tried to come up with some other topic of conversation.

"By the way," I asked, "who was that obnoxious man taking all those pictures of you at the farm stand?"

"That idiot? Devon Barnett."

The expression on my face must have reflected my confusion.

"You've never heard of him?"

I shook my head.

"Probably because you have too much sense to read those ridiculous supermarket tabloids."

"You mean those rags at the check-out counters with headlines like 'Alien Eats Milwaukee for Breakfast'? or 'Hundred-Year-Old Woman Gives Birth to Kittens'? "

"Exactly. Or 'Shawn Elliot Assaults Animal Doctor with $300,000 Car.' "

My eyes grew as big as headlights. "Is that how much your car cost?"

He didn't answer.

"Devon Barnett is one of the sleaziest celebrity photographers—paparazzi—that ever lived," Shawn went on. "In fact, it's safe to say he's one of the most hated men in Hollywood, not to mention a few other places like New York and London. Here, let me show you some of his handiwork."

He reached into a desk drawer and pulled out a stack of newspaper clippings. They were all the front pages of supermarket tabloids. Each one sported accusatory headlines, and underneath, there was invariably a photograph that was just as incriminating. In every case, the photo credit "Devon Barnett" was printed in tiny letters.

"Shawn Fights Battle of the Bottle!" the first headline read. Splashed across the page was a picture of Shawn, dressed in a bathrobe that looked just like the one I was wearing. His eyes were barely open, and he was cradling an armful of empty liquor bottles.

"The jerk snapped that the morning after I held a huge fund-raiser for the Red Cross," Shawn explained angrily. "I was taking those out to the recycling bin."

"But don't all those photographers—the paparazzi—do pretty much the same thing?"

"Up to a point. But Devon Barnett is the absolute worst. He has no sense of fair play, no notion of what it means to respect other people's boundaries. Here, look at this one."

He leafed through the pile, picking out one I'd barely paid attention to. The photograph showed Shawn scowling at a group of crazed fans huddled at the bottom of some steps, frantically thrusting pens and papers in his face.

"Shawn Elliot: 'I Have No Time For Foolish Fans!'" the headline read.

"Do you know where that was taken?" he asked.

I shook my head.

"No, of course not. That's the whole point. The answer is, outside a funeral home. I was coming out of my father's wake, for God's sake."

"I think I'm beginning to understand," I told him.

"It's not even that Barnett captures people at their very worst moments and then twists them into something they're not," Shawn continued. "I mean, that's bad enough. But what's even more despicable is the fact that he'll stop at nothing to get a photo. I've caught him sleeping in a deck chair beside my pool, waiting for me all night. Once I found him sitting in the backseat of my car at a four-star restaurant. Turns out he'd bribed the parking attendant.

"Then there was the time I was really sick. I'd been in seclusion for almost two weeks. All kinds of rumors were springing up, since one of my movies had just come out and I was expected to do the usual round of talk shows. Somehow, Barnett got hold of my private number. He called me and told me he'd just hit Rufus with his car, right in front of my house. I raced outside, half-crazed. Rufus was perfectly fine, of course. But Barnett got exactly what he wanted: a picture of me looking like a madman, running across the lawn in my underwear."

I took a moment to appreciate the fact that I wasn't famous or important. I hadn't realized what an invasion of privacy it was, having someone devote his entire life to capturing your worst moments on film so they could be plastered over every newsstand and supermarket checkout in the country.

Rufus picked that moment to waddle over to Shawn and nudge him. I guess he'd decided it was his turn to be the focus of his master's attention again.

Which made me remember I had some canine lovables of my own.

"My dogs!" I cried. "I mean, I have two of them, a Westie and a Dalmatian, and right now they're probably wondering if I've deserted them forever. If I could just get the key to the guesthouse—"

"Sorry. I know I got carried away. Just thinking about that Barnett character makes my blood boil."

He got the key, then walked me to the door.

"Keep that robe as long as you need it. Make yourself comfortable, and let me know if you need anything."

"I'm sure I'll be fine," I told him.

"And remember, it's just me and Rufus, all alone in this big house," Shawn said. He hit me again with that grin. "Don't be a stranger, okay?"

• • •

*Oh*, boy, I thought as I fumbled with the key, trying to figure out the intricacies of the lock on the guesthouse's front door. My heart was actually fluttering. I felt like the heroine in a Victorian romance novel instead of a serious, hardworking medical professional.

I glanced down at Max and Lou, who were frolicking beside me, thrilled over the prospect of a brand-new place to smell. As always, they had the power to bring me back to reality. If nothing else, marveling over their unwavering joie de vivre was a truly sobering experience.

They shot inside the moment I wrestled the door open, darting around like a SWAT team on a mission. I took a more cautious approach, flipping on a light switch and surveying the place before passing judgment.

The tiny bungalow was charming. From the doorway, I could see a small living room, a kitchenette off to one side, and a single bedroom in back. The cottage had clearly been decorated by a pro, and every inch screamed "Summer House!"

But the pastel colors, fluffy throw rugs, and white wicker furniture weren't what were making me feel so light-headed. It was that stupid heart of mine, beating as wildly as if I'd just belted down a double cappuccino.

It suddenly seemed like a good idea to call Nick.

I reached for the phone hanging on the kitchen wall, then hesitated. One of the main reasons I'd agreed to fill in for Marcus was that a week in the Bromptons had sounded like the perfect romantic getaway. Nick and I hadn't been away together for more than nine months, since the previous September—and that trip had been nothing short of a disaster. He'd caught me completely off guard by producing the engagement ring he'd packed along with his 30-SPF sunblock and his rubber flip-flops. True to form, I'd freaked—so badly that our relationship had ended. At least, for a while.

Since then, we'd decided to try being a couple again—

only this time, taking things a little more slowly. So far, so good. The past few months had been blissful.

But they'd also been busy. Between my veterinary practice and Nick's job as a private investigator, we'd had to work hard to squeeze in our dinner dates and our weekends together at either my cottage or his apartment. And with Nick starting law school in the fall, it didn't look as if our schedules were going to lighten up anytime soon. A short vacation on Long Island's East End sounded ideal—even if it did include spending a few hours at a charity dog show every day.

Of course, I'd had no idea Nick would back out at the last minute.

Even though I still hadn't completely forgiven him, the memory of Shawn Elliot's blue eyes and irresistible grin prompted me to grab the phone. First I dialed his office. No answer, just the usual recorded message explaining that Nick Burby, private investigator, was not available to take my call.

I put down the phone long enough to disengage an embroidered hand towel from Lou's jaws, then tried Nick's apartment in Port Townsend. And got another machine. I tried once more, this time dialing his cell phone. And endured one more recording.

I was on my own, with nothing to do until the fund-raiser's kick-off dinner this evening. I suddenly felt a stab of loneliness, that hollow feeling that comes from being in a new place where you don't know a soul.

Except that I did know a soul. One and only one. Shawn Elliot, who'd made a point of telling me not to be a stranger.

I suddenly had another good idea: taking a shower. I decided I'd better make it a cold one.

# Chapter 2

"One hundred people can sit together peacefully, but two dogs in the same place will pick a fight."

—Kurdistan Jewish saying

I was relieved that the organizers of the charity fund-raiser had the foresight to plan an opening-night event to keep us dog-show groupies out of trouble. I also hoped the kick-off party would provide me with my first taste of what the excitement of the Bromptons was all about.

As I cruised along Ocean Spray Drive in my clinic-on-wheels a few hours later, I wondered how I'd recognize the estate at which tonight's gala was being held. In this town, mansions were as common as telephone poles. But in the distance, I spotted two towering torches, one on each side of an open gate, glowing invitingly against the darkening sky. I had a pretty good idea I'd reached my destination.

After checking in with a guard who crossed my name off a list, I drove along a curving driveway. Looming ahead was a huge white tent that was bigger than any I'd ever seen—at least, outside a circus. The house next to it made Shawn Elliot's place look like a starter home.

A young man in a uniform flagged me down. He opened the door of my van and peered inside. "A veterinarian, huh?" he asked nervously. "Anything alive in here?"

"Just me." I hopped out and handed over the keys. "Take good care of it. It might look like a school bus with an identity crisis to you, but to me it's a dream come true. Not to mention my livelihood."

"You got it, Doc."

I watched him drive it away toward the section of the football field-sized lawn that had been converted into a parking area. The area was already filling up with cars that probably cost at least as much as my mobile veterinary unit—and they didn't even come with their own autoclave.

I felt a pang of fondness as I watched my beloved vehicle bounce along the grass. I still experienced a little thrill every time I was hit with the fact that I really had my own veterinary business. Not only did my mobile services unit give me complete autonomy; it kept me from having to spend my days cooped up inside in order to live out my lifelong goal of helping animals.

Of course, tonight my beloved van didn't exactly blend in with the other vehicles crammed together on the grass. It really was the size of a small school bus. But instead of bright yellow, it was painted white with blue letters on the door:

**REIGNING CATS AND DOGS**

**MOBILE VETERINARY SERVICES**
**LARGE AND SMALL ANIMAL**
**631-555-PETS**

A nice contrast to the gleaming DeLoreans, the dignified Rolls Royces, and the low-slung Lamborghinis, I decided with pride. *Definitely* lends a little character to the
place.

As I neared the tent, I switched gears, suddenly obsessing over my choice of outfit for the evening. Since my
fashion statement runs along the lines of chukka boots
and my customized "Jessica Popper, D.V.M." polo
shirts, I felt a little strange decked out in a flowered sundress and a pair of sandals with ridiculously impractical
two-inch heels.

I was hoping that I wouldn't stick out as much as my
van, when out of the corner of my eye, I caught sight of
someone lurking in the shadows. Someone much taller
than either a bulldog with an eye for the ladies or a half-
starved black cat.

Adrenaline pumped through my body as I checked
around. But there was no one else nearby. I was alone.

*Paranoia*, I scolded myself. After all, this is the
Bromptons. Not exactly a high crime area.

Almost immediately, someone leaped out from behind
a tree, and I was blinded by a flash of light.

For a few horrifying seconds, I couldn't see. Then I realized what had just happened—and who was responsible.

"You again!" I yelped. "How dare you?"

The man I recognized as Devon Barnett scowled. "I
thought you might be somebody." Shaking his head disapprovingly, he disappeared back into the shadows.

I just stood there, shaking with anger. I didn't know
which made me more furious: having been subjected to
my second assault with a deadly camera of the day ... or
being written off as a nobody.

*Take deep breaths*, I instructed myself. Don't let some
professional stalker ruin your evening.

My heart was still pounding with jackhammer speed

as I stepped into the tent. As if that wasn't bad enough, bursts of light kept flashing before my eyes.

But I forced myself to focus on what was going on around me. I realized I'd finally gotten to the "Glamour with a capital G" part.

The giant white tent was just the beginning. Beneath it, on the grass, was the setting for an elegant dinner party, complete with huge bouquets of flowers, glowing candles, and strings of tiny white lights glimmering in the branches of trees that spurted out of huge terra-cotta pots. Dozens of round tables, each outfitted with place settings for eight, fanned out from a podium. An enormous banner printed with "Support the SPCA!" served as a backdrop for the stage set up in one corner. I took it all in, aware that my eyes were as big as the dinner plates adorning the tables.

Thank you, Marcus Scruggs, I thought, for giving me an opportunity to see how the other half—or at least the other one-tenth of a percent—lives.

The downside was that I wasn't sure what to do with myself. Few of the other guests had shown up on time, and the catering staff was still working at a frantic pace, hurrying to get things ready. Young men and women in black pants and white shirts embroidered with "Foodies, Inc." rushed around, putting the final touches on the preparations.

I wandered around the estate, trying not to appear too awed by its grandeur. The vast lawn that stretched back beyond the party tent overlooked a tremendous crescent-shaped bay. While a few other estates bordered the inlet, most of the shoreline was land I knew was part of a wildlife preserve, hundreds of acres of protected wetlands and woodlands that served as a habitat for migratory birds and other endangered species. Aside from an occasional storage shed, the entire area remained undeveloped, providing whoever had the good fortune to live in this mansion with a spectacular, unspoiled view.

Which was probably one reason the owner had dotted the property with wooden lawn chairs, hammocks, and even a charming gazebo. The white structure was set high atop a pedestal. Between its unusual height and its intricate latticework, it looked like a giant wedding cake.

I sauntered over and climbed the steps. For tonight's event, the gazebo had been converted into a temple for worshipping the hors d'oeuvre. A long table draped in white linen ran along the back, covered with platters of exotic-looking cheeses, raw vegetables cut into flower shapes, and enough shrimp to keep an entire flock of seagulls happy for a week.

But the spread of glorious food paled beside the grouping of magnificent ice sculptures towering above it. Famous dogs from television and film had been carved from huge blocks of ice, each one easily three or four feet high. In the center, Snoopy lay across the roof of his doghouse. To his left, Lady and the Tramp eyed each other longingly as they shared a strand of crystal-clear spaghetti. They were straddled by Lassie and Rin Tin Tin, both poised to save someone's life. Benji was curled up in front, managing to look cute and furry even though he was really one giant ice cube.

I stood in front of the display for a long time, admiring the sculptor's handiwork and the attention to detail that had gone into these disposable decorations. I would have stayed longer, but suddenly my nostrils started to burn. I wrinkled my nose and sniffled, my usual reaction to the unpleasant smell of cigarette smoke.

It seemed to be wafting up from below. I peered over the railing and saw a man standing in the shadows, lighting up. I wouldn't have recognized him if it hadn't been for the large camera lying on the grass beside him.

Devon Barnett.

I was considering dropping a handful of raw cauliflower on his head just for the heck of it, when I was distracted by angry voices behind me. I turned and saw two people coming up the steps of the gazebo.

"You don't understand!" a young man cried, gesticulating wildly. "Each dog was carved from a three-hundred-pound block of ice! If one of them fell backwards from this height, it could kill somebody!"

"No way," insisted the woman beside him. She was wearing a pale pink suit and far too much makeup. "You've got to keep the display unobstructed. I want people admiring the ice sculptures, not staring at some ugly pieces of metal holding them in place!"

"Look, Phyllis, if anything ever happened, it'd be my ass on the line, not yours!"

The woman narrowed her eyes. "You listen to me, Gary. If you ever want to work on the East End again, you'll do exactly as I say!"

She turned on one ridiculously high heel, clunked back down the steps, and stalked away from the gazebo. I watched her teetering across the grass, making her way back to the tent.

"Witch!" the man muttered, turning to notice me for the first time.

"What was *that* about?" I asked.

He shook his head angrily. "Just because she's considered one of the hottest caterers in the Bromptons, she thinks she's the new Martha Stewart."

I wasn't sure she'd picked the right role model, but I kept silent.

"I mean, first she wants me to set up the sculptures here in this ridiculous gazebo," the man sputtered angrily. "Do you have any idea what it's like getting six humungous ice sculptures up eight stairs? Then she insists that they be placed right next to the railing. Hasn't she ever heard of gravity? Doesn't she know what would happen if one of these fell over?

"Besides, it's not as if I work for her!" he continued. "I'm working for Russell Bolger."

"Who's Russell Bolger?"

"The guy who owns this estate—and the guy who hired me."

"He's got quite a place here," I observed. "Who is he, anyway?"

"Only one of the most high-powered executives in the film industry. And I have a feeling that if he knew what Phyllis wanted me to do..." His voice trailed off. "I don't know why I'm telling you this. It's not your problem." He turned to the ice sculptures and studied them in silence.

"Are you the artist?" I finally asked.

He nodded.

"Your work is fabulous," I said sincerely. "You've carved the dogs so accurately! Look at the flat skull and the almond-shaped eyes on Lassie. You've captured collies perfectly. And over here on Rin Tin Tin, you've got the slightly curved tail that's typical of German Shepherds—"

"What are you, some kind of dog expert?"

"In a way," I said, suddenly sheepish. "I'm a veterinarian. In fact, I'm here for the dog show. I'm running the 'Ask The Vet' booth."

His expression softened. "Well, thanks. In that case, maybe I should bring my cat by. I keep meaning to take her to the vet, but I never have the time. Lulu's eyes have been so red lately. Almost like conjunctivitis, even though I know that's a people thing."

"It's a cat thing, too. How long has she had it?"

"Almost a week. I know I should have taken care of it by now. But June is the busiest month of the year for us. The summer season's starting up and *everybody* on the

East End is having a party. I just haven't had time to bring her in."

"If it is just a superficial eye infection, a broad-spectrum antibiotic would take care of it. But it might be chlamydia. It's not serious, but it could become chronic, something that's brought out by stress. Tell you what: how about if I come over to your studio the first chance I get? I've got a mobile services unit, and I make house calls for a living. I'd be happy to take a look at her."

"*Would* you? That would be so great! Here, let me give you my card. It's got the address of my studio on it. I'm so loaded up that I'm pretty much there from dawn 'til midnight, seven days a week. Unless I'm at an event, setting up."

I glanced at the business card he'd handed me. It was glossy black card stock, printed in silver.

*Gary Frye*
*Ice Sculptor Extraordinaire*
*Ice Castles*

Underneath was the address and phone number of his studio, which was located right in East Brompton.

"I'll try to come by tomorrow," I told him. "It depends on how busy this dog-show thing keeps me."

"Great." Mumbling, he added, "At least *something* good came out of this evening. Now, if you'll excuse me, I've got to figure out how to make these things safe."

As I headed back into the tent, I saw that the guests had started arriving in droves. I wasn't at all surprised that Devon Barnett had relocated once again. Now that he'd satisfied his nicotine craving, he'd positioned himself directly outside the tent's main entrance, where no one could sneak by without having their arrival recorded on film.

I plopped down at one of the round tables, noticing

that the brightly colored tablecloths were printed with cartoonish images of cats and dogs. The napkins, made of the same fabric, were encircled with silver napkin rings, each one in the shape of a different dog. I checked out the different place settings, recognizing a dachshund, a poodle, and a beagle.

I was puzzling over mine, trying to figure out if it was a Corgi or a werewolf, when I heard someone say, "Mind if I sit here?"

I glanced up at a tall, muscular man in his late twenties, his hair bleached a startling shade of white and painstakingly gelled so that it pointed upward like Bart Simpson's. He wore a tight T-shirt, even tighter jeans, and a gold eyebrow ring.

"Please do."

As he sat down, he, too, noticed the tablecloth.

"Just *look* at all these cute little doggies and kitties," he cooed. "Aren't they too *precious*? The effect is so wonderfully kitsch!" He leaned toward me. "I just hope they're not serving Purina Dog Chow. *Especially* at five hundred dollars a plate."

"At least they're not making us eat out of plastic food bowls." I gestured toward the fine white china.

He held up his plate and examined it. "Now that you mention it, this does look suspiciously like *bone* china."

I laughed. "Thank goodness I've found somebody with a sense of humor! Otherwise, I don't know how I'd get through this evening."

"Honey, come to enough of these and you'll start bringing along your knitting." He put down the plate and held out his hand. "I'm Chess LaMont."

"I'm Jessie Popper." As I shook his hand, I said, " 'Chess'?"

"Don't tell anybody, but I started out in life as a 'Chester,' if you can believe that. But when I left my hometown of Crabapple, Iowa, I left behind the 'T-E-R.' I picked up the extra 'S' when I crossed the Mississippi, and believe me, honey, I never looked back."

He sighed. "I know what you're thinking. You're probably like every other New Yorker. You don't believe that *anybody* comes from Iowa. You might not even believe there *is* such a place."

"I've been to Iowa," I said. "I liked it."

He shook his head dismissively. "Sweetie, you can have it. That's one place that looks best from the window of an airplane—growing smaller and smaller every second."

I smiled. "I guess you're not one of those people who romanticizes the good old days."

He pretended to shudder. "I'm sure there are people in my hometown who think I've *died* because they've seen so little of me since I graduated from high school."

"How long ago was that?"

"Would you believe ten years?" He grimaced. "I'm already getting wrinkles."

"I don't see any."

"That's because you're too polite. I can tell just by looking at you that you're one of those kind, sincere types. Which probably explains why I've never run into you out here in the Bromptons before."

"This is the first time I've ever come to one of these," I admitted. "I'm just here for the dog show."

"You're so lucky! I hope your little darling wins."

I didn't even stop to contemplate the irony of either Max or Lou being referred to as a "little darling."

"I'm not showing a dog," I said. "I'm actually a veterinarian, and I'm going to be standing at a booth, answering questions. It's called 'Ask The Vet.'"

"Then you're doubly lucky! You get to be part of the fun without all that pressure. The shampooing, the brushing, the fluffing... then there's all the work that goes into getting the dog ready." Chess's expression tightened. "You know, I wanted to enter Zsa Zsa. She's a Havanese, the sweetest little angel this side of heaven."

"Havanese?" I repeated. "They're part of the Bichon family, aren't they?

"You're familiar with them?" he asked excitedly. "They're *so* fascinating. Did you know they're originally from the Mediterranean? Spanish traders used to bring them to Cuban women as gifts. I just *love* that." He sighed. "But Zsa Zsa is special. She has the sweetest expression. Really, she doesn't look like any other dog you've ever seen. Of course, we don't use that word around her. 'Dog,' I mean. We always refer to her as a princess, because that's exactly what she is."

"Why didn't you enter her in the dog show? She might have won."

Pouting, he replied, "My significant other wouldn't let me. Nettie insists he doesn't want me getting mixed up in the celebrity scene. He seems to think it would taint me or something."

"That sounds kind of extreme."

"That's what I'm always telling him! But he's one of those macho types who thinks I should wait at home, playing June to his Ward Cleaver. At least June was on Ward's pension plan!" Chess sighed. "He even acted like he was doing me the favor of a lifetime by getting me a ticket for this dinner tonight. But so far, the only celebrities I've seen have been a bunch of washed-up has-beens who haven't made a movie practically since the talkies were invented."

As he spoke, my attention was diverted by a small commotion behind him.

"Oh, my God!" I gasped. "Isn't that Hugo Fontana?"

"Muscles, ten. Acting talent, one." Chess rolled his eyes. "Did you see him in *Pulverizer 3: The Annihilation*?

I swear, they should have annihilated his Screen Actors Guild card after that one!"

As I glanced around at the increasingly crowded tent, I realized that Hugo Fontana's face wasn't the only one I recognized. I've never thought of myself as starstruck, but it was fun to spot one celebrity after another. Then there were the people I couldn't place, but who certainly looked famous. The tiny woman dressed entirely in orange leather, for example, a jolting contrast to her cherry-red hair and glittery eye shadow.

I actually gasped when I noticed a slender blond at the edge of the tent, surrounded by a sea of admirers. Every one of them was male. Her delicate coloring was set off by the simple black dress she wore, cut low enough to intrigue without giving too much away. She threw back her head and laughed, a fluttering sound that reminded me of a bird.

"That's Kara Liebling!" I exclaimed.

"She's absolutely gorgeous, isn't she?" Chess gushed.

I was astonished to see the famous actress survey the room, zero in on our table, and head in our direction. I was even more surprised when she came right over to our table and threw her arms around Chess.

"*There* you are!" she cried. "I heard you were coming tonight!"

No air kisses for these two. The affection between Chess and Kara Liebling seemed completely sincere.

"Kara, love, you must meet my newest friend, Jessie Popper. She's a living, breathing veterinarian. Can you imagine—a person with a *real* job? Jessie, this is Kara, the brightest star in the Hollywood sky."

"Hello, Jessie." Kara held out her hands and smiled warmly. "I'm so pleased to meet you. Are you involved with the dog show?"

"I'm running the 'Ask The Vet' booth. Do you have a dog who's competing?"

"I've got a borzoi that I'm sure will win a prize." She beamed proudly. "Are you familiar with the breed?"

"Sure. They're also called Russian wolfhounds. That's because the Russian aristocracy first started breeding them in the 1400s." I also knew they were generally considered the last word in glamour breeds, but I kept that fact to myself.

"I'm very impressed," Kara said. "You'll have to meet Anastasia while you're here."

"I'll look for her tomorrow at the show."

"All this dog talk is making me furious that I can't enter Zsa Zsa," Chess said sullenly.

"Why not?" Kara asked.

"Nettie, what else? He simply *refused* to let me participate. As usual, he wants to keep all the glitter and glamour for himself!"

"That's too bad, but—oh, look, there's Russell Bolger," Kara said. "I'd better go say hello to him. After all, he was kind enough to let us use his backyard tonight. And this event is for such a worthy cause."

"Don't look now, but it's time to pay the piper." Chess gestured toward the stage, where a small group was gathering. "Speech time. My cue to disappear."

As I watched him head off in a completely different direction from the route Kara had chosen, I wondered if I was a fool not to do the same. But then I heard someone tapping a mike to get everyone's attention.

It was too late to escape. An elderly woman wearing a cream-colored pantsuit and enough makeup to qualify for Cirque du Soleil had just climbed onto the podium.

"Good evening, ladies and gentlemen," she began in a high, quivering voice. "I'm Celia Cromworthy, president of the East End Chapter of the SPCA. On behalf of our entire organization, I'd like to welcome you to the opening festivities of Funds for Our Furry Friends. I know each and every one of you shares my *complete* devotion to the puppies and dogs, kittens and cats, rabbits, ferrets, hamsters, gerbils, and even the tiny little mice who so wonderfully enrich our lives. Some people refer to them as pets, but we know they are *so* much more. They are extensions of ourselves, sweet, lovable little beings who embody the qualities that are the best of *all* of us. . . ."

Her droning voice had a hypnotic effect. I realized that Chess had been smart to duck out before the speeches began.

Glancing around, I saw that at least I wasn't alone in my misery. The tent was packed. Not only were about two-thirds of the tables full, but people stood in clusters along the edges of the tent. I looked behind me, checking the gazebo to see if it was too late to sneak back for some of that gorgeous shrimp, but I saw that the lights had been turned off, and the charming little building was empty except for one lone figure standing near the ice sculptures. Cleanup time, I figured. I'd missed my chance at the shrimp.

I was wondering how I would ever get through the rest of the night when I felt a light tap on my shoulder. I glanced up and saw Shawn Elliot smiling at me. He was dressed in a tuxedo that looked custom-made. As if the hand-stitching wasn't dazzling enough, his ensemble included a bow tie and a cummerbund that were the exact same shade of blue as his eyes.

His date for the evening, standing patiently at his side, didn't quite fit in with his elegant look. Still, what Rufus lacked in sophistication, he more than made up for with charm.

"Hello, again," Shawn said softly, leaning closer so he wouldn't disturb anyone who was actually listening to Celia Cromworthy's opening remarks. "I see they tricked you into coming tonight, too."

"I wish I'd thought of bringing a date—probably Lou, my Dalmatian. He's got both the build and the coloring to look totally awesome in a tux. Of course, Rufus here cuts a pretty mean figure in his birthday suit." I bent over to scratch the bulldog's ears and was rewarded with a big slurping kiss on the wrist. "Aren't *you* a lucky dog!" I told him. "Out having fun while all the other doggies in the show are home in bed. But I guess you're just a party animal, huh?"

"Is the guesthouse working out okay?" Shawn dropped Rufus's leash and sat down next to me. With a loud sigh, the bulldog plopped down between us, resting his chin on his paws. "Did you find everything you need?"

"... And of course, I'd like to thank Dr. Jessica Pepper, who has agreed to enlighten us all with information on how to keep our beloved animals happy and healthy...."

I jumped at the sound of my name—or at least a name close to it—amplified by a sound system that seemed to have been designed for rock concerts.

"Dr. Pepper?" Celia Cromworthy asked in her tremulous, high-pitched voice. "Are you here tonight?"

"Stand up, Jess," Shawn urged.

I rose to my feet. Hundreds of faces blurred in front of me, and I was vaguely aware of a smattering of polite applause.

When I sat down again, I could feel my cheeks burning. I suspected I looked like a shy third-grader who'd just taken her turn at a spelling bee.

Shawn wore a wicked grin. "See that, Dr. Pepper? You're famous. Practically a household name."

"Right up there with Coke and Pepsi."

"Just as sweet—and probably just as addictive," Shawn commented coolly.

I didn't know how to respond, so I was relieved that a final burst of applause signified that the speech portion of the evening was over. Shawn and I were both distracted by the catering crew, who instantly shifted into high gear. The folks in black and white swarmed through the tent, distributing salads with alarming efficiency.

When I felt a hand on the back of my chair, I expected to find a waiter hovering behind me. Instead, I turned and found Kara Liebling.

"I've got to run," she said, "but I wanted to say good-bye—"

The temperature in the immediate area suddenly dropped about forty degrees. Confused, I looked at Kara, then Shawn. The expression on both their faces told me where the deep freeze was coming from.

"Hello, Shawn," Kara said crisply.

"Kara." He nodded.

She quickly turned her attention back to me. "If you see Chess, please tell him I said—"

A loud scream suddenly cut through the pleasant din of the party. The incongruity of a sound that was so dreadfully out of place was chilling, and within moments, complete silence had descended over the entire dinner party.

Like everyone else, I swiveled around in my seat, craning my neck and trying to figure out what on earth was going on. I finally focused on a young woman dressed in the black pants and white shirt of the catering staff, standing at the back of the tent, gesticulating wildly. Her face was twisted into an expression of horror.

"Back there!" she shrieked. "Behind the gazebo...a body! There's a *dead body* lying on the ground!"

# Chapter 3

"Some of my best leading men have been dogs and horses."

—Elizabeth Taylor

W hat is this, one of those Murder Mystery Dinners?" a man behind me grumbled.

"I think it's a marvelous idea!" a woman exclaimed. "I *love* those!"

"They could have warned us," someone else complained. "I'm not big on this kind of thing."

I was as confused as everyone else. I was looking around the tent, amazed at how quickly a calm evening had turned chaotic, when I heard Shawn demand, "Where's Rufus?"

"What?" I responded distractedly. "He's right here. At least, I thought he was."

"He's gone," Shawn announced, jumping to his feet. "I hope he didn't get too far...."

I watched him dart off through the crowd in search of his wayward bulldog, then turned my attention to the podium as Celia Cromworthy took the microphone once again.

"Please, everyone, take your seats," she instructed shrilly. "There's no reason to panic. There's been an accident near the gazebo, and it appears that someone has been injured. The police have been notified, and an ambulance is on its way. If you will all just remain calm, we will relay any information we receive."

"Who's hurt?" someone called from the back of the tent.

Ms. Cromworthy hesitated. "I've been told it was Devon Barnett, the photographer."

I was instantly overcome with guilt. Less than half an hour earlier, I'd been standing in the gazebo myself, poised above the infamous paparazzo and contemplating dropping cruciferous vegetables on his head. Now he was lying behind that same gazebo, badly hurt...or maybe even dead.

Glancing around the tent, I could see from the guilty expressions on the faces of many of the other guests that I wasn't the only one having that thought. A lot of these people had undoubtedly wished bad luck upon Devon Barnett at one time or another.

The atmosphere of the elegant party had become strained. The guests appeared to be in a waiting mode, resisting the urge to dig into their salads so they wouldn't appear coldhearted. There was such a mood of uncertainty that it was actually a relief when the tension was interrupted by the wail of sirens and the flash of police lights.

The arrival of the police prompted me to stand up and make my way closer to the gazebo so I could get a better look at what was going on. Two official-looking cars had just pulled up, the words "Town of East Brompton Police Department" printed on the doors. They parked at odd angles, as if wanting to make the point that these weren't just any vehicles. A cop climbed out of each, both holding their heads at cocky angles that made it clear that *they* were in charge here. An ambulance from the East Brompton Fire Department quickly joined the two police vehicles, with a third sedan arriving a few seconds later. The police sergeant, I surmised, as I watched its sole occupant ease out of the driver's seat and make his grand entrance alone.

The cops positively strutted across the back lawn. I wondered if part of the appeal of doing police work in a town like this was feeling important. While they undoubtedly knew they were surrounded by famous actors and rock stars and supermodels with fan clubs and multimillion-dollar deals and even their own websites, suddenly *they* were the main attraction.

As for the impressive roster of guests, they had been reduced to onlookers. They moved toward the back of the tent, talking to one another in low tones as they watched the police cordon off the area with yellow tape. The EMT workers, meanwhile, rushed behind the gazebo.

From where we all stood, we couldn't see much. But the expressions on the medics' faces as they came back into view told us everything.

"Oh, my God," I gasped. "Devon Barnett is dead!"

The appearance of the county medical examiner a few minutes later verified my suspicions. The crowd lapsed into respectful silence as the EMT workers carried Barnett's body away on a stretcher.

Two women and a man, who had to be reporters, crowded around the medical examiner as he started to leave.

"What happened, Dr. Stokes?" one of them demanded.

A stocky man with enough lines in his face to indicate he'd been doing this for a long time barely glanced over. "My preliminary determination is that Devon Barnett died accidentally when a block of ice fell on him from a height of approximately ten feet. The police will be conducting a full investigation, but someone from the catering staff has informed me that he saw a small dog moving around inside the gazebo prior to the incident. I suspect that the dog bumped into the table on which the ice sculptures were displayed, causing one of the pieces to fall over and kill Mr. Barnett. We'll examine the body to determine the exact cause of death."

"Which sculpture fell?" another reporter asked.

Dr. Stokes looked uncomfortable. "I believe it was, uh, the cocker spaniel from the movie about the two dogs... *Lady and the Tramp*, I think it's called. So that would be, uh, Lady, I suppose."

"And you're convinced it was an accident?" the first reporter persisted.

"Aside from the possibility of the dog being in the wrong place at the wrong time, there's no reason to suspect foul play at this time," Dr. Stokes replied, his irritation only thinly masked. "The police can answer any additional questions, but since there were apparently no witnesses to the actual event, this is just one possible scenario. That's all I have to say."

Just then, Shawn emerged from the crowd, wearing a distressed expression and clutching Rufus's leash tightly. The sturdy bulldog trotted alongside him, his furrowed face seemingly drawn into a frown. I noticed a few people in the crowd whispering and pointing at them.

The two of them headed in my direction. "It's over," Shawn announced grimly. "Let's get out of here."

• • •

It wasn't until we'd retreated to Shawn's house and I was cradled by the overstuffed cushions of a remarkably soft couch that I realized how shaken up I was. Finding myself in a mansion that looked more like a movie set than an actual home only added to my disconcerted feeling.

My eyes traveled around the cavernous rooms, the imposing floor-to-ceiling windows framed by flowing white drapes and the silky Oriental carpets with their rich colors and intricate designs. The eclectic furnishings were all well-designed and beautifully crafted, from the stark modern pieces that somehow gelled with the fussy antiques to the carefully chosen accessories like the beaded floor lamp and the needlepoint pillows in pastel tones. Somehow, the spectacular show of wealth that epitomized the Bromptons only made the fact that a man had died here tonight seem even more surreal.

Shawn, meanwhile, looked as if he was even more upset than I was. His expression was grim and his eyes were clouded. Even Rufus seemed agitated. Somehow, I got the feeling he sensed he had something to do with his master's tense mood. The sour-faced beast refused to leave Shawn's side, and he kept looking up at him woefully, his dark liquid eyes clouded with concern—or maybe even guilt. His master reached down, distractedly fondling his ears as if to let him know there were no hard feelings.

I stared off into space, unable to shake the feeling that I was in a dream.

"It's so hard to comprehend," I mused, sounding as dazed as I felt. "One minute somebody is alive, flashing lights in your eyes with his camera, and the next minute he's..." I couldn't quite bring myself to utter the word. "And the strange thing is that I actually *knew* him. Well, maybe I didn't actually *know* him, but I encountered him three different times—and I've only been here in the Bromptons for a few hours." Apologetically, I added, "I guess even I'm surprised at how hard I'm taking this."

"And *your* dogs had nothing to do with it," Shawn interjected glumly.

I just stared at him. "Shawn, what happened tonight

was an accident. There's no reason to feel you had anything to do with Devon Barnett's death."

"Aside from the fact that if I'd hung on to Rufus's leash, he wouldn't have even *been* in that gazebo in the first place. Not only do I have to deal with feeling horribly guilty about what happened tonight, I have to consider the possibility of being sued over it."

"I'm no lawyer," I told him, "but I find it hard to believe you could get sued over something like this. Especially since the medical examiner himself said that no one can be certain that Rufus was responsible. I understand that you feel bad, Shawn, but there's simply too much uncertainty about the circumstances surrounding Devon Barnett's death for you to feel as if you're to blame—or to worry about a lawsuit."

"You're probably right," Shawn muttered. "I guess I should just chill. Anyway, there's nothing I can do about it right now. Hey, how about something to calm our nerves?"

"Maybe that's not a bad idea."

"Great. I'll open a bottle of champagne."

I was about to protest. Even though Devon Barnett hadn't exactly been the most popular guy in town, his death didn't strike me as cause for breaking out something I associated with happy times.

But it was already too late. I heard a definitive pop. The next thing I knew, Shawn was handing me a crystal flute filled nearly to the brim.

"Just a sip," I insisted, feeling guilty. But as soon as I tasted the cold bubbling liquid, I knew it was the good stuff. Much too good to waste.

I helped myself to a few serious gulps, settling back further into the comfortable cushions. But even drinking fine champagne amid palatial surrounds wasn't enough to distract me from the hard reality of what had just happened—and the person it had happened to.

"Shawn," I mused aloud, "do you think it's possible Devon Barnett's death *wasn't* accidental?"

He looked startled. "But the medical examiner seemed sure that it was an accident. It's not as if there's any reason for him to lie."

"True. It's just that... well, you told me yourself that Barnett was one of the most hated men in the Bromptons. His death is a bit bizarre. Doesn't that mean it's possible that it wasn't an accident at all? That somebody deliberately pushed that ice sculpture over the side of the gazebo?"

Shawn shrugged off the jacket of his tux and sank onto the couch next to me, draping one arm across the back so that it came dangerously close to being around my shoulders. He leaned toward me, his face so close that I was afraid I'd drown in his blue eyes. "Know what I think?"

"What?" Funny; even though I'd been drinking, my throat was suddenly strangely dry. I took a few more gulps, hoping the bubbly would help me relax.

"That you've seen too many movies." He moved even closer. Even through my champagne-induced haze, I could tell where this was going. Instinctively, I leaped off the couch, frantically searching the room for a distraction. My eyes lit on a cluster of framed movie posters hanging on one of the walls. *The African Queen,* starring Katharine Hepburn and Humphrey Bogart. *High Noon,* with Gary Cooper and Grace Kelly. *On The Waterfront,* with Marlon Brando.

"Speaking of movies," I said brightly, "which one's your favorite?"

He let out a little sigh. "As you can probably tell, I prefer old films," he replied. "Especially the classics, like *Citizen Kane* and *The Grapes of Wrath*. They sure knew how to make movies in those days. I have tremendous respect for the old-time actors, too. My idols are the truly great ones: Jimmy Stewart, Cary Grant, Orson Welles, Henry Fonda . . ."

"Want to hear something I've never told anybody before?" The champagne had seriously gone to my head. I didn't care.

"I can hardly wait."

I smiled dreamily. "Sometimes I pretend I'm Audrey Hepburn."

Shawn just nodded, as if it was the most understandable thing in the world. "She was pretty incredible. But you seem more like the *Katharine* Hepburn type to me." He pointed at the *The African Queen* poster.

"Really? Why?"

"She was strong. Accomplished. The type of woman who didn't let anybody push her around."

I was still basking in the compliment when he said, "How about if I put on some music?"

"Sure."

The romantic instrumental that filled the room surprised me.

"Recognize this?" he asked.

I shook my head.

"It's the theme song from one of my movies. *Afternoon in Paradise*. I don't suppose you saw it."

Twice, I thought. And once more on tape. But I just nodded.

"Remember the part where I dance with Jennifer Miller?"

"Sure. The scene where you confess that you're not really the billionaire's son; you're his chauffeur." But make her fall hopelessly in love with you anyway, I was tempted to add.

"That's the one."

"I remember that when I saw it, I was struck by what a good dancer you were."

"Actually, filming that scene was a breeze. For one

thing, I had an excellent dance instructor. One of the best in the business. But it's pretty simple. Here, I'll show you."

He jumped to his feet, holding out his arms as if he were Clark Gable playing Rhett Butler, daring Scarlett O'Hara to dance with him at the Confederate soldiers' charity ball.

But I was no Vivien Leigh.

"I'm not much of a dancer." I shrank into the cushions.

"I find that hard to believe."

"No, really. I—"

"It's easy. Honest."

He pulled me up, keeping one of his hands in mine and encircling my waist with the other. Just like some of America's best-known film actresses, I suddenly found myself in Shawn Elliot's arms. I wondered if they'd handled it more coolly—or if, like me, they suddenly found it as difficult to breathe as if a Saint Bernard had plopped down on their chest.

"Just follow my lead," Shawn instructed. "It helps if you look into my eyes."

Even though I had the horrible feeling my cheeks were bright red, I raised my eyes to meet his. He was only a few inches away, so close I could practically feel myself melting into the warmth of his body.

"Now relax and move with me. Just let your body follow mine. Use my hips as your guide."

Forget *Gone With The Wind*. The room was spinning so fast, I felt like I was in the opening scene of *The Wizard of Oz*.

"I can't," I gasped. "Really, I'm not a dancer."

"You're doing great!" Shawn held me tighter. Now I could feel more than the warmth of his body. I could feel his thigh pressing against mine, his chest brushing against my breasts, as gentle as a whisper . . .

The sound of someone clearing his throat loudly made me lose my concentration completely. I snapped my head around, then froze—except for my right foot, which somehow managed to crunch down on top of Shawn's.

"Nick!" I yelped.

"Ouch!" Shawn cried.

Nick didn't say anything. He just stood in the doorway with his arms folded.

It took a few seconds for the room to stop spinning. This time, my dizziness had less to do with too much champagne than it did with the sudden appearance of the last person in the world I was expecting.

"What a surprise!" I finally said.

"So I gather," Nick observed dryly.

I took a giant step backwards, away from Shawn.

Shawn frowned. "Do you know this guy, Jessie, or should I call for help?"

"I know him."

"That's a relief," Nick returned. "That you remember me, I mean."

"Shawn, this is my, uh, boyfriend. Nick Burby."

A strange look crossed Shawn's face. "A real pleasure, Mick."

"That's *Nick*," I corrected him. "And this is—"

"I know who he is," Nick interrupted. "I own a DVD player."

"In that case," Shawn asked evenly, "may I ask why you're not home watching it instead of breaking into people's houses?"

"I didn't have to break in. The door was wide open."

"My fault," I admitted. "I was the last one in."

Shawn glared at Rufus, who lay with his head on his paws, watching the whole scene with his large, woeful eyes. "Some watchdog you are," he muttered.

I was struck by the contrast between the two men. Shawn Elliot, looking as cool and sophisticated as James

Bond in his custom-tailored tux. Nick Burby, decked out in tattered cutoffs, a scruffy pair of Nikes, and a Led Zeppelin T-shirt so faded that Robert Plant and Jimmy Page looked more like ghosts than aging rock stars.

I turned to Nick. "I thought you'd decided to stay home."

He shrugged. "I changed my mind."

"Who's taking care of Cat and Prometheus and Leilani?" I persisted. An image flashed into my mind of my aging pussycat, my endearing blue-and-gold macaw, and my Jackson's chameleon languishing in my empty house.

"Betty," he replied. "They're in good hands, and they were all perfectly fine as of two hours ago."

"How did you know I was here?"

"I saw your van parked outside, and I heard the music *inside,* so I figured I'd knock."

"That would have been an excellent idea," Shawn said.

"I did knock. Several times. Tried the bell, too. It doesn't seem to work. Or else you two didn't hear it because you were so busy doing...*what* exactly is it you were doing?"

"Dancing," I said weakly.

"Actually, we were reenacting a scene from one of my movies." Shawn's cheerfulness sounded forced. For a professional actor, he wasn't doing very well. "I was trying to take Jessie's mind off the events of the evening."

"What events were those?" Nick pushed back the piece of straight brown hair that was always falling into his eyes. "Or shouldn't I ask?"

"A man was killed tonight, right here in East Brompton," I told him, certain that presenting him with such terrible news would make him realize how ridiculous he was being.

"Who did it?" Nick asked. "A jealous boyfriend?"

"Maybe you two should be on your way," Shawn suggested. "It's getting late, and I'm sure you want to fill Mick in on what happened."

"That's *Nick*," we said in unison.

•   •   •

"I didn't mean to spoil your evening." Nick walked a few steps behind me as I led the way across the lawn. He was carrying the small suitcase he'd retrieved from his car, along with his laptop and a plastic shopping bag that appeared to contain a large portion of his collection of classic rock CD's. "If I'd known I was going to interrupt—"

"Here's the guesthouse," I said pointedly. "It's pretty comfortable. It's got a little kitchen and its own bathroom—"

"Is there a reason why you're acting like a tour guide?"

"Is there a reason why you're acting like a complete idiot?"

"Hang on, Jess." Nick caught up with me right outside the guesthouse and took hold of my shoulders. "Look, I thought it'd be fun to surprise you. I had this crazy idea that it would be really romantic if I just showed up and—"

He leaned forward and sniffed. "Is that alcohol?"

"Champagne."

Nick dropped his arms to his sides. "You and that Shawn guy were *drinking*?"

"No. I mean, yes. But it was because we were upset. About what happened tonight, I mean. So Shawn opened a bottle of champagne."

"I've heard of calming your nerves with sherry. Or a few shots of whiskey. But never with champagne."

"That's because you're not a movie star."

"You're right. I'm not." The hurt look on his face instantly made me regret my flippant comment.

I opened the cottage door, expecting that Max's and Lou's reaction to the reappearance of a man they hadn't seen for almost twelve hours would give us a temporary break. I was right.

"At least these guys are happy to see me," Nick mumbled once the leaping and barking had settled down.

"They're probably not in shock, the way I was. Which leads to the obvious question: How come you changed your mind? I thought you were too busy to waste your time with something you characterized as—what was the word? Oh, that's right. 'Frivolous.' "

"I missed you. How's that for a reason? And I guess I just assumed you missed me, too, and that you'd be glad I showed up."

"I *am* glad. It's just that if I'd had some warning, I would have had the presence of mind to *look* glad."

"You looked glad, all right. It's just that it seemed like it was Shawn who was making you feel that way."

"We were *dancing*."

"I noticed. I also noticed you didn't waste any time finding male companionship. A *movie star,* no less."

"Oh, right." My voice was dripping with sarcasm. "I'm the woman of Shawn Elliot's dreams. He could have any woman in the world, but I'm the one he's drooling over."

"He certainly looked as if he was enjoying himself."

"He's an *actor*! It's his *job* to look happy, even when he's not!"

"Actually, I never thought he was a very good actor. Just another bland Hollywood hustler with decent features and a lot of ambition."

"Don't you want to hear about the man who was killed by the falling ice sculpture?" I really was glad that Nick had shown up, and the last thing in the world I wanted was to argue. Besides, I still hadn't recovered from the fact that I'd just come home from a party at which a man had been killed.

"I'm much more interested in how you ended up at Shawn Elliot's house—alone. Dancing, no less. If you can even call it that."

"That's exactly what I'd call it," I said indignantly. "Surely you don't think anything else was going on?" I tossed my head and raised one eyebrow. Maybe there was a little Vivien Leigh in me, after all.

"Why don't you tell me?" Nick's voice had changed. Instead of cranky, his tone was more along the lines of pleading. "*Was* anything else going on?"

My prickliness was suddenly gone, too. I snapped my renegade eyebrow back into position. "No, Nick. Of course not."

"Good. That's all the reassurance I need." His expression softened. "I do trust you, you know."

I nestled my head against his shoulder. "Please don't worry about Shawn Elliot. The only reason I was at his house tonight was that I ran into him at the kick-off party for the dog show. Then this terrible thing happened to the photographer, and the police showed up and we cleared out. We were both pretty shaken up, so we went back to his place to calm down. He's harmless, Nick. I promise."

"Okay." Nick put his arms around me. "If you say so."

I was about to add that if the evening hadn't been bizarre enough, the police thought Shawn Elliot's dog might have been partly responsible for the horrific accident that had resulted in a man's death. But he didn't give me a chance.

He was too busy showing me just how much he'd missed me.

# Chapter 4

"Children and dogs are as necessary to the welfare of the country as Wall Street and the railroads."

—Harry S. Truman

I expected the entire East End to be buzzing about Devon Barnett's demise and the surprising circumstances that surrounded it. Instead, as Max, Lou, and I headed to East Brompton Green, the location of the first annual Funds for Our Furry Friends Charity Dog Show, I discovered that when it came to dog-lovers, even a bizarre death right in their own backyard couldn't deter them from their passion.

The triangle-shaped stretch of grass looked as if a team of experts from the Home and Garden Channel had taken over. Beyond the huge banner out front, multicolored streamers flowed from what looked like two Maypoles on either side of the entrance to the field. Several huge tents had been set up, differentiated by masses of different colored balloons bobbing outside. A courtesy tent was well-stocked with coffee for humans, bottled water for canines, and plenty of edible goodies for both.

While I was impressed by the magnitude of the operation, I was much more interested in the dogs. I held onto Max's and Lou's leashes tightly, since they were at least as intrigued as I was. Max was barking his head off, trying to show the competition who was boss. Lou seemed a bit overwhelmed, his entire body trembling as he took in all the excitement around him. He made a point of standing as close to me as he could.

Looking around at the competitors, I concluded that although a few regulars had come out for the event, most of the entrants were new to the dog-show world. It was easy to spot the few seasoned canines. They were the ones behaving themselves. It was easy to spot the experienced handlers, too. They were the ones wearing practical shoes.

Yet all the dogs, even the pros, looked like they were having a blast. Sure, each and every one looked good enough to star in a dog-food commercial: the poodles and Yorkies with perky ribbons in their freshly shampooed fur, the spaniels with their painstakingly fluffed ears, the sleek Rottweilers and greyhounds, their flanks shining from all the brushing that had brought them to such a luminous state.

But most of the dogs couldn't help acting like . . . well, like dogs. They darted about, barking joyfully or, in some cases, angrily. I watched an incensed Chihuahua give a piece of his mind to an Alaskan malamute at least ten times his size. You had to admire his spirit, if not his common sense.

As for the breeds, I'd expected to see the usual assortment of beagles, cocker spaniels, and pugs. So nothing prepared me for the Who's Who of exotic specimens prancing around with their proud owners. An impish affenpinscher, a sturdy black little dog whose name means "monkey terrier"—and who has a mug that lives up to it. A Chinese crested dog, completely hairless except for the long, wispy fur on its head, feet, and tail. A Lowchen, or "little lion dog," that resembles a miniature English sheepdog who'd had his back half-shaved. A sturdy black Schipperke, an imposing breed that looks like the inspiration for the Big Bad Wolf.

The celebrities on parade were almost as impressive as the dogs. The first familiar face I spotted belonged to Hugo Fontana, his muscles bulging beneath a tight-fitting black polo shirt. Strutting alongside the extraordinarily popular actor was an equally muscular specimen I recognized as a Chesapeake Bay retriever.

Figures, I thought wryly, given the fact that the breed is generally considered the hardiest of the retrievers. Macho guy, macho dog.

I was pretty sure the owner of the Chinese crested dog was a soap opera star that even I'd heard of, since her career as one of the best-known villains on television spanned three decades. I also recognized a supermodel whose face had become synonymous with an expensive line of cosmetics, striding alongside a sleek, rust-colored vizsla, one of the more imposing members of the pointer family. I was trying to remember the model's name when I noticed someone hurrying across the field, heading in my direction.

"*There* you are, Dr. Pepper!" Celia Cromworthy exclaimed. Her thickly powdered cheeks were flushed with excitement. Or maybe it was just too much rouge. I noticed that she eyed my outfit for the day with approval. Of course, I was wearing the same official-looking polo shirt embroidered with "Jessica Popper, D.V.M." that I wore almost every day. But I knew that the crisp khaki shorts I'd paired with today's forest-green selection gave me a particularly authoritative look—as if I were a game warden on a preserve in the Serengheti, or at least an extra on *The Crocodile Hunter*. "Thank you *so* much for agreeing to be part of our little fund-raiser! It was *so* good of you to fill in for that *charming* Dr. Scruggs. What a shame he suddenly had a personal emergency to deal with!"

Calling the "emergency" Marcus was dealing with "personal" was a real understatement, I thought wryly. He'd telephoned me three weeks earlier, explaining that he'd had another offer—one that was too good to turn down. After plying him with questions, I learned that an admirer—a woman he described as "mature"—was desperate for him to accompany her on an all-expenses-paid trip to a tropical island. Frankly, it had taken me a few seconds to get over the shock. While the man was convinced he was God's gift to the female half of the species, to me he was more like the lump of coal that someone on Santa's "Naughty" list might find in her Christmas stocking.

But I wasn't about to bore Celia Cromworthy with the unsavory details of Marcus Scruggs' love life. I just smiled politely. "I'm glad I could help. It's for such a good cause."

"Indeed. Now let me show you to your booth. . . ."

She led me to the tent placed at the far end of the Green. It was lined with tables and booths. In addition to the representatives from local organizations like an East End animal shelter and the Guide Dog Foundation who were standing behind tables, considerably more elaborate displays had been set up by a few major dog-food companies, an "invisible fencing" firm, and a chain retailer specializing in canine-related paraphernalia. When I spotted a six-foot placard emblazoned with a giant deer tick that looked like it was posing for the cover of a Kafka novel, I had a feeling I'd found my home away from home. Sure enough, the banner draped above it read "Ask The Vet!"

"Here you go!" Celia Cromworthy beamed. "We've left some brochures on health issues that you might want to hand out. If you need anything else, just ask your assistant."

" *'Assistant'?*" I asked.

But she'd already dashed off. No matter; as I neared my booth, I understood what she was talking about. Standing inside, glancing around nervously, was a serious-looking girl about twelve or thirteen, with straight brown hair and hazel eyes. Stick-thin, she was dressed in a striped shirt and flowered shorts that even I could tell didn't go together. Every few seconds, she slid the thick eyeglasses she wore up the bridge of her nose. Overall, she had the gawky look of someone whose body hadn't yet decided upon its long-term plan.

Max and Lou bounded over to her, eager to introduce themselves. As soon as she noticed them, her face lit up.

"Hey, you cute little doggies!" She crouched down to their level, laughing gleefully as they both climbed all over her in a manic effort to cover her face with dog saliva. "Hey, cut that out!" she protested between giggles. "You're getting me all wet!"

"Sorry!" I cried as I jogged over. "Whenever they're out in public, they act like they're the most attention-starved beasts in the universe. You'd never guess they're really the most spoiled." I reached for my wild canines' collars so I could pull them off her.

"They're okay," she insisted. "I love dogs. I really wish I had one, but my parents won't let me. They say our lives are too complicated."

Much to the dismay of both my Westie and my Dalmatian, the girl stood up. It only took another two seconds before they resumed harassing her; Lou nudged her hand roughly with his nose in a desperate attempt at prolonging physical contact, and Max tried to climb up her leg.

She glanced at me shyly, grinning. For the first time, I

noticed that her teeth were covered with shiny metal braces. "They really like me!"

I wasn't about to tell her they were shameless at soliciting affection from any living, breathing being they encountered. Instead, I nodded. "I'll say they do. You have a real way with dogs. If you want, you can pick up Max. Lou'll go nuts, but that's the price you pay for being a Dalmatian. When you weigh sixty-six pounds, only weight lifters can carry you around like a baby."

"Hey, Maxie," the girl cooed, reaching for the crazed Westie. "Want me to hold you? Come here, little doggie."

Max was more than happy to comply. When she started to scratch his belly as she cradled him gently in her arms, pure ecstasy was written all over his furry face.

"What happened to Max's tail?" the girl asked earnestly. "He's hardly got any of it left!"

"Both my dogs lived with other people before they came to live with me. Their original owners weren't exactly the nicest people in the world, so somewhere along the line, Max lost part of his tail. Lou had an accident, too. See? He lost an eye."

"You poor things!" she whispered.

"By the way, I'm Dr. Popper," I said. "I'm supposed to stand in this booth all day, handing out advice."

"My name's Emily Bolger." Once again, she jabbed at her thick glasses. "I'm your volunteer helper."

"Emily, huh? I had a feeling that was your name."

"*Really?* How?"

"Your name tag."

She grinned. "Oh, yeah. Forgot."

"Glad to have you aboard, Emily. Thanks for helping out."

She studied me for a few seconds. "Are you really a veterinarian?"

"Got the diploma to prove it. *And* the scars."

"Huh?"

"Just joking. What about you? What do you do, when you're not volunteering at charity dog shows?"

"Nothing much. I'm still just a kid, you know?"

"I guess I noticed that. Do you live around here?"

"Not really. I kind of don't live anywhere. My dad has a summer place out here, but he really lives in California and New York. My mom lives in a bunch of places, too. Paris, mostly. And me, well, I don't spend much time at any of their houses because I go to boarding school in Virginia during the year."

"Do you like boarding school?"

She shrugged, sending her glasses slipping down the bridge of her nose again. She stopped scratching Max's belly long enough to push them back into place. "It's okay, I guess. I like the school part. But it's not like I have tons of friends or anything."

"Personally, I've never found that having tons of friends mattered. Having one or two really good ones always seemed a lot better."

She brightened. "Yeah, you're right. Hey, maybe you and I could be friends! I don't know a lot of people out here."

"Haven't you met other kids out here over the years?"

"This is the first summer I've spent on the East End. I usually go to summer camp. Or else one of those travel programs where you spend the summer biking around Italy or kayaking on the Colorado River."

"Wow! Lucky you!"

"I guess. Except the only reason my parents send me is to get rid of me."

"I doubt that!"

"You don't know my parents." She puckered up her face into a sour expression. "I'm kind of a disappointment to them."

"Oh, Emily! I hope you don't really believe that!"

Another shrug. "It's true. The only reason I'm here

this summer is that my father decided it was time to start turning me into somebody who fit into his world." She grimaced. "You know, the whole scene out here."

"What about *your* world?" I asked in a gentle voice. "What matters to you?"

"I think I'd like to work with animals, like you," she answered shyly. "They're so...honest. They always let you know exactly what they're thinking, you know?"

Lou chose that moment to lift his leg on the giant tick.

I moaned. "Sometimes I wish they'd try just a little harder *not* to!"

Emily giggled. I felt oddly pleased.

"So these dogs who are in dog shows like this... they're probably nervous wrecks, right? They must get all kinds of special diseases and things."

"Actually, the opposite is true," I told her. "Most show dogs adore the attention. They love all the time they get to spend with their owners and their trainers. Then there's the excitement of the actual event. If you watch them, you can see they have a pretty good sense of what's going on, and they really get into it. Of course, their owners also take very good care of them, making sure they're inoculated and taking them for regular check-ups. All in all, they're a pretty healthy, well-adjusted bunch."

"That's a relief," Emily said. "I'd hate to think that all these sweet doggies—"

"Jessie!" I glanced up and saw Kara Liebling trotting toward me, her silky blonde hair framing her face and giving her the look of an angel. She was even dressed all in white so that she matched the meticulously groomed borzoi beside her.

"Good morning!" she greeted me when she reached the booth. "How lovely to see you again!"

"Nice to see you, too, Kara. And who's this lovely creature?"

I reached down to stroke the graceful white animal. Even though she probably weighed in at seventy-five pounds and stood almost to my hip, the leggy hound with the long, silky coat was surprisingly dainty.

A good choice for Kara, I decided. They both have the same aura of elegance.

"Just look at this beautiful animal!" I turned my head toward Emily, who was standing a couple of feet behind me.

She gave a little shrug, twisting her face into a disagreeable expression. She stubbornly continued to pet Lou's head, as if demonstrating that her affections were not easily swayed.

Even so, Kara brightened. "Hello, Emily. I didn't realize that was you!"

"It's me," she said meekly.

"Do you two know each other?" I asked, genuinely surprised.

"Everybody knows Emily Bolger!" Kara said a little too heartily.

Bolger, Bolger . . . of course! Russell Bolger, the movie executive on whose estate the opening-night gala had taken place. So *he* was her father, the man she was so certain was disappointed in her. Given the glimpse I'd had of "his world," I suddenly understood this serious, uncertain girl's claim that she didn't fit into it very well.

Kara's smile faded. "How's your mom doing, Emily?"

"Okay, I guess. Right now she's in California, in one of those rehab places."

"Give her my very best, okay?"

"Sure." I noticed that Emily barely looked at her.

"Well," Kara said cheerfully, "I'd better be off. Wish Anastasia and me luck!"

A few seconds later, I spotted Shawn Elliot sauntering over in my direction. Considering that I'd been in town less than twenty-four hours, even I was impressed by all the new friends I'd made.

That didn't mean my friends were also friends with one another. Remembering the iciness I'd picked up on between Shawn and Kara the evening before, I wondered if he'd been watching, waiting for her to make her exit before he made his entrance.

"Well, well, well. If it isn't Dr. Pepper," Shawn teased once he reached the booth.

"Her name is Dr. *Popper,*" Emily corrected him crossly.

"That's okay, Em," I told her. "He's just being difficult."

Breezily, Shawn returned, "And here I thought I was being charming!"

I decided to change the subject. "How's Rufus? Any stage fright?"

"Naw, turns out he's a natural."

We both looked down at the heavyset bulldog with the James Cagney face who had flopped onto the cool grass. Rufus dug his chin into the soil and looked up at us with his big, soulful brown eyes. To me, he looked like the "What, me worry?" poster boy.

"In fact," Shawn went on, "Rufus may be getting his first acting gig. I just found out some independent filmmaker is videotaping the dog show. He's making a documentary to show at the end—probably his way of getting an 'in' with some of the suits in the movie biz. Russell Bolger's even offered to host a luncheon at his place on Sunday so everybody can come and relive their favorite moments. Hey, I wouldn't mind seeing Rufus on the big screen." His expression suddenly darkened. "Besides, maybe it'll help his reputation."

I responded with a puzzled look.

"I know it sounds kind of crazy...but people are

starting to make comments about Rufus." Eyeing Emily, he added obtusely, "And what happened last night."

She didn't seem to notice the change in Shawn's tone. She was too focused on his dog. "What a funny animal," she commented, frowning at Rufus. "He looks mean."

"Not at all! In fact, he's a real pussycat," I assured her. "Why don't you pet him?"

She scowled. "He looks like he doesn't like me."

"If you want to work with animals, it's a good idea to get used to all kinds," I said gently. "Go ahead. He doesn't bite."

Emily hesitated before crouching down to Rufus's level and tentatively patting his head. True to form, Rufus rolled over and lay on his back with his four legs limp, already in position for a quality belly-scratching.

"He *does* like me!" she squealed happily. As she obliged the affection-craving bulldog, it was difficult for me to tell who was enjoying it more.

"Why don't you take him for a walk?" I suggested. "I know he looks gruff, but he's really a teddy bear."

"Come on, Rufus!" Emily said, scooping up his leash. He didn't need to be asked twice.

Once the two of them had toddled off and were out of earshot, I turned to Shawn. "You're kidding, right? About people making comments?"

"I wish I were." He sighed. "You know, to be in this business, you have to be as tough as nails. Part of the job is having people criticize you. And I thought I'd gotten used to it. But all of a sudden, people are acting really weird about Rufus—and it's making me nuts. When you come right down to it, East Brompton is just another small town—and people are already talking about what happened last night.

"Like this morning? When I parked near East Brompton Green and got out of my car, a bunch of teenage girls were hanging around, looking for celebrities. When they spotted me, they started squealing and giggling." His cheeks turned pink. "Look, I'm not saying I deserve that kind of treatment, but it happens, okay? Anyway, they were asking for my autograph and all that...and then they spotted Rufus. They started laughing, saying he was wanted by the police, that he was one of 'America's Most Wanted,' stuff like that.

"Having people act crazy around me is one thing. But seeing them respond negatively to Rufus—who's, like, my main man—really bothers me, you know? I know he wasn't really responsible for Devon Barnett's death. If anybody's to blame, it's that ice sculptor guy."

I was about to say something consoling when Emily came trotting back with Rufus at her heels.

"Did you two have fun?" I asked her.

"Kind of." She wrinkled her nose, then paused as she pushed her glasses back into place. "At least, we were until this mom came by with her little boy. He got all excited when he saw Rufus and came running over to pet him. But then his mother started yelling, saying, 'That's Shawn Elliot's dog! Keep away from him!'" She shrugged, then handed the leash to Shawn. "I think you'd better take him."

Glancing over at Shawn, I saw that his mouth was pulled into a tense line. I didn't know him very well, of course, but I still had a sense I was seeing a side of him that didn't come out very often. I could feel my heart clench.

"This will blow over," I assured him, reaching over and putting my arm around him. I rubbed his shoulder consolingly, leaning forward so I could speak to him without Emily overhearing. "I'm sure that in a day or two—"

"*There* you are! I was beginning to think I'd never find you!"

I glanced up and saw Nick striding across the grass.

My arm dropped to my side as quickly as if I was doing jumping jacks. But it was too late. I saw his smile fade as he took in the scene he'd walked in on.

"Hey, Nick!" I exclaimed, trying to sound glad to see him. In fact, I *was* glad to see him. It's just that my timing suddenly seemed to be disastrous.

Shawn didn't help. "Hello, Mick," he mumbled.

"That's *Nick*." Glancing at Shawn coolly, he added, "I seem to be interrupting something. *Again*."

"Hardly," I said cheerfully. I took a giant step away from Shawn. "Shawn was just telling me how bad he feels that people have been acting strange toward him since his dog—"

" 'His dog'?" Nick repeated.

"Exactly. I never got a chance to explain, but the police seem to think that Shawn's bulldog—Rufus, this guy over here—might have had something to do with Devon Barnett's death last night."

"I guess trouble runs in the family," Nick observed.

When I heard a low growl, I couldn't tell if it was coming from Nick or Shawn. But then I glanced down and realized it had come from Rufus, who was probably picking up on the bad vibes between his beloved master and this interloper.

"I hope you've got that animal under control," Nick said through clenched teeth.

"He's highly trained," Shawn returned calmly. "He only bites people who deserve it."

"Uh, Shawn, I think they're getting ready to start the opening ceremonies over at the Blue Tent," I interjected. "Maybe you and Rufus had better head over—especially if you want to make sure he's featured in the videotape." Just for the heck of it, I added, "Besides, I heard they take off points if you're late."

"Then we'd better get going." His eyes fixed on Nick, Shawn said, "I always believe that, in the end, people get what they deserve. Dogs, too. And Rufus here is definitely a winner, so I don't want to stand in the way of him getting his due recognition."

"Did you actually manage to string all those words together yourself?" Nick asked pleasantly. "Or do you keep a screenwriter locked up in your basement?"

"I think I'm beginning to understand what Jessie sees in you," Shawn returned in the same cheerful voice. As he turned to lead Rufus away, he called, "Later, Jess."

"I don't like him," Emily muttered.

"Me, either," Nick agreed. "What's he doing, Jess, stalking you?"

"Why are you making such a big deal about Shawn?"

"How about the fact that every time I see the two of you together, you've got your arms around each other? What am I supposed to think, when you act all...all *gooey* whenever he's around?"

"I've never acted gooey in my life!" I insisted indignantly. Deciding not to mention the mud bath his Ferrari had given me upon my arrival, I added, "Besides, Shawn has been very nice to me ever since I got here."

Nick snorted. "I'll bet he has."

"What's that supposed to mean?"

"Just that I wouldn't trust that guy as far as I could throw him."

"Are you the veterinarian?" a woman cradling a silky gray dog in her arms asked as she emerged from the crowd milling around the booth. "My schnauzer just started limping. I'm worried that he might have stepped on something sharp. Can you take a look at him?"

I felt like hugging her. "Certainly. Just give me two seconds." I turned to Nick. "Look, I don't have time for this right now. Just trust me, okay? You have nothing to worry about where Shawn Elliot is concerned. We're just friends. I'm not the least bit impressed by the fact that he's a famous movie star. Look, it was really thoughtful of you to come by, and—"

"There *was* a reason, you know." He still sounded defensive, but his tone was softening. "I wanted to ask you if you had time to go to the beach later. When you're done here, I mean."

I blinked. " 'The beach'?"

"I thought it'd be . . . you know, romantic. That *was* the original idea in coming here, remember?"

"That's really sweet," I told him sincerely.

"Great. Then I'll be waiting for you at the guesthouse at the end of the afternoon." He leaned forward and kissed me lightly. "Hey, have fun today, Jess. And knock 'em dead. Let these snobby Bromptons folk see just how special you are."

At that moment, as I turned away and focused on the schnauzer with the bum leg, I remembered exactly why I loved Nick Burby.

• • •

The morning passed quickly. While I'd expected things to be quiet, a steady stream of pet owners stopped by the "Ask The Vet" booth, looking for information or advice. I discussed flea collars with the owner of a black Lab and advised a pug owner on how to help her overweight dog slim down. One woman with a Scottie wanted me to look at her dog's ears, which were constantly getting infected. A nervous young man was all atwitter about the safety of the chemicals in dog shampoos and the preservatives in food. I reminded him that just because something claims to be all-natural, that doesn't guarantee that it's safe.

Lyme disease was a popular topic. Deer are as abundant on eastern Long Island as tourists—and as hard to control. They're everywhere, even in people's backyards, eating their flower beds. That means deer *ticks* are everywhere, and deer ticks mean Lyme disease. While it's as much a problem for people as it is for animals, today's crowd was much more focused on their dogs' health than their own. The grotesque deer tick next to my booth turned out to be the biggest draw of the event. At least, after the booth selling collars studded with giant *faux* jewels and crocodile-skin leashes.

After a long, intense hour of fielding questions, I decided to take a short break. I left Emily in charge of both my dogs and the booth, assuring her that I'd be back soon to deal with anything complicated that came up.

I had to admit, the excitement was getting to me. Being exiled to the edge of the action, watching the dogs and their owners parade in and out of the tents from afar without being able to see what was going on inside, was making me restless. True, Funds for Our Furry Friends was what's called a "fun match." Official dog shows provide the chance to compete for points that can lead to the title of Champion—which, aside from bolstering both human and canine egos, yields cash prizes and increases a dog's value for breeding purposes. But that doesn't mean a fun match isn't as entertaining to watch, not to mention a lot more relaxing.

Both matches and shows are all about conformation—meaning how well each dog conforms to the standards for that particular breed. The American Kennel Club determines the breed standard, which includes all kinds of physical characteristics like the shape of the ears, the size of the feet, and even the texture of the dog's coat or how much his tail curves. While I always appreciate seeing a really stellar example of any breed, when you come right down to it, I just like being around all those happy, healthy dogs.

My first stop was the "Information" table, where I picked up a show catalog. I scanned the Judging Schedule and saw I was in luck. The wire fox terriers were on for ten-thirty in Ring Number Two of the Red Tent, and I was just in time.

I stepped inside the huge tent festooned with crimson flags. More than half the space had been divided into two show rings. Dogs and their hopeful owners, sporting bright blue armbands printed with a number, were packed into the rest of it, awaiting their turn in the ring. I was amazed at all the paraphernalia the owners had dragged along. Even though the temperature had already topped 90° and the air was heavy with humidity, they'd lugged giant metal crates, portable grooming tables, folding chairs, ice chests, and huge tote bags stuffed with brushes, shampoos, favorite toys, water bowls, towels, and dog treats across East Brompton Green. It made carrying my medical practice around in a van look easy.

Yet while the humans looked a little droopy, the dogs couldn't have been perkier.

"Hey, fella!" I greeted a spunky fox terrier who stood on a grooming table. Although his eyes were bright and his posture was alert, he was exhibiting remarkable patience. For a dog that had been bred to hunt foxes, chasing them down relentlessly and then digging them out of their holes with paws powerful enough to burrow through an Oriental carpet, standing still for more than twenty seconds was an unfathomable hardship.

His owner, however, didn't seem the least bit appreciative of his cooperativeness. The heavyset woman, decked out in a yellow appliquéd blouse and a bright red skirt printed with tiny fox terriers, sniffed and sighed in frustration as she pulled a wire brush through his coarse fur.

"Freddie, you're being *such* a naughty boy today," she hissed. "You *know* how important this is to Mommy! I *need* you to do this for me. Do you think you can calm down long enough to win Mommy a blue ribbon?"

I made a mental note to give Max, a fellow terrier

with the same frisky temperament, a special dog treat the instant I saw him. An extra hug, too.

"What a beautiful dog," I commented.

She looked at me with surprise. "You have *no* idea what the competition is like out there," she replied tartly. "And Freddie gets so *tense* at these things!"

The owner next to her appeared to be having a much better time—maybe because his dog's breed wasn't on the schedule until that afternoon. The lean, middle-aged man was engaged in an energetic game of tug-of-war with his sleek, white miniature bull terrier. The dog's muscular, squarely built physique made him look as if he were taking the whole thing very seriously. And he was certainly growling ferociously enough. But his mischievous expression, especially the glint in his eyes, gave away the fact that he was enjoying the moment as much as his master.

As I strolled by, he let go of the rubber toy and looked over at me expectantly, wagging his tail.

"Mind if I pet him?" I asked his owner.

"Go right ahead," he answered congenially. "Just don't be surprised when Marshmallow tries to follow you home."

An announcement came over the sound system, cutting through the din: "The wire fox terriers are now competing for Best of Breed in Ring Number Two."

The mood around me instantly shifted as a half-dozen terrier aficionados prepared for competition. I was delighted by the sight of one healthy, meticulously groomed fox terrier after another streaming into the ring. Even though only six dogs were competing, the scene reminded me of a merry-go-round—one made with spunky canines instead of horses.

The owners busily set about posing their dogs in the required position, known as "stacking." I zeroed in on Freddie, who seemed to be doing just fine. His "Mommy," however, was beet-red. I was tempted to rush over to her with a bowl of water, smoothing her ears and telling her to calm down.

The judge, an earnest-looking older gentleman in a blue-and-white striped seersucker suit and an old-fashioned straw hat, motioned for the first dog to be presented. His owner, a prim-looking young woman whose straight dark brown hair was held back from her face with a white velvet headband, leaped into action. She deftly lifted her terrier onto the table by placing one hand under his chin and the other under his tail, a strategy I knew helped avoid undoing the rigorous grooming process the dog had just undergone.

I held my breath as I watched the judge begin his hands-on examination. The anxiety in the tent was contagious. He ran his fingers over the animal, much as I was in the habit of doing. But instead of checking for irregularities like growths or enlarged organs, he was getting a feel for the dog's body structure. Next he looked into his mouth, counting his teeth and checking his bite. As he moved toward the back to check the dog's testicles, the dog's owner slipped him a snack to distract him. I made a mental note to try that little trick in my own practice.

But dog shows were like life in that appearance only got you so far. After the judge had examined each of the competitors, he instructed, "Take the dogs around."

The owners gaited the spirited terriers, trotting them around the ring in a circle as the judge looked on. Freddie's owner looked a little more relaxed, at least if her face returning to its normal color was any indication. Still, she gripped the leash tightly and her mouth was drawn into a straight line. As for Freddie, he looked as if he were having a blast. I was glad he hadn't succumbed to the neuroses of his pushy stage mother.

And then, just like that, it was over. The dogs stood by patiently, as if they understood the importance of what was going on as they waited for the judge to make his decision. The owners weren't doing nearly as well. They all looked nervous.

The judge pointed to the winner. Freddie! I let out a sigh of relief, pleased that he'd come through. I hoped his owner would finally give him a hug and play a few rounds of Frisbee or tennis ball with him, now that the hard part was over. He'd earned it.

It wasn't until I stepped outside the tent and was heading back to my booth that I realized my palms were sweaty. I'd gotten more emotionally involved in watching the competition than I'd realized.

This dog-show business is *murder,* I thought.

For some reason, having that particular turn of phrase pop into my head made me uncomfortable. But I decided I was just reacting to all the tension in the air that was the result of everyone else's dog-show jitters. I put the thought out of my head as I strode across Brompton Green, back toward the "Ask The Vet" booth.

# Chapter 5

"I love a dog. He does nothing for political reasons."
—Will Rogers

Noon rolled around quickly. Emily headed over to the refreshment tent for the hour-long lunch break, but I had a house call to make.

As my dogs and I headed across East Brompton Green, toward my van, the two of them bounced along ecstatically. The mere prospect of any activity whatsoever that has something to do with a vehicle tends to have that effect on them. As we drew closer, Max pulled on his leash so hard that he started to choke. As for Lou, he pranced around gleefully, as if the phrase "high on life" had been created with him in mind.

Once we reached the van, I made a point of giving them each a bowl of water. During the summer, hyperthermia—heat stroke—is always something to watch out for in dogs. They can't resist running around when they're outside, and high temperatures can cause them to become dehydrated. Max and Lou lapped up the water eagerly, and we got on our way.

I'd driven through the village of East Brompton before, visiting the few clients I had out here. But I'd usually been in a hurry—or else scanning the street signs, trying to locate a particular address. This time, I drank in my surroundings, wanting to get a sense of exactly what made the Bromptons such a desirable place for the rich and famous. The charming little town had a rich history. By the mid-1600s, British colonists had already figured out that eastern Long Island was a pretty congenial place. In addition to settling in Massachusetts and Virginia, they also built several communities here on the South Fork, naming them after their hometown of Brompton, England.

When I reached the intersection of Main Street and the village's major cross street, Brompton Road, I squinted, trying to imagine how this area looked to those early residents. The midday sun cast a golden glow over the landscape, and I had to admit the quaint little town looked magical.

Still, East Brompton had changed quite a bit since its early days. True, a few historic houses, churches, and wooden windmills still remained, thanks to the preservation efforts of local historical societies. And much of the area retained its casual, countrified feeling, partly because of the rustic landscape and partly because of the shabby-chic look the summer residents cultivated. But these days, the buildings lining the two intersecting streets that constituted downtown housed swanky designer clothing boutiques, restaurants that featured local produce and seafood, a few basic necessities like the public library and Town Hall, and a seemingly endless supply of real-estate brokers.

Max, Lou, and I drove to the edge of town, where the natty shops and sprawling estates gave way to a cluster of undistinguished industrial buildings. I found the Ice Castles ice sculpture studio wedged between a T-shirt embroidery establishment and a hot tub wholesaler. I was struck by the contrast between the squat, gray concrete building and the glamorous parties at which the dramatic ice sculptures produced inside were showcased.

For Max and Lou, arriving at a destination—any destination—was as exciting as driving there. Predictably, they shot out of the van the moment I opened the door.

"Be-*have*!" I commanded, fully aware that I sounded like I was doing a bad Austin Powers imitation.

I held on to their leashes tightly as my rambunctious mutts and I headed toward the front door. I tried the knob and found it was locked, so I buzzed. Peering through the small window, I saw someone moving through what looked like a front office. Still, I jumped when the door opened. The man standing on the other side was brandishing a chain saw.

I took a few steps backwards. "Is, uh, Gary Frye here?"

"Yeah. Come on in."

I followed him inside, keeping my distance. I'd shrieked through enough slasher films during my wild and crazy teenage years to know the cardinal rule about never trusting anyone carrying a chain saw. Still, this guy seemed okay. He led me through the front office, a boxy room that contained little more than a gray metal desk, matching file cabinets, and a phone. The only sign of life was a contented white cat stretched out on the sill of the sole window in the room, basking in the warmth of whatever sunlight made it through the thick pane of frosted glass. I left Max and Lou in her charge, figuring she looked self-possessed enough to keep them in line.

The real action, I quickly realized, was in back.

A large open warehouse stretched beyond the front office, cool and damp but not nearly as cold as I'd expected. One area was walled off, and through its large windows I could see two men working. One was busy transforming a block of ice into a clown, while the other used sweeping strokes to create the outline of a polar bear. Both used chain saws as their magic wands. Chips flew everywhere, and the noise from the powerful tools was deafening.

Another man, casually transporting a towering ice lighthouse on a dolly, didn't seem to notice the noise. He rolled the sculpture across the concrete floor, taking it as far as a large, imposing door. It opened into a freezer. I peeked inside and saw a statue of Neptune, a baby grand piano, and a golfer, all carved from tremendous blocks of ice.

"Gary?" my escort yelled over the noise. "Yo, Gar-ry!"

I barely recognized the man who came out from behind a partition.

It was Gary, all right, the man I'd met at the party the night before. But today, he looked so distraught that he'd practically turned into a different person. His expression was stricken, and the dark rings under his eyes gave him a haunted look.

"*Gary?*" I asked.

"Dr. Popper. I forgot you were coming," he said apologetically. "Let's talk in the other room. It's quieter there."

Back in the front office, he didn't bother to turn on the lights. The only illumination came from the small window, his cat's choice for her noontime nap. The somber ambiance seemed to fit Gary's mood perfectly.

He sank into the chair behind the desk.

"Are you all right?" I asked.

"No." He laughed bitterly. "How can I be all right when I'm probably looking at a multimillion-dollar lawsuit—not to mention being accused of causing someone's death? All because some *nut* decides to use one of my ice sculptures as a murder weapon."

I felt as if I'd been slapped. "Murder? Is *that* what you think happened?"

"There's no doubt in my mind."

My heartbeat raced. I could scarcely believe what I was hearing. Sure, it had occurred to me that Devon Barnett's death might not have been an accident, given his widespread unpopularity. But I'd chalked that idea up to my overly active imagination. Now, hearing Gary voice what I'd thought was nothing more than my own far-fetched rumination chilled me to the bone.

It also set off a little bell in my head. Murder was a subject I happened to find fascinating. I'd even put my intellectual interest into practice a few months earlier when I'd found myself smack in the middle of a murder investigation just a mile or two from my home in Joshua's Hollow. But long before that, I'd found the process of finding answers to seemingly unanswerable questions intriguing. In fact, Nick had once accused me of being more interested in the cases he handled in his private-investigation practice than he was. He'd compared me to Nancy Drew—and I had to admit that he hadn't been far off base.

"Look, I've been in this business for eighteen years," Gary went on, shaking his head in disgust. "I've done parties for the governor and for U.S. Senators and even presidential candidates who were campaigning out here in the Bromptons. I've done events for the biggest companies you can think of—and the richest, most important, most *litigious* people imaginable. Don't you think that by now I've figured out I have to do everything I possibly can to protect myself?

"Last night," he continued, "after you left the gazebo, I did exactly what I told you I was going to do: secure the sculptures so they wouldn't fall. Even though Phyllis insisted it would look bad and forbade me to do it, I stretched strips of wire behind the dogs and tied them to the gazebo's columns. They were solid—strong enough that even a Saint Bernard couldn't have shaken one of my ice sculptures loose, much less a fifty-pound bulldog.

"After that waitress started screaming and all hell broke loose, I ran back to the gazebo as fast as I could. Those strips of wire were *gone,* man. Like they'd never even existed. Somebody must have cut them down."

"What about your helper? Couldn't he—or she—have taken them down?"

Gary looked at me quizzically. " 'Helper'?"

"Your assistant, or whoever was cleaning up in the gazebo."

"I didn't have anybody else from Ice Castles with me last night, if that's what you mean. I was working alone."

I decided not to mention that I'd seen somebody lurking behind the ice sculptures after everyone else had moved into the tent. At least, not yet. My thoughts were still too muddled as I tried to sift through everything Gary was telling me, and I wasn't about to complicate things even further. "In that case, is there any chance Phyllis removed them?"

"No way. I made a point of keeping my eyes on her the rest of the time—until just before disaster struck, anyway. I made sure she didn't go near the ice sculpture display because I had a feeling she'd go nuts if she saw what I'd done."

"How about someone on her staff?"

"I kept an eye on the gazebo until the cocktail hour was over. I'm positive nobody messed with it. I watched while the caterers cleaned up the hors d'oeuvres. They took everything away except the ice sculptures. It was my job to get rid of them, and I figured I'd wait until dinner was underway."

Gary looked at me earnestly. "But once everybody was out of there, I went back to my truck to get some paperwork I needed to leave behind with Mr. Bolger. I swear on my life that the only way that ice sculpture could have fallen over is if somebody *wanted* it to fall over. Somebody had to have pushed it over the side of the gazebo. There's no other way it could have fallen."

"What about the police's theory that Rufus—Shawn Elliot's bulldog—was responsible?"

Gary shook his head. "Highly unlikely if not impossible. I'm telling you, those wires held the sculptures firmly in place."

"Have you heard from any lawyers?" I asked, struggling to sound matter-of-fact. "Or the police?"

"Not yet. But I'm sure it's only a matter of time." He sighed. "But, hey, you didn't come here to listen to me complain, did you?"

I blinked in confusion.

"Lulu? Her conjunctivitis?"

"Oh, right." For a moment, I'd forgotten all about the profession I'd spent nearly a decade of my life training for. I was too busy thinking about Gary's startling contention that Devon Barnett hadn't been the victim of a freak accident, after all, but that his death had been deliberate.

"So let's have a look at Lulu," I suggested, determined to focus on his cat—at least for now.

He retrieved the sleek white feline from the windowsill. She didn't seem happy about giving up her primo spot.

With Max and Lou in tow, I led Gary and Lulu out to my van and set the cat on the examining table. While Gary filled out some paperwork, I ran my hands along her spine, then palpated her internal organs to make sure everything was in order. She seemed just fine. Then I checked her eyes. Lulu appeared to have a superficial ocular infection.

"Your diagnosis was right on target," I told him. "I'm going to give you this oxytetracycline HCL ointment.

You need to put it right on the eyeball itself, twice a day. I'll show you how. Do it for two weeks, to be safe. I'm also giving Lulu a course of doxycycline. There's a chance it could be chlamydia, which could become a chronic problem, so I'd like you to give her fifty milligrams twice a day for fourteen days. Just make sure you give it to her when there's food in her stomach."

"Whatever you say, Doc."

"I see she hasn't had a rabies shot in a while," I said, checking her tag. "What vaccines does she normally get, just upper respiratory?"

"She got her regular shots about a year ago. That was the last time I brought her in."

"Any adverse reaction?"

"Not that I remember."

"I have to give her a rabies shot, by law, and she's due for her distemper and upper respiratory booster," I told him. "That's something we can do right now. I'll give her the rabies in her right hind leg. If you notice that a small lump develops in about a week, don't be upset. It'll go away by itself in a month. Call your regular vet if it doesn't."

I inoculated Lulu against rabies, then gave her a feline distemper booster in her right shoulder. She was surprisingly cooperative. "I'm going to give you a new rabies tag, too. They're a different color and shape every year, so if she's ever outside and bites somebody, they can see that she's had her rabies vaccine."

"Thanks," Gary said, scooping up his cat and fondling her ears. "I really appreciate this—even though I probably seem pretty crabby. This isn't exactly the best day of my life. Send me a bill, okay? I really am grateful that you came by today."

After I'd given him a quick lesson in how to apply the medicine, he grunted his thanks and turned to leave. He was halfway out the door of my van when I called, "Gary?"

"Yeah?" He barely turned, instead looking back at me over his shoulder.

"I believe you. That Devon Barnett may have been murdered, I mean."

"Great," he said sourly. "Now all you have to do is convince the police, the insurance company, the newspaper, the guy's family, and anybody else who's the least bit interested."

I didn't tell him that exact same thought had already occurred to me.

· · ·

As soon as Gary was out of earshot, I dialed the Town of East Brompton Police on my cell phone. It wasn't easy. The first obstacle was the crazed Westie in my lap, repeatedly thrusting his four spiky paws into my thighs with the force of a jackhammer as he policed the flock of birds that dared to perch in the tree right outside the window. The second was the whiny Dalmatian who was also trying to crawl into my lap, no doubt convinced he deserved some cuddling, too.

"Come on, you guys," I pleaded. "Can't you—"

"East Brompton Police," a woman's voice answered crisply.

I immediately switched to a more professional tone. "Good morning. My name is Dr. Jessica Popper, and I believe I may have been a witness to a crime. Last night, I was at Russell Bolger's estate when Devon Barnett was killed by the falling ice sculpture, and—"

"You mean the accident, right?"

I hesitated. "I'm not so sure it *was* an accident. I've spoken to the—"

"I'll have to take your name and number," the woman interrupted me, sounding about as interested in what I had to say as if I was a telemarketer. "There's nobody here who can talk to you right now. That was Dr. Pepper, right?"

"Popper," I corrected her patiently. "P-O-P-P-E-R." No relation to the soft drink, I was tempted to add. Instead, I gave her my cell phone number, repeating it three times before she got it right.

I felt an odd mixture of excitement and dread as I tucked away my cell phone and turned the key in the ignition. Murder was a subject I found absolutely fascinating, and it was beginning to look like one might have occurred right under my nose.

• • •

I checked my watch and saw I didn't have much time before I was due back at the dog show. By that point, my stomach was growling loudly enough that Lou kept staring at it, cocking his head and growling back. I decided to grab something to go.

I cruised along Main Street, hoping to find a place whose prices weren't too shocking. Nothing looked promising. I turned down a side street, wondering if I'd be lucky to find an eatery the locals frequented.

After spotting a couple of possibilities, I pulled into the first parking space I found that was sufficiently shaded. I locked Max and Lou in the van once again, pouring cool water into a bowl for them and being sure to leave the windows open. As usual, I apologized profusely for leaving them alone and assured them I'd be back ASAP.

I decided to start with the small gourmet shop on the corner, the Pampered Pantry. As soon as I stepped inside, I saw from the posted price list that this place was way out of my league. Forget the lobster salad and the caviar plate. Even a tuna on rye would have required taking on a second job. Still, stopping in wasn't a complete waste. I bought a copy of the local newspaper, *The East Bromp-*

*ton Banner,* even though it only came out weekly and was dated the previous Tuesday. And on my way out, I noticed a stack of booklets titled *Guide to the Brompt-tons.* The sign above read, "Free! Take One!" I did.

The Lucky Shamrock, half a block farther down, tucked between a video store and a dry cleaner, was a much better bet. Inside, the bar-and-grill was cool and dark, with rough wooden floors and booths with high backs. The decorations ran along the lines of a neon Bud Light sign and an inflatable Cuervo Gold bottle. Only a few patrons sat at the bar and the booths, most of them alone. Nearly all of them kept their eyes glued to the television suspended from the ceiling.

"What can I get you?" the bartender asked congenially. With his red hair, freckles, and wide grin—not to mention his bright green shirt—he looked like he belonged in a place called the Lucky Shamrock.

I ordered a sandwich and iced tea to go, then let my eyes drift up to the television screen, just like everybody else around me. The Channel 14 logo permanently lodged on the lower right told me we were all watching the local news, like it or not. I half-watched a segment on a high school cheerleading squad headed for some national competition. But the next segment snapped me to attention.

"Today, members of Norfolk County's top brass came out to celebrate the opening of a new athletic complex for children and teens." Behind the blond reporter who stood in front of the camera, I could see a sprawling collection of buildings surrounded by green fields. "The new Jose Nunez Center in East Metchogue will house a swimming pool, basketball courts, and outdoor facilities for soccer, baseball, and track."

The camera panned across a group of dignitaries standing on a podium, a half-dozen men and women who looked like they were dying for their turn at the microphone. I zeroed in on one of them, standing toward the back.

"Also in attendance at the ribbon-cutting ceremony was Lieutenant Anthony Falcone. Lieutenant Falcone became Norfolk County's new chief of homicide back in December."

My mouth dropped open as I watched Falcone practically elbow his way through the crowd of dignitaries, doggedly making a beeline for the microphone. He was a small, wiry man with eyes so dark they looked as if they could burn holes in you. I noticed that as he snaked through the crowd, he straightened his tie, then reached up to slick back his shiny, carefully styled black hair.

He had to stand on his toes to get close enough to the mike to speak. That didn't deter him in the least.

"This is truly a great day for Norfolk County," he announced in a thick Long Island accent. "Our children are our future. I'm proud to be part of this great recreational facility, which will go a long way in helping young people all over Long Island achieve their potential—"

He was still talking when the camera cut to the newsroom.

"Here you go." The bartender handed me a brown paper bag. "That's seven-twenty-five. Need a straw?"

After we'd settled up and I headed out of the Lucky Shamrock, I was still thinking about Falcone. I'd noticed his picture in the newspaper before, but this was the first time I'd seen him in action. I was struck by his intensity. I was also surprised by what a media hound he was. His predecessor, Lieutenant Harned, had preferred to stay in the background. But from what I could see, this Falcone character was something else entirely.

I wondered how he felt about amateur sleuths.

•  •  •

All afternoon I kept my cell phone in my pants pocket. I must have checked it a hundred times, anxious to make sure the battery hadn't fizzled out or that I hadn't been too distracted to hear it ring. There had to be some logical explanation why the East Brompton Police weren't more interested in hearing what a concerned citizen had to say about the possibility that Devon Barnett hadn't been the victim of an accident after all.

By the end of the day, I was debating whether to call again. Maybe my message got lost, I reasoned, not wanting to believe it had simply been ignored. I dialed the number again.

"East Brompton Police," the same woman answered in the same uninterested voice.

"This is Dr. Jessica Popper. I called earlier today—"

"Yes, I know," she returned coldly. "I'm the one who took the message."

"No one's called me back yet, and—"

"Really? I handed it to Sergeant Bangs personally. Told him what you'd called about, too. He pretty much said the same thing I told you—that pending the autopsy, we're considering the photographer's death an accident."

"Yes, I know." I had to struggle to keep the impatience out of my voice. "But I'd still like to talk to him about it. I have some information he may be interested in. Would you please leave him another message?"

The woman sighed impatiently. "Suit yourself."

Well, one thing's for sure, I thought as I tucked away my cell phone. The East Brompton Police are convinced that Barnett died accidentally—and they're not exactly in a hurry to discuss any other possibilities. In fact, from the looks of things, nobody besides Gary Frye seems particularly interested in whether Devon Barnett was murdered.

Nobody, that is, except me.

• • •

For the rest of the afternoon, I couldn't stop thinking about my bone-chilling conversation with Gary Frye. I was certain he'd been telling the truth about reinforcing the ice sculptures.

In fact, the more I thought about it, the more it made sense that Devon Barnett had been murdered, rather than the victim of a random event—especially one as unlikely as a bulldog bumping into a table. The circumstances surrounding the paparazzo's death were simply too suspicious. First, no one had witnessed the so-called "accident," a fact the medical examiner himself had stated. That, combined with the dog-proof safety system Gary claimed he'd rigged up, and the fact I was *positive* I'd spotted someone sneaking into the gazebo, constituted the physical realities.

Even more compelling was the fact that Barnett had been so universally despised.

By the end of the day, my resolve to find out more about the paparazzo's death was strong. True, the last time I'd gotten involved in a murder investigation, I'd come close to being killed. But the mere idea that someone had actually been murdered—and that whoever was responsible might go free—was simply too horrifying to ignore.

After I said good-bye to Emily and thanked her for all her help, I climbed into my van with Max and Lou. But instead of heading home, I drove back into town. I cruised along Main Street until I spotted the biggest, flashiest florist I could find. This time, I brought my two sidekicks inside with me. While they like to act tough—especially Max—the truth is that those two bundles of fur love flowers. In fact, I had to stop bringing carnations home because Max was so fond of nibbling them. But both of them loved stretching out for a nap in the middle of the lilies of the valley my neighbor and landlady, Betty Vandervoort, planted around her mansion-style home.

They appreciated the gesture. The leggy Dalmatian and the squat, feisty Westie didn't try to hide their enthusiasm as we entered the tiny shop and were immediately surrounded by the nearly overpowering fragrance of hundreds of flowers. Lou just stood there, looking enraptured and breathing in deeply, his black, wet nose pulsating in ecstasy. Max waddled over to a display of freesia and stuck his nose in unceremoniously, half his face disappearing into the profusion of soft pink petals.

A young woman with two long blonde braids, a flowered skirt down to her ankles, and purple Birkenstocks stepped out from behind the counter. "Hi!" she said cheerily. "How can I help you?" If she noticed Max slobbering over her merchandise, she was too polite to comment.

"I'd like to send flowers, but I'm afraid I don't know the person's address," I explained. My heart pounded as I wondered if my little ploy would work.

"Maybe I can help," she said. "At least, if it's somebody local."

"I want to send an arrangement to Devon Barnett's house. The photographer?"

Her smile faded. "Yeah, I heard about that. Weird, huh?"

My ears pricked up like Max's. "How do you mean?"

"Oh, just the way he died. I mean, can you imagine getting killed by an ice sculpture? It's freaky. I mean, what are the odds of *that* happening?"

I didn't tell her I was starting to wonder the exact same thing.

I picked out a dignified arrangement, then wrote out a card with the message, "Our deepest sympathy. Funds for Our Furry Friends." When it came time to settle up, I paid cash.

"About where to send them . . ." I said.

"No problem. I know where he lives—*lived*. One-forty-five Beach Lane."

The address was instantly stored in my memory bank.

"They'll be delivered some time this afternoon," she told me. "Is that soon enough?"

"Terrific. Thanks for your help."

I was about to leave the shop when the woman asked, "Were the two of you friends?"

"Not really. More like acquaintances."

"Figures."

Her response surprised me, and I guess my expression showed it.

"It's just that, from what I've heard about the guy," she said with a shrug, "I figured he didn't really *have* any friends."

As soon as I reached my van, I checked my map. Instead of driving home via the most direct route, I took a slight detour. It was only a few miles out of my way—and it took me right past Devon Barnett's house.

# Chapter 6

"There are three faithful friends—an old wife, an old dog, and ready money."

—Ben Franklin

Even though I now knew Devon Barnett's address, as soon as I turned onto Beach Lane I discovered his house would have been hard to miss. While it was similar to all the others on the block in terms of its grandeur, the bright Caribbean colors of its exterior differentiated it from all the rest. The house itself was a sunny yellow. But that was just the backdrop for its bubble-gum pink front door, apple-green door frame, and turquoise wooden shutters.

Once the shock wore off, something else caught my eye. While the grass was so green it looked as if it, too, had been painted with painstaking care, its perfection was marred by a small blotch of brown.

Even from my van, I could see that it was a badly mangled rawhide stick.

Devon Barnett had owned a dog.

The idea intrigued me. I'd already become familiar with his ruthless side, the aspects of his personality that had motivated Shawn Elliot to dub him "the most hated man in Hollywood." It had never occurred to me that the notorious paparazzo had also been a dog-lover.

I got out of my van, bringing Max and Lou with me as I gave in to the temptation to investigate at closer range. About twenty feet beyond the mutilated rawhide, alongside the house, I spotted something yellow. When I got closer, I saw it was a rubber banana, chewed almost beyond recognition.

When I saw what lay another thirty feet beyond, I gasped. I'd seen my share of doghouses in my day, but never anything like this. Even though I knew I was trespassing—probably risking arrest in a town like this—I couldn't resist crossing the grass.

The lucky canine who resided with Devon Barnett lived in a house that was an exact replica of his master's mansion. The architecture was precisely the same, down to the wooden shutters. The paint job was also identical. I got down on all fours to get a better look, not even caring about the inevitable grass stains.

*"Jessie?"*

I jumped up at the unexpected sound of my own name. I was even more surprised when I turned and saw Chess LaMont standing on the lawn. He was dressed only in a black bathing suit the size of a G-string. His muscular body, including his perfectly hairless chest, had been slathered in oil, giving his skin a disconcerting sheen.

Two distinctive accessories complemented his outfit. One of them, a gold nipple ring that matched his eyebrow ring, made me cringe. I found it much easier to focus on the other one. The perky Havanese tucked under his arm was as well-groomed as he was, her hair brushed to an impressive state of fluffiness. She, too, was dressed in black, although her tiny garments took the form of a satin ribbon tied around her neck and a matching bow atop her head that kept her fur out of her eyes.

"Chess! What a surprise!"

I was about to ask him what he was doing there when he crouched down beside the doghouse. Max and Lou immediately introduced themselves to the pretty pup. There was so much tail-wagging it created a breeze.

"Isn't it wonderful?" he cooed. "The exterior is an exact replica of the main house. We even had it painted the same colors. See, the front door is Sweet Pea Pink and the shutters are Bimini Blue."

"It's amazing," I said sincerely. "I've seen dogs with some pretty luxurious digs in my day, but I've never seen anything quite like this."

Chess beamed. "I got the idea when Nettie and I were in Key West."

" 'Nettie'?" Of course, I'd heard him refer to his lover as "Nettie" before. I just hadn't bothered to think about how it fit into the grand scheme of things.

"My pet name for Devon Barnett; Nettie . . . get it?"

I blinked. "You and Devon Barnett are—partners?"

"We were. Until that stupid ice sculpture of Lady fell on him and the cruel randomness of Fate took him away from me." Chess scooped up the Havanese and hugged her close against his bare chest, his eyes filling with tears. "And now Zsa Zsa and I are all alone. Aren't we, precious? All because of Shawn Elliot's clumsy bulldog. It's just you and me against the cold, cruel world."

I glanced around at the ostentatious estate. Chess and Zsa Zsa may have been left alone, but from the looks of things, they weren't exactly Ragged Dick and Little Orphan Annie.

"Anyway," Chess continued bravely, "while we were down in the Keys, Nettie dragged me on a tour of Hemingway's house. I thought I'd be bored silly, but it turns out that Ernest was a true animal lover. He had something like sixty cats. And he loved them so much that he had a cute little cat house built for them that was a replica of his house."

He nuzzled the white mop draped across his arm. "And Zsa Zsa deserves the very best, don't you? Oh, yes, you do. *Yes,* you *do-o-o.*"

He stopped suddenly, as if he'd just remembered I was there. "If you didn't know Nettie and I were a couple, how did you know you'd find me here?"

"I—I didn't." I struggled to do some fast thinking. "I, uh, just happened to be driving by—well, it wasn't entirely a coincidence, since I was curious about where Devon Barnett lived. I mean, I *did* know him, at least a little, so of course I'm upset about what happened. Anyway, I saw the doghouse, and I couldn't resist stopping to get a better look."

"Actually, I'm glad you're here, Jessie." Chess sounded miserable. "Maybe I look like I'm handling all this pretty well, but the truth is, I'm still in shock. I deserve an Oscar for managing to act in control enough to arrange his cremation this morning."

"Are you planning a funeral or a memorial service?" I asked gently.

"Just the cremation. I thought I'd scatter his ashes right here in the backyard, since he loved this house so much. Zsa Zsa and I will do it together." By way of explanation, he added, "Nettie didn't have a lot of friends."

"What about his family?"

"Disowned him." Bitterly, he added, "It turns out his family in Crockettsville, Louisiana, is no more open-minded than my relatives back in Crabapple, Iowa."

His expression softened. "Come inside and have some iced tea. I make it with fresh mint I grow myself, right here in my garden. I throw in a couple of secret ingredients, too, but I'll never tell." He bit his lip, his eyes once again filling with tears. "My iced tea was Nettie's favorite. He used to call me his 'Happy Homemaker.'"

"Thanks, Chess. I'd be happy to." I hesitated. "Is it okay if I bring these two monsters?"

"Of course. If this place isn't dog-friendly, I don't know *what* is."

The inside of the house that Devon Barnett had shared with his lover was as striking as the outside. The same bright colors were everywhere, splashed on the walls, in the fabrics, and in the endless clutter that gave the house a cheerful, lived-in look. I was particularly captivated by a framed picture hanging on the living room wall that featured extraordinarily bold colors.

"I have that poster, too," I observed.

"Oh, that's not a poster," Chess replied matter-of-factly. "That's the original. Don't you just love David Hockney? We have a Renoir, too. Nettie had excellent taste."

"I'll say," I muttered.

My dogs and I followed Chess and Zsa Zsa into the kitchen, taking in the granite counters, Sub-Zero freezer, and every other desirable accountrement I'd ever seen on the Home and Garden Channel. I paused in front of a shelf lined with unusual cookie jars.

Chess noticed me studying them. "Part of Andy Warhol's collection," he informed me.

Up until that point, it never would have occurred to me there could be so much money in stalking celebrities. I was beginning to understand the motivation behind Devon Barnett's relentlessness.

"This is a fabulous place," I told him sincerely as I sat down at the kitchen table. I was relieved that after Chess placed Zsa Zsa on the floor, he took a bright Hawaiian shirt off the back of a chair and pulled it on. Just looking at that nipple ring made me shudder.

"Isn't it fun?" Chess took a pitcher of iced tea out of

the refrigerator. "I tried to talk Nettie into getting a photographer from one of the design magazines in here, but he wouldn't hear of it. It's funny; he was a very private person."

"Yet he made his living publicizing the comings and goings of other people."

I was simply thinking out loud. But Chess set his lips firmly in a straight line.

"And look at the thanks he got." His tone was icier than the pitcher of frosty mint tea he held in his hands. "You'd think all those celebrities had never heard the saying, 'There's no such thing as bad publicity'—which I happen to believe is true ninety-nine percent of the time. You'd think they would have been *thrilled* with the coverage he got them. They should have kissed his feet. Instead, they treated him like something you'd find under a rock."

He sniffed indignantly. "Everybody complains about the paparazzi, but nobody acknowledges how popular their work is. I mean, look at the tabloids like the *Stargazer* and the *Gossip Gazette*. Why do you think they even exist in the first place? Because the public—you and me, Mr. and Mrs. Joe Average—can't get enough of the movie stars and the TV personalities and the other celebrities we all treat like gods!

"Those papers sell millions of copies every single week. And do you think they'd fly off the newsstands if they were full of factual tidbits about what Brad Pitt eats for breakfast? Of course not! People want drama! They want sensation! Most of all, they want reassurance that, when you come right down to it, the celebrities we've all put on a pedestal aren't any better—or happier—than the rest of us."

Chess kept talking as he poured us each a tall glass of iced tea. "Take Kara Liebling. We've all seen a million pictures of her looking like a fashion model. And we all know somebody spent two hours on her hair, giving it that flyaway look, and somebody else spent two hours on her makeup, making her look like she's not wearing any, and somebody else took some five-thousand-dollar designer gown and fit it to her like it was her own skin. But we don't think about that. We just think about her perfection. We yearn for it for ourselves, but we know that never in a million years will we come even *close* to tasting it in our lives.

"So isn't it reassuring to see a picture of her screaming at some autograph hound who's been hassling her, with her hair sticking out all over the place and a big stain on her shirt, and maybe, if we're really lucky, a big zit in the middle of her forehead? I love Kara like a sister, and I'm the first to admit that she can be made to look like an absolute princess. But the reality is that sometimes, she's just as tired and frustrated and miserable as the rest of us!"

Chess's passion startled me.

"It's not as if Nettie didn't work his butt off," he went on in the same bitter tone. "And it wasn't just standing out in the rain and the snow or sleeping in people's backyards. A lot of times he had to be extraordinarily creative. Nobody ever gave him credit for that.

"Like he came up with this really clever way of getting a person's address. He'd call up somebody who knew them and tell them that, by mistake, he'd gotten a piece of mail delivered to his house that was in their name. He'd ask for the correct address, saying he wanted to send it to them. And if they wouldn't give it out, he'd give them a little nudge by saying it looked like it was a check. At that point, they always changed their tune."

"Clever," I said. *Devious,* I thought.

Chess glanced at the pitcher of iced tea in his hands, as if he had just remembered he was holding it. He turned and put it back in the refrigerator. "Sorry if I got a little carried away. This happens to be a subject I feel very strongly about."

"Of course you do," I said soothingly. "Devon Barnett was someone who really mattered to you."

"I loved him," he said simply. "I still do. And I always will."

He bent over and scooped up Zsa Zsa. "Come here, my precious little princess. Daddy needs a great big hug."

Suddenly, he stiffened. Noticing that his eyes were fixed on something behind me, I turned to look.

Standing in the doorway was a woman the size and shape of a telephone booth. Even though she was carrying a plastic bucket overflowing with every cleaning product ever invented, she was wearing a dress. The fabric was a solemn shade of blue, and it was completely unadorned. Its high neck was surprisingly modest, especially given the warmth of the June day. The same went for the sleeves that hung below her elbows. She also wore a flowered apron, its bright oranges and yellows a jarring contrast to the rest of her outfit. Thick, dark beige pantyhose were stretched over her barrel-shaped calves, bunching up at her ankles like the skin on a shar-pei. On her feet, she wore a pair of padded black Nikes.

Her graying hair was pulled back into a tight bun. The expression on her face matched its severity. Small, light-colored eyes peered out at me from narrowed slits. Her mouth was also a narrow slit, thin lips drawn into a tight straight line.

Lou immediately retreated under the table. Max, meanwhile, let out a low growl. I scooped him up and held his tense body in my arms.

"Hello," I said cheerfully.

"I am Hilda," she barked. "I clean."

Her accent struck me as Eastern European. "Nice to meet you, Hilda."

She appeared to have finished with the pleasantries. Turning to Chess and scowling, she said, "Dogs bring dirt in house."

"That's just silly." He clasped the mass of white fur even more tightly to his chest. "Especially Zsa Zsa. She's immaculate. Besides, she's so light on her feet that her paws barely touch the ground."

"Dog carry germs," she insisted. "I clean kitchen now."

"Hilda, we're talking in here. Do you think you could work somewhere else?" Covering his mouth so only I could hear, he muttered, "Like Iceland?"

Hilda didn't budge. "I clean living room. I clean dining room. Now I clean kitchen."

"Oh, just go do the bathrooms or something. Surely you can find some of those *germs* you're always chasing after in some *other* part of the house!"

She cast him a look capable of taking the varnish off a table. Then, still clutching her plastic bucket, she stomped out of the room.

"I *hate* her," Chess hissed the moment she was gone. "Nettie insisted that we keep the house absolutely immaculate. And once he found that battle-ax, no one else would do." He shuddered. "He had a thing about dirt."

Ironic, I thought, considering he made his living reveling in it.

"I'm getting rid of her," Chess continued petulantly. "As soon as I get my bearings, I'm going to fire that monster. But for now, I'll just do what I've always done: disappear the minute she gets here. Go hang out at some restaurant like the Sand Bar or the beach or something."

The Sand Bar. I made a mental note to scope it out the first chance I got.

"If she does a good job of keeping this place clean, she's probably worth holding on to," I commented. "It's a big house."

"It's a *huge* house," Chess corrected me. "Speaking of which, would you like to see the rest of it?"

"I'd love to."

I left Max and Lou in the kitchen with Zsa Zsa, not wanting any stray dog hairs to incur Hilda's wrath. Chess placated the three of them with a few gourmet brand Milk-Bones, doled out from one of Andy Warhol's cookie jars. Then he took me on the grand tour, pointing out the highlights along the way.

"And this is the guest room. The silk wall coverings are from France; the chandelier is Venetian glass—"

"Did you decorate it yourself?"

He looked pleased. "How did you know?"

"Just a hunch. Are you a professional?"

"Oh, Jessie, you are pulling me right out of the doldrums. You're better than an illegal substance. No, honey, I'm not a professional. Not that I didn't train for it. That, and about a thousand other occupations."

He sighed. "When I moved to New York from that *pit* of a hometown of mine, I didn't have a single marketable skill. I skipped around from job to job, each one drearier than the last. But when I met Nettie, he insisted on helping me improve myself. He paid tuition at all kinds of different schools while I tried to 'find myself.' I started out in hairdressing school, but it turned out I was allergic to hair spray. Then I tried cosmetology. I thought I was a natural, but the teacher said I made everybody look like a drag queen. Then came cooking school, but we won't even go there. Decorating was next, but most people didn't share my taste." He grimaced. "The instructor told me I should get a job designing brothels. How's that for encouraging America's youth?

"Still," he went on wistfully, "it was such a happy time in my life. I was so glad to have gotten myself out of Crabapple. Still am. Every day of my life, I thank *God* for Greyhound buses. I'll never forget how ecstatic I was when I first moved to New York. I was like a kid on Christmas morning. I couldn't believe I was really there. Ever since I'd first seen it, back when I was sixteen, I just knew I had to find a way to get myself there." He sighed. "I felt like Dorothy, finally getting to the Emerald City."

"You came to New York when you were sixteen?"

He nodded. "School trip. Something I'll never forget. And once I saw the Big City, I couldn't *wait* to move there. So that's exactly what I did, the day after my high school graduation."

By that point, we'd walked the entire house, except for the master bedroom. We found Hilda there, oblivious to us as she attacked the carpet with the vacuum cleaner. Chess just rolled his eyes, then walked right by.

On our way back to the kitchen, I noticed a closed door.

"What's this?" I asked.

"That leads to the basement. It's always kept locked."

"Ghosts?" I suggested. "Or just dust bunnies?"

"That is—*was*—Dev's photo studio." He stopped, his eyes filling with tears again. Then he shook his head hard, as if forcing himself to go on. "He—he developed his own negatives down there. He used a digital camera some of the time, but he still preferred the old-fashioned way. I think he loved the process of working with the film and the chemicals, seeing the pictures appear right before his eyes. Having *control* over the whole process. Besides, you can't alter real photographs the way you can play around with digital photos, so there's no doubt that whatever you see in the picture is real."

"Could I see his studio?"

"Heavens *no!*" Chess looked horrified. "Absolutely *nobody* was allowed in there! Nettie's studio was his sacred place. We need to respect that, even now. He practically had a *phobia* about anybody ever going into his workroom!"

His vehemence piqued my interest. A locked room that Barnett didn't allow anyone to enter—not even his lover?

I was still studying the door, scoping out the lock to see how formidable it looked, as Chess prattled on. "He was crazed about so many things. I used to call him 'Nervous Nettie.' Of course, that about drove him up the wall."

The tour led us back to the kitchen. The dogs, still chomping on their high-priced doggie treats, barely noticed our return.

"Chess," I asked, choosing my words carefully, "do you think any of his phobias might have been justified?"

He frowned. "What do you mean?"

"There were a lot of people who didn't like what he did. Taking pictures of people—celebrities—at their worst moments, publishing them with the intention of making them look bad.... From what I understand, he wasn't very popular."

"What's your point, Jessie?"

I took a deep breath. "It's occurred to me that maybe Devon's death wasn't accidental."

Chess looked stricken. "You think he was *murdered?*"

"It's possible."

I told him about the conversation I'd had with Gary Frye earlier that day. When I finished, he remained silent. But the frown lines in his forehead had thickened considerably.

"Chess, has anything unusual happened lately?" I asked him. "Was Devon acting different? Did he mention anything—or anyone—that might not have struck you as odd at the time, but that, looking back, could have indicated that something was wrong?"

"Well . . ." He glanced from side to side, as if to make sure no one was listening. As far as I knew, the only person within hearing distance was Hilda, and she seemed completely focused on sucking dust and germs out of the carpet.

"Now that you mention it, there *was* something. . . ."

"Yes?"

Chess sighed. "Lately, like for the past couple of weeks, Nettie kept talking about buying another vacation home. Only this time, in the South of France."

"You didn't think that was a good idea?"

"Believe me, no one would have loved a *petite maison* in Provence more than me. But I didn't know how he thought we were going to afford it." He opened both arms, gesturing at the house around us. "You see how he liked to live. He acted as if there was an unlimited supply of money. But even *I* knew there had to be *some* limit to how much we had to spend."

"Is that the only thing you've noticed that's been out of the ordinary?"

"Well . . ." He hesitated, as if trying to sort out what he was going to say next. "A few nights ago he went out for a meeting. Someplace local, since he wasn't gone that long."

"What kind of meeting?"

"He wouldn't say. And even at the time, it struck me as odd. Most of the people out here don't want to meet with the paparazzi. They're too busy running away from them."

"Did he tell you anything more about it?"

"He wouldn't say a word. But I noticed that when he came home, he was Mr. Cranky. You couldn't get near him. Not that I tried very hard. Nettie could be sweet, but when he was in one of his black moods . . . well, I can tell you it wasn't a very pretty sight."

"So you have no idea who he met with? Or whether it was related to his work?"

Chess shook his head. "Nettie and I were really close. In fact, we were getting ready to celebrate our three-year anniversary. But even with me, there was a side of him that was very secretive. I always figured it was the nature of his business to be guarded, since a lot of what he did involved tricking people. You know, sneaking up on them when they least expected, so he could get just the right shot. The one that showed their vulnerability."

Smiling sadly, he added, "And now you're telling me somebody might have snuck up on *him*. And that he turned out to be the most vulnerable of all."

"I don't know for a fact that Dev was murdered," I pointed out. "It's just a theory."

"I wish I could tell you you're wrong, that no one could have possibly wanted Devon Barnett dead. But even though I loved him, I always knew there were plenty of people who couldn't wait to read his obituary."

I didn't mention that I happened to be one of them. Not that I'd been rooting for Devon Barnett's demise, of course. But now that he was dead—under circumstances that I, at least, considered extremely questionable—I was anxious to learn as much about him as possible. His obituary would be the first factual account of his life I'd have access to.

"Knock, knock. Anybody home?"

Both Chess and I turned at the sound of a sweet female voice at the screen door at the back of the house. It turned out to belong to a sweet female face.

"Kara!" Chess rushed across the kitchen and flung open the door. "Or is that Little Red Riding Hood, bringing me a basket of goodies?"

He took the giant-sized basket from her and put it on the table. "You are *such* a dear."

"Just a few things I picked up at the Pampered Pantry," she said breezily. "I figured you wouldn't be in the mood for cooking. Certainly not for going out. This should keep you well-fed for the next few days. I brought over a couple of videos, too. *Desk Set* and *Brigadoon.* I thought you and I could stay in tonight."

Kara turned to me. "You're welcome to join us, Jessie."

"Thanks, but I've got plans of my own."

"Kara, you are my guardian angel. Let me just put some of these things into the 'fridge...."

As Chess fussed with the food, Kara sidled over to me. "Thanks for stopping in to check on Chess," she said in a low voice. "That was really thoughtful of you. Especially since you two just met."

I just nodded. I wasn't about to admit that not only wasn't I the Good Samaritan she thought I was, but that Chess had actually discovered me spying on his property.

Confident that I was leaving Chess in good hands, I gathered up my canine cohorts and went home to Nick.

•  •  •

I was thinking about Devon Barnett's obituary and the insights it might give me as the dogs and I made my way across the lawn of Shawn's estate, toward my cottage. Suddenly, I stopped in my tracks. Once again, I had the creepy feeling I was being watched. And this time, I knew it couldn't be Devon Barnett lurking in the shadows. I didn't think it was a voyeuristic bulldog, either.

"Hello?" I called. "Who's there?"

I was almost certain I heard a rustling in the rhododendrons. The sound sent Max into a barking frenzy. Every muscle tensed as I instinctively prepared for fight or flight.

When the scrawny black cat I'd seen the day before darted out from under the bushes, I relaxed.

"Why don't you find somebody else to pick on?" I called as the cat rocketed across the lawn. Still, I was taking a mental inventory of the refrigerator, wondering if there were any tidbits I could leave out for the poor little vagabond.

I opened the door to the guesthouse, glad Nick and I had decided to leave it unlocked, since neither of us wanted to deal with the uncooperative hardware. I was pleased to hear a Talking Heads CD playing, a sign that Nick was home, waiting for me. I couldn't wait to tell him everything I'd learned.

Instead, as soon as I walked inside, I could feel the chill in the air. And unlike the main house, the guesthouse wasn't air-conditioned.

"Hi! I'm back!" I called gaily, hoping that using a cheerful tone would add a little warmth.

"That was a long day," Nick greeted me.

He was sprawled across the couch, an open copy of a Scott Turow novel lying on his chest. No doubt his way of preparing himself to enter law school in the fall.

Max and Lou made a beeline for him, acting as if they'd feared they'd never see him again. He, in turn, gave them a royal head, back, and belly scratching.

His warm welcome wasn't universal.

"I thought we were going to the beach." Even though Nick was trying to sound casual, I could hear that he was hurt.

"There's still time." I hated the defensive tone I was using.

"I thought the dog show ended at four."

"It did. I got busy. I ended up...doing something else."

"What kind of 'something else'?"

"Why am I being subjected to the third degree?" My

prickliness didn't sound any better to me than my defensiveness.

"Because you're almost two hours later than you'd said you'd be."

"I couldn't help it. Something came up."

"Something related to the dog show?"

He had me. "Actually, it was related to Devon Barnett's death." Reluctantly, I added, "Nick, I'm beginning to think he was murdered."

Nick sighed. "I thought this dog show thing was supposed to give us a chance to spend some time together. I had no idea you were going to let your obsession with investigating murders of people you don't even know, get in the way."

"Wait a minute. You're the one who backed out at the last minute!"

"I'm here, aren't I?" he insisted. "I held up my end of the bargain. What about you?"

Why are we arguing? I thought. That's not what we came to the Bromptons for.

"I'm sorry, Nick," I said, all the anger gone from my voice. "Look, let's start over. I promise not to say another word about Devon Barnett for the rest of the night, if you promise you won't, either. We'll just pile into the car with the dogs and drive to the beach. Okay?"

He looked relieved. "Okay."

By the time we got to the shore, it was nearly deserted. Even the diehards were rolling up their towels and heading toward the parking lot.

The beach was ours. The fine white sand gave off magical little sparkles if you squinted at it just the right way, and just beyond, the ferocious blue-green waves edged an ocean that seemed to stretch on forever.

"Are you thinking what I'm thinking?" I said breathlessly, barely able to utter the words.

"What, that it feels like we're the only people in the world?"

"Exactly. Adam and Eve Play Beach Blanket Bingo."

We turned into two little kids, frolicking in the waves. Nick totally got into it, splashing me until I squealed for mercy and insisting that I climb onto his shoulders and dive in. I loved every minute.

So did Lou, who was as much of a water baby as we were. He pranced in the waves beside us, his gangly legs kicking up the foam. Max, a true landlubber, raced back and forth on the sand, barking his head off. Every time the surf touched one of his paws, he leaped back indignantly and barked even louder. Nick had had the foresight to bring along a Frisbee he kept in his car, standard equipment he stashed in the trunk with the jumper cables and a can of Fix-A-Flat. We took turns throwing it, then howled with laughter as Max and Lou scrambled after it as excitedly as if they were pursuing a pound of sirloin.

Finally, the four of us sank onto the warm sand. We were all exhausted from fighting with the ocean, which won every time.

"Now what?" I asked.

"How about going into town and stocking up on groceries, and then you taking a long, hot bath while I make you dinner?"

"Hmm. That's a tough one. Let me think.... Okay!"

A half hour later, Nick and I were meandering through a small but well-stocked grocery store, examining the displays of imported cookies and weird condiments and discussing the merits of one brand of coffee versus another.

*We're like an old married couple,* I realized, then braced myself for a wave of anxiety.

It never came.

Instead, I marveled at how nice it felt, playing house. How comfortable. Not threatening at all. Shyly, I

glanced over at Nick, curious about how he was reacting. He stood with his elbows resting on the edge of the
grocery cart, reading the ingredients on a jar and looking
completely contented.

*I could get used to this,* I thought.

As for Nick, it looked as if he already had.

# Chapter 7

"Dogs act exactly the way we would act if we had no shame."

—Cynthia Heimel

I didn't sleep much that night. But it wasn't Nick who kept me awake. It was Devon Barnett.

Or, more accurately, my growing suspicion that he could well have been murdered, rather than simply the victim of a random event.

By the time I bounded out of bed the next morning, my head buzzing from a long night of ruminating, I had decided to pay a visit to the Bolger estate. And there was no time like seven A.M., when few people were likely to be around to witness my snooping. The last thing I wanted was intervention from humans.

That included boyfriends. As I padded around the bedroom, pulling on shorts and a fresh burgundy-colored monogrammed polo shirt, I made as little noise as possible. I was relieved that Nick continued to sleep soundly, sprawled across the bed with the sheet draped modestly across his loins, as if he were posing for a classical oil painting. I was happy to let sleeping dogs lie.

Not *real* dogs, however. I was busily hatching a plan, and my two canine sidekicks played leading roles. They were both raring to go, acting as if they'd already hit the espresso pot. Even though Max was curled up at the foot of the bed, his sturdy little body was tense as he watched me hopefully, wagging his stub of a tail to show he was ready for anything. Lou was also a good sport. Aside from a few yawns and stretches, he didn't seem the least bit put off by the fact that the sun looked as if it could use a little caffeine of its own.

As I drove to the palatial estate that Russell Bolger and his daughter Emily called home, I hoped that neither of them was an early riser. I also hoped they weren't as security conscious as Shawn Elliot, whose formidable iron fence didn't exactly scream "Welcome."

The moment I turned onto Ocean Spray Drive, I saw that I'd been wise to anticipate the worst. While the Bolgers' place had looked inviting at Sunday night's kick-off dinner, this morning it was shut up tight. But I immediately spotted what I hoped would be my ticket inside the grounds: a landscaper's truck, parked outside what looked like a service entrance off to one side of the property. That gate was wide open, making room for the gardeners who were busily unloading lawn mowers, leaf blowers, and other equipment off the back of the flatbed truck.

*Yes,* I thought. The force is with me.

Instead of heading directly toward the Bolger estate, I turned onto a side street, drove a couple of hundred yards, and parked my van out of sight of Ocean Spray Drive. Then I focused on Max and Lou, who were already pawing at the windows, itching to get out and explore.

"Okay, guys," I told them firmly. "I'm going to need your help. Do you think you can act like wild beasts? Oh, that's right; you *always* act like wild beasts."

Lou looked at me blankly, as if he were thinking, "Could you please translate that into Dog?" Max was too busy smearing the van's side window with nose slime to respond.

After snapping leashes onto both, I retrieved a doggie treat from my secret stash and stuck it in my pocket. Next, I pulled on a cotton sweater that hid my name, boldly embroidered on my chest. Then the three of us headed back to Ocean Spray Drive—this time, on foot and on paw.

I strolled along the street with my two charges, attempting to look as relaxed as any other local resident. Well, maybe I couldn't pass for an actual resident, but I figured I could always pretend I was a nanny—or even a professional dog-walker. Max and Lou did their usual first-rate job of sniffing every square inch of grass and the trunk of every tree, as if nothing were in the least bit out of the ordinary. When it comes to acting, they're both pros.

Even though I'd already attended an event on the studio executive's grand estate, I hadn't gotten a very good look at it—at least, not beyond the tent, the gazebo, the fabulous view of the bay and the wildlife preserve, and the police cars. This time, as I approached, I studied the mansion and the grounds that surrounded it much more carefully. After all, I was beginning to view it in a new light, considering the possibility that it now had another identity: the scene of the crime.

The mansion, set amid an immense piece of carefully manicured property, had a gray stone façade that gave it a dignified, almost stodgy look. Still, extra touches like a cupola on top, a side porch that stretched across the entire back, and at least twelve chimneys jutting up against the pale blue sky made it seem a little more friendly.

But I wasn't here to admire the architecture. It was time to put my plan into action—and my dogs weren't the only ones who had to do a little acting. *You can do this*, I told myself, fully aware that I sounded like one of those ridiculous self-fulfillment tapes.

As I neared the forbidding wrought-iron fence, I snuck the doggie treat out of my pocket. I let Lou smell it, then hurled it as far across the Bolgers' lawn as I could.

Predictably, he watched it disappear, then looked at me mournfully, whining in disbelief that I'd done such a cruel thing.

"Go for it, Lou!" I whispered hoarsely. I let go of the leash, then watched with satisfaction as he wriggled under the fence and bounded across the lawn, barking like a madman—or even a mad dog.

Good job, I thought with pride. Okay, Maxie-Max. Now it's your turn....

My Westie didn't need any prompting. As soon as he saw that Lou had been freed from the constraints of his leash and was running across the huge stretch of lawn like a crazed antelope, he went into overdrive. He began barking his head off, his indignant yelps irritating enough to attract the attention of one of the landscapers standing a hundred yards or so up ahead.

"Excuse me!" I cried, pulling an extremely unhinged Max toward the open gate by his leash. "My dog got loose, and he's running around back there. Do you mind if I go onto the property and get him?"

It didn't take the landscaper long to make up his mind. I imagined him picturing Russell Bolger storming out of the house in his bathrobe, demanding to know what all the racket was—and why his gardener couldn't be trusted to do his job without waking up the entire neighborhood.

"Go ahead, lady," he instructed, glaring at Max. Then he shot a dirty look at Lou, who was already fading into a black-and-white dot. Probably hoping his job description wasn't going to be expanded to include pooper-scooper duty.

I thanked him, trying not to look triumphant, then jogged across the immense lawn with Max leading the way. By that point, Lou was nowhere in sight. Figuring he'd probably disappeared behind the house, I headed that way, dragged by my incensed Westie.

I looked back over my shoulder and, as soon as I saw the landscaper turn away, let go of Max's leash. That first taste of freedom put an end to his barking. He was too busy running after Lou, following his scent with the determination of a bloodhound.

I headed around back, quickly discovering that while the house was impressive, the grounds stretching behind it were even more sensational. The last time I'd been here, I'd been so entranced by the view that I hadn't even noticed the huge swimming pool, edged with bright blue and yellow tile. The same color scheme was picked up in the row of cabanas that ran along one side. The back lawn was also outfitted with tennis courts and a roller-skating rink, a perfectly flat oval made of concrete. At the water's edge, a wooden dock jutted out into the water. Tied to it were a rowboat, a canoe, a Sunfish, and a small motorboat. Dotting the endless stretch of lawn were several outbuildings, including a string of garages, several storage sheds, and a guest cottage that was at least twice as big as Shawn's.

At the moment, however, the only building I was interested in was the gazebo. I glanced around, anxious to make sure none of the landscapers was watching. From what I could tell, I'd gotten far enough behind the house that I was out of their line of sight. Next, I checked the windows and doors of the house, looking for a face or even a shadow. I knew that if all that barking had woken up Emily—and if she glanced out the window and saw Lou and Max—she'd be outside in a flash. But so far, there were no signs of life. As for the dogs, I spotted them in the distance, busily sniffing every square inch of the grounds, clearly ecstatic over having a brand-new place to scope out.

As far as I could tell, I was free to snoop around the grounds. But I had to act fast. I made a beeline for the gazebo. The early morning sun, still low in the sky, cast a golden glow over the ornate white building. It also illuminated the grassy area directly behind it—the focus of my exploration.

I felt like Lou or Max as I examined the ground, crouching down to get as good a look as possible. I would have stuck my nose in the grass if I'd possessed a fraction of their sense of smell. I vaguely recalled Nick telling me that scrutinizing a crime scene this carefully had a name. A "fingertip search." Inspired by the memory, I ran my fingers lightly over the ground.

It didn't take long for me to make contact with something. Immediately my heartbeat quickened. I leaned closer to get a better look—and saw that it was a cigarette butt, nestled deep in the grass.

I picked it up gingerly and studied it. Probably Barnett's. Not only had I seen him smoking back here on Sunday night, but as far as I could tell, that was the reason he'd snuck behind the gazebo in the first place.

I debated whether to take it with me or leave it, then decided to put it back where I'd found it. I resumed my search, quickly locating two more cigarette butts.

So Barnett had developed quite a habit, I thought wryly. But it wasn't lung cancer that got him, so . . .

I froze at the sound of Lou's shrill bark.

Damn! I thought. I knew I had to move fast, but I desperately wanted to cover the entire area.

I stood up and surveyed the property. Sure enough, I spotted Lou on the dock, howling at seagulls. If I didn't quiet him down—pronto—he was going to blow my cover.

I glanced back at the grassy spot behind the gazebo longingly. So much grass, so little time...

Lou's relentless yapping cut through me as if someone were jabbing me in the ribs with their finger. I knew I had to shut him up before he woke the whole household and I suddenly had to explain to Russell and Emily Bolger what I was doing prowling around their property at seven-thirty in the morning. My eyes darted around the stretch of grass frantically as I looked for something, *anything,* that would turn out to be helpful.

And then, just as I was about to give up and go running after my frenzied Dalmatian, I saw something glinting in the early morning sunlight. At first, I thought it might just be a few drops of dew. But the pattern was too distinctive: a gentle arch, just a few inches long...

*"Woof! Woof!"* I was all too aware of Lou's incessant yelps as he did his best to rid the world of bothersome seagulls. I glanced over my shoulder, half of me feeling compelled to dash over to quiet him down and the other half unwilling to abandon my search—especially since my stomach was doing flip-flops over the possibility that I'd actually found something. I crouched down to get a better look—and let out a loud gasp.

With trembling hands, I picked up the thin piece of wire that had been half-hidden by the dense grass.

"Oh, my God!" I cried breathlessly. "Gary was telling the truth!"

• • •

My head was spinning as Max, Lou, and I sped away from Ocean Spray Drive. My two sidekicks were growling and nipping at each other, positively giddy after their exhilarating adventure at the Bolger estate, but I was too deep in thought to let them distract me. The possibility that Devon Barnett had been murdered was getting more and more difficult to ignore—especially with my conversation with Gary Frye resonating through my head, and the scrap of wire I'd found still clutched in my hand.

Then, of course, there was the inescapable fact that the number one occupational hazard of Devon Barnett's chosen profession was making enemies.

I couldn't just let it go—and my innate inability to resist poking my head in where it didn't necessarily belong was only one reason. The torrents of adrenaline surging through my body were also a reaction to the horrible injustice of Gary Frye possibly being blamed for Barnett's death. An accusation like that had the potential to destroy him both personally and financially.

Someone else had been unfairly accused, as well: Rufus. Maybe Shawn was being overly sensitive about the fact that his dog's name was suddenly mud in this town, but the possibility that Shawn could become involved in a lawsuit on the basis of that claim, even one that would be next to impossible to prove, couldn't be completely discounted. Frivolous lawsuits were a fact of life these days—especially where someone who was known to have exceptionally deep pockets was concerned.

Most compelling of all, and most responsible for my agitation, was the idea that there could be a killer out there—someone who was literally about to get away with murder. Yet the police weren't inclined to investigate any further because they were convinced Barnett's death had been an accident.

I simply had to know more. And the first place to start was by learning everything I could about Devon Barnett. As I pulled my van into a parking spot on East Brompton's Main Street, I was more anxious than ever to read his obituary.

"Stay," I instructed my dogs, ignoring their forlorn

whining as I headed toward the Pampered Pantry. Maybe I couldn't afford the gourmet grocery's lobster salad, but I could certainly spring for the latest edition of *The East Brompton Banner*. A cup of coffee wasn't out of the question, either—especially since I was as desperate for a caffeine fix as all the other coffee addicts lined up inside.

I grabbed a copy of *The Banner* as soon as I got close enough to the stack piled neatly on the counter. My suspicion about the newsworthiness of Devon Barnett's death had been correct. He'd made the front page.

*"Devon Barnett Killed By Freak Accident!"* the headline screamed.

The irony wasn't wasted on me. Even though the paparazzo had been merciless when it came to revealing other people's secrets, he had been secretive about his own life. But this time—this one final time—it was *his* name that was featured in the headlines, and *his* face that was splashed across the front page.

I dropped three quarters onto the counter and hurried back to my van with the newspaper. As soon as my butt hit the front seat, I began devouring the article.

Famed paparazzo Devon Barnett has taken his last picture. On Sunday evening, the 34-year-old celebrity photographer was killed in a bizarre occurrence that the East Brompton Police and the Norfolk County Medical Examiner have determined was accidental.

The fatal incident occurred at a fund-raiser for the East End Chapter of the Society for the Prevention of Cruelty to Animals (SPCA), held at 206 Ocean Spray Road, the home of North Star Studios President Russell Bolger. At approximately 8:45 P.M., as most of the guests listened to speeches under a tent on the lawn, an ice sculpture of a well-known canine cartoon personality fell from the side of a gazebo.

According to Sergeant Wallace Bangs of the East Brompton Town Police Department, the block of ice dropped directly onto Barnett, who is believed to have been smoking in the vicinity. The sculpture is estimated to have weighed 250 to 275 pounds.

"We do not suspect foul play at this time," Sergeant Bangs said. "Unfortunately, accidents happen. This was just one of those freak things. We expect that the season will continue, just as it does every year. There's no reason for something like this to have any effect on summer tourism."

For eighteen years, Barnett was an integral part of the celebrity scene, photographing actors, musical performers, and politicians for tabloids like the *Stargazer* and the *Gossip Gazette*.

A native of Crockettsville, Louisiana, Barnett moved to New York City at age 17 and began working as a news photographer. He started at local papers in Queens and the Bronx, using his real name, Daniel Barnes. Next, he worked as a freelancer for the *New York Post*, legally changing his name to Devon Barnett. He built his reputation by taking pictures of celebrities.

Barnett soon branched off on his own, selling photographs to popular tabloids. He quickly became known as one of the most creative paparazzi in the business, as well as one of the most determined.

"It was a terrible shock," commented Celia Cromworthy of Brompton Harbor, president of the East End Chapter of the SPCA and chair of the weeklong event, Funds for Our Furry Friends. "It's a tragedy when anyone at a party is killed—even though Mr. Barnett wasn't actually an invited guest."

Phyllis Beckwith, whose Dering Shores-based company, Foodies, Inc., catered the fund-raising dinner, said, "We are all saddened by Devon Barnett's passing. The only good thing about it was that it happened out of view, so none of the guests had to witness anything distasteful." Beckwith added, "I'd like to assure everyone that we donated all the leftover food to a local soup kitchen. That includes our signature dessert, Mocha Crème Brûlée with Chocolate Almond Drizzle, made only with farm fresh eggs and real cream—last year's Grand Prize winner in *Bromptons Magazine*'s Dessert Olympics."

Russell Bolger, on whose estate the fund-raising dinner was held, observed, "Devon Barnett was practically an institution here on the East End. His presence was an integral part of the summer experience—like humidity and mosquitoes."

Barnett is survived by his wife, photographer Sydney Hornsby Barnett, who resides in Cuttituck.

"Devon Barnett was *married*?" I cried aloud.

I reread the final line of the obituary half a dozen times, wanting to make sure my eyes weren't playing tricks on me. Now *there* was a lead worth following up on.

Then I went back and read the entire article again, pondering each paragraph and taking in the details of Barnett's life. It was clearer to me than ever that I still had a lot to learn—and that the only way I'd accomplish my goal was by being at least as creative as Barnett.

But he and I had something in common: We were both resourceful.

I picked up the *Guide to the Bromptons* I'd grabbed at

the Pampered Pantry the day before and tossed on the floor of my van. If I was going to start poking around in the Bromptons, where I had very few ties, I was going to need some help. And the best place to start was by enlisting the aid of another veterinarian. I turned to the V's, holding my breath as I read the listings, wondering how I'd ever be able to convince a total stranger to help me investigate an incident that even the police had decided wasn't worth their time. Vegan Restaurants, Vegetable and Fruit Purveyors, Vegetarian Restaurants, Veterinarians . . .

I let out a shriek when, there among the three or four listings of veterinarians with offices in the area, I saw a name I recognized. It hadn't even occurred to me that I might come across someone I knew. As if that wasn't enough of a shock, this vet happened to be one of the last people I ever expected to end up on Long Island.

I was practically jumping up and down with excitement as I glanced at my watch. It was barely eight o'clock, meaning I still had over an hour before Day Two of the dog show got underway. *More* than enough time to pay a surprise visit—and to rekindle an old and valued friendship.

I double-checked the address in the *Guide,* started up the van, and headed east toward Poxabogue.

•  •  •

Poxabogue was a sleepy community that straddled Sunset Highway, its business district consisting of half a dozen shops housed in weatherworn freestanding buildings. I spotted a health-food store, an espresso bar, and a nursery that featured kitsch garden sculptures of giant chess pieces and dinosaurs in addition to the usual azaleas and rhododendrons. Beyond the road, tucked away from view, there were scores of palatial estates that served as summer homes. The houses north of the highway were interspersed with scenic farms that hadn't changed much since the area's original settlers planted the first seeds back in the 1600s. The houses to the south, meanwhile, tended toward the mansion variety, over-looking gentle sand dunes and, just beyond, the pound-ing surf of the Atlantic.

But I wasn't here for the real estate.

I braked when I spotted the bright yellow sign jutting above the greenery: Suzanne Fox, D.V.M. Just looking at it made me grin. As I pulled into the parking lot, I imag-ined what Suzanne's reaction was going to be when she saw what the cat dragged in.

While the front door was unlocked, the waiting room was empty. Too early for office hours. Even the recep-tionist hadn't come in yet. I ventured farther inside, with Max and Lou trailing after me, looking for signs of life.

I spotted Suzanne in the surgery room. She stood with her back to me, bending over a German shepherd and finishing up what looked like a routine spaying. A sec-ond woman, another vet or maybe a technician, stood at her side. Even though I hadn't seen Suzanne for years, there was no doubt in my mind that I'd found her. True, she no longer wore her hair in a long braid down her back. Instead, it was twisted into a complicated knot and held in place with a plastic clip. But its color—a fiery orange-red—hadn't changed a bit.

She turned slightly, and I saw the familiar sprinkle of freckles across her nose. And she was still what my grandmother used to call "pleasingly plump."

I didn't say hello. Instead, I stood in the doorway, threw open my arms, and cried, "*Anassa kata, kalo, kale . . .*"

"*Ia, ia, ia, nike!*" Suzanne finished, turning around. When she saw it was her college lab partner and long-lost friend, her face lit up like a sky full of fireworks, and she let out a squeal. "Oh, my *God*! Jessie, is that really *you*?"

"It's me, all right!"

She pulled off her surgical gloves and sprinted over to me. We threw our arms around each other, laughing and hugging.

"How long has it been?" she cried breathlessly when she finally pulled away.

"College graduation—a good ten years."

Her large blue eyes, the color of cornflowers, were shining. "I can't believe it. Jessie Popper, after all this time!"

Suzanne and I had met at Bryn Mawr, a small women's college in Pennsylvania that was so rooted in the traditions of classical education that its school cheer was in ancient Greek. While dozens of young women in our freshman class had been premed students, Suzanne Fox and I made up the entire prevet population. So it was hardly surprising that we'd bonded as soon as we met in our Chemistry 101 lab. Both of us were thrilled that we'd found another Mawrtyr hell-bent on getting into vet school and spending the rest of her life caring for animals.

Together, Suzanne and I had endured more all-nighters than I cared to remember, agonizing over lab reports fueled with Diet Coke, really bad pizza, and an unflagging sense of camaraderie. Of course, we'd managed to squeeze in a little fun, too. Stealing into Philadelphia on rainy Saturday afternoons to see two movies in a row, throwing ourselves into making our class's Junior Show the best one in the college's one-hundred-year-plus history, even double-dating a few times.

Our senior year, we had literally held each other's hands as we opened the long-awaited letters that would determine how we'd each live the rest of our lives. When both turned out to be acceptances—mine from Cornell

University's College of Veterinary Medicine in upstate New York and hers from Purdue, in her home state of Indiana—we were as thrilled for each other as we were for ourselves.

After graduation, we'd kept in touch for a while. But we'd only managed a few phone calls and E-mails before the demands of veterinary school got in the way.

"I'm still in shock!" Suzanne exclaimed. Her rounded cheeks were punctuated with two big dimples as she said, "Shelley, this is Jessie Popper, one of my best friends *ever*—even though we haven't seen each other for ages. Jess, this is Shelley Howard, my technician."

After Shelley and I said the requisite "Hello, nice to meet you's" and I'd introduced Max and Lou to everyone, Suzanne demanded, "How in the world did you *find* me?"

"One of those free booklets they put in all the stores," I replied. "*Guide to the Bromptons* or something."

"But what are you doing on Long Island?"

"I live here."

"Get *out* of here! Since when?"

"Since finishing vet school. How about you?"

"I moved here last summer. It never even *occurred* to me that you might be living on Long Island!"

"You wouldn't have found me. I'm listed as 'Reigning Cats and Dogs.' "

"Where's your practice?"

"All over the Island. I have a mobile services unit. But I live in a place called Joshua's Hollow, on the North Shore. I rent a cottage on a big estate. It's small but incredibly cute, and the lovely woman who owns it has become one of my best friends."

Suzanne grinned. "So you're the competition."

"Don't worry. I only have a few clients out here on the

South Fork. Most of my work is on the North Shore, farther west."

She shook her head as if she still couldn't believe her old college pal was standing in front of her. "I'm about done in here. Let's go into my office. Shelley, would you mind finishing up?"

Leaving her technician to take charge of the German shepherd, Suzanne walked me and my canine entourage through a small cluster of rooms. Both Max and Lou were in sniff heaven, luxuriating in the smells of the hundreds of dogs, cats, rabbits, ferrets, and other animals who had passed through the building in recent times. Suzanne's office, way in back, was just as cluttered as her dorm room had once been. Ceiling-high shelves were crammed with textbooks and stacks of science journals, and catalogs for veterinary supply houses and uniform companies were scattered here and there. A haphazard stack of bills sat in the middle of a desk, along with several mugs of half-drunk coffee, by now long forgotten. The pale green walls were covered with photographs of cats and dogs doing ridiculously cute things. The same animals appeared so frequently that I assumed they were her pets.

I settled on the window ledge after moving aside a thirsty-looking plant with a gift tag dangling from a scraggly branch. "With our gratitude for all the care you gave Bootsy," it read. Lou settled down at my feet, while Max continued to explore, nosing around every corner of the room.

"It sounds like you're doing great!" Suzanne dropped into the wooden desk chair. "Wow, Jess, your own mobile unit!"

"I can't complain. But what about you?"

Suzanne sighed. "I'm just getting started. I bought this practice last summer. To be perfectly honest, sometimes I feel like I'm in a foreign country."

"What happened to Indiana?"

She grimaced. "Promise you won't think I turned into a total flake?"

"I can't wait to hear this," I said, grinning.

"A few years out of vet school, I decided I deserved a real vacation," Suzanne began. "So I took myself to the Caribbean. You know, one of those resorts where everything's included—even the condoms?"

"Not one of those singles resorts!"

"You *promised* not to laugh!"

"Hey, there's nothing wrong with a little male attention."

"Well, it worked. I mean, I met someone. Robert. And I thought he was the most charming, most fascinating guy on earth. He was an entrepreneur who opened restaurants. He'd pick out a good location, hire an architect, find a chef, and launch it. Once it got going, he'd sell it."

"Sounds like fun. And I bet you ate well."

"I'm still paying for it, too." She rolled her eyes and patted her rounded middle. "Anyway, as long as he was in that line of business, I could stay with the same practice I'd worked in since I finished vet school in Indianapolis. But then he decided he wanted a restaurant of his own. One he'd stick with, instead of selling off. He found one, all right, but it was all the way out here on the East End. So we picked up and moved to Long Island."

"So your husband owns a restaurant nearby?" I asked excitedly.

"Yup—but he's not my husband anymore. At least, he won't be for much longer. Last summer, right after we moved here and I bought this practice, Robert announced that he wanted to change more than his career. He filed for divorce. We're still agonizing over the details. Even though we don't have any kids, it's gotten ridiculously complicated."

"Oh, Suzanne! I'm so sorry."

"I was devastated at first. And I felt completely stranded in a brand-new place where I didn't know a soul." She shrugged. "But I'm getting used to it. At this point, I'm just counting the days until I'm finally divorced and that whole chapter of my life is over." Brightening, she asked, "What about you, Jess? Are you married?"

"Nope."

"Anyone you're serious about?"

I hesitated. That still wasn't a question I felt a hundred percent comfortable with. "I've been seeing a guy named Nick Burby for a few years now. He's a private investigator, or at least he will be for another couple of months. Then he's going to law school."

"Is he your Mr. Right?" Suzanne asked eagerly.

Her question caught me off guard. I hesitated a few seconds before answering, pretending I was busy adjusting Lou's collar.

"Could be," I finally said, not wanting to get into the ups and downs of our relationship. Especially since my ongoing struggle with commitment was responsible for most of the downs. "I'll tell you all about him one of these days. But in the meantime, I'm here to ask a favor."

"Anything, Jess."

"The reason I'm out here this week is because I'm running the 'Ask The Vet' booth for a charity dog show the SPCA is putting on."

Suzanne nodded. "I've been seeing posters advertising it for months."

"I got the gig through a friend of mine who's a vet. He backed out at the last minute. Seems his social life got in the way."

"You mean he's single?" Her face lit up.

I rolled my eyes. "Yes, Marcus is single—for a very good reason."

"How about if you let me be the judge of that?" Suddenly sheepish, she added, "Sorry. I can't help it. That's what happens when you're suddenly in the market again. Especially when you find out pretty darn fast that there are about six decent men out there."

Her use of the word "decent" in a conversation about Marcus Scruggs gave me pause. I was tempted to give her an earful about Marcus Scruggs—a man who thought the term "feminist movement" referred to jiggling breasts. Instead, I said, "If you insist, I'll introduce you— but only if you sign a waiver saying I'm not responsible for whatever happens. In the meantime, I'm kind of involved in a murder investigation. Of course, the police are insisting it was an accident. But I'm convinced there's more to it."

Suzanne's eyes widened. "You don't mean that photographer, do you?"

"Devon Barnett. Did you know him?"

"No. But I read about it in the paper. What does he have to do with you?"

"Actually, nothing." I filled Suzanne in on my background as an amateur sleuth, hoping she wouldn't think I'd gone completely off the deep end.

Instead, she seemed fascinated. "How can I help?" she asked enthusiastically.

"You might have access to some of the people I'm interested in questioning. There are several right here on the East End who had ties to Devon Barnett. My suspicion is that one of them might have had a reason to want him dead. Some of them might be your clients, people you've developed a relationship with. If I presented myself as your associate, they wouldn't hesitate to let me into their homes—or to trust me when I started asking questions. Would you mind if I looked through your client list?"

"Be my guest." Suzanne gestured toward a metal file cabinet pushed into the corner of the office. "I've got a folder on each client in there. And if you can't read the handwriting, don't blame me. That's what was given to me when I bought the practice. Unfortunately, the vet I bought this practice from was an older guy who thought computers were just a fad."

His handwriting didn't look any worse than mine. Methodically, I flipped through the folders, glancing at the tabs and looking for a name that might be useful. While most of them meant nothing to me, I did see that some of the celebrities I'd spotted out here were among Suzanne's clients.

"I still can't believe you found me," Suzanne exclaimed as I continued perusing her files. "Or that you live so close by. By now, I've gotten to know a few people around here, but it's hard when you're new to an area, you know? I haven't even learned all the roads yet."

"I know. It can be pretty confusing." I only half-listened as I continued mentally filing away the names I'd found.

When I slammed the heavy drawer shut, Suzanne asked, "Did you find what you need?"

"I'm not sure. You've got a few clients I might be interested in talking to at some point. Maybe you'll let me fill in for you some time."

"I could use the help. We can get pretty busy around here, especially during the summer. Just let me know what I can do."

"Thanks, Suzanne," I said sincerely.

"In fact, why don't I just give you an extra key to my office? That way, you can come and go as you please while you're here in the Bromptons. Feel free to use the copying machine, the fax, whatever you need. The same key opens the front door and the one in back, down at the end of that hall. Let me explain how the security system works. . . ." She jotted down the code on the back of one of her business cards. I glanced at it before tucking it safely into my wallet, noting that the card was printed with her fax number, as well as her phone number—a resource I knew might prove helpful at some point.

"Suzanne, you're a doll. If there's anything I can do in return—"

She waved her hand in the air. "Glad to help. In the meantime, let's get together *soon*. I live close by, in West Brompton Beach. At least, for now." She grimaced. "Whether I'll get to keep the house or not depends on how the divorce negotiations end. For now, my lawyer has advised me to act like a model citizen. Apparently good old Robert has hired an investigator to watch me, some guy in a beat-up Ford who's spending his life parked outside my house. That means no wild parties, no men traipsing in and out at all hours of the night . . . But I could still meet you and Nick for dinner in town."

"Thanks. It sounds great."

"And if you want to bring along your friend Marcus . . ." Suzanne added with an unmistakable twinkle in her blue eyes.

I didn't have the heart to tell her that, in the jargon of our chosen field, she was barking up the wrong tree.

• • •

By the time I got to the dog show, Emily was already standing at her post. She'd neatened the piles of brochures the SPCA had supplied on the importance of regular rabies shots and the keys to good nutrition. She'd also pushed forward the giant tick so that it was more prominently displayed. I was pleased she was so excited to be part of the dog show. Emily Bolger was a special little girl, and she deserved to have a good summer.

"Hey, Dr. Popper!" she greeted me.

As I grew nearer, I noticed she was wearing a huge smile and her eyes were shining. For the first time, I caught a glimpse of the future—and what a pretty young woman she was going to be.

"You certainly look happy this morning," I observed.

"I got a letter from my mom!" She pulled out a note, handwritten on pale pink stationery.

"How's she doing?"

"Terrific! The rehab's going really well. She says she's doing even better than they expected!"

"That's good news!" I said enthusiastically. While I didn't know all that much about drug and alcohol rehabilitation programs, I was aware of how difficult they were. "You must really miss her."

Emily nodded. "We usually spend half the summer together. I'm still hoping I can go to Paris with her during August. In the meantime, I'm going to ask my dad if I can fly out to California to visit her."

I was silent, wondering if it was the best idea for a vulnerable twelve-year-old like Emily to visit her mother in a place like that. It was probably as luxurious as a spa, but that didn't mean it wouldn't be traumatic for a patient's young daughter.

I was curious to hear more, but the owner of a fluffy Old English sheepdog descended upon us. "Oh, good, I'm glad you finally got here," she said pointedly. "Barnaby keeps acting really funny whenever he chews something. It's almost like his teeth hurt. Is it possible for dogs to get cavities?"

"It's more likely he's fractured his tooth—probably a slab fracture of the major cheek tooth. It happens when dogs chew things that are too hard, like stones."

I knelt down to examine Barnaby's teeth. Sure enough, it looked as if he'd fractured his major premolar. I instructed her to schedule an appointment with her regular veterinarian as soon as she could. I also gave her my business card, in case she was looking for a new vet for Barnaby.

My next consultation was with a college-age young man with spiky bleached hair and a pierced eyebrow. At his side was a sleek, muscular dog I recognized as an American bulldog.

"Beautiful animal," I commented. "Is she competing in the dog show?" The breed was relatively new and hadn't yet been recognized by the American Kennel Club.

"No, Bailey and I just came to watch," he informed me. "She's only five months old. But I wanted to ask you something. She's not great at stairs, and sometimes she has trouble jumping up onto the couch. Do you think she could have hip dysplasia?"

"Let's take a look. Hey, Bailey! How's the dogger?" I crouched down to get a sense of the puppy's bone structure, running my hands over her silky-smooth fur and feeling the structure of her bones. "You could be right," I told her owner. "Her hocks turn inward. Keep an eye out for signs, like hearing a clicking when she walks or noticing that she seems stiff in the morning, before she's had a chance to move around. But CHD—canine hip dysplasia—can be tough to diagnose in American bulldogs. For one thing, they have an exceptionally high tolerance for pain. And their hindquarters are often strong enough to compensate, holding their hips together even in the presence of CHD. Her regular veterinarian should probably take X rays and do a thorough orthopedic exam under sedation."

"Thanks," he replied. I could see he wasn't happy with my answer, and I didn't blame him. I was experiencing the beginnings of that sad, defeated feeling that crept up on me sometimes after I'd doled out bad news, when I glanced up and saw that the next person waiting to talk to me was Shawn.

"Hey, stranger!" he said cheerfully. "Thought I'd stop by and see how you're doing."

It felt good to see a familiar face. "Busy, believe it or not. I've been handing out advice nonstop."

He chuckled. "I'm glad that, in my line of work, I just have to *pretend* to know stuff, without actually having to learn it." Turning to Emily, he asked, "How about you, kiddo? Are you having fun helping out Dr. Dolittle here?"

Her sullen expression had returned. "I guess," she said with a little shrug.

To smooth over the uncomfortable silence that followed, I said, "How's Rufus bearing up under the pressure?"

His expression darkened. "Are you talking about the pressure of the dog show or the thing with Barnett?"

Knowing how bad Shawn felt about the accusation against Rufus, I saw no reason to belabor the subject. "Actually, I was curious about the documentary. Is he going to be in it?"

Shawn smiled. "He's one of the stars! That guy who's making the videotape of the dog show got some great footage of my boy. I can't wait for you to see it on Sunday. This documentary is turning out to be a pretty big deal. Even the TV stations are coming to the screening this weekend. You'll be there to see Rufus on the big screen, won't you?"

Shawn cast an adoring look at the squat, wrinkled beast waddling beside him, his tongue hanging down like a necktie as he panted loudly, no doubt a response to the warmth of the sunny June morning. I noticed that the look of devotion in the bulldog's eyes was almost identical to his master's.

"Wouldn't miss it for the world." I crouched down to

give the sturdy bulldog a total body scratch. "How're you doing, Rufus, old boy?" Glancing up at Shawn, I said, "What a charmer! I wouldn't be surprised if he won Best of Show."

"As long as it's based on looks." In a stage whisper, he added, "Maybe I shouldn't admit this to you, since you're an insider and all, but I'm afraid Rufus is what you'd call an underachiever."

I stood up, laughing. "Most dogs are. Fortunately, the only thing most people expect of them is unquestioning devotion and never-ending cuteness—both areas in which they happen to excel."

"Yeah, it's great to have someone who's so into you."

"Rufus looks thirsty," Emily suddenly said in an accusing tone.

"You're absolutely right, Emily, my friend. Got any ideas about what we can do about it?"

"I can bring him over to the courtesy tent, if you want," she offered. "They have water for the dogs there."

"Would you do that for me?"

She scowled. "I'd do it for Rufus."

"I'm sure he'd love it." Shawn handed her the leash. Emily, meanwhile, never looked him in the eye, instead grabbing hold of the leather strap and trotting off with her head down, her squat little friend in tow.

"I get the feeling that little girl doesn't like me very much," Shawn commented.

"She's just been having a difficult summer," I replied. "She doesn't have any friends around here. Besides, her mother's in a rehabilitation center out in California. That can't be fun."

"Yeah, I heard all about that. Tough break." A strange look crossed his face. "So...I guess that boyfriend of yours—Mick—has been keeping you busy."

"Nick. Yeah, we've been managing to squeeze in a little fun."

"I'll bet. By the way, I've been thinking about what you said the other night. About the possibility that Devon Barnett might have been murdered."

"Really?" I was surprised he even remembered, much less that he'd taken my comment seriously.

"I still don't think the police would miss something like that. But the thing is, I know he had a lot of enemies. The idea that somebody might have bumped him off isn't all that crazy. Besides, I do have kind of an ulterior motive. If Barnett really was murdered, that would mean Rufus had nothing to do with it. Look, I have no idea if your theory's correct or not, but if you're interested in getting more information about the guy, I might be able to help."

"How?"

In a casual tone, he said, "I was thinking that maybe I could get you into some places you might not have access to otherwise. I mean, while you're here at the dog show, you're kind of on the sidelines, just somebody who's standing around, handing out free advice. But I know a lot of people in the Bromptons, and they'd look at you differently if you were with me. You might be able to get people to talk to you more openly if you were perceived as more of an insider."

"Thanks," I said sincerely. "I just may take you up on your offer. And if I can help clear Rufus's name, so much the better."

He grinned. "Cool. In the meantime, I'd better get this guy over to the ring. They've got the Nonsporting Group scheduled in the Red Tent first thing this morning. 'Nonsporting.' Boy, is that ever an understatement! Rufus is so lazy, he considers Frisbee a spectator sport!"

I laughed. "First, you'll have to pry him away from Emily."

He shielded his eyes with his hand, gazing off at Emily and his beloved dog. "The two of them do look pretty happy together, don't they?" Sighing, he added, "I just wish I had a fraction of that guy's good looks and charm."

I didn't dare touch that one. Instead, I watched Shawn Elliot stride toward the courtesy tent, where Emily was stroking the bulldog's head lovingly as he lapped up water from a plastic bowl.

Shawn's offer had left me feeling oddly elated. But as much as I hated to admit it, the chance to delve into Devon Barnett's past, gaining access to the hidden nooks and crannies of the paparazzo's life was only partly responsible. At least as attractive was the idea of having Shawn as an escort. I was positively giddy over the idea of being his . . . well, if not his date, then something very much like it.

It was all I could do to keep from giving myself a kick in the pants.

*What on earth is wrong with me?* I wondered. One minute, I'm contemplating walking hand in hand into the sunset with Nick. The next minute, Shawn Elliot is making my heart go pit-a-pat.

I didn't understand what was happening with me. Even so, I had the disturbing feeling that whatever it was, it was dangerous.

It was time to consult an expert.

• • •

As soon as Emily returned to the booth, I stepped into a corner away from the milling crowd, pulled out my cell phone, and dialed a very familiar number. Betty Vandervoort didn't pick up the phone until the fifth ring. When she finally did, I could hear a recording of *42nd Street* in the background, the bouncy music echoing off the walls of her cavernous mansion in Joshua's Hollow.

"Hello?" she answered breathlessly.

"Betty? It's Jessie."

"Jessica! How lovely to hear from you!"

"Are you all right?" I asked solicitously. "You sound out of breath."

"I'm on a treadmill."

"Betty, we all feel that way at one time or another—"

"No, *really*. I got myself a treadmill. To help me get in shape."

"I didn't realize you'd gotten *out* of shape."

It was true. From what I could see, Betty still had the same trim figure she'd had back in her days as a Broadway dancer—and that had easily been a good five decades earlier. In fact, putting on a little performance for me every now and then, showing off her tap routines from musicals like *South Pacific* and *Oklahoma*, still gave her a kick—no pun intended.

But for someone who'd once enjoyed a glittering life—complete with parties that ran until dawn, weekends at Newport mansions and Havana hotels, and an endless supply of adoring stage-door Johnnies—Betty Vandervoort was surprisingly down to earth.

She was also full of surprises.

"Jessica, I've got good news. *Exciting* news."

"What?" I asked, bracing myself.

"I'm getting back into show biz."

"*What?*"

"I realize I've been away from it for far too long. When you have a passion for something, why not indulge it? Of course, I'm keeping my expectations realistic. I'm starting small. There's a community theater group in Port Townsend that's holding auditions the day after tomorrow. I've been putting together a terrific new routine, and I have every intention of knocking 'em dead."

"What show are you auditioning for?"

"*Chicago.*"

"Which part, Roxy or Velma?" I was only half-teasing. Knowing Betty, I wouldn't have been at all surprised if she'd set her sights on one of the two leads.

"Oh, I'm not ready for starring roles." I couldn't tell if her breathlessness was from her excitement over her new adventure or the treadmill. "At least, not yet. I'm planning to get back into it with something smaller. Actually, I've set my sights on the jailhouse song-and-dance scene, 'Cell Block Tango.'"

"That's wonderful, Betty." Even though I was having a bit of trouble picturing the whole thing, I had to admit I was thrilled. "I won't keep you, since you sound so busy. I was just calling to see how Cat and Prometheus and Leilani are doing."

"They're fine." Betty still sounded slightly out of breath, and I could hear the rhythmic rumble of her treadmill in the background. "In fact, Cat's right here, watching me as if she can't figure out why anyone would work so hard to move without getting anywhere. I've let her take over the couch—I think the soft cushions are easy on her arthritis. And Prometheus has developed a taste for tortilla chips. He particularly likes the salsa. I didn't know parrots knew how to dip. As for Leilani, well, the lovely thing about chameleons is that all they need are a few crickets every day and they're happy."

"Thanks for taking care of them, Betty."

"My pleasure—especially since it's giving you and that Nick of yours a chance to be alone together. Speaking of which, how's life in the glamorous Bromptons? Is the dog show going all right?"

"It's fine." I hesitated, wondering whether or not to mention Devon Barnett. I decided not to. I knew from experience that when it came to my interest in investigating murders, Betty wasn't exactly my greatest supporter. She felt I'd be better off putting my energy into more productive things—like my relationship with Nick. So instead, I simply said, "It's turned out to be a lot more interesting than I thought."

"I bet you're having a grand old time, hobnobbing with all those celebrities."

"Well . . . I have met one or two."

"I can't wait to hear all about it!" she said enthusiastically, the treadmill still droning on and on. "As soon as you get back, I'll make us a pot of tea and you can tell me everything. Of course, I'll probably be busy, what with rehearsals and all. But you know I always have time for you."

"It's a date."

Betty paused before asking, "Are you *sure* everything is all right, Jessica?"

"Of course. Why wouldn't it be?"

"Because it's not like you to worry about your pets. Not when they're in my care. Besides, I know you well enough to hear it in your voice when there's something on your mind."

My dear friend had seen right through me. Still, coming clean was turning out to be more difficult than I'd anticipated. "Actually, I've been feeling kind of . . . confused."

Across the wires, Betty let out a deep sigh. The rumble of the treadmill had stopped, and the upbeat music had come to an end. "This doesn't have anything to do with Nick, does it?"

"As a matter of fact—Betty, there's this . . . *person* here who's been paying a lot of attention to me."

"You mean flirting."

"Not flirting, exactly. More like . . . Well, yes, flirting."

"And you're enjoying every minute."

"Yes," I admitted miserably.

"And he's somebody a little bit famous?" Betty probed.

"Somebody a *lot* famous."

"I see. So you're wondering how the fact that you're

flirting right back fits in with your relationship with Nick. A relationship that, I might add, is still somewhat fragile."

Betty was only telling me what I already knew. Even so, that didn't make it any easier to hear.

"Just remember, that Nick of yours is worth a hundred movie stars any day." While her voice was gentle, her message was coming across loud and clear. "Don't get caught up in the glamour of somebody whose face you've seen on the big screen, Jessica. It's dangerous. Believe me; I know."

I could feel one of Betty's reminiscences coming on. But I didn't mind. Especially since I was hoping it would give me some insight into the ridiculous roller coaster of emotions I was experiencing.

"You know about Charles, of course," she began.

"Yes." Betty must have told me the story of the love of her life a few hundred times. But it was one I never tired of hearing. It was easily one of the most romantic tales I'd ever heard—certainly better than anything I'd seen in a movie.

"I was smart enough to know from the very beginning that Charles was special," Betty went on wistfully. "That he was the one. There was something magical between us, Jessica. Something difficult to define—and even more difficult to find. It was there from the start, from that first night I spotted him at the front table at the Copa while I was onstage with that ridiculous pile of fruit on my head. Our eyes met, and I just *knew*. The air was electrified. *I* was electrified. The point, Jessica, is that I can see that you and Nick have the same thing."

"You were never interested in anyone else?"

"Sure I was. After Charles died, there were other men. Lots of them. And there are few things that feel as marvelous as having a man you find attractive show interest in you. I can assure you that, over the years, I've been involved with a lot of charmers. Even some you might have heard of. But none of them was like Charles. Even after he was gone, I never had any doubt he was the one.

"In other words, Jessica," Betty said gently, "don't take Nick for granted. Don't make the mistake of thinking the connection you two have is something that's easy to come by. I'm more than twice your age, and I've learned a few things along the way. My greatest desire is to have the people I care about benefit from whatever knowledge I've gained."

"Thanks, Betty," I told her sincerely.

"You know, deep down, that I'm right, Jessica, don't you?"

"Yes."

"Good," she declared in a firm voice. "Then I'll be able to sleep soundly tonight."

I hoped I'd be able to do the same.

# Chapter 8

"A dog is not 'almost human,' and I know of no greater insult to the canine race than to describe it as such."

—John Holmes

To improve my chances of doing just that, next I dialed Nick's cell phone. "Hey, hot stuff. What are you up to?"

"Missing you. Other than that, I'm lying on a lounge chair, soaking up the sun and reading John Grisham. My way of getting psyched for law school."

"Any way I could tear you away with an offer of lunch?"

"Hey, I'm easy," he replied breezily. "Just say where and when."

"I heard about a place I'd like to try." I hesitated, waiting for a momentary flash of guilt to pass. "How about meeting me at the Sand Bar around noon? I've got the address right here...."

All right, so maybe I could be faulted with blurring the lines between cultivating my love life and investigating Devon Barnett's murder. But while I'd promised Nick I wouldn't let my snooping get in the way, I hadn't said anything about not doing it at all. Besides, as far as I could tell, it didn't matter where our lunchtime rendezvous took place, as long as I made time for the two of us to be together. So what if I chose the place Chess had named as one of his retreats when he hid from Hilda and her maniacal cleaning? The fact that a bartender or a waiter might be able to shed a little light on the relationship between Chess and Devon wouldn't detract from the romance *that* much, would it?

As for Devon, I was still puzzling over the factoid I'd picked up in his obituary. Its claim that a man who had been openly gay was also married buzzed at me like a mosquito that wouldn't take "No" for an answer. I was beginning to understand that there were more layers to him than I'd first realized.

En route to the Sand Bar, I made a slight detour. The fact that the chic café was right around the corner from Chess's house created an ideal opportunity to do a little more poking around the love nest he and Devon Barnett had shared. Even though I found him tremendously engaging, I couldn't rule out the possibility that as the person who was closest to the photographer, he could also have been his killer.

I left Max and Lou in the car, then headed for the Sweet Pea Pink front door. As I rang the bell, I hoped that, this time, I'd find Chess lounging around the house in an outfit that was a little less revealing than what he'd worn the last time I'd paid him a visit.

When the door finally opened, it wasn't Chess who was standing on the other side. Instead, I found myself face-to-face with Hilda. And just like last time, the expression on her face was anything but welcoming.

She stood at attention, clutching her plastic bucket overflowing with bottles of Windex, Lysol, Tilex, and half a dozen other cleaning products. This time, her dress was a remarkable shade of yellowish-green that I doubted would complement any skin tone. Over it, she wore the same garish orange-and-yellow flowered apron I'd seen before. Only this time, its pockets were stuffed with rags. The same heavy black running shoes gripped her feet to the floor. Her thick beige stockings, meanwhile, seemed to bag around her ankles even more than the last time I'd seen her.

"Hello, Hilda," I greeted her, plastering on the friendliest smile I could manage. "Remember me?"

"I pay no attention to who comes and goes," she returned gruffly. "Is not my business."

From what I could tell, Hilda had left all her charm back in the Old Country, along with her fashion sense. Still, I did my best to act cheerful.

"Is Chess here?" Keeping the smile on my face was getting more and more difficult.

The gesture wasn't reciprocated. "Mr. LaMont not here. I clean."

"Yes, I can see that."

During a short lull in our otherwise fascinating conversation, I could hear the sound of muffled barking.

"Is that Zsa Zsa?" I asked, trying to poke my head through the doorway so I could hear better.

Hilda took a step to the left, blocking me. "Dog is fine. I clean."

Zsa Zsa didn't seem fine to me. Even from where I stood, I could hear that her frantic barks had turned to whimpers. The sound made me cringe.

"It sounds as if she's in trouble," I insisted. "If you don't mind, I'd like to see if—"

"Dog is fine," Hilda repeated, drawing her thin lips into an even straighter line.

I pictured poor Zsa Zsa stashed away in a kitchen cabinet or a breadbox, somewhere she couldn't get underfoot while Hilda battled the armies of germs she seemed convinced lurked in every corner of Dev and Chess's immaculate home. The image infuriated me.

"In that case, you probably wouldn't care if—"

Hilda took a step forward, placing her Mack truck of a body more firmly between me and the doorway. I could see I wasn't about to win this one, especially since Hilda had a right to be inside Chess's house—and I didn't. Still, the first chance I got, I resolved to inform him of how his housekeeper treated his beloved canine during her impassioned cleaning sessions.

But for now, I was the picture of politeness. "Do you know when Chess will be back?"

"I pay no attention to who comes and goes," she repeated.

"So I understand. Would you at least tell him I stopped by?"

"Yah, yah. Busy. Very busy." She slammed the door in my face.

I stood on the front steps for a few seconds, stunned. I'm glad we had this little chat, I thought, irritation rising inside me like a bad case of indigestion.

I headed back to my van, thinking that I didn't blame Chess for making himself scarce whenever Hilda showed up. Hiding out at the Sand Bar or the beach while she buffed and polished and scrubbed and whatever else she did in there made perfect sense.

I only hoped I'd learn more at the bistro than his favorite variety of margarita.

• • •

"This is nice, isn't it?" I commented as Nick and I headed toward the Sand Bar's outdoor seating area with the dogs. I glanced around, checking to make sure Chess wasn't hiding out here today. The coast was clear. He wasn't sitting at any of the small round tables that lined the sidewalk, shielded from the noonday sun by red-and-white umbrellas that were printed along the edge with the name of a popular European beverage. "It feels so . . . *French*."

"Can't tell yet," Nick returned cheerfully. "It depends on how rude the waiters are." He and I plunked ourselves down on two wrought-iron café chairs, carefully arranging the dogs' leashes to keep them from getting their paws tangled up in them. Nick had taken charge of Lou. At the moment, my sweet-tempered Dalmatian seemed content to sniff everything around him, the tiny muscles of his nose on overdrive as he struggled to take in all that exciting new square footage. Max, meanwhile, was in my care. His sturdy little body positively trembled with excitement. Not only were there other dogs within ten blocks of where he stood; layer upon layer of residual scents from dogs who'd been on the premises hours and days and probably even weeks earlier covered the sidewalk, creating a virtual archeological site of canine presence from times gone by.

"For a place to feel *really* French," Nick continued as he put a calming hand on Lou's back, "the waiters should have that certain air of superiority that comes from distributing *pommes frites* to tourists all day."

I laughed. Still, I remembered that during my high school trip abroad, the young, good-looking Parisian waiters had seemed like gods with trays. Their arrogance only made them seem more unattainable—and more intriguing. Gazing across the table, I reminded myself that I no longer had to yearn for the day my prince would come. He was sitting across from me, frowning over the wine list he'd idly picked up.

"Geez, will you look at these prices?" Prince Charming grumbled. "A magnum of champagne—Cristal Brut Rosé, 1988—costs more than a month's rent!"

"Which is why we'll stick to iced tea." I glanced around the Sand Bar's outdoor seating area admiringly.

It really did remind me of France—largely because its patrons clearly loved their dogs as much as Parisians did. Just like on the Boulevard Saint-Germaine, many of the people having lunch today had animals at their feet—or, in the case of the devastatingly good-looking couple two tables away, in a baby seat. Their snow-white Maltese, her long coat brushed until it was as soft and fluffy as cotton candy, perched in a high chair. Two yellow satin ribbons were tied high atop her head, holding her silky hair out of her eyes. Every few seconds, she lurched forward, greedily grabbing at the morsels of paté and roast duck her owners kept offering up.

As for the man at the table next to us, he had two luncheon companions. His Afghans were much more sedate. They lay beside him contentedly, lounging on the sidewalk like giant lawn ornaments—at least until the white powder puff of a Maltese lunged at a piece of duck his mistress offered him and missed.

The Afghans were instantly on their feet, scrambling toward the coveted morsel. Both Max and Lou immediately picked up on what was happening. Lou strained toward them, so determined to get in on the action that he pulled his leash taut, nearly knocking Nick's chair over. He was barking his head off, completely destroying the peacefulness of what, up until that point, had been a relaxing afternoon. As for Max, his leash was so tangled up in the chair legs as he attempted to become part of the action that he practically strangled himself. His yelps were punctuated with choking sounds that became increasingly hoarse as he watched one of the Afghans inhale the tiny scrap of food—much to the dismay of the other Afghan, the Maltese, and the Maltese's owners.

"Quiet, Lou!" Nick commanded. "Stop acting like a tourist!"

As I unraveled Max's leash, restoring his air supply as quickly as I could, I noticed that a busboy clearing a table nearby had paused long enough to watch the scene. He was short and stocky, with beach ball-sized biceps that tested the limits of the white T-shirt he wore with his white apron. His piercing black eyes, completely bald head, and tattoo-covered arms made him look better-suited to a career as a bouncer in a biker bar than a bus-boy.

I offered him an apologetic smile, remorseful over having played even a small role in the chaos that had just disrupted the restaurant's tranquility. In response, he shook his head, wearing a look of utter disdain.

I was relieved that our waiter finally emerged from inside the restaurant. The tall, fair-haired young man glanced at the scene of the canine commotion, and then pointedly looked away. I got the feeling that the time of his arrival had been carefully planned. Good strategy, I decided. After all, scolding the customers—not to mention their beloved pets—was hardly the route to good tips.

"I'm Steve," he began, dipping down to present each of us with a lunch menu. Up close, I saw that he was as well-built as he was good-looking. Probably another wannabe actor, I figured, just like the sales clerk at the roadside farm stand who'd helped me find Shawn's house. "I'll be your waitperson this afternoon. May I tell you about our specials? Our appetizer is a seafood Napoleon made with bay scallops, baby shrimp..."

The dogs quieted down as soon he launched into his monologue. Maybe they found all that talk of confits and reductions soothing.

After we ordered, I casually asked Steve the Waitperson, "Are things always this crazy? With the dogs, I mean."

He rolled his eyes. "You have no idea!"

"I guess the food makes up for it," I continued. "I

have a friend who just raves about this place. Chess LaMont?"

"Sure, I know Chess," the waiter said, nodding. "He comes in here a lot, sometimes with his—"

He suddenly looked stricken. Of course he'd heard the news about Devon Barnett. In a gossipy summer community like this one, I couldn't imagine that anyone hadn't.

"Yes, it's tragic, isn't it?" I offered as a means of getting him off the hook.

"Devastating."

"Did you know them well?"

"Sure. They used to come in all the time. Sometimes, we'd get to talking. Devon knew a lot of famous people, and the stories he used to tell were fascinating."

I noticed that the owner of the two Afghans had left. But the busboy had moved closer. In fact, the way he'd positioned himself—mere inches away, with his back to us as he checked salt and pepper shakers to see if they required refilling—gave me the impression he was doing his best to eavesdrop.

"What about Chess?" I prompted.

"He's great, too," Steve gushed. "The ideal couple. One of those matches made in heaven, that make you believe there really is such a thing as destiny."

I was about to ask another question when I noticed that the busboy had turned his head so that he was facing us. He was smirking. Maybe I was reading too much into his expression, but I got the feeling he couldn't believe we were actually buying what Steve was telling us.

"Excuse me, will you?" Steve said abruptly. The owners of the Maltese were desperately waving their hands in the air to get his attention. They were probably ready to order raspberry soufflé for their dog's dessert.

"He wasn't much help," I commented to Nick.

"Actually, I thought old Steve was pretty impressive,

the way the list of specials rolled off his tongue. Personally, I always trip over the word 'arugula.' "

"I wasn't talking about the food. I was talking about getting information out of him."

The look on Nick's face told me I'd just said the wrong thing.

"Not that dead paparazzo again," he said, sounding exasperated. "What is it, exactly, that you find so fascinating about this case?"

"Lots of things," I replied excitedly, wondering where to begin. "First of all, there's the fact that everyone has been so quick to assume he died accidentally. Even the police don't seem interested in considering the possibility that he was murdered. I can't even get them to return my phone calls! Then there's the fact that Shawn Elliot's poor dog, Rufus, is being blamed for—"

Even before I'd gotten the words out, I realized I'd made a mistake.

"Is that what this is about?" Nick asked archly. "Shawn Elliot?"

"No," I replied, doing my best to sound indignant. "The role Shawn's dog played in this is just one small piece of what I think is a very intriguing situation. Think about it, Nick," I went on quickly. "Devon Barnett wasn't just anybody, He was one of the most hated men in Hollywood—not to mention New York, London, and here on the East End."

"Really? Who told you that?"

I wasn't about to mention Shawn again. "I read it somewhere."

Nick frowned. "Look, just because this guy had a lot of enemies doesn't mean he was murdered. I mean, you'd hope the police had already come up with this theory."

"But the local police have an agenda of their own," I insisted. "The Bromptons' season is just beginning. That means tourist dollars, big time. If word got out that people were being murdered around here, that wouldn't be very good for business, would it?"

Nick's eyebrows shot up. "You really think they'd cover it up?"

I shrugged. "Maybe they're just not inclined to look for foul play as hard as they could. As long as Devon Barnett was simply the victim of gravity, it's a local matter. A tragedy that doesn't warrant much more than a couple of articles in the local paper. But murder—that would be something else entirely.

"For one thing, crying 'murder' and bringing in Norfolk County Homicide would mean the local police would completely lose control over what happened from that point on," I continued. "Even worse, it would be a question of *minutes* before the New York media were all over the story. We're talking major headlines here, lead stories on the six o'clock news, nonstop speculation about whether the murderer would strike again. Not exactly the best public relations for—"

"Hey, Jess?" Nick interrupted. "Aren't you forgetting something?"

I looked at him and blinked.

"We're supposed to be taking a little vacation here. I thought this was our chance to get away together."

"We *are* together."

"But it's a little crowded. You, me, this Barnett character . . . I'd rather it was just the two of us."

"Don't worry, Nick. I won't let this get in the way. I just want to poke around a little, ask a few questions . . . that's all."

As if to prove my point, I didn't mention Devon Barnett for the rest of the meal. When Steve brought our entrees, I even resisted the temptation to say they looked gorgeous enough to photograph for a food magazine. All in all, I thought I did an admirable job of behaving myself.

"I've got to get back," I finally said, glancing at my watch. "You'd be amazed at how many people have questions about their dogs' health. But first, I've got to make a pit stop. Iced tea has no mercy."

I left Max and Lou in Nick's care as I maneuvered around the tables and into the restaurant. I was certain I'd find a rest room with my name on it—or at least my gender. Sure enough, I spotted the door I was looking for, tucked away at the end of a short hallway in back.

The hallway happened to pass by the kitchen. As I reached the swinging doors, they flew open with such force I was glad I hadn't been standing in front of them. Out came the tough-looking busboy I'd noticed hovering near our table as Steve the Waitperson sang the praises of Dev and Chess's remarkable relationship. His biceps ballooned under the weight of the huge plastic bin of clean cappuccino mugs he was hauling, the steam from the dishwasher floating above them like a cloud.

"Was I imagining things," I asked him in a low voice, "or were you listening in on our conversation about Devon Barnett and Chess LaMont?"

The busboy looked shocked, but only for a moment. Then he shrugged noncommittally.

"Did you know them?" I asked.

He let out a contemptuous snort. "We weren't exactly pals. I mean, it's not like I hang around with them types."

"But they were regular customers, weren't they?" I persisted. "You must have seen them here all the time." And probably eavesdropped on their conversations, I thought.

He glanced around, as if wanting to make sure no one was within earshot. "Let's just say those two fags weren't exactly the happy couple everybody thought they were. Sure, the really effeminate one—Chess or somethin'?— *he* liked to put on a good show. But people like us, who saw them practically every day, knew they weren't exactly Romeo and Juliet."

"I guess no couple has a perfect relationship," I said noncommittally. "They're all bound to have the occasional argument—even gay couples."

"Yeah, right. Except most arguments don't get rough enough to involve the police."

My heart started to pound the way it always does when I'm about to learn something potentially incriminating about someone who's made my top-ten list of murder suspects. I stepped closer, trying to look interested but not overly eager.

"The police?" I repeated.

The swinging doors burst open again, nearly smacking me in the nose. This time, a man in a jacket and tie flew out. An owner or manager, most likely, rather than simply another member of the happy family of Sand Bar employees.

"Hey, Gus, wanna put those over by the espresso machine some time before next week?"

The busboy cast him a scathing look.

We both waited until the boss man hurried off. "Look," I said evenly, "I'd really appreciate hearing about what happened that night."

He looked me up and down appraisingly. Maybe to see if I was someone who could be trusted, but more likely to see if I was someone who was worth his time.

"How about meeting me later tonight?"

I blinked. I wasn't sure what I'd be getting into. But if it was a chance to learn something about Devon Barnett, I was willing to take the risk.

"If I do," I countered, "will you tell me what you know?"

"I got no reason to protect those fags," he said. "Tell ya what. I work nights at a place called Raffy's. It's over in West Brompton, right on Sunset Highway. Come tonight around closing time, right before ten. I gotta hang around anyway to lock up. We can talk then."

"A few minutes before ten at Raffy's," I repeated. "I'll be there."

I tried to act matter-of-fact as I returned to the table, as if the most dramatic thing that had happened to me in the past five minutes was running out of paper towels in the ladies' room. But my cheeks must have still been flushed from my unexpected encounter with the Incredible Hulk.

"Everything okay?" Nick asked me the moment I sat down.

"Everything's fine," I replied quickly. "Why?"

"You were gone for kind of a long time. And you look . . . excited."

I couldn't resist. "Nick," I said, leaning forward and lowering my voice, "you won't believe what just happened! I ran into the busboy in there—you know, the one who was listening in on our conversation with the waiter?"

"I hadn't noticed."

"Well, *I* did. And it turns out he knows something about Dev and Chess! He said they had an argument one night, right here at the restaurant, and the *police* got involved—" I stopped. Nick was wearing his grumpy expression again. "What's wrong?"

"What's wrong is that I still feel like I'm vying for your attention. And *losing*."

"All right, so I'm not perfect," I said, not even trying to hide my exasperation. "I happen to have this little flaw. You said yourself that I've always been even more interested in the cases you've investigated in your PI business than you. I admit it: I find investigating murders irresistible."

"Do you need to be reminded that you almost got killed the last time you decided to play Nancy Drew?"

"No." I swallowed hard, instantly sobered by the memory. Nick wasn't exaggerating in the least, and coming horrifyingly close to having my own life snuffed out wasn't an experience I would ever look back on lightly.

"But I didn't," I pointed out. "As a matter of fact, I think I handled myself rather well." Before he had a chance to come back with a counter argument, I added, "You know, you're not perfect, either."

Nick shifted in his seat. "What do you mean?"

"You're going to law school."

"A lot of people would consider that admirable."

"That's because they don't feel the same way I do about lawyers."

"Right. You think they all drink martinis and drive BMW's—both offenses you feel should be punishable by law."

"Okay, so maybe I'm guilty of stereotyping. But you know that's not what bothers me most. It's the way they prey on other people's misery."

"Isn't that what a murder investigation is all about?" Nick countered. "Getting your kicks from the fact that some poor bastard got iced?"

"I don't 'get kicks'!" I protested. "I consider it an intellectual challenge! Plus, I happen to believe that people should be held accountable for their actions."

"That's precisely why I want to be a lawyer." Nick reached across the table to take my hand. Begrudgingly, I let him. "See, Jess? Maybe we're not so different, after all. Except I intend to protect the rights of the living, while you're interested in justice for the victims of the very worst crime there is."

"Well . . . I guess I never thought of it that way," I admitted.

"Maybe it's time you started doing just that."

"I suppose I could. I mean, you do have a point."

"So are we okay with this?"

"I am if you are."

"I'll try. That doesn't mean I'm willing to sacrifice my vacation among the beautiful people, but I'll try to be more patient. And Jess?"

"Umm?"

"I don't like martinis. But a BMW—"

I punched him in the arm. But only very lightly.

· · ·

I left Max and Lou with Nick, figuring spending the afternoon inside the guesthouse eliminated any possibility of heat stroke. Besides, I knew he'd enjoy their company.

As soon as I got back in my van, my cell phone trilled. I grabbed it, certain the East Brompton Police were finally returning my call.

"Jessica Popper," I answered crisply.

"Hey, Jess! How's it going?"

*"Marcus?"* Hearing his voice caught me completely off guard. I was astonished at how clearly he was coming through. Still, I made a point of speaking loudly and clearly, in case the tropical island he'd been whisked off to didn't share our abundance of cell phone towers. "WHERE—ARE—YOU?"

"On the Island. Thought I'd check in and see how it's going."

"IT'S—GOING—GREAT!" I replied, enunciating each word. "HOW—ABOUT—YOU? ARE—YOU— HAVING—FUN?"

"I always have fun," he returned coolly. "So how are the chicks out there in the Bromptons? Pretty hot, I bet!"

"NO—CHICKS," I returned. "JUST—DOGS."

"Maybe I'll come out there one of these days. You know, check things out for myself."

The wheels in my brain were turning. "Wait a minute. When you said you were on the island, which island did you mean?"

"Long Island, of course. I'm back home."

"What happened to your tropical vacation with the mature woman?" I was back to using my normal cell phone voice, which is still about ten times louder than my normal telephone voice. I felt like a fool for picturing Marcus lying under a palm tree, sipping a pink drink garnished with a tiny paper umbrella, when he was probably calling me from his flashy Corvette as he topped eighty mph on the Long Island Expressway.

"Didn't work out. It turned out that what she *really* wanted was—"

"That's okay," I interrupted. "You don't have to explain."

"No, get this," he insisted. "Turns out what she wanted me for was to make some old guy jealous! Some white-haired dude on this yacht that was, like, as big as Cleveland!"

"And the fact that her intentions weren't honorable troubled you?" I couldn't resist asking.

"I can't tell you how many times she paraded me up and down the dock, like I was some kind of prized *poodle* or something." He took a long, deep breath. "Popper, she *used* me!"

"Imagine!"

"She's history, man. Anyway, it's definitely time to move on, and I thought that since you're out on the East End, maybe I'd come out and, you know, make the scene."

I didn't bother to tell Marcus that no one "made the scene" anymore. I was too busy trying to think up an excuse. "Well . . . they don't give me much time off—"

"That's okay. If there's one thing the Marc Man excels at, it's making his own good time."

*The Marc Man?* I was glad he wasn't there to see the way I was rolling my eyes.

"So listen, Popper, I'll be in touch," he continued. "But

I wanted you to know I'm back in the good old U.S. of A. and ready to par-*tay.*"

And I'm ready to vo-*mit,* I thought grimly after we hung up. All I needed was a visit from Marcus Scruggs to complicate my life even further. But as I turned on the ignition, I pushed the thought aside. Knowing Marcus, he probably wouldn't make good on his threat. Since he had the attention span of a two-year-old toddler combined with the libido of a fifteen-year-old boy, it probably wouldn't be long before he'd moved on to some other distraction—undoubtedly of the female variety, and hopefully much closer to home.

• • •

I was humming as I strolled across East Brompton Green toward my bug-bedecked booth. My lunch with Nick had put me in such a good mood that even the possibility of a visit from Marcus Scruggs couldn't ruin it. Or maybe something else had elevated me to such an optimistic state: the promise of a clandestine rendezvous with a mysterious busboy that would yield me some telling new information about Chess and Devon's dark side.

Lost in thought, I suddenly became aware of someone walking beside me. Glancing over, I saw it was Shawn and his sidekick, Rufus.

"Hey, Rufus!" I chirped. "How's our star?"

"Aw, so it turns out he's not the only pretty face in this town," Shawn answered glumly. "But even though he didn't win any ribbons, I'm still his number one fan."

"And he's clearly yours." I didn't mention that the loyal bulldog undoubtedly had a lot of competition. "Speaking of animals, you never mentioned you had a cat."

"*A cat?*" Shawn looked puzzled for a few seconds before saying, "Oh, you must mean that nasty black cat that hangs out on my property. I call him Lucifer."

My eyebrows shot up. "Interesting name for a pet."

"He's no pet," he insisted. "He just kind of moved in."

"Poor thing. You might want to make his adoption official. By feeding him, I mean."

"I guess there's no harm in that—as long as he stays outside," Shawn mused. "I don't think Rufus is interested in sharing me. *Especially* with a feline!"

I glanced at the adoring pet at his side, who at the moment was gazing at him with moist, soulful eyes. "I think I have to agree. Speaking of man's best friend, I'd better get over to my booth—"

"Actually, there was a reason I was looking for you. I realize this is short notice, but I was wondering if you were free tonight."

I guess I looked shocked. He quickly added, "What I mean is, there's a party this evening. I thought it might be a good opportunity for you to learn more about Devon Barnett and the circles he traveled in. Their edges, anyway."

"Well, I—"

"We wouldn't have to stay that long," he insisted. "I just need to put in an appearance. In fact, you'd be doing me a favor, since I have nobody else to go with."

Right, I thought. Like Shawn Elliot has trouble finding a date—especially for a glamorous soiree in the Bromptons.

The fact that he could have taken practically any woman in the Free World made me realize he really was doing me a favor.

"It sounds great," I told him sincerely. "What kind of party is it?"

"It's a screening, over at Russell Bolger's." He grimaced.

"Hugo Fontana's got a new movie opening next week: *Pulverizer 4: Armageddon.*"

"A comedy, huh?"

He chuckled. "Yeah, right. Unfortunately, you'll probably have to sit through the whole thing. But there'll be a cocktail party afterward that'll give you a chance to mingle. Who knows what you'll find out?"

"Shawn, I'd love to." It really was an offer I couldn't refuse.

"Why don't I pick you up at the guesthouse around six?"

I hesitated, imagining Nick's reaction. "Maybe it would be better if I picked you up."

"Sure, whatever. Just knock on my door when you're ready. I'll be waiting."

I was absolutely thrilled over the opportunity to go to a party that would give me a closer look at the celebrity scene that Devon Barnett had found so intriguing—especially one that was being held at the scene of the crime. And most of the guests would probably be people who had known him—if not personally, then by having their names smeared by him at some point in their careers.

Of course, first I had to overcome a major stumbling block. Nick.

I'll just be straightforward, I decided as I headed toward the guesthouse late that afternoon. Surely Nick won't begrudge me the chance to go to a Hollywood party that will probably be the most glamorous event I've ever attended. And he'll just have to understand that Shawn is doing me a real favor, that he's turning out to be a good friend. . . .

All my resolve to be strong slipped away the moment I opened the door.

Nick stood in the middle of the living room, holding what looked like a white towel. He was studying it, the expression on his face puzzled, enraged, and hurt, all at the same time.

It took me a few seconds to realize that the bundle in his arms was Shawn's bathrobe, embroidered with the initials "S.E."

"Hey, Nick," I said with forced cheerfulness.

He just glanced at me questioningly.

"It's not what you think," I said. It took me about two seconds to realize how ridiculous those words sounded. "I wore that here the day I arrived because my clothes got splattered with mud. . . . It's kind of funny, actually. See, when I was driving here, I got lost and—"

I noticed then that Lou was lying under the coffee table, his eyes moving back and forth between the two of us, no doubt picking up on the tension that was sending invisible sparks flying around the room. I was relieved when Max came trotting in from the bedroom with his favorite squeaky toy, a hot pink plastic poodle, dangling from his jaws.

"Not only am I competing with a dead guy," Nick said coldly. "I'm also competing with some Tinseltown Don Juan!"

"It was completely innocent!" I insisted.

"So you keep saying," Nick replied. "Again and again and again."

"If you don't trust me, I don't see how we can have much of a relationship!"

"Maybe that's the bottom line. Maybe we *don't* have much of a relationship!"

I opened my mouth to protest, but Nick held out both hands to stop me. "Wait. Let's not do this. Look, Jess, you and I have the whole evening ahead of us. Why don't we find a nice, quiet restaurant, someplace romantic, and you can tell me the whole story behind that idiot's bathrobe being in *your* bedroom, and—"

"I have a feeling you're not going to like this very

much, either," I interrupted. "I'm going to a screening tonight. With Shawn."

I braced myself for a tirade. Instead, he just blinked. "You're joking, right?"

"Nick, it's a really good chance for me to talk to people who knew Devon Barnett," I went on, speaking too quickly, "and even a few who—"

"Tell you what, Jess," Nick said icily. "You do whatever you want, with *whomever* you want. But do me one small favor: Let me know if you ever decide, once and for all, that you want me to be part of your life. Okay?"

He grabbed his car keys and stormed out.

I stood frozen to the spot, not quite able to believe what had just happened. My eyes stinging, I told myself he'd come back.

He *has* to, I insisted, biting my lip. He left behind all his CDs.

# Chapter 9

"The more I see of the depressing stature of people,
the more I admire my dogs."

—Alphonse de Lamartine

As Shawn and I zoomed into Russell Bolger's driveway, the tires of his red Ferrari sending up a spray
of tiny pebbles that set the valet parking staff
jumping, I saw I wasn't the only one who'd started
thinking of the estate as the scene of the crime. Russell
had summoned an impressive amount of extra security
for the evening. In addition to the legions of guards from
a private security firm, there was also a Town of East
Brompton Police car parked discreetly behind a clump of
trees.

Once inside, I saw that the studio executive had good
reason to worry about keeping the premises safe—and
tumbling ice sculptures were only part of the picture. The
artwork he owned—including a Picasso, a Matisse, and a
Monet I could only assume were the real thing—could
have been the basis for a small museum. In addition, I
spotted a glass chandelier that looked like a Chihuly and

an egg, most likely a Fabergé, placed unassumingly on an end table.

Given the impressive collection Russell Bolger had amassed, I suppose I shouldn't have been surprised that his house also had its very own theater, with a large open area outside it that served as a lobby. The room was the size of a small auditorium, with a large stage, complete with thick velvet curtains the color of an expensive burgundy. But it was also suitable for viewing movies. In fact, it was equipped with plush, dark red velour seats, plastic cup holders, and a screen as big as the ones I'd seen in my local multiplex. It even had its own popcorn machine, made to look like an old-fashioned red cart with oversized wheels.

Yet as I followed Shawn into the theater, a glass of champagne in hand, I noticed that there was one very distinctive feature that differentiated this theater from your average, run-of-the-mill movie house: the audience. Tonight's crowd was as star-studded as Oscar night. Aside from my own celebrity date for the evening, I spotted at least a dozen other actors I recognized from television and film. I also saw a Pulitzer Prize-winning journalist, a few well-known novelists, and a Swedish fashion model who'd retired at age twenty-two after marrying the head of a record company.

Despite the impressive guest list, the focus of the evening was undoubtedly Hugo Fontana, the star of the film and tonight's guest of honor. All eyes were upon him as he sauntered into the theater after everyone else had taken a seat. He was dressed casually in khaki pants, a black polo shirt, and a loose-fitting wheat-colored linen jacket whose clean lines emphasized his broad shoulders and massive chest. His square jawline was accentuated by a serious five o'clock shadow, giving him an air of insouciance that belied the importance of the evening.

A tall, lanky man strode into the theater beside him, trying to look just as relaxed but not quite succeeding. Russell Bolger, no doubt. While Hugo took a seat in the front row, the man I assumed was our host for the evening stepped in front of the screen and motioned for everyone to quiet down. He was exceptionally good-looking, the type of individual who exuded such confidence that he automatically became the center of attention. His dark hair was peppered with gray, and his tanned skin had the weathered look of someone who'd spent a lot of time on a yacht. Even from a distance, I could see that he had the same hazel eyes as his daughter. When he smiled, I saw the resemblance even more clearly.

"I'd like to thank you all for coming tonight," Russell Bolger began, his voice filling the room as he spoke into a microphone he'd pulled from out of nowhere. The sound system in the modest-sized auditorium was so powerful I half-expected him to introduce the Rolling Stones. "It's exciting for me to see so many familiar faces. I promise you're in for an action-packed evening. In case anyone doesn't know why we're here, it's because we're about to have the pleasure of watching one of the greatest actors of all time, Hugo Fontana, do what he does best."

After pausing for some light applause, he continued smoothly, "Just to give you a little background, Hugo is one of those rare individuals in Hollywood who truly was an 'overnight success.' I'm proud that I'm the person who discovered him, back when he was working as a waiter. I knew the minute I laid eyes on him that he had real star quality. Good thing, too, since I seem to recall he couldn't get my order straight."

Russell waited until the polite laughter died down. "Even though he'd only come to L.A. from New Jersey a few weeks earlier, I cast Hugo in the first *Pulverizer* movie. It was simply called *The Pulverizer,* since none of us dreamed it would turn out to be such a phenomenon. But the film was more than a box-office smash that set new records. Its star immediately struck a chord with his audience. Men loved his movies for the action. They saw Hugo Fontana as someone they'd like to be. But women loved him, too. He is amazingly charismatic, someone female ticket buyers couldn't get enough of. Suddenly, everybody was saying Hugo's signature expression, *"In—your—dreams!"* He punched out each syllable, using a distinctively New York accent. The audience laughed appreciatively.

"The rest, as they say, is history," he continued. "The success of *The Pulverizer* led to two equally successful sequels, *Pulverizer 2: The Devastation* and *Pulverizer 3: The Annihilation.* Together, these films put my production company, North Star Studios, on the map. I hope—and expect—that this fourth *Pulverizer* movie will be just as big a hit. I owe Hugo Fontana a lot—as do movie-lovers all across America and throughout the world."

"Hey, Russ!" someone called from the back of the room. "Is there going to be a *Pulverizer 5*? I want to know if I should invest in North Star!"

Amidst the laughter that broke out, Russell shot back, "It's hard to say. After all, who knows what comes after Armageddon? And now, without further ado, I invite you to enjoy the long-awaited *Pulverizer 4: Armageddon.*"

He sat down amid enthusiastic applause. The lights went out, and I sat back to watch my first *Pulverizer* film.

While I hadn't given much thought to what the next two hours would hold, I realized immediately that the movie's title should have tipped me off. I gripped the armrests so tightly my fingers ached as I watched Hugo—a.k.a. Dino Gigante, "the Pulverizer"—in action. He ferreted out a cowering drug dealer by wresting open the trunk of a Mercedes with his bare hands, then twisting the sheet metal into a cylinder and bonking him on the head with it. He picked up a second villain by the ears, held him at arm's length, and twirled him around a half-dozen times before lobbing him directly in the path of an oncoming garbage truck. He stacked a few hundred pounds of heroin in front of a fire hydrant, crouched down to open it with his teeth, and watched with satisfaction as the bad guys' booty was reduced to a dangerously addictive pool of oatmeal.

And that was just the first five minutes.

By the time the movie was over, I was exhausted. I'd seen more blood and guts in those 118 minutes than I'd encountered in my entire career as a veterinarian. It was a relief when the lights finally came back on, the last of the screen credits still rolling up on the screen, accompanied by the loud, menacing music that constituted *The Pulverizer*'s theme song.

"Another blockbuster!" I heard someone say as I filed out of the screening room with the other guests. "I just *love* the way he says, '*In—your—dreams!*'"

"Hugo's done it again," the woman heading up the aisle in front of me gurgled. "They sure don't make men like *that* anymore."

"How'd you like to jump in the sack with him?" her friend countered, giggling. "I bet pulverizing drug dealers isn't the *only* thing he's good at!"

My head hadn't yet stopped spinning, and it wasn't only from all the Hollywood-style violence I'd just been subjected to—enough to guarantee that *Pulverizer 4* would be a box-office hit with his macho, action-loving fans. While Hugo Fontana was certainly the embodiment of power, at the same time he managed to generate an amazing amount of sex appeal on screen.

When it came to muscles, nobody had him beat. His

arms and torso were perfectly formed, as if Michelangelo himself had created the man out of marble. Although his muscles could best be described as "bulging," there was a certain beauty, and even grace, to his rounded biceps and triceps and his well-developed abs. Either sweat, oil, or some other Hollywood trick gave his olive-toned skin a sheen that made him look even more unreal—and more powerful. He was also classically handsome, with a Roman nose, that remarkably strong jawline, and intense dark brown eyes fringed with extraordinarily thick black lashes.

I hated to admit it, but I'd come to understand Hugo Fontana's appeal. I could even imagine plunking down a pile of bills for a movie ticket, just to see him in action once again.

A splash of cold water on my face was definitely in order.

"I'm going to pop into the ladies' room," I told Shawn. "I'll catch up with you in a minute."

I headed down a short hallway and opened a door I suspected would take me where I wanted to go. But instead of finding myself in a bathroom, I confronted black walls, thick velvet curtains, looping ropes, and electrical boxes.

"Oops," I muttered, realizing I'd accidentally stumbled upon the entrance to the backstage area. I backed out and tried again, immediately spotting a door labeled "Actresses." When I noticed a second door that said "Actors" right across the hall, I knew I'd found the right place.

I ducked inside, then stood in front of the large mirror hanging above the three sinks. I was checking to see if I looked as drained as I felt, when the door opened and Kara Liebling floated in.

"Jessie!" she greeted me brightly. "What a nice surprise!"

I was just as pleased to see her. "I noticed you in the audience, but I was sitting toward the front."

"Funny how our paths keep crossing, isn't it?" she commented.

"I guess when you come right down to it, the Bromptons are really like a small town."

She stepped over to the mirror so that the two of us were standing side by side. "I see we have something else in common," she said, her eyes fixed on her reflection as she reached up to smooth her perfect hair. "Besides our social calendars, I mean." I guess I looked as puzzled as I felt, because she added, "Shawn Elliot?"

I didn't respond.

"I saw the two of you sitting together during the screening," Kara went on, her eyes still fixed on the mirror. "I don't know if Shawn has said anything to you, but he and I were together at one point."

I could feel the blood draining from my face. Sure enough, when I checked my reflection, I saw that I looked like an extra in a horror movie. My impulse was to correct her, to tell her that Shawn and I were "just friends." But I knew if I tried to explain, my words would come out sounding weak and defensive.

Then there was the fact that the only reason Shawn had brought me here tonight was so I could seek out information that might help me with my murder investigation. I wasn't exactly anxious to confess that I was playing private detective.

"I suppose he's giving you the royal treatment," she continued. "Shawn is one of those rare men who really knows how to treat a woman."

I glanced over at Kara's reflection and saw she was smiling. Yet there was a distinct undertone to her voice that exposed an entirely different side of her. Still, I supposed that jealousy could have that effect—on *anyone*. I decided to try being honest.

"Kara, I'm only going to be here in the Bromptons for a few days," I told her, my voice as even as I could manage. "The people who are running the charity dog show were kind enough to find me a place to live while I'm here, and it happened to be the guesthouse on Shawn's estate. He's simply being neighborly by making sure I have something to do in the evenings."

"That's *so* considerate of him." She paused only for a second before adding, "And how does your boyfriend feel about Shawn's generosity?"

I stiffened. Kara had clearly put some effort into dissecting my social life. But while my initial reaction was irritation, I told myself that it was nothing personal. It was obvious that she still had strong feelings about Shawn.

Fortunately, I never had to answer her question about Nick. The door flew open again, and a group of three women who'd clearly hit the champagne a little too hard burst into the room, laughing and screeching.

"It's getting crowded in here," I said, flashing her a smile that I truly meant to be sympathetic. "I'll catch up with you later, Kara."

I was relieved that I spotted Shawn the moment I stepped back out into the lobby. I made a beeline in his direction. But before I had a chance to engage him in conversation, a tall, dark-haired woman wearing a dress that revealed considerably more than it covered, cut me off.

"Shawn Elliot! *There* you are!" She grabbed his arm, wrapping both hands around it possessively. "I need you to settle a bet. Alicia and I were just arguing over which one of your movies came out first, *Afternoon in Paradise* or *Rocky Mountain High*. You *must* clear this up before we break into a fistfight—"

Shawn cast me an apologetic look as he allowed himself to be led away. But as far as I was concerned, he'd done enough just by getting me in the door.

Still, I found myself in the uncomfortable position of having no one to talk to once again. I wandered over to the food table, a lavish display of sushi, raw vegetables, and other food that had never seen the inside of an oven or the top of a stove. I had just picked up a plate and was trying to decide where to begin, when a sharp female voice caught my attention.

"Not *there*!" the familiar voice hissed. "The beluga belongs over *there*, next to the osetra!"

Phyllis Beckwith, the mistress of Foodies, Inc., was standing a few feet behind me, her hands on her hips. Once again, she was dressed in a tailored, expensive-looking suit—this time, lemon-yellow—and a pair of spiky high heels. And once again, her carefully madeup face was twisted into an angry scowl.

"You *know* how important this movie is to Mr. Bolger!" she continued in the same angry tone. "He's got a lot riding on it. Now put *this* caviar next to the *other* caviar, where it's *supposed* to be, before I put them both where they *really* belong!"

Phyllis's habit of talking to her employees as if they were cockroaches irritated me. But if I'd learned anything in life, it was that the old saying about catching more flies with honey than with vinegar couldn't be more true.

"Are you the culinary genius who's responsible for all this fabulous food?" I asked, easing over to her and doing my best to look admiring.

"Why, yes." Her voice had softened so dramatically it was hard to believe this was the same person who, seconds before, had been barking orders like a drill sergeant.

I narrowed my eyes and looked pensive, as if I was

thinking really hard. "Now wait a minute..." I said tentatively. "Aren't you the same caterer who did that magnificent spread at the dinner for the charity dog show? The *other* event here at Russell Bolger's?"

Phyllis beamed. "You have an excellent memory."

"Well, I was so *impressed*," I gushed, horrified at how good at this I was turning out to be. "But I suppose you knock yourself out for every event you cater."

"Definitely. But especially for Russell. He's much more than a client. He's a *friend*. Russell Bolger has been very good to me over the years. Why, he was practically the person who got Foodies off the ground!"

"Really! How did he manage that?" I prompted.

"He took a chance by hiring me back when I was just starting out, trying to get my catering business off the ground with nothing but a few quiches." Her eyes got glassy, as if she were taking a momentary trip back in time. "Back then, I didn't even have my own kitchen. I used to get up at five A.M. to make my quiches at a friend's restaurant before her regular staff came in. I owe him a lot. I was in the middle of a divorce, and after twelve years as a stay-at-home wife and mother..."

"What an amazing success story!" I exclaimed. "Well, you've certainly gone all out tonight."

Phyllis glanced around, as if wanting to make sure no one overheard. In a much softer voice, she said, "Of course, this movie is *very* important to Russell."

"Why this one, in particular?" I asked.

She reacted to my question with surprise. "Don't you read the trades?"

"Uh, no. I'm a veterinarian. I'm only out here on the East End for the dog show."

"How refreshing! I sometimes forget there are people in the world who aren't connected to the entertainment business in some way."

I leaned forward, hoping she'd be willing to fill me in, even though I had no connection to Hollywood.

"Russell's production company, North Star, has been having some . . . financial difficulties," she told me in a near-whisper.

"Really? I had no idea!"

"North Star's last few pictures flopped at the box office," Phyllis went on in the same low voice. "In fact, in the last five years or so, the *Pulverizer* films are the only ones that have made any money. Russell is counting on *Pulverizer 4* to pull his company out of its financial slump. If, for some reason, it *doesn't* break a few records for ticket sales . . ."

She shook her head. "Well, I'm not even going to *think* about that. I'm sure Hugo's got another huge hit on his hands. I was too busy in the kitchen to come to the screening. What did you think of it?"

I smiled brightly. "It certainly had all the elements required to make it a success." I silently congratulated myself on my diplomacy. "And Hugo Fontana definitely possesses star quality." At least I was sincere about that last part.

Phyllis looked relieved. "I *knew* it. I've got a good feeling about *Armageddon*. I've been telling Russell all along that this is the movie that's going to do it for him—"

"I'm sorry to interrupt, Ms. Beckwith," interjected a Foodies staff member, dressed in the signature black pants and white shirt, "but the oregano dipping sauce looks a little watery."

Phyllis immediately looked stricken. "Oh, my God. I *told* Antonio he was getting a little heavy-handed with the balsamic vinegar!" She turned to me, all smiles again, and said, "Will you excuse me? It seems we're having a little crisis. But let me give you my card. You veterinarians have conferences and parties and things, don't you? Foodies can even do a completely vegetarian menu!"

She produced a business card from out of nowhere and pressed it into my hand. Then she scurried off to put things right with the uncooperative dipping sauce.

So Russell Bolger's production company isn't doing very well, I mused. I glanced around the palatial room with new interest. That little tidbit, combined with the luxurious lifestyle that Bolger had clearly become accustomed to, made for an interesting juxtaposition.

I was still pondering what I'd learned from Phyllis Beckwith, pretending it was the intriguing selection of uncooked food on my plate that was making me so pensive, when I heard a high-pitched voice squeal, "*There* she is!"

I glanced up and saw Emily physically dragging our host for the evening in my direction.

"She's over *here*, Daddy," Emily told him. "You *have* to meet her!"

"Hello, Emily," I greeted her. "How nice to see you!"

"Dr. Popper! I'm so glad you're here!" The little girl threw her arms around me and gave me such a big hug she nearly knocked me over. She reminded me of one of those Great Danes who's nearly fully grown but still thinks she's a puppy, with no idea of her strength.

She was all smiles as she presented me to her father. "This is Dr. Jessica Popper, Dad. My new friend that I told you about. She's a veterinarian!"

"So you're the famous Dr. Popper," Russell Bolger said, smiling warmly and extending his hand. "My daughter has talked about very little else since she met you."

"Emily is a terrific girl," I told him sincerely as we shook hands. "Getting to know her has been one of the highlights of this event."

"Isn't she great?" Emily asked him. "I told you she was the nicest person in the world!"

Russell patted his daughter's shoulder affectionately. "Sounds like the feeling is mutual, Emmie."

As I'd expected, Emily's conclusion that her parents were disappointed in her was completely inaccurate—at least, if the pride I saw in her father's eyes was any indication.

"Guess what, Jessie!" Emily demanded, her wide eyes focused on me.

"What?"

"My dad says I can go visit my mom next week!"

"That's wonderful news!" I smiled at Emily, still uncertain about the wisdom of a twelve-year-old girl visiting a rehab center. But I reminded myself that it wasn't my call.

"It's been a rough few months for my daughter," Russell Bolger told me, putting a protective arm around his daughter. "I think it'll mean a lot to her to be able to spend some time with her mother."

"There you are, Russell! Where *have* you been hiding all evening?" One of the other guests—a nearly emaciated redhead in a white dress that was intentionally see-through—came up and planted a wet kiss on his lips, meanwhile pressing her disproportionately large chest against him. I watched Emily's face fall. My impulse was to distract her. But before I had a chance, one of the other guests grabbed my arm.

"Terrible, isn't it?" a woman in her late sixties said in a stage whisper, yanking me closer to her side. She was wearing a huge turquoise hat, and I was forced to keep one eye closed to avoid being poked by the oversized brim. "What that poor little girl must have gone through! Not to mention poor Delilah!"

" 'Delilah'?" I realized, for the first time, that I'd never

bothered to find out who Emily Bolger's mother *was*.
"You don't mean—"

"It's *so* tragic! After all, Delilah Raines is one of the
biggest stars in Hollywood! At least, she *was* before she
hit forty and the really good roles stopped coming in. It's
such a sad story; one you see getting replayed again and
again. Actresses are under so much more pressure than
actors when it comes to aging. And then *this*! I mean, it's
bad enough that it happened in the first place. But the
way the newspapers carried on and on, reporting every
single *detail*—"

I was about to volunteer that I'd missed the event she
was talking about completely—and that, in fact, it
wasn't until this very moment that I'd even realized that
Emily Bolger's mother was the movie actress Delilah
Raines—but I never got the chance.

"Oh, my God," the woman gushed. "There's Hugo.
Doesn't he look *fabulous* since the surgery? I swear, that
doctor took ten years off his face. I simply *must* tell him
how magnificent he looks. . . ."

She was gone as abruptly as she arrived. Emily and
her father, meanwhile, had disappeared into the crowd.
But my head was spinning. Of course, I did my best to
keep up with the news. But I tended to concentrate on
the stories in the front of the newspaper, rather than the
ones in the back. Even finding out that Emily's mom was
Delilah Raines didn't give me much information—aside
from being impressed by what a truly star-studded set of
parents the sweet little girl had. Maybe everyone else
knew "every single detail" about whatever had happened to Emily's mother, but somehow I'd missed the
whole thing.

I glanced at my watch and saw it was getting late. If I
was going to make it to West Brompton in time to meet
Gus the Tattooed Busboy before Raffy's closed, it was
time for me to go.

I was about to seek out Shawn when he burst into the room, nearly spilling the glass of champagne he was carrying. From the sloppy grin on his face, I surmised that it wasn't his first.

"Here she is!" he cried when he spotted me. "I been lookin' for you!"

Any doubts I may have had about his state of inebriation were instantly dispelled by his slurred speech. I only hoped he'd allow me to drive us both home without an argument. I'd never driven a Ferrari, but I couldn't imagine it was any trickier than a van—especially one stocked with medical equipment.

"You know, Dr. Pepper—I mean, *Popper*—is quite a girl," Shawn went on. By this point, he was talking loudly enough that most of the people gathered in the room had stopped their own conversations, instead focusing on him. "Not only is she a helluva veteran—hah! I mean, veterinarian. At least, I don't *think* she's ever been in the Army. Have you, Jess?"

"Shawn, I think—"

"*Have* you?"

By this point, the room was completely silent. I could feel my cheeks burning. "No. But I think it's time to—"

"Not only is she smart enough to be an animal doctor. This woman is also a private investigator!"

"Please, Shawn!" I begged, grabbing his arm.

"It's not like she's not a professional or anything. But that's not stopping her from invezzi—I mean, *investigating* murders! I'd bet my Ferrari she's gonna figure out who killed that bastard Bevon Darnett—"

Several people in the crowd gasped. I could feel a tidal wave of anger rising up inside me.

"Shawn, we're leaving," I said firmly, tightening my grasp and practically dragging him out of there.

"Wait, that doesn't sound right," he muttered, as he allowed me to pull him along beside me, practically tripping over his own feet. "Kevin Larnett...no, that's Mevon Carnett..."

I was prepared to give him a piece of my mind as I backed his sports car out of its parking space so fast the tires sputtered against the dirt. As I drove off, my jaw was tightly clenched and my eyes were burning from the tears of anger I refused to let fall. But even before I'd made it out of the driveway, Shawn fell into a deep sleep, slumping over in the seat beside me and snoring more loudly than Lou.

• • •

Even though I was infuriated over Shawn's announcement to a crowd of possible murder suspects that I had taken it upon myself to investigate Devon Barnett's death, I tried to put my anger aside. Instead, I concentrated on getting Shawn safely into his house and onto his couch, where he immediately launched into the next item on his agenda: sleeping off his overindulgence in Russell Bolger's expensive champagne.

"He's all yours," I told Rufus, dropping the keys to the Ferrari on the coffee table.

The squat bulldog eyed me warily, then plopped down on the floor next to his master with a loud sigh. The look on his face made me feel he understood completely that he was in for a long night.

Next, I got into my van and headed for West Brompton to meet Gus. I had a pretty good idea where Raffy's was. As for *what* it was, I wasn't nearly as certain. I figured it was probably a restaurant, one of those places with twelve varieties of hamburger, each with a name that's cuter than the last. Or maybe a tuxedo rental place, nicknamed for its suave, continental owner, Rafael.

A half hour later, I pulled into the strip mall I'd envisioned when Gus had given me the address. Methodically, I checked out the sign above each store. "Raffy's, Raffy's . . ." I muttered.

And then my heart stopped.

Raffy's. There it was, all right, exactly where Gus had said it would be. Only he hadn't given me the whole name.

*Raffy's Reptile-A-Rama.*

My heart started up again. Only this time, it was beating so fast I felt dizzy.

Personally, I have nothing against the Reptilia class. I'm quite fond of lizards, invariably appreciative of the charms of the dignified iguana, the energetic gecko with its funny feet that look like asterisks, and even the ferocious-looking monitor. And ever since Nick and I went to Hawaii, I've been pleased to count Leilani, the most charming Jackson's chameleon this side of Polynesia, among our pets. Turtles? I can hardly imagine anything cuter. Gators and crocs hold an endless fascination for me, and I can't get enough of those cable TV shows they star in.

It's snakes I have a problem with.

I'm not saying it's admirable, and I'm not saying it's based on logic. All I'm saying is that it's *there*. And idling outside Raffy's Reptile-A-Rama, doing my best to peer inside through its giant display window, I had a feeling that Raffy had amassed a huge inventory of boas, pythons, and all those other creepy, slithery members of the Serpentes suborder.

"You can do this," I told myself as I pulled into a parking spot, sounding like one of those self-help tapes. I held my head up high, pushed open the glass door, and strode inside.

My first maneuver was glancing around Raffy's, curious to see what I was up against. Even though the shop wasn't very big, its inventory was impressive. Over two dozen tanks were on display, lined up on the built-in shelves covering two of the walls. Most of them housed small reptiles, harmless critters I could readily identify. A black-and-brown Abbots tree dragon. A black timor monitor covered with white speckles. A Jackson's chameleon that was cute, but not nearly as engaging as Leilani. I noticed that Raffy had also expanded into amphibians. One tank was filled with tiny arrow frogs, each one smaller than a Ping-Pong ball, in such bright neon colors they looked like ceramic decorations for a fish tank instead of living, breathing beings.

I jumped when I caught someone staring at me with cold, unblinking eyes. He hovered in the corner of Raffy's, as big as a large coffee table, but standing so still I couldn't tell if he was alive or not. Then the five-foot-long land iguana moved his head. He was real, all right. Not particularly dangerous, I knew, but disconcerting nonetheless.

Still, I hadn't yet encountered anything I couldn't handle—or even anything that would send my blood pressure soaring.

"So far, so good," I breathed.

As the old saying goes, I spoke too soon.

I had already spotted the busboy, standing behind the counter and chatting with a couple of men I presumed were customers. Gone was his tight white T-shirt. In fact, Gus wasn't wearing any shirt at all. Instead, his torso was partially covered by a black leather vest that showcased not only his bulbous biceps, but a chest and stomach so rippled with muscles they looked like a graphic relief map of Tibet.

While his upper body definitely fell into the "fascinating" category, for some reason the two customers were focused on his waistline. A particularly attractive belt? I wondered as I ventured over. It was a distinct possibility, given his obvious passion for leather.

"Hello, again," I said, my voice uncharacteristically weak.

Gus barely glanced up. I, meanwhile, couldn't resist looking to see what was monopolizing the men's interest.

I found out fast, stopping dead in my tracks as I did. That was no belt wrapped around Gus's waist. It was a reticulated python. And it was probably close to eight feet long.

I guess I gulped pretty loudly, because all three of the men suddenly glanced over at me.

"Remember me?" I squawked. I hoped we could get this over with—*fast*.

"Hey, check this out," Gus said cheerfully. "You like snakes?" He gestured toward the gray-and-black tube slithering ominously around his torso.

I immediately looked down at my shoes, hoping he didn't see me shudder. "Well . . . not particularly."

"But this is a great snake," he insisted.

"And believe me," one of the men added, "Gus knows his snakes."

I glanced up long enough to see that the busboy *cum* snake charmer was beaming proudly. I, meanwhile, was hoping we could change the subject, if not the entire locale.

"But listen, it's just about closing time," Gus said. "Sorry, guys, but we gotta call it a night."

"Sure, Gus. Whatever," one of the men muttered. He turned to me, looked me up and down, and leered. I half-expected his tongue to dart out like one of the lizards' in the tank behind him.

This time, I didn't care *who* saw me shudder. Flesh that touches snakeskin shall never touch mine, I thought, horrified by what was obviously going on in his mind.

I watched the two men wander out of the store, assuming that Gus's next step would be putting away his writhing accessory. Instead, he kept the python wrapped around him as he scooped up a key ring and sauntered around the shop, shutting off lights.

"So what's your interest in those two fags from the Sand Bar, anyway?" he asked casually. "They friends of yours?"

I could hardly stand to look at him. I tried fixing my gaze on the display of paperback books on the counter, then realized that most of them had snakes as cover girls. I turned—and leaped into the air when I found myself face-to-face with the king-sized iguana. Without the benefit of fluorescent lighting, even he was starting to look ominous.

"Yes. Well, no, not really. I—look, I don't want to take up a lot of your time," I said, eyeing the door nervously. It suddenly seemed very far away, and I noticed that the air inside Raffy's was growing noticeably warmer. Whether Gus had turned off the air-conditioning or his playful pet had caused me to break out in a sweat, I couldn't say. "I can see you're busy. If you could just tell me more about that incident you mentioned, the one with the police . . ."

"There's not much to tell." Gus had reached the five-hundred-gallon tank that was tucked into the back corner. With surprisingly gentle hands, he began unraveling the python from his muscular trunk. My mouth became drier and drier as I watched. I'd been way off when I'd estimated that the snake was eight feet long. Fifteen was probably more like it. "The two of them came into the Sand Bar one Saturday night, maybe three, four weeks ago. Maybe less. Anyway, they sat down at their favorite table. It's inside the restaurant, way in the back. That Barnett guy always insisted on sitting against the wall so he could see everybody who came in. He always had his eye out for a celebrity, somebody he could pounce on. He'd snap some pictures, make a few bucks . . . can't blame him for that, I guess."

"It *was* how he made his living," I interjected, surprised that my mouth still worked.

I'd lost Gus's attention, at least for the moment. Instead, he was focused on his serpentine friend. He had apparently encountered a glitch in his attempt at unraveling the snake from his person. Instead of cooperating, Buddy was writhing upward along Gus's chest, toward his neck.

"Come on, Buddy," Gus murmured, sounding positively affectionate as he wrestled with the slithering beast. "Time to tuck you in for the night. Don't play games with me."

Please, Buddy, I thought, taking deep breaths and looking away. No games.

"Anyway, the place was pretty crowded that night," Gus continued, "so I was running around, clearing one table after another. The boss was in, too, so I had to hustle. You know, look like I was keeping busy. But every time I passed their table, I heard them talking about the same thing."

"Which was? ..." I prompted, forcing myself to look at him.

"Y'ready for this?" Gus's mouth twisted into the same smirk I'd seen at the Sand Bar when he was eavesdropping on my conversation with Steve the Waitperson. "The guy with the yellow hair, Chess, is working on the photographer, trying to convince him that the two of them should make their relationship *legal*."

"You mean ... like a marriage?" I asked, not bothering to hide my surprise. "A same-sex union?"

"Yeah, I think that's what they call it. Chess keeps saying that him and Barnett should get a weekend house in Vermont, establish themselves as residents, and throw a big wedding. The guy even volunteered to plan the whole thing. I swear, it sounded like he'd already picked out his wedding dress."

I chose to ignore that last comment. Besides, I was too busy wondering if Chess knew that Devon had already taken his vows once—only that time, with a woman. "I take it Dev—uh, Barnett—didn't think it was such a good idea."

"You could say that. In fact, he just about froze Chess out. He wouldn't even talk about it. Chess keeps chattering away, trying all these different ways to convince him, and Dev just sits there. Then he starts saying 'No,' giving Chess a hard time. Their voices keep getting louder. Meanwhile, I'm listening to them, cleaning up the table right next to them. I can see that Chess is getting more and more upset. And finally, he picks up a knife—"

I gasped. "A steak knife?" At this point, even the snake had lost its power over me. I was too focused on what Gus was telling me to take more than a casual interest in the fact that the python was finally allowing himself to be lowered into the tank, shooting its tongue out every few seconds and looking more evil than the devil himself.

"Actually, it was a butter knife." Gus, now free of the python, slammed down the lid that would keep Buddy out of trouble for the rest of the night. "Look, it was the only utensil on the table. But that didn't keep the guy from acting really ferocious. He stood up and starting jabbing Dev in the shoulder—"

"With a *butter knife*?"

Gus just shrugged.

"Did he break the skin?"

"I think the worst he did was get grease all over the guy's shirt." Gus let out a harsh laugh, clearly scornful of Chess's effectiveness as a warrior. "But my boss called the police anyway. At that point, we didn't know what the guy was capable of. I mean, we got *forks* in that place!"

"Did the police come?"

"Sure. They gotta answer every nine-one-one call. They talked to Dev; they talked to Chess; they talked to me and the boss... 'Course, by the time they got there, everybody had calmed down."

"Did Dev press charges?"

"Nah. Personally, I don't get it. Seems to me somebody attacks you, you should make sure it goes on the record. You know, in case there's a next time."

I thought for a few seconds. "Do you know why Barnett was so strongly against the idea of a same-sex union?"

"Beats me. Like I said, those two weren't exactly my best friends." He turned his attention to the giant iguana, who was still lurking in the shadows, right behind me. I'd forgotten all about him, but all of a sudden, the place was giving me the creeps. Too little light and too many creepy crawlies. It was definitely time to get out of there, even with the huggable python put back in his tank for the night.

"Well, thanks for the information," I told Gus, edging toward the door. Gesturing toward the glowering iguana, I added, "I, uh, guess you'll be putting this guy away next."

"Molly?" Gus asked, looking surprised. "Naw. She comes home with me."

I eased out of there as quickly as I could, climbing into my van and making a left turn out of the parking lot. Already the details of my experience at Raffy's were fading. Instead, I focused on the new information I'd gathered.

So sweet little Chess has a history of violence, I mused as I veered onto Sunset Highway and headed back to East Brompton. For at least a few moments, he completely lost control. He physically attacked Devon.

Very telling, I thought. Even if it *was* assault with a deadly condiment spreader.

• • •

It was after eleven by the time I reached the guesthouse. I was relieved to see Nick's car outside, a sign that he hadn't given up on us completely and gone back home to Port Townsend.

As I headed toward the front steps, I was glad that he and I had decided to do without the house key. The dim porch light was enough to keep someone from stumbling, but hardly the best for rifling through a jam-packed purse.

I kept my eyes down, wary of maneuvering the uneven steps while wearing shoes with heels. Which is how I happened to notice the small, shadowy mass on the small landing.

I leaned forward to get a better look—and gasped.

It was only a mouse, I realized right away. Still, it was a *dead* mouse, and it was lying directly in my path.

Poor little guy, I thought, leaning over to study the tiny rodent more carefully. You didn't need a D.V.M. degree to see that his little neck had been snapped. Lucifer's handiwork, no doubt.

I scooped the critter up with some leaves, then found a soft spot under the shrubs. Using a stick, I dug a small hole and buried him.

That's how nature works, I thought grimly. There are the hunters, and there are the hunted.

I reminded myself that human beings were no exception.

I crept inside the guesthouse, not wanting to wake Nick. It wasn't a question of being considerate. It was more that I was so tired and so overwhelmed by all the information I'd been barraged with that evening that I didn't have the energy to argue.

"Hey, guys," I greeted my dogs in a whisper. They were both waiting for me, descending upon their lord and master as soon as I walked in the door. I crouched down, hugging and scratching each of them. Lou's tail thumped loudly against the wooden floor, while Max's nails skittered noisily across its smooth surface.

"Sh-h-h," I warned. "Nick's sleeping. Don't wake him."

I found him lying in bed, so far over on his side that his feet hung off the mattress. He'd left the light on for me, draping one side of the shade with a dark T-shirt. The dim light cast the room in eerie shadow.

"Are you okay?" he asked softly as I tiptoed into the room. He didn't move, and he kept his eyes closed.

"Sure," I answered. "Why wouldn't I be?"

"It's late." He was silent for a long time before adding, "I was worried."

I felt a pang of regret that we couldn't simply sink into each other's arms and fall asleep. But I knew from Nick's tone—and his posture—that he wasn't ready to do that. At least, not yet.

I slipped in beside him, taking care not to let our bodies touch. "I went to the screening," I said, snapping off the light. "I saw Hugo Fontana's new *Pulverizer* movie."

"How was it?"

"Violent."

"Figures."

I didn't mention Shawn or Gus the Busboy or anyone else connected to Devon. Instead, I lay in the dark, contemplating whether to say anything at all or to simply go to sleep.

I suddenly felt Lou's nose poking against my hand. As usual, he was looking for an invitation.

"Come on, Louie-Lou," I instructed.

He leaped onto the bed and dropped down between Nick and me, letting out a contented sigh. Max followed without hesitation, jumping up and then turning around half a dozen times before settling at my feet.

I nestled my head against Lou's warm body, glad that at least somebody still wanted to sleep with his body close to mine.

# Chapter 10

"It's not the size of the dog in the fight, it's the size of the fight in the dog."

—Mark Twain

The temperature was still unseasonably frosty early on Wednesday morning—at least, inside the guesthouse. Nick was polite, answering my questions about breakfast, dogs, and plans for the day with single syllables. I was actually relieved that by the time I got out of the shower, he'd already left for the beach, taking Max and Lou and John Grisham with him.

The Grand Canyon-size distance between Nick and me, combined with the dog show's one-day hiatus, made this the perfect opportunity to find out what I could about Sydney Hornsby Barnett. I'd already managed to locate the woman who held the dubious distinction of being Devon Barnett's wife by combining my sophisticated investigative skills with my natural insightfulness. In other words, I called Norfolk County Information.

I had to restrain myself from letting out a squeal of joy when I found out there was a listing for a Sydney Barnett

at 25 Windmill Lane in Cuttituck. Just to be sure, I dialed the number on the spot.

*"You've reached Sizzle. Living during the technologi-
cal age has taught you what to do and when to do it.
You've also learned to wait for the beep."*

" 'Sizzle'?" I repeated aloud, wondering if I'd dialed
wrong. Just to be sure, I tried again—and got the same
recording.

I didn't leave a message. Instead, I copied the address
and phone number into my notebook.

The drive to Cuttituck was much more relaxing than
I'd expected. The North Fork, Long Island's other fish-
tail, is less developed and less overtly prosperous than
the South Fork. Once a rich farming area, the flat stretch
of land still retains its peaceful rural quality, even though
the local growers have switched from potatoes to wine
grapes. Back in the 1970s, an inventive couple who'd
been college sweethearts realized the region's climate and
soil were similar to those of France. They bought some
land, figuring they'd plant a few grapes and see what
happened.

What began as a brave experiment turned into a vi-
brant industry. The North Fork is now home to more
than two dozen wineries. The immense fields of neatly
planted grape arbors lining both sides of the country
road provided me with a pleasing view as I headed east
in my van. Every few miles, a sign identified a different
winery, inviting travelers to stop in for a tasting or a tour.

I'd been on the road less than forty-five minutes when
I reached the town of Cuttituck. Actually, "town" was
an exaggeration. It was more of a hamlet, with a central
business district that consisted of two antique shops, a
video store, a red brick fire house, and the Cuttituck
Diner, a classic-looking eatery from the 1950s that you
just knew had terrific meat loaf.

As I turned off North Shore Road onto Windmill

Lane, I suddenly had an attack of butterfly stomach. It was one thing to mingle with strangers at a party or a dog show, sprinkling the conversation with a few carefully crafted questions. Knocking on a stranger's door without any introduction and certainly without any legitimate reason for being there was in another league altogether.

I reminded myself that I'd managed just fine at Chess's house, doing such a good job of thinking on my feet that I actually got myself in the door. Still, I questioned the wisdom of this entire trip as I bumped along the side road, the badly paved surface giving way to dirt as I neared the North Coast. Then I spotted a lone mailbox, handpainted in purple with the number twenty-five. Underneath, in hot pink, were the words, "SIZZLE/BARNETT."

"This is the place," I muttered, making a sharp left into the driveway. I drove only a few more feet before rounding a bend and spotting a squat, dilapidated-looking farmhouse covered with weatherworn cedar shingles. Between its architectural style and its advanced state of decay, I figured it had to be at least a hundred years old. The white paint on the windowframes was peeling, and the roof looked as if it might collapse if I huffed and puffed just a little too hard. Farther back on the property was a barn of the same vintage. The grass in between was overgrown, happily living side by side with an impressive crop of weeds.

The grounds seemed deserted, the silence broken only by the chirping of birds and the thud of my footsteps. Fool's errand? I wondered. But I took a deep breath and knocked on the door.

Then groaned when there was no response.

I tried again, this time knocking harder. Finally, I resorted to banging.

I stood with my fist in midair, about to give the door one more pounding, when I heard a voice behind me.

"You don't give up, do you?" someone growled. "You've already broken my concentration, so this better be good."

I turned around and saw that the person who'd spoken was standing in the doorway of the barn. For a few seconds, I just stared, caught completely off guard by the incongruity of the gravelly voice and the woman who produced it. Even though she sounded like a trucker with a cigar habit and a sinus infection, Sydney—*Sizzle*—was barely five feet tall and probably weighed about ninety pounds. Purple velour stretch pants clung to her bottom half like skin, while her tiny torso was encased in an equally tight white shirt printed in black with words and photographs so that it looked like a newspaper. Layer after crusty layer of mascara made her eyelashes stand out like spikes, and her lips were thickly smeared with scarlet lipstick. She was sucking on a cigarette—the reason behind the rasping voice, I concluded.

Yet it was her hair that was her most outstanding feature. It was dyed the color of overripe cherries and shaved into a crewcut.

I couldn't stop staring. But it wasn't simply her bizarre appearance, or even its jarring contrast with such a rustic setting, that intrigued me. I couldn't shake the feeling that I'd seen her before.

"Ms. Barnett?" I asked, trying to get a grip.

She just looked at me, not saying yes but not saying no, either. I went on.

"My name is Jessica Popper." I walked toward her slowly, the way I do when I approach an animal whose temperament is still in question. "I, uh, knew Devon."

I studied her face, wondering what kind of reaction I'd get. I was prepared for anything except the one I got: icy laughter.

"I noticed you didn't say you were a *friend* of Devon's. Probably because the man didn't have any friends. Or know the meaning of words like 'friendship' or 'loyalty' or—God forbid—'love.' "

"Uh, I was wondering if I could speak with you for a minute."

She sucked up more smoke as if it were the only thing keeping her alive, then studied me as she slowly breathed it out. "Since you're here, I suppose you might as well come into my studio. It's not like I'll be able to get any-more work done *now*."

I stepped into the barn, an expansive space that looked as if it hadn't been updated since the day it was built. Its walls were made of wood that was so rough that simply touching them practically guaranteed a seri-ous splinter. The floor, made from even wider slats of wood, was just as crude.

Sydney apparently used the space to produce artwork. Or at least her version of it. In addition to an expensive-looking camera and a tabletop setup edged with a sophis-ticated lighting system, dozens of framed black-and-white photographs leaned against the walls of the barn.

At first glance, they looked like ordinary still lifes, at-tractive groupings of everyday items. But as I focused on them, I saw that each one told a story. One featured a tube of lipstick, a lacy bra, a strappy shoe with a spiked heel, a champagne glass, and a pregnancy test. Another was a photograph of pastries slathered in whip cream, chocolate truffles, delicate petit fours, and a prescription bottle of heart medication.

I turned to Sydney. "I had planned to start out by of-fering my condolences," I told her, "but I get the feeling that may not be appropriate."

"Probably not, considering I haven't even seen the man for at least a year."

"You were Devon's wife, right?"

"Technically. Although we've been separated for close to four years, so I tend to think of myself as his ex-wife."

That explained a lot.

She leaned against a table, puffing away maniacally and peering at me more closely. I hoped there was a fire extinguisher on the premises. "What's *your* interest in Devon?"

"He and I got to know each other a bit because I, uh, was his veterinarian. At least, when he was out at the East End. You know Zsa Zsa, don't you? The Havanese?"

Sydney's mouth twisted into a sneer. "Most vile beast I've ever encountered. But that ridiculous lover of his simply had to have it. Checkers, or whatever his name is."

"Chess."

"Like I said, whatever." She ground her cigarette into the coffee cup sitting on the edge of the table. It was stained with brown, and its edges were smeared with blood-red lipstick. Just glancing at it was enough to make my stomach convulse. "So you live in the Bromptons?"

"Actually, I live on the North Shore. But I have a mobile services unit, so I have clients all over Long Island. How about you? Do you spend much time on the South Fork?"

She shook her head as she lit up another cigarette. The acrid smell of the sulfur irritated my nose. "I can't remember the last time I was there. I absolutely despise the entire scene, all those pretentious people who flock there like lemmings every summer. It's gotten as bad as Manhattan—which is why I don't live *there* anymore." She paused for only a second before asking, "How did you find me?"

At least I could be honest about that. "You're listed in the phone book. And I knew Devon had a wife because it was mentioned in his obituary in *The East Brompton Banner.*"

"My, my. Somebody did their homework." She narrowed her eyes. "That Checkers person probably told them about me. What did it say, exactly?"

"Not much. Just that Devon Barnett was survived by his wife, Sydney Hornsby Barnett."

"'Barnett,'" she repeated, sneering. "I never should have changed my name. Now I'm stuck with Devon's name for the rest of my life. It's like a tattoo."

"But people know you as 'Sizzle,' don't they?"

"Hah!"

I jumped. The raw sound of her laughter jabbed me in the ribs.

"Actually, I got the name 'Sizzle' from Dev, too."

"So it was his idea?"

"Only indirectly." She lit up another cigarette. "He loved that tired old line from the advertising world, 'Sell the sizzle, not the steak.' It was his motto. To me, it epitomized his whole disgusting attitude toward concentrating on the superficial—the *flashy*—instead of on substance." She shrugged. "But he influenced me. I admit it. And as soon as my work started generating some interest, I decided to follow his lead. Of course, we were already separated by then."

"How long were you married?"

"Seven years." Sydney stared at me in silence, the only sound in the room her relentless puffing on her cigarette. "You still haven't told me why you're here. What exactly are you trying to find out?"

"I'm anxious to learn as much as I can about Devon. I'd like to find out who killed him."

She froze, refraining from breathing cigarette smoke in and out for the first time since she'd opened the door. "Say again?"

"The medical examiner ruled his death accidental, but I suspect otherwise."

In a strained voice, she asked, "Because of who he was?"

"Partly. And partly because of the circumstances. The block of ice that fell on him had been secured with wires.

There's no way it could have fallen unless someone deliberately cut them and pushed it over." I hesitated. "Do you have any idea who might have wanted him dead?"

"*Hah!*" she barked.

Once again, I jumped.

"I could give you a list as long as my *arm* of people who would have loved to see Devon Barnett dead!"

"I'd love to see that list," I told her sincerely.

She grimaced, once again bringing her cigarette to the brilliant red gash on her face that constituted her lips. "I didn't mean that literally. I only meant that half the people on both coasts are probably celebrating the fact that he's dead with a champagne toast. Surely you know he wasn't exactly Mr. Popular."

"From what I've heard, that's a real understatement. Which is why I'm curious about what motivated him."

"Money, mainly," Sydney replied with a shrug. "Isn't that pretty much what motivates everybody?"

"Not necessarily. For example, I became a veterinarian because I love animals and find it very rewarding to make things better for them. You probably do what you do"—I gestured around the studio vaguely, not quite sure how to describe what she did—"because you're naturally creative and having an outlet for that creativity is as vital to you as breathing." Or at least your version of breathing, I thought grimly, wondering how much time all this secondhand smoke was taking off my life.

"Well, Dev sure didn't love animals," she said scornfully. "Or people or plants or anything else that's alive. And he was no artist. I'd say I knew him pretty well, and he was just greedy. He went where the money was.

"Believe it or not, Dev started out as a legitimate photographer. In fact, that's how I met him. He was working for the *New York Post* and I was with the *Daily News*. We both ended up covering the same stories— usually crimes." She smiled coldly. "There's nothing like snapping pictures of a mutilated corpse lying on a river-bank at two o'clock in the morning to bring people together."

"Is that how you two got together?"

"Pretty much. We kept running into each other, through our work." She grew pensive as she paused to take a few puffs. "And it wasn't just the drama and the emotion of seeing humanity at its lowest levels. It was also that we understood each other. You know, the strange life we'd both chosen. Sure, some of it was the horror of what we saw every day, although you do get used to it. Kind of. But also the craziness. Running around the city at all hours of the night, schmoozing with homicide cops and DEA guys and the medical examiner, the people who are also out there as part of the circus...At the time, I was fine with it. But after a while, you start to realize how insane the whole thing is.

"Anyway, at the beginning Dev and I used to joke that we had to get married since we were the only two people in New York City who could tolerate each other, given what we did for a living." She snorted. "Pretty romantic, huh?"

"It probably seemed that way at the time," I told her. "Like you said, you both lived in a world that most people don't understand. Something like that can bring two people close together very quickly."

"Right, like a fairy tale. Happily ever after." Sydney lapsed into silence.

"So what happened?" I asked gently. "To your 'happily ever after,' I mean?"

"Are you married?"

"No."

"Ever have a serious boyfriend cheat on you?"

"No."

"Then you have no idea what it feels like to find out the one person you love is cheating on you."

"I guess not."

"Even if you'd been through it, I'd tell you to multiply that horrible feeling by about a thousand to imagine what it's like finding out that person is cheating with another *man*."

Before I had a chance to say something sympathetic, she mused, "Actually, make that men, not man. It wasn't just one man with Dev. Once he came out, he started screwing a different guy every night of the week. And acting really giddy, like he had this wonderful little secret.

"At first, I thought he was just happy with the success he was having with his new job at the *Stargazer*. He'd just started working for them around that time, and I assumed the long nights he was putting in were because he was working hard to impress them. But then I started finding these little clues that told me he was out 'til all hours because of his blossoming social life. I'd get up in the morning and find a matchbook from some club sitting on the counter, next to the coffee pot. Places with names like 'Rod's Ramrod Room' or 'The Leather Lounge.'

"He never came right out and told me, the bastard. But he made it obvious enough that I figured it out before long. The man was gay, and he was suddenly New York's number one party boy. Talk about a slap in the face."

"I can't imagine how painful that must have been," I told her sincerely.

Sydney didn't seem to have heard me. She had a faraway look in her eyes, and she was staring off at something I couldn't see.

"But it's funny," she mused. "Looking back, dealing with the fact that Dev was out screwing a different stranger every night was a lot better than Dev suddenly announcing he was in love. Can you imagine? *In love—* with another man."

"Wow," I breathed.

"Of course, I felt like an absolute fool," Sydney said bitterly, waving her cigarette in the air. "I mean, it's bad enough when your husband's running around, and every one of your friends has heard about it. You know they feel sorry for you, but at the same time you suspect that they think you're an idiot because you never saw it coming. But when he starts flaunting the fact that he's fallen in love with another man, especially such a high-profile personality—"

I blinked. "Who did he fall in love with?"

She smiled coldly. "That little fact has always been my ace in the hole. At least, I believed it was. I thought that as long as I kept that little secret, I could use it for leverage with Dev."

"Leverage for what?"

"The negotiations. I told you we'd been separated for almost four years, but I didn't mention that during most of that time, we've been involved in ugly divorce proceedings. Somehow, they never seemed to go anywhere. For reasons I could never understand, Dev was in no hurry to get divorced—even though I was anxious as hell to get it over with."

"So you were holding on to this information about who Dev's lover was?"

"Yes. But there's no reason for me to keep it a secret anymore. I could make a few phone calls, and the whole world would know." She shook her head. "But there's nothing for me to gain from it. Not now, not with Dev gone.

"I admit that I've never forgiven Dev, not for what he put me through," she continued. "But somehow, I've never really been able to blame Hugo."

My ears pricked up like Max's do whenever he hears

the crinkle of cellophane. "*'Hugo'*?" I repeated. "Hugo...
*Fontana*?"

Sydney shrugged. Smiling sardonically, she said, "So
now you know. The first major love of Dev Barnett's life
as a gay man was the Pulverizer himself."

• • •

As I drove along a winding country road back to the
South Fork, my head was spinning. Hugo Fontana...
*gay*?

I marveled over Sydney's claim, wondering if it could
possibly be true. I pictured America's number one action
hero at the dog show, trekking across East Brompton
Green with his tough-looking Chesapeake Bay retriever
beside him. Then I thought back further, to the first time
I'd seen him. It had been the night of the party under the
tent, the night that Devon had been murdered....

"Oh, my God!" I cried as a lightbulb flashed on in my
head. "Sydney was *there*!"

My heart was suddenly pounding. Of *course*. That
was why I hadn't been able to take my eyes off her when
I'd first seen her standing in the doorway of the barn.
She'd been at the opening night party, dressed in an orange leather pantsuit that clashed horribly with her
bright red hair and glitter eye shadow.

Devon Barnett's wife had lied to me about having
been in the Bromptons—on the very night her estranged
husband had been murdered.

My head positively buzzed as I wondered what other
lies she had told me.

First the revelation about Hugo Fontana, now the re-
alization that Sydney was hiding something.... My ob-
servation that there had been more layers to Devon
Barnett than I'd ever imagined, was simply the tip of the
iceberg. I was discovering that the people he'd surrounded himself with were just as complex.

As I stared out the window at the passing scenery without really seeing anything, I replayed the demise of Sydney and Devon Barnett's marriage in my head. I pictured her spending long evenings at home alone, trying to convince herself that her husband was working, but little by little putting the pieces together—and realizing that what he was really doing was sleeping with half the gay men in New York. And then the humiliation and heartache of learning that he had fallen in love with one of them.

As I turned off the quiet back road onto Sunset Highway, Sydney's words reverberated through my head: "I admit that I've never forgiven Dev, not for what he put me through."

I'd just added another name to my list of suspects.

• • •

I still felt dazed as I trudged across the lawn of Shawn Elliot's estate toward the guesthouse.

As far as I could see, there were no signs of life. Nick and the dogs were probably still at the beach—which would give me some time to unwind. I was thinking about how much I was looking forward to a glass of something wet and frosty when I noticed the square of white, stuck in the middle of the front door where I couldn't possibly miss it. My first thought was that it was a note from Nick, trying to smooth things over. Or maybe it was from Shawn, an apology for his outrageous behavior the night before.

As I unfolded the single sheet of paper, I thought about the desperate call I'd made to Betty, just the day before. If I remembered correctly, I was all in a tizzy over being pursued by two fabulous men. In an impressively short time, I realized, I'd gotten myself down to none.

I saw immediately that neither of my estranged love interests had left me the note. In fact, my stomach lurched as I read the three short sentences that were neatly typed on the page.

*Chess isn't who you think he is. Check into his past. Start with his hometown—and Mr. Sylvester.*

It wasn't signed.

My instinctive response was to check behind me and peer into the bushes that surrounded the guesthouse, just to make sure whoever had left me the note wasn't lurking in the shadows, watching for my reaction. Then I held the single 8½" x 11" white sheet closer, scrutinizing it and trying to find something—anything—that would give me a clue as to who had tucked it into my front door. As far as I could tell, it was an ordinary piece of paper, the kind used in just about every computer printer in the world. In fact, the only thing remotely distinctive about it was a barely noticeable streak running along the left side—a sign that the printer's owner would soon be in need of a new ink cartridge. Either that, or shaking the cartridge side to side in a high-tech version of the Macarena.

As I stepped inside the guesthouse, I discovered I'd been right about Nick and the dogs still being absent. I was glad to have the opportunity to follow up on the note's suggestion. An idea of what ruse to use was already forming in my mind as I dialed Information again.

"What city and state?" the voice at the other end of the line asked.

"Crabapple, Iowa. The public library."

I waited, gripping my pen as I heard the clicking of computer keys at the other end of the line.

Finally, the operator said, "I'm sorry. I don't have a town by that name."

I frowned, wondering if I'd remembered the name of Chess's hometown incorrectly. "Is there anything that sounds like it?" I asked. "Or maybe some other spelling—like maybe 'Crab' starts with a 'K'?"

"I need an exact name," the operator told me impatiently.

Thank goodness for the Web, I thought, after I gave up on that approach. Instead, I set up Nick's laptop on the kitchen table and logged on. One good thing about the Internet is that it never gets snippy, no matter how many questions you ask.

I typed in the key words "Crab" and "Iowa." What came up wasn't very helpful.

Next, I tried "Tree" and "Iowa." Maybe I hadn't heard everything Chess had said correctly, but I was pretty sure I got at least that part right. Nothing. I started trying other combinations with "Iowa," like "Pine," "Maple," and "Elm."

"Bingo!" I cried as "Sweet Elm, Iowa" appeared in half a dozen listings.

"So there's no such place as Crabapple, Iowa, but there is a Sweet Elm," I mumbled, thinking aloud. "Could be a play on words, the result of Chess LaMont's off-beat sense of humor."

But I wondered if that was all it was. Another possibility was that Chess was deliberately trying to mislead people. It was certainly a good way of making it harder for someone to find out anything about his past.

Still puzzling over whether I'd managed to stumble upon Chess's actual hometown, I forged ahead, punching in more words to see what I could learn. The Sweet Elm Chamber of Commerce treated me to a pretty comprehensive overview of the town I suspected Chess had fled a decade earlier. In addition to a park with a baseball field, picnic grounds, and public rest rooms near the bandstand, it had six restaurants including two that weren't chains, two hardware stores, and five churches. And there was plenty to do. This summer, in addition to the Fourth of July parade, the town was sponsoring "I'm Sweet on Sweet Elm" Day, an annual event that featured a blueberry pie eating contest, music by the Sweet Elm Sweeties, and of course, the ever-popular Miss Sweet Elm pageant.

From what I could see, it was a wholesome Midwestern town out of a Norman Rockwell painting. Not necessarily the most comfortable place for a young man who was anticipating coming out of the closet.

Fortunately, in addition to a war memorial, an historical society, and a senior center, the town also boasted a public library. Its phone number was right there on the Website, and I copied it into my address book. Then I dialed it, glancing at my watch and hoping that the fact that it was an hour earlier in Iowa would work in my favor.

"Sweet Elm Public Library," answered a voice so sugary that its owner clearly belonged in a town with that name. "How may I help you?"

"Could you please connect me with Reference?"

"Oh, I'm sorry," the young woman said sincerely. "I'm afraid our Reference librarian, Ms. Pruitt, has left for the day."

So much for the benefit of the time difference. "Maybe you can help me. I live in New York, and I'm planning a surprise party for a friend of mine who grew up in Sweet Elm. I thought it might be fun to get hold of some pieces of his past, like the picture from his high school yearbook. He graduated ten years ago."

"We keep all the Sweet Elm High School yearbooks on file, all the way back to 1928," the young woman informed me, "but you'll still have to talk to Ms. Pruitt. That kind of research is really her area."

And so much for immediate gratification. "When will she be in?"

"You can probably reach her tomorrow. She comes in at ten."

"Thanks for your time. I'll try her then."

Next to the phone number of the Sweet Elm Public Library, I jotted down, "Call Ms. Pruitt, Reference. Thursday, 10:00 A.M., Central Time."

•  •  •

Given what I'd learned about Hugo Fontana earlier that day, the handsome action hero with the bulging muscles held new interest for me. I made a beeline for Poxabogue.

"Dr. Fox is in surgery," Shelley informed me when I appeared, unannounced, in Suzanne's office. "She's removing a mass...."

"It's okay," Suzanne called from the back of the office. "Jessie's always welcome."

I found her suturing a black shih tzu whose tiny body lay limp on the stainless-steel table. The dog's tongue hung motionless from her slackened jaw, and her fur was matted against the side of her skull as if she'd been in that position for some time. Her intravenous catheter was hooked up to a clear plastic IV bag with a narrow tube.

Even though I'd performed surgery hundreds or even thousands of times myself, I was struck by how vulnerable the helpless pup looked. Out of habit, I glanced at the digital reading on the purple pulse oximeter nearby on the counter to make sure the animal was stable. Even though she looked like a rag rug, she seemed to be doing fine.

Suzanne glanced up. "This is a hard one," she told me grimly. "Charley here was one of my first patients. Sweetest little dog you ever saw. And now, we've got this mass to deal with. I was hoping it was just a cyst, but we weren't that lucky. I'm really going to sweat it out, waiting for the pathologist's report to come back."

"That's tough," I commented, knowing how difficult it always was to deal with the probability of cancer.

"I'm just about done here.... I'll be right out, Jess."

Two minutes later, Suzanne and I were sitting in her

office. "A long day," she said with a sigh, leaning back in her chair.

"Most of them are," I observed.

"At least this one's almost over. So what brings you to beautiful downtown Poxabogue?"

"I'm here to ask you a favor," I replied with a grin. "What else?"

"Shoot."

"When I looked through your files the last time I was here, I noticed that Hugo Fontana is a client of yours."

For the first time since I'd walked in the door, she smiled. "I'm one of the few people who knows the Pulverizer can't stand the sight of blood. He can barely watch me cut Brutus's toenails."

I decided not to mention that there were a few other facts about the Pulverizer that most people didn't know.

"I'd like the opportunity to talk to him," I told her. "Is there any way we could set up a house call?"

"Sure. I could call him and remind him that Brutus is due for a rabies shot. I remember that his last one was a year ago, just after I bought the practice. He was one of my first clients. I still remember how impressed I was when he walked in! Anyway, I could tell him it's time for a booster and that I'll be sending an associate with a mobile unit to his house to take care of it."

"Perfect. Thanks a million, Suzanne," I said sincerely.

She pulled a file from the metal cabinet, plopped back into her desk chair, and dialed the number handwritten on front.

"Mr. Fontana?" I heard her say in the same professional tone I used with clients. "This is Dr. Fox, Brutus's veterinarian. . . . I'm fine, thank you. The reason I'm calling is that I happened to check Brutus's chart and I see that he's due for a rabies shot. I'm working with a mobile services unit this summer, to see if it's an addition that might benefit my practice. Rather than having you bring him into the office, I can have a veterinarian come right to your home, whenever it's convenient.... Tonight? If you hold a moment, I'll check my schedule...."

She glanced at me, her eyebrows raised questioningly. I nodded.

"Tonight looks fine. How does six-thirty sound?"

I gave her the thumbs-up. I guess Hugo did, too.

"I'll be sending an associate, Dr. Jessica Popper... Yes, as a matter of fact, she is involved with the dog show.... Yes, the SPCA *is* a worthy cause.... You're right; the way some animals are treated is horrendous. Okay, then, Dr. Popper will see you and Brutus this evening at six-thirty."

"Thanks, Suzanne," I told her sincerely once she'd hung up the phone. "I owe you."

"I'm glad you feel that way," she replied, "because now I've got a favor to ask *you*."

"Anything."

"I'd like you and Nick to have dinner with me Friday night."

"That's the kind of favor it's easy to say 'Yes' to."

"There's a catch."

I raised my eyebrows expectantly.

"Remember that guy you mentioned the other day... the single one?"

"Marcus?" His name came out like a gasp. True, I hadn't forgotten about the interest my college pal had expressed in Marcus Scruggs the last time I'd dropped in. But I was hoping against hope that *she* had.

"Yeah, that's the guy." Suzanne's tone was casual, but there was a glint in her blue eyes I remembered seeing before. I knew her well enough to recognize it as a sign of determination. "Do you know if he's back from his trip yet?"

I couldn't bring myself to lie. "As a matter of fact, he is. Apparently, it didn't work out the way he expected."

"Great. In that case, I was wondering if you'd invite him along as a fourth."

"But I don't even know if he's free—"

"Try him," she urged. "Tell him you've got someone you want him to meet."

"But Marcus is . . . he's . . ." How could I possibly put it into words?

Suzanne didn't wait. "Look, Jess, just because you don't like him doesn't mean *I* won't." Impatience had crept into her tone. "Besides, he's a vet, right? He and I already have something in common!"

She had me there.

With a little shrug, Suzanne added, "I figure this Marcus guy is young, available, and breathing, so how bad could he be?" Young, more or less, I thought morosely. Available, definitely. Breathing, probably. As for answering Suzanne's last question, I wouldn't have known where to begin.

.   .   .

Suzanne went back to work, and I went back to my van. I dialed Marcus as soon as I got inside, figuring I might as well get it over with.

"Scruggs here."

"Is this the Marc Man?" I asked dryly.

"You got him," he replied, his tone morphing into a seductive murmur. "And what lovely lady am I lucky enough to have calling me today?"

"It's Jessie."

"Popper." I could hear the disappointment in his voice. But it only took him a few seconds to remember that I was stationed in the Bromptons—as in "Glamour with a capital G." "How's life on the East End?"

"Fabulous. Famous stars of stage and screen, champagne flowing like water, luxurious mansions . . . it's like being in a movie." A *Hitchcock* movie, I thought, deciding not to add the part about the dead body. "In fact, the reason I'm calling is to invite you to dinner. I've got a friend out here who's very anxious to meet you."

"A movie star?"

"Uh, no."

"Supermodel?"

"Not exactly. She's a vet."

"I get it. The brainy type."

Once again, I could hear his disappointment. I wanted to reach through my cell phone and strangle him. Unfortunately, the technology hadn't yet developed to that point.

"Come on, Marcus," I insisted. "You owe me. I filled in for you at the last minute so you could run off to a tropical island with somebody's oversexed grandmother, remember?"

"All right, all right," he grumbled. "If the evening's a total waste, I can always hit the bars afterward."

"Right. You can 'make the scene.'"

I gave him the name and address of the restaurant Suzanne had picked, then experienced a sinking feeling as I ended the call. I hope I'm not making a mistake, I thought. Then I reminded myself that my pal Suzanne was a grown-up—old enough to make her *own* mistakes. And in this case, I was certain it wasn't going to take her very long to figure out she'd made a whopper.

• • •

I hurried home, figuring I'd grab a quick snack before jumping in the shower and heading over to Hugo's. I hadn't counted on running into Shawn. He was poking around the flower beds in front of his house, brandishing a large pair of scissors.

Given the way my mind was working these days, my first thought was that he was acting awfully suspicious. Then I realized he was simply cutting flowers.

He brightened when he saw me. "There she is!" he cried. "The inimitable Dr. Pepper!"

"That's Popper," I corrected him crossly.

A look of confusion crossed his face as he thrust a bouquet of bright pink peonies at me. "These are for you," he said. "I thought they'd cheer up the guest-house."

I ignored the flowers. "I don't know how you can look me in the eye," I challenged, making no effort to hide my anger.

Shawn blinked. "What am I missing here, Jess?"

I could see that his confusion was sincere. That didn't make me any more forgiving. "Last night? The *Pulverizer* screening?"

He shrugged. "I thought we had a good time. I know I did—at least until I woke up this morning and realized that somewhere along the line, a rhino had trampled on my head."

"You really don't remember? Then allow me to refresh your memory," I said crisply. "First of all, you had way too much champagne. And then you announced to everybody that I'm investigating Devon Barnett's murder!"

"Is that bad?" he asked, looking baffled.

"Of *course* it's bad!" I cried. "It would be one thing if I were a . . . a homicide detective, with an entire police department behind me. It wouldn't even matter if I were a real private investigator. But I'm just doing this on my own! Now, when I go around asking questions, the people who know what I'm doing are going to be suspicious. They'll probably be more careful of what they say to me—which means I'll find out a lot less than I would have if they'd thought I was just a veterinarian making conversation!"

"I see your point." Shawn's face fell. "Gee, Jess, I'm really sorry. I hope I didn't screw things up for you *too* badly." He thought for a few seconds before adding, "Is there any way I could make it up to you?"

Startled, I asked, "What do you mean?"

"I was thinking...I found this stretch of beach that, believe it or not, nobody else seems to know about. I go there all the time, and I almost always have it all to myself. I'd love to show it to you."

"Shawn, I'm not really sure—" I was thinking of Nick, of course. But I stopped midsentence. At the moment, I reminded myself, Nick wasn't speaking to me. He wasn't even *around*. So much for *me* spoiling our romantic little getaway.

Then again, I was furious with Shawn. At least, I was supposed to be. But he was looking at me with those intense blue eyes of his, waiting for my answer. I could feel my anger melting away.

"Shawn, I'd love to see your private beach," I finally said, telling myself I was only human, after all. Human— and of the female gender. "Right now, I've got to make a house call—veterinarian stuff. But as soon as I'm done, I'll stop over. How does that sound?"

"It sounds...terrific." He smiled at me, that same smile that had made millions of women all over the world instantly fall in love with him.

I wondered if I was any different.

# Chapter 11

"Speak softly and own a big, mean Doberman."
                                        —Dave Miliman

Hugo Fontana's house was a dignified Tudor so big that Henry VIII himself would have undoubtedly felt at home in it. Just beyond the expansive property, the calm waters of East Brompton Bay provided the summer hideaway with another one of the spectacular water views the Bromptons were so famous for.

The house was so vast that I expected it to be staffed with uniformed servants. So I was surprised that Hugo answered the door himself when I showed up promptly at six-thirty. He was dressed casually in jeans and a navy-blue polo shirt. True to his usual style, the shirt looked as if he'd purposely bought it one size too small to show off his cantaloupe-sized biceps and his massive, sculpted chest. His thick, shiny black hair dissolved into a mass of tiny curls at the back of his neck. No doubt a team of hair stylists agonized over those recalcitrant locks every time a director shouted "Action," forcing them to blend in with the rest of his sleek, black hair.

"I'm Dr. Popper," I announced in my professional voice. "I'm working with Dr. Fox—"

"Yeah, yeah, she told me all about it," Hugo interrupted.

I was interested to hear that he really did talk in the gruff, heavily Brooklyn-accented voice that had become his signature. I was also struck by the fact that, up close, he had the same bigger-than-life presence in person that he projected on-screen. The way he fixed his dark, smoldering eyes on me definitely had a jarring effect.

My focus quickly shifted to another muscular being covered with exceptional hair. Brutus stood at Hugo's side, eyeing me suspiciously. He kept glancing up at his master, as if he wanted help deciding whether he should growl or cover me with dog kisses.

"She's okay, Brutus," Hugo told him.

Right on cue, he stepped forward and stuck his nose in my crotch. Nothing I hadn't dealt with more times than I could count. I sidestepped him, crouching down so that he and I were at eye level.

"Hey, Brutus," I greeted him, giving him an expert neck-scratching designed to show him I was someone who knew her way around dogs.

"What a fine animal," I commented, glancing up at Hugo. It was true; the Chesapeake Bay retriever was beautifully proportioned, with a broad head, an oily brown coat, and small amber eyes. Like all retrievers, he had well-developed hindquarters, designed to put him in good stead for swimming.

The breed had an interesting history. In the early 1800s, two Newfoundland puppies were rescued from a shipwreck off the Maryland coast. After they turned out to be exceptional water retrievers, they were bred with several other types of dog to create a brand-new breed. Their nickname was "Chessies"—wonderfully ironic, I thought, given what I now knew about Hugo's romantic history.

"Brutus must love it out here," I said, rising to my feet. I gestured toward the tremendous property and, behind it, East Brompton Bay. "All this room to run around."

"This guy's in heaven," Hugo agreed heartily. "He's always jumpin' into the bay. The seagulls drive him nuts."

I laughed. "Those are Chessies for you. Born to retrieve. But let's take a closer look at him. If you could just bring him into my van..."

"Sure. Come on, boy. Let's follow the lady."

Once the three of us had crossed the immense lawn to the driveway and climbed into my van, Hugo looked around and let out an appreciative whistle.

"Whoa. Nice place you got here," he said. "And I thought the trailers we get when we shoot on location were nice. You got everything you need right here, dontcha?"

"Pretty much. Now, let's just get Brutus up here...." I stepped on the foot pedal that lowered the mechanized examining table, steadying the dog and wondering how my back would ever survive without such a valuable invention. "How're you doing, Brutus? You sure are being brave. Thatta boy. You're doing fine." I continued to murmur encouragement as I checked Brutus's eyes, then looked in his ears with an otoscope.

"I'm glad I'm having the chance to chat with you, Mr. Fontana," I commented congenially. "I was afraid I'd be dealing with a handler." I had to resist the urge to say "one of your people." "I always like to speak directly with the animal's owner, since that's usually where the real bond lies."

"I'm very involved in Brutus's care," Hugo assured me. "I wouldn't trust my dog to nobody. He's too much a part of my life, y'know? Always has been, ever since the days he was eatin' canned dog food and I was livin' on peanut butter. These days, we're both filet mignon guys."

I couldn't resist giving him a quick lecture on the importance of giving a dog a balanced diet, one that included calcium rather than just meat. Hugo listened, but he didn't look convinced. Meanwhile, I ran my fingers along Brutus's spine and belly, palpating his internal organs to see if anything felt out of the ordinary. Everything seemed fine—until I noticed a moist area on his left hind.

"Looks like we've got a hot spot," I noted.

Hugo looked alarmed. "What's that?"

"See this moist area, over here?"

"Sure. I figured it was just a bruise."

"It's infected, no doubt an allergic reaction." The sturdy retriever had decided he'd had enough of being poked and prodded. He made a move toward the edge of the table, skittering across the stainless-steel surface. Fortunately, I'd maintained a strong hold on him just in case it turned out he didn't enjoy being in the spotlight as much as his master. "It's okay, Brutus. Just hang in there...."

"'*Allergic*'? To what?" Hugo sounded a little defensive, as if I might be questioning his ability to care for Brutus responsibly.

"It's very common," I assured him. "It could be from swimming in the bay, or even just a reaction to pollen."

"So what do we do?" he asked nervously.

"First, I'm going to clip the hair around the wound to keep the infection from creeping under the hair coat. Then, I'm going to use an antibiotic anti-inflammatory spray on it.... Would you hold onto him? He's a little skittish, poor guy." The apprehensive animal looked at me woefully, and his entire body shook. "Hey, Brutus, we're not going to hurt you. Mr. Fontana, come around to this side, so he can see your face. He'll feel a lot more comfortable that way."

I noticed that as Hugo held eighty pounds of well-developed muscle in place, his own muscles bulged impressively. I remembered the female audience member who had walked out of the screening ahead of me, practically swooning over Hugo Fontana, Hunk Extraordinaire. The thought made me smile.

"All done, Brutus!" I finally announced, turning to Hugo. "Mr. Fontana, I'll give you this corticosteroid spray to use for at least another week. At that point, you should bring him into Dr. Fox so she can have a look. We won't bandage it, because it's important to keep it open to the air. I'll also give you an antibiotic for him to take orally, twice a day for a week. First, I'll weigh him, so I can determine the correct dosage...."

When I was done, I fondled Brutus's ears. "All done, sweetie. What a good boy! Yes, you're a *very* good boy...."

Hugo was patting the pockets of his jeans. "Shoot. Guess I left my checkbook in the house. D'ya mind coming in for a sec?"

"Not at all." I thought you'd never ask, I was tempted to add.

Not surprisingly, the inside of the house was as grand as the outside. Just past the foyer, I could see a gigantic room with cathedral ceilings. The entire back wall was glass. A large swimming pool stretched beyond, framed by the awe-inspiring water view.

The heavy furnishings stood in sharp contrast to the expansive sea and sky. Hugo had decorated his house with bulky leather furniture, dark wooden tables, and lamps with black wrought-iron bases. The look was more along the lines of a hunting lodge than a seaside retreat. The only thing missing was a pair of elephant tusks and the mounted heads of a few trophy animals.

A stack of magazines and newspapers lay on a coffee table made from tree branches lashed together with strips of leather. I half-expected to find neatly-stacked copies of *Soldier of Fortune* on top. I wasn't too far off. Along with recent issues of *Gun Collector* and *Field and Stream,* I spotted that week's issue of *The East Brompton Banner.* From where I stood, the headline "Devon Barnett Killed By Freak Accident!" screamed at me.

I took it as my cue.

"Too bad about Devon Barnett," I commented, doing my best to sound casual.

"Yeah." Hugo's eyes narrowed. "I understand you think it wasn't no accident—and that you're tryin' to find out who was responsible."

"Shawn exaggerated," I insisted. "I'm just curious. The entire incident strikes me as suspicious." I watched him closely as I added, "Apparently, he had a few enemies. Then there's the fact that the way he died was so bizarre."

He shrugged. "Things happen. That's why they call 'em accidents."

I simply nodded. Innocently, I asked, "Did you know him?"

"No. Yeah. I mean, everybody knew *of* him. It was impossible not to. The guy was everywhere, snappin' pictures wherever you went."

"I'm sure his friends are devastated," I added, trying to bait him.

He wasn't biting. "Yeah, I guess." Impatiently, Hugo said, "You know, I think my checkbook's upstairs. You mind waitin'?"

"Not at all. In the meantime, is there a rest room I can use?"

"Sure. Right down that hall."

I'd learned early on that trips to the lavatory were a great way to gather information. You never knew what you'd find simply by wandering around somebody's home or office, pretending to look for a bathroom.

So far, it appeared that the only good this foray was going to do, was to prove that Hugo's taste in home furnishings was consistent. I passed a huge dining room with a ridiculously long, rough-hewn wooden table and twenty leather chairs with metal studs, giving them a definite Wild West flavor. A spiky wrought-iron chandelier that looked like something from the Spanish Inquisition hovered above. The adjacent room was packed with electronics, including a television with a screen that was almost as big as the one in Russell Bolger's screening room.

Expensive toys for very rich boys, I thought.

I slowed my pace considerably as I approached the next room. This one looked like a home office, outfitted with a computer, fax machine, and scanner. All the equipment looked spanking new and state-of-the-art. I glanced back to make sure Hugo wasn't tailing me, then ducked inside.

I figured you could learn a lot about a person by his home office. But why someone like Hugo Fontana even needed a home office was beyond me, aside from the fact that so many high-tech machines had wheedled their way into our lives that most of us had come to believe there was no way we could survive without them.

I looked around quickly, afraid to linger. My heart pounded wildly, the way it always does when I venture into a place I know I'm not supposed to be. I figured I'd just take a few seconds to see if anything interesting caught my eye.

Something did. Aside from the various machines, the long, sleek L-shaped desk that hugged two entire walls was completely bare except for a single stack of papers held together with two gold fasteners. I stepped over and scanned the front page.

*Pulverizer 5: The Aftermath,* I read.

A script. So there *was* going to be a sequel, something the modern world clearly couldn't manage without.

I felt a little thrill over having access to information that even most insiders didn't have. Still, I couldn't see how knowing that Hugo Fontana planned to star in another ridiculously violent film would help the progress of my investigation.

I was about to abandon his home office and find the bathroom when another piece of paper caught my eye. Even though it appeared to be the only other one in the room, it was harder to spot because it was still in the printer. Just for the heck of it, I reached over and pulled it out.

And practically fell over.

Skimming it, I saw that it was a poorly written letter, addressed to someone in Los Angeles I surmised was his agent. It was from Hugo, confirming his interest in appearing in *Pulverizer 5* as long as some additional conditions were met.

But it wasn't the letter's content that nearly made me lose my balance. It was the barely perceptible streak that ran along the left side—the same imperfection I'd noticed in the anonymous note I'd found tucked inside the cottage door.

•  •  •

As I pulled into the driveway of Shawn's estate, I was still mulling over my unexpected discovery that Hugo Fontana had left me that anonymous note. Was there really a skeleton in Chess LaMont's closet, something in his past that Hugo thought I should know about now that I was investigating Devon Barnett's murder? Or was the Hollywood hunk simply seeking revenge against the man who, for reasons I might never know, had replaced him as the object of Dev's affections?

I was more anxious than ever to find out.

At the moment, however, I had something much more pressing to deal with: my trip to the beach with Shawn Elliot. I was torn between wanting to enjoy myself and being afraid I might enjoy myself too much.

Too late now, I reminded myself as I rang Shawn's doorbell.

"Hey, Jess!" he cried as he threw open the front door. I gulped, taken aback by finding him naked. At least, I thought he was naked. When I dared to lower my eyes, I saw that in between his bare chest and his muscular thighs was a pair of short beige bathing trunks. I hoped Shawn hadn't noticed that all the color had drained from my face.

Rufus waddled over to greet me, wagging his tail enthusiastically.

"How're you doing, Rufus, old boy? How's the dogger?" I crouched down to scratch the thick folds of his neck. The chunky bulldog basked in the attention, making joyful wheezing sounds and covering my arm with wet dog kisses. He no longer saw me as a threat, I supposed, someone who might become a rival for his master's attention. I hoped he was right.

"All set?" Shawn asked cheerfully. "Or do you want to change into a bathing suit?"

"I'm fine," I assured him, glancing down at the gray Cornell sweatshirt I'd pulled over my "Jessica Popper, D.V.M." polo shirt and my khaki shorts, thinking it was probably better if at least *one* of us had clothes on.

I'd assumed we'd take the Ferrari. Instead, Shawn led me to his Jeep, parked in the garage behind the house. As we climbed in, he pulled on the shades and the Dodgers baseball cap he'd been wearing the first time I'd encountered him.

I tried not to think about how much had happened since then—with Nick, with Shawn, with the people who had known Devon Barnett. I decided I was due for a little R&R. So I sat back and tried to enjoy myself as he turned the radio up and we blasted out of the driveway.

I had to admit it was fun, careening along the empty residential streets toward the water, with the wind whipping through my hair. I tried to let the sea breezes blow away all the tensions of the past few days. Instead, I let myself get lost in the scenery: the endless stretch of sandy white beach, the swirling blue-green waves, the astounding beach houses that sprang up from the tall sea grass.

Shawn slowed the Jeep as we neared an orange cone stuck in the middle of the road. "Do Not Enter," the sign just beyond read.

"I guess we've reached the end," I commented.

"Nah," he insisted. "That sign's for other people."

He swerved around it, driving the Jeep onto the sand. "You don't get very far in my business without taking risks," he said, grinning.

He stopped a few hundred yards beyond, jerking to a halt behind a sand dune so high that it blocked the view.

"Okay," he announced, jumping out of the front seat and jogging around the Jeep. "Close your eyes."

"Then how am I going to find the water?" I protested.

"I'll guide you."

"But—"

"*Trust* me," he said, gently taking hold of my arm. "I'm a *very* trustworthy guy."

I didn't answer. I was too caught up in the dangerously wonderful sensation of walking alongside Shawn, shoulder to shoulder, thigh to thigh. I swallowed hard and tried to concentrate on the fresh, salty air and the cooling breezes.

"Open your eyes," Shawn finally instructed.

I did—then blinked a few times, overwhelmed by the beauty of the spot he'd led me to. White sand curved around a blue-green cove, forming a perfect half-circle. There was absolutely no one around. In fact, the only sound was the screeching seagulls flying overhead, occasionally swooping down and dipping into the water.

"What do you think?" he asked anxiously.

"Wow." Not very original, but the most accurate statement I could come up with.

"Come on. Let's walk along the beach. You can usually go a half-mile or so without running into anybody." Pulling off his rubber flip-flops, he yelled, "Race you to the shore!"

Squealing like a preschooler, I ran toward the water, managing to keep a few paces behind Shawn. He threw himself into the waves. I ventured in knee-deep, relishing the feeling of the cold water swirling around my legs.

He finally emerged, dripping wet but wearing a huge grin.

"You look like a sea monster!" I cried.

"But I feel great! Come on, let's head up that way."

As we kicked our way through the surf, I saw that Shawn was right. There wasn't another person around as far as I could see. Given the fact that he spent so much of his life on display, it was no wonder he loved this hideout so much.

After we'd walked in silence for a minute or two, Shawn said sincerely, "You know, I feel really bad about last night. I'm sorry I acted like such a jerk. I hope I didn't totally screw up your murder investigation. I know it's important to you. Heck, it's important to me, too. I'm the one who asked you to help clear Rufus's name. Not to mention mine—especially given the possibility of a lawsuit."

"It's done," I said with a little shrug. "At this point,

I'm just hoping that the fact that a lot of people now know what I'm up to won't make that much difference."

"What about Nick?" The tone of Shawn's voice had changed. "What does he think about all this?"

"You mean Mick?" I asked, eyeing him slyly.

"Mick, Nick ... whoever." He chuckled, aware that he'd been caught.

"Nick wishes I'd find another hobby."

"I guess I don't blame him." He hesitated before adding, "I take it the two of you are pretty tight."

I nodded.

"How long have you been together?"

"About four years. On and off."

Shawn raised his eyebrows. "I'd be interested in hearing what the 'offs' were about."

I kicked at the sea foam, sending up a little spray. "My own insecurities, mainly."

"*You?*" Shawn sounded genuinely shocked. "You seem like one of the most centered, self-possessed people I've ever met!"

I grinned at him. "Then I guess you're not the only actor around here."

"So tell me: What's behind these so-called insecurities of yours?"

"The usual. Fear of commitment gets the number one spot. The result of growing up with parents who weren't exactly about to give Romeo and Juliet a run for their money."

"Then how does Nick fit in?"

"Nick is—how can I explain? He's somebody I'm so comfortable with, that being with him just feels right. Since the day we met, we've been able to talk for hours on end about absolutely anything. But what amazes me most is that we never seem to get bored with each other. Irritated, maybe, or even furious on occasion, but never bored." I laughed nervously. "Sounds like a romance novel, right? And I guess it is, a lot of the time. It's just when I step back and think about it that it gets scary."

"Sounds like a kind of 'scary' that most of us would give our eye teeth for."

"What about you?"

Shawn shrugged. Gazing out at the horizon, he said, "I'm pretty much on my own these days."

"That's not the impression I've gotten! I've seen the headlines from *People* and the tabloids at the supermarket. Your name's been linked with at least half a dozen actresses in the past year. Lily James, Heather McBane, Beebee Montez, Kara Liebling—"

"Beebee and I are 'just good friends.'"

"Aha!" I cried triumphantly. "So you *were* involved with the others!"

"That depends on how you define 'involved,'" Shawn replied lightly. "Some of them were just dates for high-profile events, like opening nights or fund-raisers for charity. Usually, my public relations firm set them up. Some of the others, I really did take out a few times."

"Which category did Kara Liebling fall into?" I asked, trying to sound casual.

He hesitated. "That one was real."

A crushing feeling immediately washed over me, a reaction that felt dangerously like jealousy.

"But she turned out to be kind of a nutcase," Shawn added.

I started at his use of such a strong word. "What do you mean?"

"She was incredibly ambitious. You know the type. Whenever she's looking deep into your eyes, you can't help feeling she's checking out her own reflection in your contact lenses."

He shrugged. "The problem is, most of the people I meet are more interested in themselves than they are in anybody else. There aren't a lot of real people in the world I travel in. Everybody wants something."

"Speaking as somebody who happens to live in the 'real' world," I interjected, "I can assure you that finding someone who truly cares about you—and loves you for yourself—isn't that easy out here, either."

"What about Nick? Does he fit into that category?"

"Yes." I answered quickly. So quickly, in fact, that I questioned my own motives. Especially since something about Shawn's tone had told me he was asking a trick question.

I decided it was time to change the subject. "What about Devon Barnett?"

Shawn looked startled. "What about him?"

"What do you suppose he wanted?"

He laughed coldly. "You mean, besides destroying people's lives?"

"Even if that was his goal, there had to be something in it for him."

"Besides satisfying his vicious streak, you mean."

"That could have been his main motivation, if he really was just a mean guy who liked to make trouble," I said thoughtfully. "But somehow, I get the feeling there was more to it."

"Then you're a much more generous person than I am."

"There's so much I don't know about him," I said, sounding as frustrated as I felt. "I've become pretty friendly with his partner, Chess LaMont. But it's almost as if the more I learn about Dev—about both of them, actually—the harder it seems to figure out who wanted him dead badly enough to do him in. I've even hoped that being inside his house would help provide me with some clues, but so far, it's gotten me nowhere."

"You've been inside?" Shawn asked. "I always

thought that place looked like something out of *Ripley's Believe It Or Not*. What's it like?"

"Very nicely decorated, as a matter of fact. It's not garish at all. There are a few fun touches, but for the most part it's pretty tasteful." I sighed. "I guess the only thing I've learned from being inside is that Devon Barnett was pretty wealthy. Making money was clearly a priority in his life. He's got an actual Renoir...*and* a David Hockney. Can you imagine?"

Gently, Shawn said, "I know a lot of people who own valuable artwork. Rembrandts, El Greco's, Van Gogh's—"

"I own a few of those, too," I teased. "Of course, they're in postcard form. And they're stuck to my refrigerator with magnets from the gas company."

Shawn grinned. "I'd love to see your collection some time."

I chose to ignore that comment. "But something about the possessions Devon chose to surround himself with tell me that he was also starstruck."

"I find that hard to believe. I mean, if that were true, wouldn't he have had a little respect for celebrities?"

I shrugged. "Could be that it's something else, then. Envy, maybe. But he has so many valuable things that have ties to the rich and famous. Like Andy Warhol's cookie jars. He kept a few pieces from the collection on display in his kitchen."

"So you're saying that poor old Devon Barnett may have just been a wannabe," Shawn mused. "Somebody who was so enthralled with fame that he spent his life trying to be part of it in whatever meager, pathetic way he could."

"It's just a theory."

"Personally, the theory I subscribe to is that he was nothing more than a greedy bastard."

"Maybe."

Shawn suddenly stopped walking. He put his hand on

my arm and drew me closer. "Hey, Jess?" His voice suddenly sounded different. Tight, somehow, as if he were having trouble getting the words out. The expression on his face was also one I hadn't seen before. His blue eyes glowed with such intensity I found it difficult not to look away.

I was suddenly very aware of the fact that the two of us were still standing ankle-deep in sea foam. The sun was hovering just above the horizon, fading to a pale yellow that complemented the streaks of pink and lavender that filled the sky. The effect was spectacular, as if someone with a very large brush and a few tubs of watercolor paints had gone wild. No one else was around. The only sounds were the crashing of the waves against the shore and the seagulls, screeching overhead.

"I think what you're doing is terrific," Shawn went on in the same husky voice. "In fact, I think *you're* terrific."

He was suddenly holding me in a gentle embrace, his eyes burning into mine. His face was only inches away from mine, yet I saw him drawing even closer. . . .

I knew where this was heading. I'd seen this movie before.

"I'd better get back," I said brusquely, looking away. "It's getting late, and Nick is probably home by now."

"Nick." Shawn gave a sharp little laugh, then dropped his arms to his sides. "Right. We wouldn't want to keep old Nick waiting, would we?"

We were both silent as we started back to the Jeep. As I walked barefoot through the waves, I noticed for the first time that the water was uncomfortably cold. We also kept ourselves at least two feet apart, so there was no chance we'd bump into each other.

"Shawn," I said, trying to break the awkwardness, "I—"

"It's okay, Jess," Shawn said evenly. "I guess that old saying about timing being everything is really true."

· · ·

As I crossed the lawn to the guesthouse, I was still dazed over what had just happened at the beach. I felt confused— not by Shawn as much as by my own reaction. I hated to admit it, even to myself, but I'd *wanted* to kiss him. Maybe it was curiosity, maybe it was genuine attraction, and maybe it was just who he was: a gorgeous star of the big screen who also starred in a lot of women's fantasies.

I half-hoped Nick hadn't come back yet. Not now, when facing him after my unexpected interlude with Shawn seemed like more than I could handle. I was thinking that it was probably time to put another call in to Betty Vandervoort as I neared the guesthouse.

*"Yeow!"* I let out a yelp as I came close to stepping on a misshapen mound of dark gray fur lying in the middle of the front porch.

It took me a few seconds to realize that it was a rat. A dead rat, placed in the same spot as the mouse I'd encountered the day before.

My stomach lurched as I leaned over to examine the animal more closely. I noticed that once again, it had been killed by a neck injury. But this time, its windpipe had been cut. The wound was a straight incision. No blood, no teeth marks, no raw flesh in the poor dead animal's neck. Instead, the wound looked as if a human had inflicted it, using a sharp metallic tool like a razor or a knife.

My mind raced and the tightening in my stomach had let loose into a series of cartwheels. When I'd encountered the dead mouse the day before, I'd just assumed it was the handiwork of Lucifer, the stray cat that had adopted Shawn's estate as its territory. This time around, I sensed that whoever had left me this little gift wasn't any four-legged animal. It was much more likely that the perpetrator was the two-legged variety.

I pulled off my sweatshirt, using it to wrap the dead animal and move it to the side of the guesthouse, beneath some shrubs. My mouth had become uncomfortably dry, and the pounding of my heart was making me feel light-headed. Someone had been watching my comings and goings—and that someone wasn't happy about it.

"Nick? *Nick?*" I cried, storming inside the cottage. I was suddenly desperate not to be alone. But while I was hoping to find Nick and the dogs home, I wasn't at all prepared for what I encountered.

The front rooms of the guesthouse were aglow in candlelight. The tables, the counters, and even the windowsills were lined with white votives, their flickering flames drenching the living room and the kitchen in soft light. A bottle of champagne and two long-stemmed glasses sat on the coffee table. The kitchen table was set for two, with a tablecloth, a circle of candles, and, in the middle, a huge vase of yellow roses.

Nick stood in the doorway, searching my face for a re-action. Max stood on one side of him and Lou on the other, wearing the same expectant looks—as if the three of them had cooked this up together.

"What's all this?" I asked, blinking.

"My way of saying 'I'm sorry,'" Nick replied. "I've decided that I've been acting childish. My jealousy over that Shawn guy is just dumb. I know you don't give a hoot about him."

"Oh, Nick," I said in a breathless voice. "This is all so...so unexpected."

"I can tell by the look on your face!"

"I—I just need a minute to catch my breath."

"You look flushed," he observed. "I didn't mean to catch you off guard like this."

I wasn't about to tell him that the real reason I was so flustered was a dead rat, not a live boyfriend. I stood woodenly as he came over and took me in his arms.

"Can you forgive me for being an idiot?" he asked gently. "Is it enough to tell you that I'm sorry?"

Don't say it, a voice inside my head insisted. Don't start, Jess. . . .

"Don't you owe me a second apology?" I suddenly heard myself saying, as if I'd lost the ability to control what came out of my mouth.

I felt Nick stiffen. "For what?"

"For giving me such a hard time about investigating Devon Barnett's murder."

"Wait a sec." He pulled away, his hands still around me, but suddenly in what seemed like an awkward embrace. "This murder business is something else entirely."

"Not really," I said lightly. "I thought we'd reached an agreement that time we had lunch at the Sand Bar. We decided that my fascination with murder investigations and your decision to become a lawyer weren't that different."

"That may be true on some intellectual level," Nick countered. "But the fact of the matter is, that what you're doing is just plain dangerous! When you start poking your nose around in places where it doesn't belong—"

"Who are you to tell me where my nose belongs?"

"Who am I? Who am *I*?"

Our voices had gotten so loud that someone who didn't know any better might have concluded that we were fighting. In fact, Max had begun barking, as if saying, "Cut it out, you two!" Lou ducked under the coffee table, never very comfortable with disagreement. Frankly, I wasn't that good at it, either. By this point, I'd decided to deprive Nick of the knowledge that some unknown individual had gotten in the habit of sneaking dead animals onto my porch when no one was looking. If he wasn't going to support me, then I could manage without him.

"Jess, you're just being stubborn," Nick insisted.

"You took it upon yourself to find out who murdered Devon Barnett. Well, guess what? You haven't been able to do it! The poor guy was probably nothing more than the victim of a freak accident, anyway. But would you ever admit that? Would you ever back down and say you'd been *wrong*?"

"I'm *not* wrong!" I shot back. "He *was* murdered, and I'm going to find out who did it!"

"Even if pigheadedly insisting on doing it ruins our entire vacation?"

"The only thing that's ruining our vacation is your mood swings—and your insistence that you know more about what's good for me than I do!"

"If that's how you feel, then *fine*," Nick shouted.

"*Fine!*" I countered.

He started toward the front door. I knew this conversation was over.

"Aren't you going to blow out all these candles?" I called after him. "You could start a fire!"

"I thought I could," he answered, "but I guess I was wrong."

He slammed the door hard, making the entire guesthouse shake. Lou began to whimper, while Max went into a frenzy as he tried to climb up to the window to watch him leave.

So much for kissing and making up, I thought sullenly.

I scooped Max into my arms so the two of us could stand in front of the window and watch Nick storm toward his car and drive off. Instead of feeling triumphant or even angry, I suddenly felt empty.

I also doubted my own motives.

Was I really angry that Nick wasn't crazy about me playing detective during our romantic little getaway? I wondered, blinking hard to keep my eyes from stinging. Or was this argument the result of my own insecurities, my compulsion to find a new and complicated way of pushing him away?

One thing was for certain. If Devon Barnett hadn't gotten himself murdered the first night I was on the East End, Nick and I would have spent an idyllic week together, splashing in the waves and pigging out on seafood. In a way, this whole thing was Devon Barnett's fault.

At least, I hoped it was. After all, the dead paparazzo was a much better fall guy than Shawn.

# Chapter 12

"Women and cats will do as they please, and men and dogs should relax and get used to the idea."

—Robert A. Heinlein

Some time after midnight, I heard Nick come in. Max, Lou, and I all lay in bed, our muscles tensed and our ears pricked as we listened to him move around the living room. My two dogs kept their eyes on me, wagging their tails as they silently begged for permission to run out and give Nick the royal welcome.

"Don't even *think* about it!" I whispered, feeling slightly bruised by how easily they could shift loyalties.

My heart pounded as I waited to see what would happen with Nick next: an apology followed by a *real* session of kissing-and-making-up . . . or a standoff.

The creaking of the wicker couch gave me my answer.

I didn't sleep very well, so I was glad when the clock finally told me it was a respectable time to get up. I pulled on some clothes, brushed my teeth, and tiptoed out with Max in my arms and Lou at my side. A cat burglar couldn't have made less noise. As I opened the door, I glanced back at Nick. He lay sprawled across the couch, wearing nothing but the ridiculous boxer shorts I'd bought him for Valentine's Day, neon yellow covered with red hearts and pink pigs. He was fast asleep. Or at least pretending to be.

Arriving at the dog show on Thursday morning was a relief. Even Max and Lou seemed to feel it. As the three of us headed toward the "Ask The Vet" booth, they pranced around gleefully, barking and nipping at each others' butts and having a grand old time.

When they spotted Emily, they strained at the leash so hard that I let go. They raced across the field. As soon as they reached her, Lou jumped up, pushing his paws against her shoulders and nearly knocking her over. Max kept leaping into the air, his body twisting into a different formation every time he came down.

"Hey, doggies!" Emily cried, obviously delighted by their no-holds-barred greeting. "I sure missed you guys!"

She glanced up, her hazel eyes sparkling. "I missed you, too," she said, quickly adding, "and coming here, of course. I had nothing to do yesterday."

I pictured the swimming pool, the tennis courts, the roller-skating rink, and the boats that were all right in Emily's backyard. I was about to protest when I realized that none of them would be much fun without someone to enjoy them with.

"Looks like we're going to make up for it today," I commented, nodding toward a man making a beeline in our direction. He had no fewer than five dogs in tow, ranging in size from a toy poodle to a Saint Bernard. He also had an extremely determined look on his face.

"That's why we're here," Emily replied proudly. "To help people. We're the experts, right?"

The man with the eclectic taste in breeds turned out to be just one in a series of dog owners who were anxious to talk to us "experts." As I answered their questions and examined their dogs, Emily handed out brochures, gave directions to the "Refreshments" tent, and admired the animals so enthusiastically that most of their owners left our booth with big smiles on their faces.

The independent filmmaker Shawn had mentioned also wandered by. From what I could see, the intense young man never stopped looking at the world through the lens of his video camera. I made a point of ignoring him as he shot some footage of Emily and me talking to one of the dog-owners, not wanting to ruin the *cinema verité* effect. I didn't even look up when he leaned over to place a sheet of yellow paper on our table. When I finally glanced at it, I saw it was an invitation to the screening of his documentary at Russell Bolger's estate at one o'clock on Sunday.

Even though Emily and I dealt with a steady stream of visitors to our booth, I managed to steal away for a few minutes. Leaving her in charge of both the booth and my dogs, I hurried over to the Yellow Tent, where the Group judging was underway. According to the schedule, I was just in time to catch the end of the Toy Group.

While I've treated my share of the miniature breeds that fell under this classification, I couldn't help melting over the spectacle of so many cute little animals in the ring. Seeing them together instead of one at a time, cheerfully parading around the circle with their handlers, was as much fun as peering into the window of a toy store.

Yet while they all had the same small size in common, that was about the only characteristic they shared. The frisky black-white-and-tan cavalier King Charles spaniel with the shaggy fur and long ears of all spaniels bore no resemblance to the sleek black-and-white Italian Greyhound that barely stood a foot high. The fluffy Pekingese that reminded me of one of those woolly bedroom slippers was light-years away from the toy Manchester terrier that looked like a tiny Doberman.

Still, each one was already a winner, having captured Best of Breed in the event's earlier competitions. They were all beautiful dogs, groomed to perfection and well-versed in dog show etiquette. How a judge would ever manage to choose just one as the group winner, I couldn't imagine.

"Every one of them is absolutely darling, don't you think?"

I turned, curious about who had been reading my thoughts. Glancing over, I saw that Kara Liebling had joined me.

"Hello, Kara," I said. Sincerely, I added, "Running into you like this is certainly a nice surprise."

"I'm glad I ran into you, too, Jessie."

For today's event, Kara was dressed casually, her pale blond hair piled on top of her head and fastened with a clip that left soft tendrils curling around her face. She wore white capris, a sky-blue tank top, and canvas tennis shoes, with a white sweater tied loosely around her shoulders. Every article of clothing looked expensive, with handstitching and unusual detailing. Even on a day like today, she managed to look radiant. I reminded myself what Chess had said: that Kara was simply another human being, just like the rest of us.

Another dog-lover, as well. I reached down to pet Anastasia, who stood regally at Kara's side, wagging her tail and gazing up at me with her clear, brown eyes.

"And how about you, Anastasia?" I asked, caressing the silky white fur of the Borzoi's small folded ears. "Are you having fun?"

"She's doing more than that," Kara said, beaming. "She competed in the Hound Group event this morning—and won second prize."

"That's great! You must be so—"

My thought trailed off as the Pekingese that had been gliding around the ring in a spirited manner suddenly stopped, turned, and let out an indignant yip. His owner, a middle-aged man in green golf pants and a loud plaid shirt, instantly looked panicked. At the same moment, the dog right behind him, the greyhound, skittered forward, growling angrily. The two canines appeared to be after the same booty—whatever it was. The greyhound's owner, a gaunt-faced woman with the same spindly build, let out a shriek, snapping the leash and pulling her dog back.

Misbehaving in the ring was the ultimate no-no. Just like everyone else who'd witnessed the scene, my eyes automatically traveled to the judge. I recognized him as the same man who'd judged the wirehaired terriers on Monday. He was wearing another seersucker suit, this time white with narrow green stripes, and the same straw hat. But this time, the expression on his face was one of pure displeasure.

Almost immediately, he pointed to the cavalier, identifying him as the winner. The dog's handler, a fit young man in shorts and a tight white T-shirt, broke into a huge, triumphant smile.

Instead of the polite applause I expected, I cringed at the sound of the greyhound owner's shrill voice piercing through the din.

"This competition was sabotaged!" she shrieked. "Someone threw something—food, probably—into the ring! Someone *cheated*!"

As for the Pekingese's owner, he just looked confused. I couldn't help examining the faces of all the other dog owners who'd been competing—especially the cavalier's handler. I wasn't certain, but I thought that for just a fraction of a second, I saw a smug look flicker across his face.

"Just like show business," Kara commented, smiling slyly. "The best actor for a particular role isn't necessarily the one who gets it!"

I laughed. "I guess it really is a dog-eat-dog world."

"Which brings me to the real reason I'm glad I ran into you. I owe you an apology." In response to my blank look, she added, "For the way I acted at the screening the other night."

I waved my hand in the air. "It was nothing, Kara. Not even worth mentioning."

"It wasn't 'nothing' to me," she insisted. "I'm sorry I sounded so catty. I'm afraid Shawn Elliot is a bit of a sore spot."

"I don't blame you for being upset. But I meant it when I said that he and I are just friends."

"I know, and I hope you can forget about how I acted."

"Absolutely."

"Good." She smiled sincerely. "There's another reason I'm glad I ran into you. I keep meaning to invite you over. I'd love the chance to just sit and chat. Even though the whole point of coming to the Bromptons for the summer is to relax and 'get away from it all,' it's much too easy to get involved with all the same people that I see at home. It's really refreshing to get to know somebody who's not in the business. How about stopping over for a drink this evening around seven?"

"That sounds great," I told her sincerely.

"Here, let me just jot down my address. . . ."

I had to admit, I was surprised by her invitation. After our encounter at the *Pulverizer* screening, I thought my friendship with Kara was over. Yet I genuinely liked her. Aside from that surprising encounter, she had always seemed like such a warm, sincere person.

But as much as I hated to admit it, I had an ulterior motive, as well. Kara was one of Chess's closest friends, and I hoped she might be able to provide me with some clues about the life he shared with Devon Barnett. Then there was Shawn's puzzling claim that appearances aside, Kara Liebling was actually a "nut case." Tonight, maybe I'd have a chance to find out for myself.

. . .

By the time noon rolled around, I was more than ready for a break. I was wondering how to spend my long lunch hour when Emily said, "Could I ask you a favor?"

"Anything, Em."

"Would it be okay if I brought Max and Lou home with me during lunch? My dad's picking me up in a couple of minutes, and I want him to see how great they are to have around. That way, maybe he'll let me get a dog."

"Be my guest."

Her face lit up. "Thanks! I'll take *real* good care of them. I *promise*!"

Her expression grew serious. "But what should I feed them? We don't have any dog food at home."

"They eat once a day, at dinnertime," I told her. "Just make sure they have plenty of water and they'll be fine."

I watched Emily skip across the field happily with her two charges in tow. Lou loped beside her on his long, spindly legs, while Max scurried along in fourth gear, his short legs moving so quickly they were a blur. I couldn't tell who was the most excited.

I decided to take advantage of my free time to drop in at 145 Beach Street. Between my meeting with Sizzle and Hugo Fontana's contention that Dev's current heart-throb had some interesting skeletons in his closet, I was anxious to scrutinize Chess a little more closely.

I stood on the steps of the pastel-colored mansion, ringing the doorbell repeatedly and hearing it echo through the cavernous first floor. Even though Chess's car was in the driveway, there was no response.

Just for the heck of it, I tried the door. Surprisingly, the knob turned easily in my hand.

"Hello?" I called, stepping inside. "Anybody home?"

Nothing. I ventured a little farther inside the house. I moved cautiously, afraid of suddenly finding myself face-to-face with a bucket-wielding Hilda—or something worse.

I jumped at least three feet into the air when I felt something brush against my leg. Letting out a yelp, I looked down—and was instantly relieved to see that my attacker was nobody more threatening than Zsa Zsa.

"Hey, Zsa Zsa," I crooned, picking up the little ball of fur. My face was immediately drenched in dog kisses, her postage stamp-sized tongue working overtime to cover the expanse of my left cheek. Despite the fluffed fur and the faux leopard-skin bow perched atop her tiny head, the sweet-faced Havanese was just another puppy dog, looking for affection. "Where's your daddy, huh? Where's Chess?"

While the soft bundle in my arms didn't answer, the sound of a crash somewhere on the second floor gave me a clue. Zsa Zsa and I both jumped.

"Go find Chess," I instructed, depositing her gently on the ground.

Dutifully, the dog trotted toward the dramatic round staircase. I followed her upstairs, calling, "Chess? Are you up here?"

If he was, he still didn't seem to have heard me. I continued trailing after my guide, turning a corner and following Zsa Zsa into the master bedroom. It was a large, sunny space with trendy *toile* wall coverings. The white silk was printed with deep red renderings of horse-drawn carriages attended by footmen, and refined ladies who looked as if they spent way too much time in front of a mirror. I'd learned all about *toile* by watching the Home and Garden Channel. Very expensive stuff, as were the coordinated drapes, bedspread, carpets, and every other element that picked up the same deep tones and Marie Antoinette ambiance.

While I'd been impressed when Chess had first shown it to me, I was even more bowled over this time. But the sudden lump in my throat had nothing to do with the décor. Instead, it was the tableau I found in the walk-in closet.

Chess was standing amid the linen shirts and Armani suits and Gucci loafers, holding a shoebox in his hand. It was white, printed in green with what I figured was probably some hotshot designer's name, Emilio Fratelli.

But it wasn't only the lettering on the box that was green. So were the bundles of cash that had clearly just spilled out of it and were now lying haphazardly all over the closet floor.

"Chess?" I asked quizzically. Searching his face, I saw an expression of astonishment.

"*Look* at this, Jessie!" he cried. "They're all twenties and fifties. There are thousands and thousands of dollars here!"

Zsa Zsa hovered outside the closet, eyeing the pile of greenery suspiciously. She looked just as confused as the rest of us. She tried barking at it, and when it didn't respond by either attacking her or running away, she eased a little closer, sniffed it a few times, and immediately lost interest.

Not so with Chess and me.

"Where did all this money come from?" I asked.

"Jessie, I have *no* idea. I was just scrounging around on the closet shelf, looking for a pair of sandals I remember buying last year when Dev and I were at the Cannes Film Festival." Defensively, he added, "Well, with him snapping pictures all day, what *else* was I supposed to do but shop? Anyway, I couldn't find them anywhere, so I thought I'd check the shelves on *his* side of the closet— and the next thing I knew, *this* came tumbling down on my head!"

"Gee," I muttered, "the only surprises I ever find in *my* closet are pants that don't fit anymore."

Zsa Zsa leaped onto the bed with amazing ease, flopping down and resting her head on the soft fabric as she watched Chess and me gather up the neat packets of bills, each one bound with a strip of cream-colored paper. Chess placed them neatly in the shoebox, probably putting them right back where he'd found them because he didn't know what else to do with them.

"Maybe this was just cash Dev kept around the house for incidental expenses," he mused.

"Sure, we all need pocket money," I said. "Two thousand dollars here, another thousand there . . ."

He stopped. "You're right. This looks *very* suspicious, doesn't it?"

"Do you know how long that box has been there?"

Chess shook his head. "I never paid attention to Dev's side of the closet. I mean, my feeling was always what's his is his and what's mine is mine. Besides, we didn't exactly have the same taste. He dressed *so* conservatively. Of course, being a bit older than me, he was starting to put on a little weight around the middle, if you catch my drift."

"What about this shoebox? Do you remember Devon bringing home a new pair of shoes by this designer?" I checked the box again, having already forgotten his name. "Emilio Fratelli?"

"I never heard of Emilio Fratelli."

I didn't mention that I hadn't, either. Personally, my favorite designers were L.L. Bean and J.C. Penney.

When all the money had been put back into place, Chess sank onto the bed, still cradling the shoebox in his arms. Looking at me helplessly, he asked, "*Now* what should I do? With all this money, I mean?"

A few possibilities immediately came to mind. Then I realized that Chess probably wasn't in the market for a better X-ray machine or a new set of snow tires. But it only took me a few seconds to come up with an even more practical idea.

"Chess," I said tentatively, "would you consider having that money fingerprinted?"

He blinked. "What on earth for?"

"To help us find out where all that money came from."

He still looked baffled. "What do you mean, where it came from? It must have come from a bank, right?"

"Not necessarily. Someone could have given it to Devon."

"But who would..." I could practically hear the wheels turning in his head. And then the muscles in his face loosened. "Oh, I get it. You think whoever gave him this money might have had something to do with his death."

"Exactly. At the very least, tracing it to a particular person might give us some idea of what Dev was involved in. Aside from taking pictures of celebrities for the tabloids, I mean."

"What makes you so sure that he was involved in something bad?" Chess's tone was suddenly defensive. Icy, even. I realized I'd gone too far.

"I'm not sure at all, Chess," I said gently. "But it's something we have to at least consider if we want to find out the real reason that Dev is dead."

Chess frowned. "You know, Jessie, I've been thinking about what you said. About the possibility that Nettie was murdered, I mean. And I'm not so sure you're right. I mean, how do you know that ice sculpture guy wasn't just lying to cover his own butt? You don't know anything about him!"

The vehemence of his reaction surprised me, especially since there was no longer any doubt in my mind that Devon Barnett had died under extremely suspicious circumstances. The more I learned about the photographer, the more convinced I became that the man had too many enemies to assume that the "freak accident" that had killed him had been an accident at all.

Besides, I'd heard the argument between Gary Frye and Phyllis Beckwith, and I'd talked to Gary myself the day after the incident. I wasn't exactly Dr. Phil, but I thought I had a pretty good sense of what people were about. And at the time, I'd been completely convinced of his sincerity. Of course, I'd also seen someone lurking in the shadows of the gazebo just before the ice sculpture had fallen, then found the piece of wire at the crime scene, which backed up Gary's story.

But what really piqued my interest was Chess's sudden interest in steering me away from investigating Barnett's murder.

After all, what did I really know about Chess? There were certainly enough indications that he wasn't quite as sweet and easygoing as he pretended to be to make me wary. For one thing, there was that anonymous note about him not being "who I thought he was." Then there was Gus's report that he'd physically attacked his lover in the restaurant. True, he hadn't exactly used a machete, and I was pretty sure the statistics would bear out my hunch that very few people were actually killed by butter knives every year. But the point was, that Chess had gotten angry enough to become violent—and that Devon had been the target of his outburst. And just minutes before, I'd walked in on him and found him holding a box of cold, hard cash that he swore he knew nothing about, even though it had been stashed right there in his closet.

My head was spinning. That, combined with Chess's fervent rejection of the idea that Devon's death had been anything but the result of an inept ice sculptor and a clumsy bulldog, motivated me to abandon any discussions of Devon Barnett's murder, at least for now.

Still, I was dying to get my hands on some of that money. And buying new toys for my van had nothing to do with it.

I watched mournfully as Dev put the cover on the green-and-white shoebox and stepped back inside the closet. Standing on his toes, he slid it back onto the top shelf, between the Kenneth Coles and the Giorgio Armanis. It seemed like the ideal time to change the subject.

"How about some of that fabulous iced tea of yours?" I suggested cheerfully.

Chess brightened. "I *told* you it was good. People have told me I should go into business. Become the Mrs. Fields of iced tea."

We sat at the kitchen table amid Andy Warhol's cookie jars, a big icy pitcher of iced tea between us. Zsa Zsa lay sprawled across Chess's lap, sighing as if she were in doggie heaven as he distractedly played with her ears.

"I had an interesting day yesterday," I said in what I hoped was a casual tone. "I went to Cuttituck to meet Devon's wife."

Chess froze. The steeliness that came into his eyes made me recoil.

"What on earth did you do *that* for?"

"Just curious, I guess. I have to admit, I was pretty surprised when I read Devon's obituary in the local paper and learned that he had a wife."

He sniffed disapprovingly. "I bet that witch with a 'B' gave you an earful."

"She certainly didn't have a lot of positive things to say about him."

"I suppose she told you all about their battle over the annulment."

I frowned. I didn't remember Sydney saying anything about an annulment. "Actually, what she said was that

Devon had been in no hurry to end the marriage. Apparently, their divorce proceedings had been going on for years."

Chess looked surprised. "You mean, she didn't tell you the *reason* it went on for so long?"

"No. As a matter of fact, she said she couldn't understand why he wasn't in more of a hurry to get the whole thing over with."

"Liar, liar, pants on fire! I can't *believe* that wicked woman is rewriting history that way!"

I leaned forward, nearly knocking over my glass of iced tea. "What really happened?"

"What *really* happened is that, by the end, Nettie hated that woman's *guts*." Chess's tone had become scathing. "And the *last* thing he wanted was for her to walk away with even a *cent* of his money. Believe me, by that point, he had quite a bit."

"But if they'd been husband and wife, she was entitled to half of everything he had. What could he do about it?"

A smug look settled on Chess's face. "Have the marriage annulled, of course."

"I see." And I *did* see, a whole lot more than I was letting on. Now *my* mind was clicking away madly. With Sydney and Devon's divorce stretching on endlessly, and the threat of an annulment, that would leave Sydney with absolutely nothing from her ex. She was bound to be frustrated and angry. Perhaps even frustrated and angry enough to kill him—especially since, as the surviving spouse, she'd be likely to inherit his entire estate.

"She's some piece of work," Chess went on bitterly. I noticed that his grip on Zsa Zsa had tightened. Instead of caressing her ears, he was tugging at them. The little dog kept glancing up at him anxiously, her entire body tense. "You wouldn't *believe* what a big deal she made about Nettie finally coming out of the closet! She took it personally, when it really had nothing to do with her. The way she threatened to ruin him and to destroy Hugo's career—not that I have any fond feelings for Hugo, of course..."

Nor he for you, I thought.

"She's a mean, vengeful woman," Chess went on, his teeth clenched and his voice practically a hiss. "In fact, maybe you're right. Maybe somebody really *did* murder poor Nettie, and maybe that someone was—"

Suddenly Zsa Zsa let out a yelp, leaping out of Chess's lap so abruptly that she knocked over his tumbler of iced tea with her tail. A stream of clear brown liquid shot across the table, sending me springing to my feet.

"Oh, Jessie, I'm so *sorry*! I hope I didn't get you!"

"No, I'm fine. Not a drop on me."

"And you, my poor precious puppy. What have I *done*?" Chess scooped up the wary Havanese. "I am *so, so* sorry. I never meant to hurt you!"

It seemed like the ideal time to make my exit. The more time I spent with the love of Devon Barnett's life, the more I found myself wondering who Chess LaMont really was.

I pretended to glance at my watch. "Look how late it is!" I exclaimed. "I had no idea the time had passed so quickly. I'd better get going or I'll be late for the afternoon session at the dog show. Thanks for the iced tea. You really should go into business."

I said my good-byes, then made a hasty retreat from Chess and Dev's love nest. I was still wondering about the true character of Chess LaMont as I climbed into my van and drove away. And there seemed like no better time than the present to find out.

•   •   •

Driving away from 145 Beach Lane filled me with re-lief. Curiosity, as well. I wondered what I'd find out by following up on Hugo Fontana's suggestion that I check into Chess LaMont's past.

I drove my van into East Brompton, then pulled into the parking lot of a small supermarket where there were plenty of empty spaces. I whipped out my cell phone and dialed the phone number I'd jotted down the day before.

"Sweet Elm Public Library," a cheerful voice greeted me. "How can I help you?"

"Can you connect me with Reference, please?"

"Certainly. Please hold."

A few seconds passed before I heard a different woman's voice, this one considerably more crisp. "Reference. Ms. Pruitt speaking."

"My name is Jessica Popper," I began before launching into the same story I'd given yesterday. "I live in New York, and I'm planning a surprise party for a friend of mine who grew up in Sweet Elm. I thought it might be fun to get hold of some pieces of his past, like his picture from his high school yearbook."

"We keep all the Sweet Elm High School yearbooks on file, all the way back to 1928." Ms. Pruitt's voice had softened, and a distinct note of pride had crept in. "What year did your friend graduate?"

"I believe it was about ten years ago. I'm afraid I don't know the actual year."

"In that case, what's his name?"

"Chester LaMont."

The silence at the other end lasted so long I thought we'd been cut off.

"Hello?" I asked.

"Who did you say you were?" Ms. Pruitt asked. By this point, all traces of friendliness were gone.

"A friend. I'm just trying to find out something about Chester's years in Sweet Elm."

"If that's what you want, I've got plenty of information," Ms. Pruitt said frostily. "I've got pages and pages I can send you that spell out the whole story. In fact, if you've got a fax machine, I'd be more than happy to send them right now."

I thought quickly, then pulled Suzanne's business card out of my wallet. I read off her fax number slowly as, far away in Sweet Elm, Iowa, Ms. Pruitt jotted it down.

"I'll be sending you articles from our local paper here in Sweet Elm," Ms. Pruitt said crisply. "I believe they'll tell you everything you need to know."

"Thank you." I was debating whether to ask her for a clue as to what they contained when she said, "I don't recognize that area code. Where are you calling from?"

"East Brompton, New York."

"That's on Long Island, isn't it?" Ms. Pruitt asked.

"Yes."

"One of those fancy summer communities, right?"

"Well . . . yes."

"Is that where Chester ended up?"

"Part of the time, anyway. He spends his summers out here."

"Sounds like he landed on his feet. That type usually does." She sniffed disapprovingly. "Well, I suppose none of that is any of my business. All I care about is the fact that he's gone. I know the Montgomery boy—or 'LaMont,' as he calls himself now—is your friend. But I say good riddance to bad rubbish."

What was *that* about? I wondered. But she hung up before I had a chance to say another word. Hopefully, I'd find out soon enough. I called Suzanne's office, told her about the fax I was expecting, and sat back in my seat to ponder the situation.

The more dealings I had with Chess, I thought, the more complicated he seemed. My first impression of him was that he was a sweet, charming guy. But he clearly got into some kind of trouble back in his hometown, maybe even something bad enough that he packed his bags and hightailed it out of there.

Then again, Ms. Pruitt's definition of "bad rubbish" could very well be different from mine. Maybe Chess's unforgivable offense had been nothing worse than organizing a Gay Pride parade or showing up at the Senior Prom in drag.

While I was sitting in my car, cell phone in hand, I decided to try the police again. First I dialed the East Brompton Police Department.

"Hello, this is Jessica Popper." I fought the temptation to add the word "again." "I've already left a couple of messages, but—"

"You mean, you *still* haven't heard back?" The woman at the other end of the line sounded accusing, as if somehow it had been *my* fault.

"No, I haven't," I told her politely. "I wouldn't keep calling if I didn't—"

"I'll leave Sergeant Bangs a message," she interrupted crossly. "That's really all I can do. It's not up to me whether or not he returns his calls."

"We live to serve," I muttered into the phone. Fortunately, she'd already hung up.

I closed my eyes, leaned my head back against the front seat, and pushed a tremendous amount of air out through my lungs in what turned into a loud, frustrated sigh. But instead of feeling defeated, I felt a renewed sense of purpose. I poked at the buttons of my cell phone again, this time dialing Norfolk County Homicide.

"Homicide," a deep male voice answered flatly. "Officer Bongiovanni speaking."

"This is Dr. Jessica Popper," I said crisply. "I have some information about the death of Devon Barnett in East Brompton. I'd like to speak to someone—"

"I'll have to take your name and number." I wondered if Officer Bongiovanni had attended the same charm school as the woman who answered the phone for the East Brompton Police. "There's nobody here right now to take your call."

"Nobody *there*?" What did the Norfolk County Homicide Squad have to do that was more important than investigating murders? I wondered.

Fortunately, Officer Bongiovanni seemed to be in a chatty mood. "There's a press conference today, over at the courthouse," he explained. "They got all the TV stations and the newspapers there. They'll probably be tied up for a while."

Of course, Lieutenant Falcone wouldn't miss *that* for the world, I thought wryly. How could the chance to find a killer or two possibly compete with a photo op?

"Let me take your name and number—"

As I recited the information as calmly as I could, I was certain there had to be steam coming out of my ears. In fact, I was surprised the van's windows didn't fog up. There *has* to be a way to get Falcone's attention, I thought. I just haven't figured out what it is yet.

●　●　●

As I pulled into the parking lot of Suzanne's office in Poxabogue, I glanced at my watch and saw it was getting late. If I was going to get back to the dog show in time to meet Emily and my dogs right after the lunch break, I had to hustle.

I rushed inside and found a waiting room full of clients and their pets. My frenzied state elicited near-hysteria from a tiny Pekingese, who barked at me shrilly from the safety of his owner's designer pocketbook. The immense Rottweiler next to him just eyed me, as if he knew he didn't have to work quite as hard to show us all who was really boss.

Shelley was standing at the receptionist's desk, perusing the papers in a folder. She brightened when she spotted me.

"Hi, Jessie," she greeted me. "I'm afraid Suzanne's with a client right now. But if you can wait—"

"That's okay. I'm just here to pick up a fax."

She looked at me strangely. "I was wondering what that was all about."

The expression on her face warned me that I'd better brace myself. And as she handed me several pages held together with a paper clip, I thought I was prepared for anything.

But I could practically feel my eyes popping out of my head as I read the headline that screamed at me from the front page of the *Sweet Elm Examiner*:

## SWEET ELM STUDENT QUESTIONED IN ENGLISH TEACHER'S MURDER

# Chapter 13

"When the mouse laughs at the cat, there's a hole nearby."

—Nigerian proverb

A re you okay, Jessie?" Shelley asked, her face tense with concern.

I just nodded, unable to respond.

"Do you want some water?"

"No, thanks. But is there someplace quiet I can sit for a few minutes while I read through this?"

"Sure. There's a bench in the back room, where we store supplies," she replied, pointing. "No one will bother you there."

Clutching the stack of papers in my hand, I dashed to the back room and sank onto the wooden bench I found pushed into a corner. I sorted through the pages, putting them in order. I had a feeling I was about to read quite a story, and I wanted to reconstruct the events exactly as they'd occurred.

I noted that the newspapers they'd been copied from were ten years old, with dates that ran from April to May. I started with page one.

## SWEET ELM TEACHER MISSING

A Sweet Elm High School English teacher is missing, according to Sheriff Clarence Colby of the Sweet Elm Police Department. Sheriff Colby reported that the school principal, Marion Carson, contacted the Sweet Elm Police Department at approximately 4:15 P.M. on Monday and reported that no one had heard from Edmund Sylvester, 32, since the previous Friday afternoon, when he left the building for the day.

Sylvester, a native of Ernst, Kansas, has been teaching at Sweet Elm High School for three years. He previously taught at schools in Kingsboro, Ohio, East Stonington, Nebraska, and Kirby, Illinois. In addition to teaching English, he runs the Drama Club after school. Two years ago, he instituted an annual school trip to New York City so his students could see plays performed by professional actors.

Sheriff Colby told the *Sweet Elm Examiner,* "Everybody in this town knows the worst thing that ever happens around here is that somebody runs the stop light at the corner of Sweet Elm and Main. At this point, there's no suspicion of foul play. I have a feeling this Sylvester fellow has simply taken it upon himself to skip town. Maybe he just decided he needed a change of scenery. I guess it's possible that he's in some kind of trouble, but as far as I know, it's not with anybody around here."

Edmund Sylvester lives alone, and no family members could be located for questioning. Anyone who has any information about his whereabouts is asked to call Sheriff Clarence Colby at the police station.

I checked the date: Friday, April 7. The second article that Ms. Pruitt had faxed, had run the following Friday, in the next edition of the *Sweet Elm Examiner*. This one didn't make the front page. It had been clipped from page five, where it was wedged between an advertisement for wheelbarrows at Harris Hardware and a coupon from The Butter Barn, two dollars off the "Lip-Smackin' Rib-Ticklin' All-You-Can-Eat Breakfast Bar."

## ENGLISH TEACHER STILL MISSING

The plot thickens, I thought, frowning as I skimmed the article.

I was trying to reserve judgment until I got the whole story, but the uncomfortable gnawing feeling I'd had in my stomach ever since Shelley handed me the fax was quickly becoming more intense. The next article, dated exactly two weeks after the newspaper's initial report of Edmund Sylvester's disappearance, didn't help.

## ENGLISH TEACHER FOUND MURDERED

The body of Edmund Sylvester was discovered in the woods behind The Butter Barn late Saturday night, according to Sergeant Bradford Beene of the Ardmore County Homicide Squad. Sergeant Beene said yesterday that an autopsy performed by the Ardmore County Medical Examiner, Dr. Jonah Brooks, determined that Sylvester was murdered.

According to the medical examiner's report, Sylvester had been dead for approximately three weeks. The cause of death was massive head injuries from repeated blows with a large, heavy object. Police have not yet determined the murder weapon.

An investigation is ongoing. Anyone who has

any information is asked to contact the Ardmore County Homicide Squad at 555-3000.

I swallowed, which wasn't easy. My mouth was so dry that even the metallic taste was gone. I already knew the saga of Mr. Sylvester wasn't leading anyplace good—and that sooner or later Chess LaMont was going to appear as one of the players.

I didn't have to wait much longer. The next article, the fourth, was the one whose headline had originally caught my eye. I forced myself to read it slowly so I wouldn't miss a single word.

## SWEET ELM STUDENT QUESTIONED IN ENGLISH TEACHER'S MURDER

A 17-year-old high school senior is among the suspects that Ardmore County Police have identified in the murder of Sweet Elm High School English teacher Edmund Sylvester. Chester Montgomery, a student at the school, was brought in for questioning on Tuesday, but was later released, Sergeant Bradford Beene of the Ardmore County Homicide Squad said.

"We've been questioning people at the school and around town, and we've learned that Mr. Montgomery and Mr. Sylvester had a very close relationship," Sergeant Beene stated. "Sources close to the investigation say the two were inseparable." He added that the police have been focusing on Montgomery since two teachers at the school came forward and said they overheard a heated argument between Sylvester and Montgomery on Friday night. According to the two witnesses, the argument ended with a threat. Sylvester and Mont-

gomery were subsequently seen leaving school together in Sylvester's car.

Students at Sweet Elm High School were stunned
to hear that a fellow student was being questioned
by police. Another student in the Drama Club, who
wished to remain anonymous, said, "Mr. Sylvester
and Chester spent a lot of time together after
school, discussing plays and talking about Chess's
aspirations of moving to New York and doing
something creative. I used to see them together all
the time, driving around in Mr. Sylvester's car and
taking walks on the trails behind the stores. Chester
really liked Mr. Sylvester. I can't imagine why he
would want to hurt him."

My mouth was dryer than ever. But as I turned the
page, I noticed my hands were clammy. The next article
was dated a week later.

### JUDGE'S SON PROVIDES ALIBI
### FOR SWEET ELM STUDENT

Sergeant Bradford Beene of the Ardmore County
Homicide Squad has announced that Chester
Montgomery is no longer a suspect in the murder
of Edmund Sylvester. According to Sergeant Beene,
a classmate at Sweet Elm High School, Ted Welling,
came forward to provide Montgomery with an alibi for the weekend that Sylvester is believed to
have been murdered.

Ted Welling, the son of Judge Theodore Welling
of the U.S. Court of Appeals in Iowa City, told police that he and Montgomery spent the entire weekend at the Welling family's house at Shimmering
Lake. According to Sergeant Beene, Welling said
that Montgomery had not been out of his sight the

entire weekend, from the time that Edmund Sylvester dropped him off at his house shortly after school ended on Friday until Monday morning, when the two boys returned to Sweet Elm and went straight to school.

Ted Welling's parents, Judge Welling and his wife Juliana, were out of town that weekend, vacationing at a golf resort. But Judge Welling told police he had no reason to doubt his son's claims.

"I stand by the statement I made to the police, that Teddy is a boy of integrity," Judge Welling told the *Sweet Elm Examiner*. "The two boys are such close friends. They often spend time together at the cabin, hunting and fishing. It sounds to me like those two rascals were too caught up in enjoying some good, old-fashioned boyish fun to have gotten mixed up in something like this business with Sylvester."

Sergeant Beene stated, "We are still actively pursuing all leads, and the investigation is ongoing."

The final article that Ms. Pruitt had faxed over almost seemed like an afterthought.

## MURDER WEAPON FOUND

An extensive search of the home of Edmund Sylvester, the Sweet Elm High School English teacher who was recently murdered, uncovered what police believe to have been the murder weapon. Sergeant Bradford Beene of the Ardmore County Homicide Squad said that on Wednesday, police discovered traces of blood that matched Sylvester's on a book they found in his study.

According to Sergeant Beene, police determined that a large, heavy book, *The Plays of William*

*Shakespeare,* had blood on the left corner, and that the cover was dented. "Forensics matched the blood to that of Mr. Sylvester," Sergeant Beene said. "No fingerprints belonging to Mr. Sylvester or any other person were found on the book, which leads us to believe that either the weapon was wiped clean of prints or that the perp wore gloves."

Although no one has been charged at this time, Sergeant Beene said the investigation is ongoing.

As I read the final words of the last article, I felt completely drained. From what I could tell, Edmund Sylvester's murder had never been solved. Yet it was possible—maybe even likely—that Chester Montgomery, a.k.a. Chess LaMont, had been responsible.

Even I could see that his alibi was weak. A close friend—and I could only imagine *how* close—had come forth and claimed that Chess had been with him the entire weekend. Yet from what I could tell, no one had actually seen them together.

The likelihood of intrigue springing from a love triangle between Chess, Ted Welling, and Mr. Sylvester was impossible to ignore. And it would have been so easy for Ted Welling to lie. The boy who'd provided Chess with an alibi was the son of a judge, a man whom the residents of Sweet Elm undoubtedly respected. The idea of the police or anyone else calling his son a liar was probably unthinkable.

Then there was Ms. Pruitt's take on the whole thing. From her attitude, it was clear she thought Chess was guilty. Of course, she could have simply been expressing antigay sentiments. But another possibility was that, as someone who knew the town of Sweet Elm well, someone who had watched Chess grow up and had access to town gossip, she was simply forming a knowledgeable opinion.

"*There* you are!" The cheerful sound of Suzanne's voice as she came bustling into the room pulled me out of my ruminations. "Shelley just told me you were back here, reading a fax. Did you find what you were looking for?"

The look on my face must have given her the answer.

"My God, Jessie! You look like you've just seen a ghost!"

"Not a ghost," I said hoarsely. "But very possibly a murderer."

• • •

Late that afternoon, as I staggered toward the guesthouse with Max and Lou romping beside me, I felt like a zombie in a 1950s horror movie. I was still shocked by what I'd learned about Chess, and the dull pain that had lodged itself in the pit of my stomach as I'd read the newspaper articles showed no signs of budging.

I was convinced he had murdered Barnett. There was simply too much evidence that pointed to him to ignore. His recent argument with Barnett at the Sand Bar, which had escalated into violence, the unsolved murder of a man who'd been his close friend and very possibly his lover, his feigned surprise over "discovering" a box of cash on Barnett's side of the closet...

"Should I go to the police?" I muttered, thinking aloud as I neared the front door. Max and Lou had already raced ahead, and for some reason were barking furiously. "If I presented all the facts to Falcone, would he believe me? Or would he think I—"

I stopped in my tracks abruptly, focusing on the dark mass a few feet ahead of me. It took me a few seconds to make sense of what I was seeing. As soon as I did, I let out a cry, instantly understanding what my dogs were so upset about.

Another dead animal lay on the front steps.

"Quiet!" I commanded, feeling my stomach wrench as I grabbed my dogs' collars. This time, there was no doubt in my mind that the unfortunate animal had been left there for my benefit. This was no random rodent or wild animal that had been killed for the sheer joy of the hunt. The black mass of fur carefully positioned in the center of my front porch was Lucifer, the feral cat who had made Shawn's property his own.

"No!" I cried, my voice reduced to a whimper. Leaning forward, I saw that his throat had been slit. The horror of what had been done to this poor, unfortunate animal, an innocent kitty who had simply been trying to survive, washed over me. I'd treated animals that had been the victims of atrocious accidents or reprehensible owners. But this was an animal I'd *known* . . .

And then another thought occurred to me. One that suddenly made it difficult to breathe.

This harmless feline had been slaughtered and placed in that spot to send me a message, loud and clear.

First the mouse, then the rat, then the cat . . .

First the mouse, then the rat, then the cat . . .

I rushed into the guesthouse, leading my hysterical canines around the poor homeless feline that had been forced to live in the shadows as he fought for his own survival. As soon as I opened the door, I was assaulted by The Who, the volume of the CD player turned up enough to make the walls vibrate. Nick stood at the stove, stirring the contents of a huge pot with a wooden spoon. He was dressed in a baggy Hawaiian shirt and tie-dyed boxer shorts featuring every color of the rainbow, his hips gyrating and his bare feet slapping against the tile floor in time to the music.

"Oh, Nick!" I cried, throwing my arms around him and burying my face in his shoulder. I vaguely remembered that we were in the middle of an argument—and that we weren't even speaking. None of that mattered as

I struggled to grasp the horror of that poor cat with his throat cut.

Fortunately, it didn't seem to matter to Nick, either. He dropped the spoon into the pot and hugged me tightly. "Jess, are you okay?"

I nodded. As I pulled away, I noticed that my two dogs were gazing up at me with the same concerned look in their eyes.

"What happened?" Nick demanded.

"There's a dead animal on the porch," I began in a choked voice. "It's not the first time. First, it was a mouse. Then, a rat."

He frowned. "Are you sure they didn't just get caught by that scraggly cat I've seen hanging around?"

"That's what I thought, too. At least, at first. But I just found him. The cat, Lucifer. With his . . . with his throat cut." I took a deep breath. "Somebody's been sending me warnings."

Nick closed his eyes and breathed in sharply, as if he were trying to maintain control. "You should have told me, Jess. For God's sake, you should have told the police!"

"Maybe." I swallowed hard. "But I guess I thought I could handle it on my own. And I was afraid it would complicate things between us. I know you haven't exactly been crazy about me investigating this murder."

"Look, I think we should file a report," Nick insisted. "Maybe the East Brompton Police won't get excited enough to launch a full-scale investigation, but this should be on the record. I'll make the call, if you want."

I nodded. "Thanks, Nick. I'd better call Kara Liebling, too. I ran into her today, and she invited me over for a drink this evening. I'll let her know I'm not coming—"

"Go, Jess," Nick urged. "Look, I can see how upset you are. If you've got something to do tonight, something to take your mind off all this, why don't you go ahead with your plans? I can deal with the East Brompton Police myself."

I realized that at this point, it really was a good idea to involve the police. My foray into the intriguing world of murder investigations was escalating, and even I had to admit that things were getting out of control. Yet I knew in my gut that a few dead animals weren't going to do much to get Sergeant Bangs excited.

Which was precisely why it was time to go one step further.

• • •

The headquarters for the Norfolk County Police Department were less than half an hour's drive from East Brompton. I drove as fast as I dared, keeping one eye on the clock. Five o'clock was drawing dangerously close, and I didn't want to rush into Lieutenant Falcone's office only to discover that he'd already left for the day. In fact, I'd taken Nick's car, knowing I'd make better time in a Maxima than in my van.

Police Headquarters was located within a complex of undistinguished office buildings just south of the Long Island Expressway, all of them housing county offices and agencies. The gigantic gray brick boxes stood against a stark, treeless horizon, as if they'd suddenly sprung up amid vacant fields that were once used for farming.

By the time I pulled into the tremendous parking lot that surrounded the complex on three sides, it was two minutes after five. It looked as if most employees had already left for the day, leaving behind only a sparse patchwork of cars. I scanned the buildings until I spotted one labeled "Norfolk County Police Headquarters," with the county's logo right below. After pulling Nick's car into the closest parking space, I scurried inside.

A burly police officer sat behind an elevated counter,

looking about as friendly as Cerberus, the mythical three-headed dog guarding the gateway to Hades. I squared my shoulders and strode over, no doubt looking as determined as I felt.

"I'd like to see Lieutenant Falcone," I told the desk sergeant.

He eyed me warily. "And you are? ..."

"Jessica Popper. *Dr.* Jessica Popper."

"He expecting you?"

"No."

"You don't have an appointment?"

"No." I held his gaze, unwilling to let him stare me down.

Finally, he picked up the phone, his deliberate movements indicating that it was so heavy he could barely lift it. After punching in a few numbers, he drawled, "Hey, Joe. I got a Jessica Popper—a *Dr.* Jessica Popper—who wants to see Lieutenant Falcone. *No,* I'm not pullin' your leg. Dr. Popper. *Not* Pepper, *Popper.* Uh-huh ... uh-huh ... Thanks, Joe. Later."

As he hung up, he returned his attention to me. "He's in a meeting. You're gonna have to make an appointment. Here, I'll write down the number—"

"I already have the number," I interrupted. "Listen, this is really important. I have to talk to him *now.*"

"Look, lady, I can't help you."

"But you don't understand! Somebody's been killing animals! First a mouse, then a rat, now a cat—"

"You want Animal Control, not Homicide. The lieutenant can't help you with that."

"But there's more to it! Whoever is killing these animals is sending me a warning! A *threat*! And it was probably because he was the person who murdered Devon Barnett!"

The desk sergeant sighed tiredly. "Look, I don't care if

the guy whose buggin' you killed Jimmy Hoffa. You *still* gotta make an appointment."

"If I had time, I'd be happy to—"

" 'Night, Lieutenant," I heard somebody behind me say. "Have a good one."

I whirled around in time to see a short man with the posture of a four-star general ease out of the building through the revolving door. The arrogant way he carried himself, combined with his slick black hair and the equally slick fabric of his blazer, told me I'd struck gold.

"Lieutenant Falcone!" I cried, running after him.

By the time I made it through the revolving door, he was halfway across the parking lot. He was pretty fast, for such a little guy. I dashed after him, almost catching up with him as he neared a dark blue Crown Victoria parked in the back corner of the lot.

I was about to call out his name, when he turned sharply and reached beneath the fabric of his double-breasted jacket. As he did, I caught sight of the leather shoulder holster he wore underneath.

"Don't shoot me!" I cried instinctively, holding out both hands. "I just want to talk to you!"

"Instinct," he returned, looking me over before dropping his hand. Both his facial expression and his body posture relaxed. "Don't you know better than to sneak up on somebody like that—especially somebody with a gun?"

"Sorry," I said with an apologetic shrug.

He peered at me suspiciously through narrowed eyes. Up close, I could see they were as dark and shiny as two black olives. "Who the hell are *you*?"

"My name is Jessica Popper. *Dr.* Jessica Popper."

He didn't react, a sign that he'd never been told about the phone message I'd left earlier. Either that or he had a very short memory.

"I've been trying to get in touch with you," I continued. "I have something important to discuss."

"Call my office," he returned gruffly. "Make an appointment."

He turned and strode toward the four-door sedan. I darted after him.

"I've already tried calling your office," I countered. "They blew me off." I paused a moment for dramatic effect, then added, "For a Homicide Department, they don't seem very interested in the fact that someone's been murdered."

He stopped short next to the driver's side of his Ford. Eyeing me skeptically, he repeated, " 'Murdered'?"

"That's right." I stood up a little straighter, encouraged by having finally gotten his attention. I was surprised to discover that I towered at least three inches above him. "Devon Barnett? The photographer who was killed on the East End?"

"His death was determined to be accidental."

"I have evidence that proves otherwise."

The word "evidence" worked like magic. "What evidence?" Glancing at his watch, he added, "And this better be good. I got a press conference in twenty minutes. ABC is supposed to be there!"

I took a deep breath. "The man who installed the ice sculpture that fell on Barnett, Gary Frye, swears he strung wires behind it to hold it in place. The Tuesday after the murder, I searched the crime scene and found a piece of wire hidden in the grass, which corroborates his claim. Look, the simple fact is that the only way that block of ice could have fallen was if someone deliberately cut the wires and gave it a shove."

Lieutenant Falcone's tiny eyes narrowed into slits again. "Go on."

"And it just so happens that I'm an eyewitness."

"To a murder? You saw it?"

"Well...not exactly." I steadied myself, having just noticed that I was squirming. "Actually, what I saw was somebody lurking in the gazebo where the ice sculpture had been set up, right before it fell on Barnett and killed him. Nobody was supposed to be in there. It was pretty dark, and—"

"Let me make sure I got this right," Lieutenant Falcone interrupted. His sarcastic tone told me I wasn't going to like whatever came next. "First of all, you got a guy who's probably about to get sued up the—up the *kazoo*, swearing on his life that it wasn't his fault that a ton of ice fell on Barnett and killed him. And you're sure he's telling the truth because the next day—two days later what, twenty-four, thirty-six hours after—you go to the crime scene and there just *happens* to be a piece of wire, right where you can find it. Then I got you, my 'eyewitness,' telling me that you're sure it was murder because you saw somebody standing next to the *food table*?"

"You're twisting the meaning of my words," I countered. But while I did my best to sound forceful, I could see where this was leading.

To a dead end.

I decided to forge ahead anyway. "There's something else. I've been poking around a little bit, asking questions, to see if I could find out who's responsible for Devon Barnett's murder. And somebody's been trying to scare me off the case."

"Yeah? Like how?"

"Like leaving dead animals for me to find, animals that had their throats cut. First a mouse, then a rat..." I paused to catch my breath. "And just a while ago, I found a feral cat that's been prowling around the neighborhood, dead on my doorstep."

His dark eyes cut through me like daggers. "A couple of dead rodents? *That's* why you're convinced the person you saw sneaking a couple of crackers murdered Barnett?"

"And a dead cat," I persisted.

"Have you talked to the local police about this . . . *theory* of yours?" Falcone asked.

I hesitated. "They weren't very interested."

Falcone opened the car door with an angry jerking motion. "I got no patience with people who waste my time," he said curtly. "As far as your claim that Barnett was murdered, all I can say is that the East Brompton Police know what they're doing. So does the medical examiner. These guys know the difference between a murder and an accident. The Barnett case is *closed*."

He slammed his car door, turned his key in the ignition, and rolled down the window a couple of inches. "Like I said, Dr. Popper, if you come up with anything solid—about this murder or any other murder—just call my office." He reached into his pocket and pulled out a business card, then handed it to me through the window. "If you ever get to that point, I'll be happy to listen."

I watched him drive off, standing alone in the parking lot and clutching his card in my hand. At least he remembered my name, I thought morosely.

It didn't make me feel any better. While Lieutenant Falcone now knew who Dr. Jessica Popper was, he was convinced she was a total flake.

# Chapter 14

"Our perfect companions never have fewer than four feet."

—Colette

I stopped at the guesthouse to pick up Max and Lou before heading over to Kara's, figuring that a "playdate" with Anastasia would do them good. They were strangely subdued, as if they sensed how distraught I was, not only over the most recent addition to the threats someone was making, but by Falcone's refusal to take them—or me—seriously.

Ten minutes later, the three of us drove along Sand Dune Road, peering at house numbers. I rolled down the car windows so we could breathe in the fresh sea air. When I spotted the address that matched the one she'd written down for me, I was surprised. I'd expected Kara Liebling's summer retreat to be just like its owner: cool, sophisticated, and extraordinarily pretty. Yet the section that faced the street was nothing more than a solid wall of rough-hewn wood, with few windows. In fact, the most remarkable thing about it was how *unremarkable* it was.

"Kind of modest, don't you think?" I asked Max and Lou, who were sitting on the seat beside me.

But the smell of the salty sea air had energized them. They were already shifting into higher gear in anticipation of another romp at the beach. I was beginning to worry that they were getting spoiled. Of course, that was the danger of being in the Bromptons. Just being amid such wealth and privilege exposed you to a lifestyle more luxurious than anything you'd ever dreamed of. At first, it was startling. But it sure didn't take long to get used to it.

It wasn't until I pulled my van up alongside the house that I understood the appeal of Kara's oceanside hideaway. The multileveled structure, a Chinese puzzle of decks and balconies, sat right on the beach, offering a view of the Atlantic and a stretch of pearl-white sand that literally made me gasp. And the back and sides of the building were made almost entirely of glass, so that the spectacular view was actually part of the décor.

I opened the car door to climb out—and nearly *fell* out as Max and Lou pushed their way ahead of me. They leaped around the driveway, barking wildly.

"Quiet, Lou!" I commanded. "Max, calm down!"

They just ignored me, sniffing every surface within reach. And then I saw the cause of their temporary insanity: a large white Abyssinian, draped across the top of a low stone fence, surveying the canine interlopers with distrust.

"Come on, you two," I said impatiently, grabbing their collars and dragging them away. "I don't think that cat is interested in making any new friends today."

As we neared the house, the dogs strained toward a path that ran alongside it, leading to the beach. This time, I let them run free. They loped toward the endless stretch of sand, still barking their heads off. I was pleased to see they were taking full advantage of our seaside visit.

"Knock, knock!" I yelled as I tromped up a wooden staircase. It led to a deck that swept across the entire back of the house. "Anybody home?"

The sliding glass doors opened and Kara poked her head out. "You made it! Come on up, Jessie."

As Kara stepped out onto the porch, I saw that she was still dressed in the same casual outfit she'd been wearing in the supermarket parking lot. But even in loose-fitting capris, a simple tank top, and canvas sneakers that looked as if they'd taken a few too many trips around the block, she managed to look as if she'd just stepped off a magazine cover—or off the poster for one of her blockbuster movies. An ocean breeze blew a strand of pale blonde hair across her face, and her eyes were as blue as the sea. Her delicate features and pale, perfect skin gave her the look of a porcelain doll. It was no wonder half the men in America were in love with her.

Anastasia came bounding out from behind her, scurrying down the wooden steps with amazing agility. She headed toward Max and Lou, barking her greeting. Within seconds the three of them were running around in circles on the sand, yelping excitedly as they played a canine version of tag.

Kara smiled. Gesturing in their direction, she said, "Want to join them for an invigorating game of Frisbee?"

"Thanks, but right now, Frisbee sounds a little strenuous." I didn't bother to explain that I'd had what most people would characterize as a trying day. "I think I'd just like to sit in one of those deck chairs and take in this incredible view."

She smiled. "It *is* nice, isn't it? It's the main reason I bought the house. These huge windows make me feel as if I'm actually part of all this, instead of just some bystander. If it weren't for the time I spend here during the summer, I don't know how I'd cope with all the stress of the other nine or ten months of the year. I think of this beach house as my own personal spa. Just being here is magical." As if to demonstrate, Kara lowered herself gracefully onto the wooden lounge chair next to me. With a dramatic sigh, she stretched out her long legs and leaned back.

"You're filming a new movie in the fall, aren't you?"

"*Day of the Unicorn*. I'll be playing Catherine the Great. Do you know much about her?"

"As a matter of fact, I have a cat named after her. But I don't know all that much, aside from the fact that she was one of the strongest, most powerful women in history."

"It's truly the role of a lifetime. I still can't believe I got the part." Grimacing, she added, "Of course, that's the upside. The downside is that I'm ridiculously nervous about how it's going to be received. My plan is to spend the next couple of months relaxing so I can really focus on the role when I go back to California in September."

I nodded. "My boyfriend's doing the exact same thing. He's starting law school in the fall, and he plans to take a few weeks off in August to relax before jumping in with both feet."

"You mean he's not a veterinarian, like you?"

"He's a private investigator."

"How fascinating!" Kara exclaimed. "What does he investigate?"

"He handles all kinds of cases. Missing persons, background checks on employees, insurance fraud . . . A lot of his cases are domestic: trying to find out if a spouse who's been acting suspiciously is having an affair, that kind of thing."

"That must be interesting."

"Actually, it's not nearly as exciting as they make it look in the movies. Most of what he does is pretty routine. Which is one of the main reasons he's going back to school. He wants to do something more challenging."

"He seems to have a good head on his shoulders."

"Yeah," I said thoughtfully. "Nick's pretty great."

"Then you're very lucky."

"How about you, Kara? If you don't mind me asking, I mean."

She hesitated before replying, "There's no one special in my life. At least, not now. Not since Shawn." Her tone had become wistful. "For almost a year, Shawn and I were practically the poster children for romance. Our pictures were everywhere: holding hands at the Academy Awards, kissing at Spago . . . We were America's darlings. Except, instead of it just being for the sake of publicity, it was *real*. At least, I thought so. I still think it was real— at least, up until the end. We were madly, desperately in love, and I was convinced I'd finally found my soul mate. I believed he felt the same way. That's certainly what he told me at the time."

She paused, as if she were picturing it all in her mind. I sat in silence, knowing that there was a great big "but" coming.

"But then . . . then he changed. He started acting different. Showing up late, not picking up the phone when I called, even though I was positive he was home . . . I was beside myself. I could feel him growing more and more distant, and I just assumed I was doing something to make him react that way. I tried being more affectionate, I tried giving him more space . . . but nothing I did seemed to make any difference." Her voice choked with pain, she added, "I knew I was losing him, but I couldn't understand why."

She lapsed into silence. I was trying to think of something sympathetic to say, when she said, "It was Devon Barnett who solved the puzzle for me."

I sat up straighter at the mention of the paparazzo's name. "Devon Barnett?"

Kara nodded. "It's hard to believe anyone could owe

that man anything, isn't it? But thanks to him, I finally found out what was going on—along with everybody else who reads the tabloids. I was clued in the week of the Cannes Film Festival, when Shawn flew to Europe to promote his new movie. I was making an independent film, so I stayed behind. Three days after he left, there it was, right on the front page of the *Stargazer:* a photograph of Shawn and ... and another woman, lying on the beach at Cannes. She was wearing this teensy little bikini, and his hands were all over her, and his tongue was halfway down her throat...." Her voice broke off with a choking sound.

"Oh, Kara," I said, my voice nearly a whisper. "How awful for you. And what a way to find out!"

"Like I said, I really owed Barnett. If it weren't for him, I would have made an even bigger fool of myself by letting Shawn two-time me indefinitely." She looked over at me, her eyes clouded. "And that's the story of Kara Liebling's broken heart. One more reason I was so looking forward to a quiet summer here at the beach house. At least, that was the plan. But it seems as if I can't get away from my past. Wherever I go, I run into Shawn."

"It does seem like it's an awfully small world out here," I commented sympathetically. "Everybody seems to know everybody else." And to have some past entanglement with them, I thought.

Kara had become silent again. It seemed like the perfect time to do a little digging—digging that had nothing to do with all the sand stretching out before me. "Speaking of Devon Barnettt," I said, trying to sound casual, "I know you're close to Chess, but what about Dev? Did you know him well, too?"

Kara thought for a few seconds, her perfectly smooth forehead wrinkling pensively. "I never got to know Devon as well as I would have liked. He was away so much of the time—or at least, busy with other things.

The man had unlimited energy, and he was on the go constantly. In fact, that's the main reason Chess and I became such good friends. We were both alone, so naturally we just gravitated toward each other. But Devon was always a bit of a mystery to me."

She smiled sadly. "It's hard to understand why someone would choose to make a living that way: following celebrities around, waiting endlessly outside clubs and in parking garages, hoping to snap a few pictures... Frankly, it sounds like a boring, *lonely* way to spend your time. Even worse than sitting around, waiting for your boyfriend to come home from film festivals."

Kara sat up abruptly. "Will you listen to me, going on like this? I'm sure you didn't come over so you could listen to me cry on your shoulder. And I just realized that I never even offered you something to drink. What would you like, Jessie? I've got lemonade, orange juice...."

The rest of our visit was considerably more upbeat. Kara entertained me by telling me stories about shooting on location in remote spots where the insects were as big as birds, filming scenes in a winter coat and mittens even though the temperature topped 110°, and getting up at four A.M. to endure two excruciating hours of hair and makeup. My short stay in the Bromptons was certainly making me appreciate my own life.

As Lou and I drove away, I mulled over the different impression I'd gotten of Kara, now that I'd had the chance to spend some time with her. It stood in such sharp contrast to the chilling report Shawn had given me. He'd insisted that she was unstable, going so far as to describe her as a "nutcase."

Does that other side of Kara Liebling really exist? I wondered. Or was Shawn just portraying her that way to convince *me* that she wasn't as sweet—or as stable—as she seemed? And if that's the case, *why*?

The possibility that Shawn was trying to create doubts

in my mind about Kara Liebling's stability could have had more to do with him than with Kara. I found myself wondering if he was simply trying to make *her* look like a suspect in order to divert suspicion away from himself.

• • •

"No new developments?" I asked Nick anxiously as soon as I got back to the guesthouse.

The despondent look on his face gave me my answer.

This much was clear: while the person I believed to be Devon Barnett's killer was trying damned hard to scare me off the case, even going so far as to kill innocent animals, I'd only become even more determined than ever to see this thing through. My mind was running on fast-forward. Tomorrow, Friday, was the last day of the dog show. I had a lot of ground to cover, and I wouldn't be able to do it if I was standing next to a giant tick, answering questions about heartworm. It was time to call in the reserves.

I dialed the familiar number on my cell phone.

"Scruggs here."

"Marcus! I'm so glad I got you!" Words I never thought I'd utter. "I need a favor."

"Wait a minute. I thought coming to meet your friend for dinner tomorrow night was the favor."

"Yes, but this one's more of a favor to *you*. It's your big chance to meet those actresses and supermodels you've been obsessing about."

*"Supermodels?"*

I'd clearly gotten his attention. "Tomorrow's the last day of the dog show, and I need a stand-in at the 'Ask The Vet' booth. You were already planning to come out to the East End. Besides, you'll meet more gorgeous, attention-starved females than you'll know what to do with." You may meet a few of their owners, too, I thought.

"Okay, okay. I guess I owe it to the SPCA."

Not to mention your elevated testosterone level. "Thanks. You won't regret it. And Marcus? There's one woman in particular you should look out for. I have a feeling she's exactly your type, and that you two are really going to hit it off."

"Yeah?" I could hear the optimism in his voice. "What's her name?"

"Celia Cromworthy."

I didn't sleep very well that night. I tossed and turned as I struggled to make sense of the information I'd collected about the people who had known Devon Barnett—and who may have wanted him dead. An entire cast of characters starred in my ruminations. I pictured them all standing in a lineup, then focused on each of them, one at a time.

First of all, there was Chess. He occupied the number one spot. Not only were there signs of major conflict in his relationship with his lover, but he had a major skeleton in his closet—a skeleton that had once belonged to his teacher and very special friend.

Next came Hugo Fontana, whose career would have been destroyed if Barnett went public with the fact that the macho movie star was gay. Standing right next to him was Russell Bolger, whose movie production company was likely to fold if the Pulverizer was ever outed. Phyllis Beckwith was wedged in there, too. She was loyal to Bolger because he had helped her get her start in the catering business. If Barnett had been on the verge of telling the world Hugo's secret, how far would she have gone to protect Bolger and his baby, North Star Studios?

Sydney Hornsby Barnett, a.k.a. Sizzle, came next. She stood to inherit a huge amount of money if Barnett died while he was still married to her. But if he'd been successful in getting the annulment he was seeking, she'd have been spit out of the marriage without a cent. On top of that was the fact that she had lied to me about being out in the Bromptons the very night he was murdered.

Then there was Shawn, who was part of my lineup simply because he had hated Barnett so much. And I couldn't forget that Rufus *had* been near the scene of the crime—even if I knew he couldn't have been responsible for Barnett's demise. Even Hilda was a suspect—mainly because of the way she crept around his house in her gigantic Nikes, a mysterious presence who always seemed to be looming in the background.

Of course, I also had to consider everyone else I'd met in the Bromptons. Even someone like Gary Frye could have had a vendetta against Barnett—and he certainly had the access and know-how to use an ice sculpture as a murder weapon. But there were also hundreds of other people who had known and hated Barnett, victims of his merciless lens who might have been at the party that night—and who could have iced the unethical paparazzo.

As I lay in the dark, I also examined the bits and pieces of information I'd acquired about Barnett himself. His secret rendezvous a few nights before his murder, his sudden plans to buy a vacation house in the South of France, the shoebox full of cash he kept stashed in his closet...I was convinced he'd been involved in something besides snapping photographs of celebrities and selling them to tabloids. I was becoming increasingly certain that the basement he was so meticulous about keeping locked was a very good place to find out what that "something" was.

I was also aware that I was running out of time. Sunday afternoon's luncheon and video screening marked the end of the dog show. After that, I'd be on my way home to Joshua's Hollow and back to my usual busy schedule. Investigating Barnett's death while I was in the Bromptons had been difficult enough. Once I was an hour and a half away, continuing would be close to impossible. If I was going to identify the murderer and gather enough evidence to convince Lieutenant Falcone that I'd solved the crime, I had a little more than two days left to do it.

It was no wonder I couldn't sleep.

• • •

First thing the next morning, even before Nick was awake, I left the dogs nestled against him in bed and headed over to Ice Castles. I was anxious to talk to Gary Frye again, to see if he had learned anything new about Devon Barnett's death. As I pulled my van into his parking lot, I was struck by the fact that something felt different this time. Only two or three cars were parked outside, and the area had the desolate feeling of a ghost town.

I knocked on the door, meanwhile peering through the small window. I saw Gary inside, sitting at his desk and talking on the phone. He gestured for me to come inside.

"Yes, Mrs. Donner, I understand that you're concerned. But let me assure you that—*cancel*? Well, it's a little late for that. If you look at the contract you signed when you first engaged Ice Castles' services for Brittany's birthday party ... Yes, there *is* a cancellation clause, but if you look at the date, I believe you'll see that it's already passed.... Mrs. Donner? Hello, Mrs. Donner? ..."

Gary slammed down the phone, yelling *"Damn* it!" He took a long breath, meanwhile staring at the offending piece of machinery. When he finally glanced up at me, he was scowling.

"Wanna buy a six-foot ballerina made of ice—*cheap*?"

"I'm afraid not," I replied apologetically. Glancing at the white cat stretched across the windowsill, I added, "Actually, I stopped by to see how Lulu was doing."

"A hell of a lot better than I am." He picked up the thick wad of paper sitting in the middle of his desk. "I'm being sued."

I felt as if I'd just been punched in the stomach. "Gary, no!"

"Not that I'm surprised," he went on in a dull voice. "I've been waiting for this since the night it happened." He held up the front page of a document labeled *Chester Montgomery* v. *Gary Frye, Sole Proprietor, Ice Castles.*

"I've got insurance, of course," he continued, "so this probably won't ruin me financially. At least, in theory. The reality is that all the horrendous publicity will probably destroy my business. We've been getting cancellations all week, but in the back of my mind, I've been thinking I could always relocate and start over. But now—"

He sighed, a deep, exasperated sigh that made my heart wrench. "I don't suppose you know a good lawyer."

*Not yet,* I thought. *If only this could wait a few years.* For the first time, it occurred to me that maybe what Nick had chosen to do with his life wasn't so bad, after all.

"No, but I know a pretty good veterinarian: me. Let's have a look at Lulu. I can check her out right here."

"Be my guest."

I reached up and gently removed Lulu from what I gathered was her favorite spot.

"Hey, Lulu," I said softly, not certain of how she'd take to being disturbed. "You remember me, don't you? Thatta girl. I'm not going to hurt you. I just want to see if your eyes are doing any better."

Sure enough, the oxytetracycline HCL ointment seemed to be doing the trick. Lulu's ocular infection was on the mend.

"Lookin' good, Lulu," I informed her, largely for her

owner's benefit. I ran my hands along her sleek body, checking her internal organs. She seemed just fine.

"You've been giving her the doxycycline, right?" I asked Gary as I returned her to her lounging spot.

"Yeah," he replied sullenly.

"Good. Keep up with that until the bottle's empty, and continue putting the ointment on for a total of seven days. She'll be fine."

"Thanks, Dr. Popper. I know I'm not exactly jumping up and down with joy, but I appreciate all you've done."

"Glad I could help." I eyed the ominous stack of papers on Gary's desk. That, along with his grim expression, fueled my determination to do a lot more for him than take care of a simple eye infection.

• • •

Driving away from Gary's by way of downtown took me past East Brompton Green. Even from the road, I could see that swarms of eager participants and spectators had turned out to enjoy the dog show's final day.

I experienced a pang of guilt over the fact that having Marcus fill in for me meant that poor Emily was spending the day with him. I wondered what other difficulties she'd been forced to deal with, replaying all the references I'd heard about her mother being in rehabilitation. When I spotted an empty parking space a few hundred feet from the public library, I pulled in.

Entering the library, I discovered, was like taking a step back in time. The East Brompton Public Library was one of those institutions that hadn't changed much in over a century—thank goodness. Sure, computers had been added, and one small room was devoted entirely to CD's and DVD's. But it also had walls that were paneled in dark wood, overstuffed upholstered chairs ideal for curling up with a good book, and even a few stained-glass windows. A distinctive smell that could only be found in libraries—library paste, mixed with dust—permeated the air.

Since I didn't know my way around the East Brompton Library, I began by seeking out the reference librarian. The woman sitting behind the big, important-looking desk fit right in with her surroundings. Not only did she talk in whispers, but she wore her glasses on a chain around her neck. Her cheeks were gaunt and her mouth was permanently pursed, as if all those years of whispering "Sh-h-h!" had reshaped it.

"May I help you?" she asked, peering at me over the top of her eyeglass frames.

"I'm trying to find some fairly recent articles from *The New York Times* about a health-related incident involving the movie actress, Delilah Raines. I believe they'd have been published in the last month or so."

"Let me do a search." With crisp efficiency, she pushed her glasses into place and began punching keys on her computer's keyboard.

"Hmm...here we are. I think this is probably what you're looking for." She hit a few more keys, then pointed halfway across the room. "The printer is over there. The citations should be coming out shortly."

"Thank you." I was about to make a comment about the wonders of technology, when I realized this woman could have probably found the information I wanted just as quickly in the days of ink pots and quills.

By the time I reached the printer, it was already spewing out a page. I waited until it was completely finished, then grabbed it up and scanned the headlines in the six or seven citations.

I thought I knew exactly what I'd find. Instead, I let out a cry that sounded like one of Lou's yelps.

My heart was pounding as I made a beeline for the microfilm machine. I perused the orange storage boxes until I found the back editions I needed, threaded the first plastic reel into the machine, and watched page after page of the *Times* flash by in a blur. My head was spinning almost as fast.

I stopped the machine when it reached page one of the May 25 edition.

## ACTRESS ATTACKED OUTSIDE HOLLYWOOD CLUB

Hollywood, California—Actress Delilah Raines, the star of such blockbuster films as *The Hurricane* and *Jennie's Story,* was attacked by two men carrying large, blunt objects late last night while walking through a parking lot behind the trendy Café Au Lait, according to Sergeant Luis Rodriguez of the Los Angeles Police Department. The assault occurred at approximately 11:45 P.M., just after Raines left the club on Sunset Boulevard. Police said she was alone at the time of the incident.

The assailants repeatedly struck Raines on both legs after leaping out from behind parked cars as she neared her vehicle. A witness described the men as two white males over six feet tall. One had long, straight blond hair and was wearing blue jeans and a dark blue T-shirt. The other had short dark hair and a mustache, and was dressed in black pants and a black shirt. According to the witness, both men fled immediately after the attack, disappearing into an alley behind the club.

Raines, 37, of Brentwood, California, and Paris, France, sustained serious injuries on both legs. An orthopedic surgeon at Cedars-Sinai Hospital in Los Angeles, where she was transported by ambulance, said that X rays showed breakages in several bones, especially the left kneecap. She will require surgery, and a lengthy period of rehabilitation is expected.

While the Los Angeles Police Department has not released any information on the attackers' possible motives, a department spokesperson has announced that the identities of the two assailants are still unknown.

So I was dead wrong in assuming that Delilah Raines was in a drug or alcohol rehab center, I mused. She was brutally attacked, and she'd been undergoing physical rehabilitation.

The next article, from the May 30 edition, was further proof of my mistaken presumption.

## DELILAH RAINES ADMITTED TO LA JOLLA REHAB CENTER

La Jolla, California—Actress Delilah Raines was admitted to the La Jolla Rehabilitation Center earlier today, where she is expected to undergo several weeks of intensive physical therapy. Raines sustained serious injuries in both legs after two men attacked her in a parking lot outside a Hollywood club five days ago. A team of orthopedic surgeons at Cedars-Sinai Hospital in Los Angeles performed surgery later that day.

Although she left the hospital through a back entrance and was driven to La Jolla in a friend's car, a crowd of fans was waiting for her when she arrived at the medical facility. They carried banners that read "We love you, Delilah!" and "Get Well Fast!" The posh La Jolla Rehabilitation Center is a favorite with prominent sports figures and other celebrities who are undergoing rehabilitation following physical injuries.

Friends report that Raines has been suffering

from mild depression since the attack by the two assailants, whose identities are still unknown.

"Delilah wants her fans to know that she is looking forward to a speedy recovery," Raines' publicist, Sheila White of White & Forrest, said at a press conference yesterday. "She also wants to thank them for all their support."

Gigi Fitzgerald, a close friend, said, "Delilah keeps asking, 'Why would anyone do this?' Frankly, those of us who know and love her are asking the exact same question."

The Los Angeles Police Department is investigating all leads, including fan mail, said Deputy Chief William Santos. No suspects have been identified at this time.

The next article had run on June 3. I waited impatiently while the machine whirled away, then began devouring it the moment I located it.

## TWO MEN ARRESTED IN ASSAULT

Hollywood, California—A Hollywood bartender and an unemployed man with a criminal history were arrested yesterday and charged with attacking 37-year-old actress Delilah Raines.

Christopher Vale, 27, a bartender, and Richard Strathe, 33, both residents of Redondo Beach, were arrested in Santa Monica and charged with assault. The weapons the police believed were used in the attack against Raines, a wooden baseball bat and a tire iron, were found in the trunk of Strathe's car. Police believe the motive was robbery.

Vale and Strathe were arraigned this morning at the Santa Monica Courthouse. Bail was set at $50,000 cash, $100,000 bond.

The article continued, but I stopped reading. Instead, I concentrated on the photograph of the two handcuffed suspects, walking with their shoulders slumped and their heads down. The witness to the assault had given the police a good description. They were both hulking men, well over six feet tall. Christopher Vale did have long blond hair, although I would have described it as "scraggly." As for Strathe, his unruly dark hair and thick, uneven mustache gave him a look I would have summarized as "unkempt."

Poor Delilah—and poor Emily! I skimmed the rest of the articles, but learned little aside from the fact that Vale and Strathe were still awaiting trial. The articles about the two suspects kept getting smaller, and they kept appearing farther and farther back in the newspaper. There was nothing more about Delilah Raines.

Tucking the last reel back into its orange box, I pondered the fact that finally tracking down the truth about Emily's mother had helped me understand why she was in a rehabilitation center in California while her daughter was with her father, three thousand miles away. But my efforts hadn't done a thing to further my investigation of Devon Barnett's murder. I flipped off the machine and hurried back to my dogs, sorry I'd wasted my time.

# Chapter 15

"Dogs are not our whole life, but they make our lives whole."

—Roger Caras

My next stop was Chess's house. While I'd always found myself looking forward to chatting with him before, this time I was a little more wary—on four different counts. First, I was still reeling from what I'd learned about his past, courtesy of Ms. Pruitt of the Sweet Elm Public Library. Then there was my last visit, when I'd caught Chess with a shoebox full of cash. I still hadn't decided whether his apparent surprise was sincere—or merely another charade designed to conceal who Chess LaMont really was. Next, there was his lawsuit against Gary Frye, who I was convinced was innocent. I still didn't know Chess well enough to have a sense of whether he truly believed Gary was responsible or he was simply trying to cash in on his lover's demise.

Then there was the fact that he was still high on my list of suspects in Devon Barnett's murder.

I took a deep breath before ringing the bell of the sprawling Beach Street mansion. Not only was I worried about confronting Chess, but I was also braced against the possibility of another unpleasant encounter with Hilda.

This time, Chess flung open the door, cradling Zsa Zsa in his arms. His face lit up as soon as he saw it was me.

"Jessie, what a nice surprise!" he cooed.

"And having *you* answer the door is a nice surprise, too." I stepped inside, lowering my voice as I asked, "Is Hilda here?"

"I gave her the day off." Chess shuddered. "I told her she deserved a three-day weekend after such a trying week. But the truth is that I simply couldn't *stand* having her around anymore!" He beckoned for me to follow him into the kitchen. "That woman gives me the *creeps,* Jessie. I'm getting rid of her—as soon as I get up the nerve. From the way she reacted when I told her to take the day off, you'd think I'd banished her from the Garden of Eden, for heaven's sake! Doesn't she have a *life*? Isn't there *something* she'd rather be doing besides vacuuming up other people's dust and killing their imaginary germs?"

After putting Zsa Zsa on the floor, Chess poured us each a glass of iced tea, then joined me at the kitchen table. Staring into his boyish face made it difficult to believe he was capable of murder. I had to remind myself that I'd been wrong before.

"How have you been, Chess?" I asked earnestly.

I expected a diatribe on how deeply the grieving process was affecting him. Instead, he replied, "Jessie, the phone's been ringing constantly. I had no *idea* Nettie was so well-known!" From the way his eyes glittered, I got the weird feeling he was actually enjoying all the attention.

"Of course, the *Stargazer* and the *Gossip Gazette* both want to do big stories on him, since he was one of their favorite photographers," he gushed. "The *Stargazer* is even talking cover story! But I've also gotten calls from *People, USA Today*...I even heard from a British journalist who's considering writing a book about him! Can you *imagine*? He wants to call it something like, 'Devon Barnett: Snapshots from the Life of a Paparazzo.'" Chess made a grand sweeping motion with his hand to highlight the title. "I'd be in it, of course. In fact, the writer would practically move in here, interviewing me and looking through all our snapshots.... Isn't it exciting, Jessie? This could make me *famous*!"

"That's great," I responded, not sure I sounded any more enthusiastic than I felt. "Chess, there's something I'd like to talk to you about. I just came from the Ice Castles studio. I was talking to Gary Frye, and he mentioned—"

The temperature in the room instantly dropped about twenty degrees. "Jessie, how *could* you? That man is responsible for Nettie's death! Him, and that Shawn Elliot. If he'd managed to control that vile bulldog of his, Nettie would still be alive today. I'm suing both of them!"

"Gary's a client, Chess. I've been treating his cat for an eye infection. From talking to him, I'm convinced he's not at fault. And even the police were never one hundred percent certain that Rufus had anything to do with what happened. Would you at least hold off a little longer with the lawsuit?" I pleaded. "You're still in shock, for heaven's sake. You've got enough to deal with right now. Besides, you might feel differently in a few weeks. Why don't you let it go for now?"

Before he had a chance to answer, the shrill ringing of the phone interrupted us.

"I have to get that," Chess said, springing up from his chair. "It could be *anybody*." He flounced off to the next room, leaving me alone in the kitchen.

As I sat tapping the kitchen table distractedly, a colorful

swatch near the door caught my eye. I focused on the blur of yellows and oranges that, up to this point, had just been part of the scenery. A jolt shot through me as I realized what it was.

Hilda's apron. Hanging on a hook, unattended.

"Yes, of *course* I'm the person you should be speaking to," I heard Chess insisting in the next room. "I was closer to Devon Barnett than anyone else in the world...."

I glanced through the doorway, wanting to make sure he wasn't wandering from room to room as he held court on the cordless phone. He was nowhere in sight. I shot across the room and began patting down Hilda's apron.

One of the pockets was bulging. My heart began to race as I wondered if my hunch about what I'd just stumbled upon would prove correct.

"Of *course* I know the show," Chess was cooing. "I watch it every Sunday night."

Glancing around anxiously to make sure Chess wasn't lurking in the doorway, I plunged my hand into the apron pocket—and realized I'd struck gold. Actually, the metal I'd just found may have been worth a lot less than gold, but to me, the collection of keys bound together on a silver key ring was priceless.

Hilda's keys. Maybe my big chance to find out, once and for all, what was hidden away in Devon Barnett's locked basement.

" 'Overexposed: The Life and Death of a Paparazzo'?" I heard Chess gurgle. "Yes, it sounds like an *excellent* title. And when are you thinking of putting the segment on the air?"

By this point, my telltale heart was beating wildly. True, in the Edgar Allan Poe story, the troublemaker had been somebody *else's* heart—somebody dead. In this case, it was mine. Still, the last thing I wanted was to be done in by the *thump-thump-thump* that, to me, sounded as if it were being broadcast on Dolby sound.

I knew I had to act fast. I made a beeline for the locked basement door, my fingers curled tightly around Hilda's keys. I was pretty confident that Chess was too busy basking in his fifteen minutes of fame to check up on me. But I couldn't shake the creepy feeling that Hilda was going to appear at any second, coming up behind me in those big padded sneakers of hers.

With trembling hands, I tried fitting one of the keys into the lock. Not even close. I tried a second. Much to my surprise, it slid into the lock just fine. I drew in my breath sharply—but let it out again when the key wouldn't turn.

"I'm thinking of getting an agent," I heard Chess chirping in the next room. "Tell you what: Why don't you give me your number and I'll have my people call your people...."

I worked as fast as I could, even though my shaking hands put me at a disadvantage. I kept going, trying another key, then another...

I'd already gone through almost all of them with no success when I heard Chess say, "Thanks for calling. We'll be in touch!"

I was about to give up, but figured I'd try one more in the few seconds that remained before Chess reemerged. I inserted one last key into the lock, felt it slide in with ease, then tried to turn it.... My knees got weak as I felt the lock give way.

I heard footsteps. Chess was coming back.

I pulled the key off the ring and stuck it into the pocket of my shorts as I stepped through the short hallway, back into the kitchen, and returned Hilda's keys to her apron pocket. I'd found a way to get into Devon's locked studio. The clock was ticking, and this was my last hope for uncovering new information about what he might actually have been involved in—and whether it was something that may have brought about his demise.

All I needed now was an opportunity to use it.

• • •

As I drove away from Chess's house, I could feel the key to Devon Barnett's studio jabbing into my hip. I didn't even care that it was probably giving me a black-and-blue mark.

Having it in my possession fueled me with optimism over finding Barnett's murderer. I realized it was possible that Devon's insistence upon keeping his studio locked, could have been nothing more than another aspect of his passion for cleanliness. But it was equally possible that in finding the key to Devon's carefully guarded photography studio, I'd actually found the key to the paparazzo's murder. I tried to imagine what I might discover down there, picturing everything from pornographic photographs to human body parts, sealed up in Ziploc bags.

As soon as I turned the corner and was certain I was out of sight, I pulled over to the curb and dialed Norfolk County Homicide. But this time, I had something up my sleeve other than trying to convince Lieutenant Falcone that Barnett had been murdered.

"Homicide. Officer Bongiovanni speaking."

"Good mornin'. Mah name is Mary Louise Highland, and I work for a public relations firm—Louis Max Associates? I have a press release I'm about to send over to Lieutenant Falcone, inviting him to a charitable event in the Bromptons. We'd be *ever* so pleased if he'd join us. There'll be lots of press coverin' the event, not to mention celebrities like Hugo Fontana, Shawn Elliot, Kara Liebling..."

"I'll put him on."

"Wait! I don't really need to speak—"

I was gripped by anxiety when less than three seconds

later, I heard a familiar voice. "Lieutenant Falcone. How can I help you?"

He sounded a little friendlier than last time—probably because Bongiovanni had clued him in on the fact that he was being invited to a star-studded event that was bound to get an impressive amount of media coverage. Even so, I had no choice but to stick to my deep-fried, honey-coated Southern accent. The last thing I wanted was for Falcone to figure out who was *really* calling him.

"Good afternoon, Lieutenant," I cooed, stretching my words out so that I sounded like a contender for the Miss Alabama title. "Mah name is Mary Louise Highland. I'm with the public relations firm Louis Max Associates, here in New Yoke City?"

"Sure," Falcone said heartily. "I've heard of them. Good agency."

It's true that no one's ever said a bad word about us, I thought wryly. "I'm callin' to tell you about an event we have scheduled out in the Bromptons this Sunday. It's a luncheon at Russell Bolger's house, the final event of the charity dog show that's been runnin' all week."

"I'm kind of busy this weekend—" he interrupted.

"So *many* local celebrities are goin' to be there—and of course, all the *media* from Long Island and New Yoke..."

I could practically hear him sit up straighter in his seat. "Media?" he repeated, his voice filled with reverence.

I'd clearly said the magic word. "ABC, NBC, CBS... even CNN. And we have a 'Maybe' from Regis—"

"What time did you say this lunch thing was?"

"One o'clock, at Russell Bolger's estate on Ocean Spray Drive. I'll fax you over a press release...."

I felt warm and fuzzy as I hung up the phone. I'd just taken a giant step toward putting all the pieces in place to present my evidence and expose the murderer to Lieutenant Falcone.

But the feeling faded as soon as I reminded myself that I didn't *know* who had killed Devon Barnett, much less have any evidence.

My next stop was Suzanne's office, where I'd have easy access to a computer and a fax machine. After assuring her she should feel free to ignore me, I typed up a one-page press release, using a flowery font to invent an address for the imaginary public relations firm Louis Max Associates.

*Louis Max Associates*
*255 Third Avenue*
*New York, New York 10025*

East Brompton, New York—Hugo Fontana, Shawn Elliot, and Kara Liebling are just a few of the stars who will light up the final event of the SPCA'S Funds for Our Furry Friends fund-raising dog show, a luncheon this Sunday at 1:00. The luncheon will be held at the home of Russell Bolger, president of North Star Studios, at 112 Ocean Spray Drive, East Brompton.

The gala will include the screening of a video made during the dog show, featuring such highlights as the Best of Breed and Best of Show competitions, plus interviews with many of the entrants' celebrity owners.

Along the bottom, I scrawled, "Hope you can make it! Besides ABC, CBS, NBC, and CNN, we now have a 'Probably' from Regis!"

I reread it several times to make sure it sounded professional, then pulled out a small white business card from my wallet. "Lieutenant Anthony Falcone, Chief of Homicide" it read, the embossed letters lined up evenly beneath the official Norfolk County seal. I located the fax number, punched it into the fax machine, and waited for the paper to feed.

"Fax is complete," the machine informed me in its robotic voice.

*Done,* I thought, experiencing a twinge of anxiety. It wasn't that I was worried about delivering what I'd promised Falcone—except the part about Regis, which was completely made up. But I *was* concerned about whether or not I'd manage to come through on what I'd promised myself: using the occasion to resolve the mystery of Devon Barnett's murder.

I checked my watch and felt another flutter of fear in my stomach. I now had exactly forty-six hours—and the ticking of that imaginary clock was starting to give me a headache.

• • •

As I trundled along East Brompton Road, a shop I hadn't noticed before caught my eye. On impulse, I stepped on the brake, then eased into the next parking space I found.

I craned my neck and studied the sign above it more carefully. The word Giorgio's was written in large gold letters in an elaborately curving script. Underneath, smaller, easier-to-read letters spelled out, "Fine Italian Footwear."

"Time for some shopping," I muttered, opening the van door.

As I neared the store, I got a better look at the display window beneath the blue-and-white striped awning. From what I could see, Giorgio's specialized in high-heeled sandals, barely-there slips of shoes that were held on by narrow strips of supple leather. It wasn't until I ventured inside that I saw any price tags. Behind each pair of shoes on display was a white card not much bigger than a postage stamp, printed with the price. Without leaning over to study them, I could see that most of them had four digits on them—as in $1200 for the *faux* leopard skin and $1800 for the shiny gold.

The shop had the air of an expensive restaurant. Every element was elegant and understated, done entirely in subtle shades of beige that I suspected had names like Buff and Ecru. Plush upholstered chairs were clustered in five or six separate groupings, as if each and every customer was treated to a private consultation on how best to maximize the fashion potential of her feet. The carpeting—a shade I'd call sand—was so thick it probably made *every* pair of shoes feel comfortable. Then again, I thought, glancing at the flimsy bits of leather that passed for soles and the long, spindly heels that resembled nine-inch nails, maybe that was the idea.

Within seconds after I'd entered, a trim, well-groomed man emerged from out of nowhere. His hair, dark with dignified streaks of gray, looked perfectly cut, and his suit fitted him so well it had to have been custom-made. I was glad I'd left my two sidekicks home. I could picture them pouncing on the expensive leather sandals, mistaking them for chew toys.

"Good morning. I am Giorgio," the man greeted me in a thick continental accent. "How may I be of service today?"

I half-expected him to kiss my hand. Instead he gave a curt little bow. I was tempted to curtsy in return.

I decided not to waste this gentleman's time. Not when the Bromptons were undoubtedly filled with feet that were much more likely to benefit from Giorgio's podiatric expertise than mine.

"I'm not here about shoes," I began. "I mean, not to *buy* shoes." Especially since doing so would require taking on a second job, I thought. "I was wondering if you'd be kind enough to give me some information about a particular brand of shoe."

"Yes, of course." Giorgio gestured grandly toward the first cluster of chairs. "Please, sit down. Can I get you something? Coffee? Tea? How about a nice cappuccino?"

"Thanks, I'm fine." I did take him up on his offer to sit, however, and sank into one of the velvety chairs. It was so comfortable that I half-expected it to start vibrating. The only negative was that my half-sitting, half-lying position thrust my own feet into center stage. My shoes were a dramatic contrast to all the Cinderella slippers around me. My sturdy, practical sandals, designed for trekking in the Himalayas, looked as out of place as a plastic mug embossed with Ronald McDonald amid a display of Baccarat crystal.

If Giorgio noticed, he was much too polite to let on. Instead, he perched on the chair next to mine and focused on me as if I were the most fascinating creature in the universe. "Now, what brand of shoe are you interested in?" he asked.

"Have you ever heard of an Italian shoe designer named Emilio Fratelli?"

"But of course. His shoes were very much in style three or four years ago. Fratelli made a name for himself working for some of the best-known designers in Europe. Paris, Milano, all the top houses. Then he tried branching off on his own, but..."

Giorgio gave a little shrug, as if Emilio's foolhardiness were something that people in the shoe biz still gossiped about.

"What happened?" I prompted.

"At first, it looked as if he had a promising future as a designer. His shoes began gaining popularity because they were so distinctive. The designs themselves were simple. He started with comfortable shoes, the type someone would wear every day. Low-heeled pumps, espadrilles, some athletic footwear, even loafers. But he added a special little touch to each one—a ribbon or some beading on the women's shoes. Tassels or even buttons on the men's. And he priced them high, very high. Of course, the materials he used were all of the very finest quality. Unfortunately, before long, his shoes got a reputation for being...how do you say, 'shoddy'? They did not hold up."

Giorgio shook his head sadly. "I believe his designs were good, but he had bad advice from his manufacturers. I seem to recall hearing something about a factory that was cutting corners to save money because of its own financial hardships. But people in the high-end shoe market are very unforgiving. Once they have paid one or two thousand dollars for a pair of shoes that lasts only a few weeks, they are not likely to buy shoes from that designer again. Emilio Fratelli was out of business in a matter of months. The last I heard, he was designing shoes for one of the big discount stores, working out of their headquarters in Des Moines."

"I see." I was already feeling deflated. While Giorgio's story might have made an interesting case study for students at the Harvard Business School, it didn't provide me with much insight. All I'd learned was that paying big bucks for designer shoes wasn't necessarily a guarantee of quality.

"Well, thank you for your time," I said politely, grabbing hold of the padded arms of the chair and pulling myself up. "And the information."

"I am sorry I could not be of more help, although I don't know exactly what you were hoping to learn."

"To tell you the truth," I told him sincerely, "I'm not sure, either."

"You are certain I cannot interest you in a cappuccino?"

"Thank you, but I've already taken up enough of your time."

I felt much more at ease the moment I walked out of the store. While having unlimited wealth at one's disposal no doubt had its rewards, being able to buy shoes that cost as much as a first-class ticket to Australia didn't impress me as one of them. I figured it was just as well that I was destined for a life of shopping at the outlet mall.

Of course, I was a little disappointed over not having found out anything particularly helpful. Then again, I'd been telling the truth when I'd told Giorgio I didn't exactly know what I was hoping to learn. But my short interview hadn't been a complete waste of time. At least I'd gained a new appreciation for my Himalayan trekkers.

# Chapter 16

"Not Carnegie, Vanderbilt, and Astor together could have raised money enough to buy a quarter share in my little dog."

—Ernest Thompson Seton

M y morning's errands completed, I retreated to the guesthouse. As I stepped out of the van my hand went automatically to the key I'd removed from Hilda's key ring earlier that day. It was still tucked into my shorts pocket.

But instead of feeling encouraged, I was filled with apprehension. I was running out of ideas, and the key was my last hope for solving the mystery of Devon Barnett's murder. The problem was, I was acting on nothing more than a hunch. My greatest fear was that the paparazzo's photography studio, like the truth behind Emily's mom's hospitalization, would turn out to be a dead end.

That is, *if* I ever found a way to sneak in.

As I neared the guesthouse, my heart sank at the sight of a white square of paper, wedged between the door and the jam. *What now?* I thought.

Fortunately, the note turned out to be from Nick. "Ran out to do a few quick errands. Dogs inside. Back soon. N.," I read. At the bottom, he'd scrawled "I love you," underlining the words three times.

"Glad I got you," a voice behind me said.

I turned, startled. Shawn was standing on the lawn, wearing a shiny black Speedo. Aside from the pair of shades and the fluffy white towel draped around his neck, that was *all* he was wearing.

"Oh, it's only you." Realizing how bad that probably sounded, I stammered, "I mean, it's only somebody I *know,* as opposed to somebody *frightening,* somebody who—you know what I mean, don't you?"

He frowned. "You seem really stressed, Jessie. Hey, why don't you put on a bathing suit and join me at the pool? It's such a great day, and you'll be leaving the day after tomorrow. Besides, you seem like you could use a break."

I opened my mouth to present him with my excuse. The problem was, I couldn't think of a single one. "Okay."

I took the dogs out for a quick walk, then headed into the bedroom. I wriggled into my bathing suit, then checked the mirror hanging above the white wicker dresser. Somehow, my two-piece suit seemed to have gotten tinier and more revealing since the last time I'd worn it.

*Stop,* I told myself firmly. There's a murderer at large; someone is sending you anonymous threats in the form of dead animals; Gary Frye is about to watch his ice-sculpting business go down the tubes; and you've got less than two days to set everything right before you go back home to all the demands of your real life. A plunging neckline is the *least* of your problems.

Still, I pulled on a big, baggy button-down shirt—one that just happened to belong to Nick.

"Come on, doggers," I said to my Dalmatian and my Westie while grabbing my cell phone, a towel, and a comb and tossing them into a tote bag. "We're going to a pool party." Max let out a shrill bark, while Lou wagged his tail hopefully before loping after me.

I found Shawn lying on a teak lounge chair, a glistening glass of lemonade in his hand. Rufus lay underneath, having zeroed in on the only shady spot around. The bulldog had flattened his stocky body so that his belly was pressed against the cool concrete. He thumped his tail at Max's and Lou's arrival, but didn't budge.

A second lounge chair was placed next to Shawn's, with a glass of lemonade waiting for me on a small table.

"Most people come to the Bromptons to relax," he greeted me with a grin. "Seems to me you've been doing anything *but.*"

"Believe it or not, relaxing was my original intention." Gingerly I sat on the lounge chair, tugging at the big shirt and wishing it were a little bigger. My dogs were busy sniffing Rufus as the three of them sized one another up.

"I know exactly what you need." Shawn leaped up, planted himself behind me, and put his hands around my neck.

I jumped. "What are you doing?"

"*Relax,* Jess! It's just a massage!"

"But—"

"I won't bite. Trust me."

I sat stiffly, irritated by the feeling of his strong fingers kneading my neck and shoulder muscles. But little by little, the motion began sending rivers of warmth through my tense upper body.

"There. I told you this would be good for you. In fact, why don't we flatten this thing out so you can lie down. . . ."

Before I had a chance to protest, Shawn lowered the back of the lounge chair. Then he motioned for me to lie on my stomach.

"I don't think—"

"You're always taking care of other people—and animals," he insisted. "Now it's your turn."

I realized I was acting ridiculous. Shawn was a friend, and he was only trying to help me unwind. Besides, he was right about me being tense. I hadn't even realized *how* tense until he'd started to undo some of the damage.

I even pulled off the shirt before lying down.

Shawn began working on me right away. He started by making small circles with his thumbs, up and down my spine. I could feel him gradually intensifying the pressure as my frozen muscles gave way. The warmth flowing through me was already reaching flood proportions.

"How am I doing so far?" he asked in a gentle voice. I just grunted. Despite my initial resistance, I was already so relaxed I didn't think I was capable of making my lips form an actual word.

"Boy, you're really tense. I can feel it in your muscles." Shawn's fingers dug harder as he worked out knots that were so deeply submerged I hadn't even realized they were there. "I guess taking it upon yourself to investigate a guy's murder is enough to do that, huh? Especially since I get the feeling Mick isn't all that supportive of what you're doing."

That's *Nick,* a little voice inside my head whispered. But I didn't bother to correct him. I was too busy luxuriating in the sensation of each of my neck muscles melting into mush. I closed my eyes, aware that I was sinking into such a relaxed state that I was practically in a trance.

"But I bet anything you'll find out who killed Barnett," he went on, using the same soothing tone. His hands were traveling lower and lower down my spine. "In fact, I have no doubt that you're one of those rare people who can pretty much accomplish anything you set your mind to."

As long as it doesn't require movement, I thought,

blissfully descending deeper and deeper into what could only be described as Nirvana.

"You know how special you are, don't you?"

My eyes flew open.

"*Relax*, Jess," Shawn insisted, chuckling. "I'm simply paying you a compliment."

I grunted again. At least, that's what I intended. Instead, I ended up making a noise that sounded dangerously like purring.

"Actually, now that I've got you here, I'll admit that I've been hoping to get you alone." His fingers had worked their way upward again, and were nearing the back of my neck. I could feel his thumbs making those delicious circles again. "There's something I want to say."

No tension this time. In fact, I was ready for more compliments. A whole stream of them, even. Like the massage, I was really getting into this.

"If things don't work out with Mick, I want you to promise you'll get in touch with me. I really care about you, Jessie. I don't know what you may have heard about me, but—"

"Stop!" I cried, flipping over like a seal and bolting upright. "You and I shouldn't be having this conversation!"

Shawn looked stricken—and completely embarrassed. He stood with his hands frozen in midair. "I—I'm sorry, Jessie. I didn't mean to . . . I just thought there was something kind of, I don't know, *special* between you and—"

"Don't even say it," I begged.

I glanced around nervously, wondering why this had turned out to be one of the few times Nick hadn't suddenly appeared without warning. Max sat up, the sudden change in mood instantly putting him on alert. Even Lou cocked his head questioningly.

"Am I wrong?" Shawn demanded. "Jessie, have I been misreading your signals all week?"

"Yes. I mean, no. I mean, I don't know, Shawn. But I do know I have to get out of here." I grabbed the big shirt—*Nick's* big shirt—and held it against my chest protectively. "Nick and I are . . . we're . . ."

"What, Jess? Madly in love? Engaged? On the verge of making a lifelong commitment to have and to hold, in sickness and in health?"

"Doing our best to make this work," I answered crisply. "And frankly, you're not helping!"

I flounced off, my two dogs trailing after me. My chest heaved with emotion, and for some ridiculous reason, my eyes were stinging.

That . . . that *playboy*, I thought angrily. Coming on to me like that . . .

But I knew perfectly well it wasn't Shawn who was to blame. It was me. He hadn't been misreading my signals. I really had been enjoying his company. And flirting with him. And maybe even having thoughts about . . . well, thoughts I shouldn't have been having.

Then again, I reminded myself, Nick hadn't exactly been what you'd call "supportive" lately.

The week had started out badly when he'd decided at the last minute that he wasn't even going to join me in the Bromptons. Next, even though I was clearly intrigued over the mystery behind Devon Barnett's death, he had done everything he could to discourage me. Then, of course, there was the childish way he'd reacted to Shawn. Not that his jealousy was completed unfounded. I couldn't deny that I'd developed a crush—a teeny, weeny one—on Shawn.

One thing was certain: It was time for another consultation with my expert on affairs of the heart.

•   •   •

As I strode across the immense lawn of Shawn's estate, I took my cell phone out of the tote bag and dialed.

"Betty? I hope I haven't caught you at a bad time."

"Of course not, Jessica. I'm always pleased to hear from you!" The warmth in Betty Vandervoort's tone told me how sincere she was. "And it's not a bad time at all. I was just having a lovely conversation with that charming parrot of yours."

"How is Prometheus?" I asked, suddenly missing him terribly.

"Couldn't be better. In fact, he's right here on my shoulder. Say hello to Jessica, Prometheus."

"Awk! Shake your booty, Mamma. Shake your booty!"

"Sounds like he's fallen in with a bad crowd," I commented, laughing. "Next thing I know, you'll be telling me Leilani has turned into a lounge lizard. What about Cat? Has she taken to hanging out on street corners?"

"She's not doing nearly as well as the others, poor thing," Betty replied seriously. "Her arthritis seems to be getting worse, Jessica. Right now, I've got her lying on the heating pad."

A flash of guilt shot through me. I wondered if I was suddenly getting all my priorities wrong. Leaving my poor pussycat behind while I went galavanting off to the Bromptons, getting massages from movie stars who whispered sweet nothings into my ear . . .

"But I have wonderful news!" she went on. "Remember the audition I told you about?"

I cringed. I'd completely forgotten—something else to feel guilty about. "Did you get the part you wanted?"

"I certainly did. You're talking to the latest addition to the Port Players! I got the role of Katalin, the condemned woman—exactly what I wanted."

"That's wonderful news!" I exclaimed. "Not that I'm the least bit surprised, of course."

"I'm going to have to brush up on my ballet, but that's part of the fun," she went on, sounding more and more excited. "I'm ready to expand as a performer, and this is the perfect opportunity. But what about *you*, Jessica?" Betty asked earnestly, reinforcing my belief that she was capable of reading minds.

I took a deep breath. "Remember that . . . that person I told you about? The one who's in the movies and—"

"I believe you're referring to the handsome Hollywood heartthrob who—as Prometheus would say—makes you want to 'shake your booty.' "

"That's the one. He just told me that if Nick and I ever break up, the first thing he wants me to do is call him."

"May I ask what the two of you were doing at the time?"

"Swimming," I answered quickly. "We were, uh, at his pool."

"I see." Betty hesitated. I could only imagine the picture she was conjuring up in her mind. Then again, whatever it was, it couldn't have been too far from the truth. "Jessica, I'm going to give you an assignment."

"You mean . . . like homework?"

"Exactly. You only have a little time left in the Bromptons, right?"

"We're coming home on Sunday."

"Then I want you to put aside some time between now and then to spend with Nick. And while the two of you are together, I want you to focus on all the things you like about him. All those little details that made you fall in love with him in the first place."

"Okay," I agreed. "Then what?"

"That's it, Jessica. That's the assignment."

It sounded too easy. But I knew Betty well enough to sense that what she was proposing had a lot more to it than met the eye.

"Sunday night," Betty went on, "when you're back in

Joshua's Hollow, you can come over and tell me what you discovered."

Not only do I have an assignment, I thought glumly as I hung up. There's going to be a quiz.

• • •

I was beginning to wonder if I'd bitten off more than I could chew. Having only a day and a half left to figure out who had murdered Devon Barnett was bad enough. Now, thanks to Betty, I was also supposed to make myself fall in love with Nick all over again.

Speaking of Nick, his car was nowhere in sight. Frowning, I glanced at my watch. He was late. I wasn't any happier than he was over the prospect of spending an entire evening stomaching Marcus Scruggs. But Suzanne was a good friend. I wasn't about to leave her to the wolves—and *especially* not to just one wolf.

"Here I'm trying to focus on all the things I love about Nick," I grumbled, "and he doesn't even have the decency to help me get through this evening."

Still muttering to myself, I marched inside, fed the dogs, and hurried into the shower. At least *one* of us could manage to be on time—and to look presentable.

As I yanked off the shower knobs, I heard the front door slam shut. *Nick's home,* I thought. *Finally.* I wrapped one towel around my dripping head and another around my damp torso, then stepped out of the bathroom, prepared to give him a lecture on the virtues of punctuality.

"Nick, where on earth *were* you? Have you forgotten that—"

I stopped dead in my tracks. No, Nick hadn't forgotten. No, he hadn't carelessly left me on my own to cope with Marcus's gushing hormones.

*Au contraire.*

Nick was decked out in a tuxedo. Not just any tux, either. If I remembered my movie trivia correctly, his suit looked a lot like the tux James Bond had made famous. Black vest, no cummerbund, smart black bow tie. With his lean frame, he looked as if he'd leaped off the cover of *GQ*.

As for his dark hair, it had been cut—and styled. From the looks of things, Nick had actually allowed someone to put gel in his hair. True, he had been known to flirt with hair products on rare occasions. But it wasn't something that came naturally—not to mention something he'd ever been particularly good at. This look definitely indicated professional intervention.

If I hadn't known better, I might have thought he'd also had his eyebrows tweezed.

Even the dogs seemed impressed. Max sniffed his pant leg respectfully, probably picking up on the scents of all the other individuals who'd worn that suit. Lou hung back, as if he wasn't quite sure this was the Nick he knew.

"*Wow!*" I finally uttered.

"I thought you'd be pleased." Nick looked uncharacteristically smug. "At least, I hoped you would."

"You look . . . *wow!*"

"You already said that." He grinned. "But please, feel free to say it as many times as you'd like."

As I walked over to him, I sniffed the air suspiciously. At first, I assumed I was just smelling the fragrance of his hair products. Then I realized it was cologne.

He'd really gone all out. And the fact that he was wearing a tux, just as Shawn had that first night, wasn't lost on me.

"I'm afraid to touch you," I told him.

"In that case, all this was a complete waste."

I laughed, then kissed him on the cheek. "I'll do my best to get past that," I assured him. "But first, we've got a serious social obligation ahead of us. I'll be ready in two minutes."

I dashed into the bedroom, towel-drying my hair and twisting it into a knot I hoped would pass for sophisticated. Then I pulled on the flowered sundress and high-heeled sandals that had prompted Devon Barnett to think I was "somebody"—however briefly.

When I stepped back into the living room, I got a pretty favorable reaction myself. Maybe Devon Barnett had decided I wasn't anybody. But Nick clearly felt otherwise. In fact, if we'd had another half hour or so before we were scheduled to meet Suzanne, there's no telling what would have become of his carefully gelled hairstyle.

"You're going to put Marcus to shame," I commented as the two of us drove to the restaurant.

"From what you've told me about him," Nick observed, "that doesn't sound very difficult."

That was true enough. It was also a reminder that while we looked as if we were both dressed to kill, we were actually in for a killer of an evening.

• • •

"Come on," I said with a sigh as we relinquished Nick's Maxima to an eager parking attendant. "Let's get this over with." My enthusiasm over Nick's conversion from Raggedy Andy to Prince Andrew was already fading. I was too busy bracing myself for the evening ahead.

Suzanne had chosen one of the Bromptons' trendiest restaurants for our rendezvous. As we headed inside, I remembered reading that it stood out from all the other chic, expensive eateries because of its Farmer in the Dell décor. In fact, it was housed in a building that had once been an actual barn. It still had the rough-hewn wooden walls, the cavernous ceilings, and—if I wasn't mistaken—the subtle smell of horse sweat and manure.

The prices, however, were definitely Bromptons-style.

The same went for the clientele, who were dressed for a night of Manhattan-style clubbing instead of a hoe-down. I was surrounded by so many designer labels I felt as if I'd wandered into the Academy Awards.

I spotted Suzanne perched on a banquette in the back corner, half-hidden by a haystack.

"Over here!" she called, waving madly.

As we neared the table, she added, "Do I look nervous? I sure *feel* nervous! Anyway, I'm glad you two could make it!"

"I don't recall being given a choice," Nick observed cheerfully, pulling out a chair.

My worst fears were being realized. Suzanne was dressed to the nines, a sure sign that she'd already made an emotional investment in the evening ahead. The thick waves of her flame-red hair curled around her face and shoulders voluptuously, and her cheeks were tinged with pink—maybe from too much blush, but more likely from excitement. Her round blue eyes were fringed with thick lashes that told me she'd gotten a little carried away with the mascara. The same went for her lipstick, a deep red shade that gave her full, sensual mouth the pouty look of a model.

But it was her dress that was the killer. It was a 21st century variation of the classic Little Black Dress, with the emphasis on "Little." In fact, it appeared to be modeled on those wide rubber bands that are frequently wrapped around the stems of broccoli. Suzanne's abundant curves tested the limits of the stretchy fabric, like a boa from Raffy's Reptile-A-Rama who'd just swallowed a large mammal. It also exposed enough thigh and cleavage that I seriously feared for Marcus's ability to remain in control.

"You look great!" I said sincerely as I sat down, my heart aching over all the effort she'd put into an evening that was guaranteed to disappoint her. "By the way, this is Nick. . . ."

"Hi, Nick." Suzanne didn't seem particularly interested in meeting my possible Mr. Right. She was too busy watching the restaurant's entrance for the person she seemed convinced would be hers. Her face lit up like Max's every time the door opened, then sagged with disappointment.

"Marcus is late," she moaned. She was clearly doing her best to act cheerful, but I could see that her ability to maintain a stiff upper lip was fading fast. "I hope he's not lost. Are you sure you gave him the right directions, Jess?"

My stomach churned with anger—anger that was directed more at myself than at Marcus. Why did I even *mention* him? I wondered. Why couldn't I have kept my big mouth shut, at least this once? . . .

"Oh, my God," Suzanne suddenly cried. "Is that him?"

I followed her gaze to the front door. There he was: the one and only Marcus Scruggs, striding in on long, gangly legs that reminded me of Lou's. For the occasion, he'd donned jeans, a white T-shirt, and what looked like a very expensive sports jacket. *Miami Vice,* a couple of decades too late. He kept running his fingers through his blond hair, cut so short it could be mistaken for stubble, in a pointless effort at grooming. In his other hand, he held a single red rose. The Marc Man clearly meant business.

Which was bound to be bad news. My heart sank. I glanced over at Nick, looking for some moral support. He didn't notice. He was too busy making a huge dent in the basket of rolls the waiter had just placed on our table.

"You must be Marcus," I heard Suzanne coo, using a voice I'd never heard emerge from her lips before.

"Well, *hell*-o, Suzanne Fox." Marcus, meanwhile, sounded like he was imitating a sleazy nightclub emcee.

As she stood up to give him a polite kiss on the cheek, he looked her up and down without the slightest trace of subtlety. "Whoa! Jessie said your name was Fox, but she forgot to tell me that you *are* a fox."

I suppressed the urge to groan. *I'm sorry, Suzanne,* I thought woefully. I am so, so sorry. . . .

"And Jessie forgot to tell *me* that *you're* an absolute *charmer!*"

My mouth fell open. I could hardly believe what I was witnessing. Suzanne, the serious, accomplished medical professional—someone with whom I had once mapped genes and agonized over matrix algebra—was giggling like a geisha girl.

"So tell me: What other attributes of yours did Jessie fail to mention?" Marcus asked, leering as he slid onto the banquette beside her.

Her cheeks flushed and her blue eyes gleaming, Suzanne countered, "I'm afraid you're going to have to find *that* out for yourself!"

I nearly fell off my chair.

I snuck another peek at Nick, curious to see if I was the only one who felt as if I'd just entered a parallel universe where everything was turned upside down. But he'd moved onto the crudités, looking as if he wasn't minding this half as much as he'd expected.

I wished I felt the same way. Instead, I let out a deep sigh, resolving myself to the fact that I was in for a long evening.

But at that point, I had no idea that the giggling, teasing, and knee-squeezing would turn out to be the least of it.

• • •

"Still afraid to touch me?" Nick murmured as we stumbled toward the guesthouse, draping his arm around me and drawing me close.

My head was spinning, no doubt the result of Marcus's insistence upon ordering a third bottle of wine. That, combined with the massive infusion of hormones that had permeated the air throughout dinner, made the idea of climbing into bed with Nick an exceptionally attractive proposition.

"Now that the social portion of the evening is over," I returned, "I don't have to worry about mussing your hair. As for untying that bow tie, I've been waiting for the chance to do that all evening."

Nick and I slid through the front door, glommed onto each other. Lou immediately bounded over, sticking his nose in my hand and, as usual, insisting on being the focus of my attention.

"I'll let the dogs out," I told Nick. "It'll only take a minute." I moved aside to let Lou out.

My Dalmatian just stood there, staring up at me anxiously.

"Great," I muttered. "Lou's suddenly decided he's afraid of the dark. And where's Max? What on earth has he gotten into?"

Lou barked, as if answering my question. Then he skittered around me in an agitated fashion.

"Quiet, Lou!" I ordered. "For goodness sake, where's Max. Max?"

I headed into the bedroom, impatient over my Westie's uncharacteristic lack of cooperation. It was late; I was tired; and all the wine I'd consumed as a way of getting myself through the unsavory evening had caused cobwebs to form in my brain. Wherever I went, Lou insisted on charging after me. I ignored him as I scanned the small bedroom, looking for Max. There was no sign of him.

"Max?" I called again, becoming increasingly frustrated. I strode into the kitchen, nearly tripping over Lou.

"Come *on*, Louie-Lou," I pleaded. "I really don't have time to—"

"Did you find him?" Nick asked.

"No. You haven't, either?"

I looked at Nick and saw the stricken look on his face.

"We have to find Max," I insisted, a flash of heat shooting through me. The cobwebs were gone. "Where is he?"

Lou barked again. I looked down, focusing on him for the first time since I'd gotten home. And realized he'd been acting strange from the moment I walked in.

"I'll look outside," Nick suggested, striding toward the door. "Maybe he got out."

"Max?" I cried, my eyes darting around the room. The feeling of panic was escalating. "Max? Where are you, Max?"

Lou barked once more, a sharp, staccato sound that cut right through me.

I went through the house once again, with Lou scrambling beside me everywhere I went. "Max?" I called again and again as I checked under the bed and in the closet. I even dropped to the floor to peer under the dresser. It was only three inches off the ground, a space that was much too small for a Westie to fit into. But I was growing increasingly desperate.

"Max? *Max?* Where *are* you?"

My voice had been growing more and more shrill as my feelings of panic escalated. At this point, I was practically shrieking.

Nick came back in, his expression pinched. I knew the results of his search without asking. I could no longer ignore what was obvious.

Max was missing.

# Chapter 17

"Man is an animal that makes bargains; no other animal does this—no dog exchanges bones with another."

—Adam Smith

A horrible sick feeling came over me, twisting my stomach into such tight knots I had to wrap my arms around my waist to keep from doubling over. My mind raced, as if a bizarre slide show was running out of control, flashing one horrific image after another on a screen. I pictured every mistreated animal I'd ever seen, from heartbreaking pictures in textbooks to emergency cases I had treated with my heart in my throat. Only this time, every one of those scenarios featured my precious Westie.

Interspersed among the slides I dredged up from my memory were more current shots: images of the dead animals that someone had left on my front porch. First the mouse, then the rat, then the cat . . .

"Oh, my God!" I gasped, blinking hard to stop the stinging in my eyes. The gesture didn't keep the tears from streaming down my face. *"Max!"*

A more rational voice emerged from my despair, trying to take over like a responsible parent. *You're jumping to conclusions,* the voice insisted. You don't know what actually happened. Maybe Max simply managed to escape from Shawn's property. Maybe he's running around the neighborhood, chasing squirrels and having the time of his life.

I darted out the front door, ignoring Nick's pleas that I stop a minute to think.

"Max!" I cried, sprinting across the lawn. Lou loped alongside me, barking furiously. "Maxie, where are you? Max, *please*!"

I ran blindly in the darkness, darting around without paying attention—until I turned abruptly and collided with something.

"Whoa, hold on!" Shawn cried, grasping me by my shoulders. "What's going on? I heard you out here, yelling your head off.... Are you okay, Jess?"

"No!" I returned. "My dog is missing! I'm afraid something awful has happened. I'm afraid that somebody—"

Shawn ran his hands up and down my bare arms. "Hey, he's probably just off sniffing around some female dog in the neighborhood. Chill!" The matter-of-factness of his tone, combined with his easy grin, only irritated me.

"But somebody's been killing animals! Somebody's been—"

"Hey, what's all this?" Shawn clutched my shoulders more tightly. "This isn't like you!"

"You don't understand!" I exclaimed. "I'm afraid somebody took him!"

"That doesn't make any sense," Shawn interjected. "I mean, who would—?"

"I hate to say this," Nick muttered, coming up behind us, "but you never should have gotten involved in Barnett's murder."

"Maybe." I swallowed hard. "But I thought I could handle it."

"*'Handle it!'* Jess, we're talking about *murder*! If you didn't learn anything the first time you were crazy enough to get involved in something like this—"

"You're really not helping, Nick," I shot back. "In fact, I probably should never even have told you about what I was doing in the first place. I guess this is what I get for thinking that maybe, just maybe, you'd actually *support* me—"

"Sounds like you two don't exactly have much of a communication thing going on," Shawn observed.

"Hey, can't you see the lady's upset?" Nick snapped.

"Sure," Shawn came back, "but it sounds like you've got some major issues. Like I said—"

"This is none of your damn business!" Nick took a step closer to Shawn. "If you had any sense, you'd keep your nose out of this—"

"If *I* had any sense! Seems to me *you're* the one who—"

"Do the two of you think you could control your testosterone for just a minute?" I shrieked. "My dog is *missing*! Max is *gone*! Isn't there anything we can do?"

The ringing of the phone inside the guesthouse shot through me like gunfire. I jerked my head in that direction, but stood frozen.

"Stay here," Nick said evenly. He sprinted inside, with Lou cantering beside him on his long, spindly legs. Shawn and I were left alone together on the lawn.

"If anything's happened to my dog..." I told Shawn. "I'm going to search every inch of the neighborhood. Maybe I've got this whole thing wrong. Maybe he's hurt, or lost, or ... or ..."

"I'll help," Shawn offered. "Want me to see if I can find a couple of flashlights?"

I didn't have a chance to answer. Nick was already

coming out of the guesthouse. He walked toward me with a determined stride, Lou still at his side.

It wasn't often that I saw Nick look shaken. So the expression on his face—and the way all the color had drained from it—set my heart pounding.

"Who was it?" I demanded.

"I'm not sure. All I heard was a tape."

"A tape?"

"Music. And then they hung up."

"What 'music,' Nick?" I asked, bracing myself.

He hesitated. "It was that old song, 'How Much is That Doggy in the Window?' "

"Hey, I know that one!" Shawn said brightly. "From when I was a kid. I remember the part about the 'waggily tail.' "

"Oh, my," I breathed. "How did they know the phone number?"

"Easy," Nick replied. "When they went in to get Max, they probably checked the phone. The number's written right on it."

"Sure," Shawn said. "Since I mainly use the place to put up friends, they have no way of knowing the number otherwise." He frowned. "Hey, what do you mean, 'When they went in to get Max?' Don't you guys keep the guesthouse locked?"

"We haven't bothered," I admitted. "The lock is so tricky, and we only have one key. . . ."

A lightbulb suddenly went on in my head. *The window!* I cried. "Maybe it's a clue!"

Nick put his arm around my shoulders. "I'll go inside with you to check."

*"A clue?"* Shawn seemed baffled. "What is this, some kind of game?"

Nick cast him a cold look. "Believe me, this is no game."

As I walked into the guesthouse with Nick on one side

of me and Lou on the other, I didn't know what I dreaded more: finding something or finding nothing. The same sick feeling still enveloped me, and terrible fantasies about what could have happened to my sweet Maxie played through my head.

Our first stop was the living room window. With shaking hands, I pulled back the curtain.

Nothing. Nick and I stared at the ordinary windowsill for a few seconds, studying it as if it were a fascinating painting.

"The kitchen," I suggested, my throat so dry it was difficult to utter even those few syllables.

Lou stuck close, following us the few steps it took to reach the next room. This time, Nick reached up above the sink, pushing away the cheerful flowered fabric. I was prepared to find the same empty windowsill we'd encountered in the living room. This time, we weren't as lucky.

The cry that escaped my lips sounded primal, a sound of deep and unchecked fear.

Max's collar. Sliced to shreds.

"It's gonna be okay, Jess," I heard Nick say. But he sounded far away as I reached up and grabbed hold of the revolting little surprise that had been left behind, just for me. I was also dimly aware of Lou, his barking now persistent and shrill.

I grasped the strip of red leather, just staring. Trying to process the fact that some despicable person had put a great deal of effort into slicing the thick piece of leather into ribbons—and trying *not* to think about what else that person might be capable of.

I was vaguely aware of the sound of heavy footsteps on the front porch.

"Hey, did you guys find anything? Or was that sick phone call just—*whoa*." Shawn stopped in his tracks. He leaned over to get a closer look at the mutilated remains of Max's collar that I still clutched in my hand. "Boy, somebody really got off on this!" he marveled. "Looks like they used a razor. Wow, it's like they're *deranged*!"

"You're not being very helpful," Nick told him sharply. "And Lou, be quiet!"

"It's okay," I insisted, my voice a hoarse whisper. "Shawn's right." I reached down to soothe Lou with my free hand, stroking his velvety ears the way he liked and pulling his head close so that it rested against my thigh. The motion seemed to calm him. I glanced down and saw him gazing up at me, looking mournful and confused.

"This is really creeping me out," Shawn continued. "I mean, this *is* my property. What if all this has something to do with *me*?"

"I don't think it has anything to do with you," I said in a low, even voice. "I think it's all about Devon Barnett's murder—and the fact that I've been trying to find out who's responsible."

"I get it," Shawn said, more to himself than to Nick or me. "Like somebody wants you to butt out."

"Exactly," Nick replied with surprising patience. "Somebody like the murderer."

Shawn nodded solemnly, as if he had developed new respect for the seriousness of the situation. "Listen, Jessie, if you want, I can put you in touch with a great bodyguard. A couple of them, in fact. I use them from time to time, like if I'm going to a premiere or a high-profile party. Believe me, there's nothing like some six-foot-three guy who weighs in at two-eighty and knows a few karate moves to keep things nice and peaceful. Just say the word."

"Thanks, Shawn," I said, and I meant it. It wasn't a bad suggestion. "I don't think I'm quite at that point yet, but—"

"Jess," Nick interjected, "I think that—maybe for the first time in his life—this guy's got a good idea."

"I'll keep it in mind," I assured them both. "But for now, I just want to..." I laughed hollowly. "To tell you the truth, I don't know *what* to do. I don't know where to begin, where to start looking—"

"Look, we've got to call the police again," Nick insisted. "It's one thing to dial nine-one-one to report that you can't find your dog. But it's something else entirely when somebody starts making anonymous phone calls—and leaving behind little 'gifts' designed to scare the shit out of you."

I simply nodded.

"In the meantime, I'll drive around the neighborhood. Max could still turn up."

"Okay," I agreed. "Thanks."

I made the call to the East Brompton Police, then waited an eternity until a uniformed cop showed up to take my statement. He looked a lot more impressed by the fact that Shawn Elliot was with me than he was by my claim that my dog had been kidnapped. Nick came home an hour later, reporting that he'd seen no sign of Max.

For the moment, at least, there was nothing else to be done.

• • •

I slept fitfully that night, enduring an endless stream of nightmares. In each one, I chased Max through various locations, ranging from endless stretches of barren land to East Brompton's chic downtown. I would catch a glimpse of him every now and then, just long enough to realize that no matter how fast I ran, the distance between us kept growing larger and larger.

I was actually glad when the shrill ringing of my cell phone dragged me out of my restless state of unconsciousness. But I was immediately swamped by anxiety—and the memory of what had happened the night before.

"Hello?" I gasped, my heart pounding at a sickening speed. I hoped against hope it was good news.

"Hey, Popper. It's the Marc Man."

My spirits plummeted. "Marcus?" I croaked. I glanced over at Nick, who was still snoring. Like me, he'd spent most of the night tossing and turning, and I didn't want to deprive him of whatever sleep he could grab. Then I checked Lou. Not only was he awake; he was watching me anxiously. A feeling of horror descended upon me with such force I was finding it difficult to breathe.

"Just calling to say thanks," he went on smoothly. "You know, Popper, you really did me a favor. Fixing me up with Foxy Suzanne was one of the best things anyone's ever done for me."

Given the fact that my Max was missing, celebrating my success as a matchmaker wasn't a very high priority. The fact that I'd regretted getting involved in the role of social director from the instant I'd first uttered his name only made the whole thing seem more irrelevant.

"Marcus, I didn't 'fix you up,'" I mumbled, rolling out of bed and moving into the living room. Lou padded after me, clearly not about to let me out of his sight. "I just happened to mention you to Suzanne in passing, and she—"

"Oh-h-h, Su-san-nah . . ." he began to croon. "I can't believe I'm going out with a fox!"

I sank onto the couch. "Marcus—"

"Der der der! Der der der!" Much to my horror, he'd started making weird sounds, doing a pathetic imitation of the late Jimi Hendrix's electric guitar. Lou's ears twitched, moving back and forth as he tried to process the odd noises coming through the phone. "*Fox-y ladeee...*"

"That's *Dr.* Fox!" I corrected him sharply. By this point, I was wide-awake. While Max's disappearance was first and foremost on my mind, I was starting to remember that there were other individuals I cared about—and that I was just as concerned about their well-being. "Listen to me, Marcus. Suzanne happens to be a very good friend of mine. She also happens to be at an extremely vulnerable point in her life right now. If I find out you've treated her badly—"

"The Marc Man—treat a foxy lady *badly*?" Marcus cried indignantly.

"You're not exactly Mr. Sensitive when it comes to the opposite sex," I pointed out.

"I'm a new man, Popper! I've *changed*!" Marcus sighed. "I never thought the day would come, but I believe that foxy lady has turned me into a one-woman man!"

At least, for *this* week, I thought grimly.

After he'd hung up—certain that the annoying beep that kept interrupting us was a call from Suzanne—I lay on the couch, the phone still in my hand as I stared at the ceiling, thinking. Even in the midst of everything else that was going on, I definitely had to make time for a woman-to-woman talk with Suzannne—the sooner, the better.

The opportunity arose more quickly than I expected.

"Jessie?" Suzanne asked in a squeaky voice after my cell phone rang a second time. "I didn't wake you, did I?"

Thanks, Marcus already took care of that, I thought. "Nope. I'm awake."

"Jessie, how can I ever thank you for introducing me to Marcus?" she cooed. "You never let on what a sweet guy he is!"

That was true enough. But it was probably because I

didn't generally classify character traits like an inability to raise one's eyes above a woman's chest long enough to make eye contact as "sweet."

"Suzanne," I said, trying to be delicate, "slow down. Are you sure you're reading him right? I've known Marcus for a few years now, and he's kind of a ... womanizer."

"Oh, he told me all about that after you and Nick left last night. We stayed at the Stable for a second cup of cappuccino."

*That* explained why sleep didn't seem to have been on the schedule for either of them.

"All that wild stuff is all in the past," she went on breezily. "The women, the outrageous parties, the kinky stuff ..."

My eyebrows shot up. Please, *please* don't say any more, I begged silently. *Especially* about the kinky stuff.

"I'm glad it's working out so well," I said quickly, anxious to cut her off. "I wish the two of you the best."

Once I finally managed to get her off the phone, I remained on the couch, fondling Lou's ears distractedly and trying not to let myself feel overwhelmed. Even though my head felt like the Long Island Rail Road was rumbling right through the middle of it, I forced myself to think.

Before, I'd felt pressured by the fact that I had only one day left to figure out who had murdered Devon Barnett. Now, I had that same pathetically small number of hours to find Max. I was convinced Barnett's murderer had taken my beloved dog as a last-ditch effort at scaring me off the case. Unless I figured out who that person was, I might never see my sweet little Westie again.

The thought was unimaginable. I had to get myself into fourth gear—fast. And that meant coffee.

• • •

As Lou and I drove to the Pampered Pantry in search of caffeine, the clock in my head was louder than ever. Instinctively, I reached down to touch the hard piece of metal in my pocket. I'd taken to carrying the key with me at all times so I'd be ready to sneak into Devon Barnett's basement whenever the opportunity arose. Now, with Max missing and finding the murderer my only chance for getting my dog back—hopefully unharmed—the need to find out what Barnett was so determined to keep hidden was more important than ever.

But I knew, deep down, that I'd never get that chance unless I figured out a way to set it up. The question was, how on *earth* would I manage to pull it off?

I was still wracking my brain, trying to come up with an answer, as I dragged myself into the Pampered Pantry. Lou, held captive in the van, whimpered loudly, reminding me to hurry. And I had every intention of getting in and out of there as fast as I could.

But when I stepped inside, I encountered a long line. While the Pampered Pantry had been nearly empty early on weekday mornings, the place was hopping on a Saturday. As I waited, I kept myself occupied by watching the frazzled young woman behind the counter, a girl who didn't look much older than Emily, struggle to keep the orders straight.

"Let me make sure I got this right," she said, frowning with concentration. "That was one decaf latte, one cappuccino with extra foam, one tea, and two chais?"

"For the third time," huffed a man in lime-green Bermuda shorts and an olive-green polo shirt embroidered with "Bromptons Golf Club," "that was a *regular* latte with *skim* milk, a *decaf* cappuccino with extra foam, and *three* chais. I thought you people were supposed to be professionals!"

By the time I reached the front of the line, I was almost as exasperated as she was. Still, I made a point of being polite to the flustered coffee girl. "Two coffees, please. Just regular old coffee."

"Excuse me," a woman who appeared from out of nowhere snapped. "I believe *I* was next. I need three cappuccinos and two lattes."

The young woman behind the counter cast me an apologetic look. I just shrugged and stepped aside to make way for the customer whose caffeine addiction appeared to be even more serious than mine. But the crazed atmosphere of the place was starting to get to me. As I waited amid more frothing and foaming and mixing and pouring, the tiny spark of anxiety I'd started carrying around with me wherever I went began escalating into panic.

I now had less than thirty hours before I left the Bromptons. And I still didn't have a plan for sneaking into Devon Barnett's basement.

I was agonizing over how I'd solve this seemingly unsurmountable problem when I was interrupted by a high-pitched voice calling, "Miss? Miss? Did you say you wanted tea or coffee?"

"Coffee," I replied, focusing on the girl behind the counter. "Not tea."

But saying those words had a remarkable effect on me. In fact, a lightbulb had just gone on somewhere in my brain—one that had the word "tea" written on it.

*Inspiration!* I thought, a sudden burst of optimism sending my heart pounding. If I can only get it to work....I hurried back to my van as quickly as I dared, given the fact that I was juggling two cups of dangerously hot coffee and a couple of croissants so light they were in danger of floating away.

As soon as I settled into the driver's seat and smothered Lou with enough affection to return him to relatively calm state, I pulled the business card Phyllis

Beckwith had given me out of my wallet and dialed the number of Foodies, Inc.

"*Please* be there," I muttered as I waited for an answer. "Saturday morning has got to be one of the busiest times in the catering business...."

"Foodies," a voice answered cheerfully.

"Phyllis Beckwith," I said, doing my best to sound important. "Just tell her Dr. Popper is calling."

I held my breath as I waited to see if I'd get her on the line. As soon as I heard, "Dr. Popper! How nice to hear from you!" I started breathing again.

"I'm glad you remember me," I said. I'd been counting on the fact that she'd seen dollar signs when she'd pictured that vegetarian buffet for an entire conference of veterinarians.

"Of *course* I remember you," Phyllis replied, her voice as sugary-sweet as Foodies' Mocha Crème Brûlée with Chocolate Almond Drizzle. "How could I forget a veterinarian who's capable of appreciating really fine cuisine? Now, what can I do for you?"

"Actually," I drawled, hoping against hope that my little scheme would work, "it's more a question of what I can do for *you*."

•  •  •

The good news was that Phyllis Beckwith took the bait. The bad news was that I was going to have to wait almost twelve hours before I'd have a chance to sneak into Devon Barnett's basement undetected. And *that* was assuming I managed to carry off the other details of my plan without a hitch.

As I opened the door to the guesthouse and heard the water running in the shower, I remembered Betty's assignment.

As if I didn't already have enough to deal with, I thought, my stomach fluttering with anxiety. But deep down, I felt guilty for shortchanging Nick. After all, this was supposed to be a vacation, a chance for the two of us to be together. Yet we'd ended up spending so little time together—and so much of it arguing.

Of course, since Max had vanished, *nothing* felt right.

Nick sauntered out of the bathroom, a large white towel wrapped around his waist. "Hi," he said, blinking. "You're back."

As I put breakfast on the kitchen table, I shook my head tiredly. "I feel so overwhelmed, Nick. I have to find Max. I feel like a piece of string that's been pulled tighter and tighter. . . ."

"Let's get out of here for a few hours," he suggested. "I know the perfect spot."

"But—"

"We've got the police looking for him, and I made a few calls around town while you were out." He came over and wrapped his arms around me. "I'm afraid there's nothing else for us to do right now, Jess. And I don't want that piece of string to snap."

I nodded, then buried my face in his shoulder.

We drove in silence to the stretch of beach we'd found the other night. Nick was right; it was the perfect spot. I knew we'd never manage to recapture the feeling of freedom and fun we'd experienced there before. But I was already looking forward to the chance to stretch out on the sand, enveloped by the warmth of the summer sun.

Even Lou relaxed, sunning himself on the edge of our towel as if he didn't dare go back home without working on his tan. Nick had brought his portable CD player, and his entourage of classic rock legends, everyone from Jimi Hendrix to Jimmy Page, kept us company.

The only one missing was Max. But I allowed myself to feel at least a little bit heartened for the first time since his disappearance. I now had a plan, and all the pieces were in place. All that remained was for me to pull the whole thing off without a hitch.

By late afternoon, we were famished. We drove around, looking for something to eat, passing up the chic restaurants until we found the right spot. Skipper's was right on the water, a ramshackle fish-and-chips establishment with weatherworn shingles that looked as if it was patronized by locals rather than Manhattan's A-list. We sat on the deck, shaded by a faded umbrella with a tired-looking fringe, scarfing down the best fried clams and fries we'd ever encountered. Lou loped around the sand, barking at the seagulls, but sounding more playful than threatening.

As we watched the sun head toward the water's edge, I forced myself to stop worrying about Max long enough to start making a mental list of the things that made Nick Burby special, all the little idiosyncrasies I'd observed throughout the day. The way that unruly lock of dead-straight hair kept falling into his eyes—and the nonchalant way he brushed it away. The way he hummed his favorite songs without even realizing he was doing it. The way he automatically took my hand whenever we walked side by side, as if touching me was as natural to him as breathing. The way he didn't mind that I reached over and picked French fries off his plate.

The list kept getting longer. In fact, I wasn't sure I'd be able to remember all of it by the time I saw Betty. But I realized that her intention hadn't been for me to tell *her*. It had been for me to tell *myself*.

As we got back to the guesthouse, I began checking my watch, counting the minutes until it was time for me to go to Chess and Devon's house.

I sank onto the couch, silently reviewing my strategy. Nick dropped down next to me. "So what are we doing tonight?" he asked.

"*Tonight?*" I repeated, surprised. Despite all the planning I'd done, I'd forgotten to include Nick in the equation.

"It *is* our last night in the Bromptons, after all. I was thinking you and I should do something special. Go to a really fancy restaurant, maybe, or take a moonlit walk on the beach. I know you can't stop worrying about Max, but..."

"There's, uh, something important I have to do tonight."

Nick shifted slightly, just enough that we were no longer pressed against each other.

"I don't suppose this has anything to do with that Shawn guy."

"*No,* it has to do with getting Max back." I twisted around so that I faced him. "Nick, I've got to solve Devon Barnett's murder. Don't you see, it's my only chance of getting Max back? I'm convinced that whoever killed Barnett took Max as a threat, a warning that I should butt out."

I braced myself for an argument. Instead, he nodded.

"What are you planning?"

"Something...important."

" 'Important.' " He frowned. "Does that mean 'dangerous,' by any chance?"

"Actually, it just means 'nosy.' I'll be fine. *Promise.*"

I was prepared to argue my case further. So I was dumbfounded when Nick said, "Anything I can do to help?"

I felt as if my heart were melting. I knew perfectly well how Nick felt about me investigating murders. The simple fact was that he was worried sick about me getting hurt—or worse.

Even though his disapproval irritated me to no end, in calmer, more logical moments, I was able to appreciate the sentiment behind it. But this time, Nick had gone beyond his instinctive concern for me. He knew exactly what was at stake here: Max. And knowing how much I loved my Westie, and how important it was for me to do whatever I could to get him back, he was willing to put his own fears aside to support me in what he knew really mattered to me.

"Thanks, Nick. I don't think so. But just asking is enough."

Okay, Betty, I thought. You've made your point. The playful lock of hair, the passion for classic rock . . . that's all well and good. Those endearing traits are what first attracted me to Nick.

But the fact that, deep down, Nick really understands me—and accepts me for who I am—is the thing that's really rare. That's what *keeps* us together.

I had a feeling I'd just earned myself an "A."

• • •

"Jessie! What a nice surprise!" Chess greeted me a few minutes later, standing in the doorway with Zsa Zsa in his arms.

He was dressed in a purple silk robe, as if he'd settled in for the evening. I experienced my first pangs of self-doubt since I'd come up with my plan for getting him out of the house. But I didn't let on.

"Chess, you'll never believe what happened this morning!" I gurgled as I barged inside. "I had a brainstorm, and . . . well, I hope you don't mind, but I set up a meeting for you with Phyllis Beckwith."

His eyes grew wide. "Phyllis Beckwith . . . of Foodies?"

I nodded. "I told her all about your spectacular iced tea and how much everyone just loves it, and suggested that she sample it herself. She's expecting you at her office at nine. She apologized for making it so late, but she couldn't fit you in until after she set up a dinner party for two hundred somewhere in Drooping Harbor. Anyway, I told her I couldn't promise, but I thought you might be willing to give her exclusive rights to your fabulous iced tea all summer—until you go national with it. Of course, I hinted about there being some serious competition." I named three of the other East End caterers I'd seen listed in the *Guide to the Bromptons,* including one whose ad had included a gushing quote from *Gourmet* magazine.

"Oh, my *God!*" Chess's hands flew to his cheeks. "I'm...I'm shaking all over, Jessie! You are such a dear! I *never* would have thought of something like that, but you're right: It *is* a brainstorm. I could become the talk of this town with my iced tea. And if someone with Phyllis Beckwith's reputation began featuring it at her affairs, there's no telling *where* it could go! Mrs. Fields, move over!"

"And this is the perfect time to strike, Chess," I added, urging him on. "You've already got the media calling you on the phone...even *People* and *USA Today.*"

Chess jeté'd over to the refrigerator. "Fortunately, I made a fresh pitcher a few hours ago. It's probably just cold enough." He took out the pitcher, wrapped both hands around it, and closed his eyes reverently. "Yes, yes...that feels about right. Oh, I hope I added just the right amount of mint. The *worst* thing I could do would be to make it too minty...."

"Let me taste it," I offered, my mind clicking away.

Chess poured me a tall glass from the large pitcher, then watched anxiously as I raised it to my lips.

"Perfect!" I pronounced.

"Oh, good!" Relief washed over his face. Still grasping the pitcher, he glanced around the kitchen. "Now what can I put this in? Something attractive, yet not too showy..."

Suddenly, he froze. "Oh, my God. Jessie, I just had the *perfect* idea for a name!"

I looked at him expectantly.

"*Chess-Tea!*"

Within ten minutes, Chess had found just the right container for his iced tea, changed his clothes, and doused his hair and body with a variety of scented products. As I watched him bustle around excitedly, sipping my tea slowly, I was pleased that in doing something to further my own cause, I'd also managed to do something good for Chess.

I had to remind myself that he might be a murderer.

"How do I look?" he asked, skipping into the kitchen. I surveyed his stylishly spiky hair, his bright Hawaiian shirt, and the hot pink Thermos he clutched possessively in his hands.

"Like the Donald Trump of iced tea," I said. "Chess, do you mind if I sit here for a few minutes and finish this?" I gestured toward my glass. "It's so good, I don't want it to go to waste. I'll lock up on my way out."

"Of course," he agreed. "Enjoy! And now I'm off. Oh, I'm a nervous wreck! Wish me luck . . ."

As soon as he left, I gulped down the rest of my iced tea and hurried over to the basement door. My heartbeat was racing, and the caffeine I'd just consumed had nothing to do with it.

*Please work,* I instructed the key I'd pulled from deep inside my pocket, suddenly afraid it had lost its magical ability to gain me entrance into Devon Barnett's secret world. I could feel the blood throbbing in my temples as I put the key into the lock and gave it a turn. The tumblers moved without hesitation, and the knob turned easily in my hand.

*There.* I'd done it. Now all that remained was to venture into Devon Barnett's private space to see what he'd been so determined to keep hidden from the rest of the world.

I opened the door wide and glanced at the small white Havanese who'd been watching me curiously. "Want to come, Zsa Zsa?"

She immediately backed away, making little whimpering sounds. Not a good sign, I decided.

I forged ahead anyway. I began creeping down the stairs, treading carefully in the dark and feeling my way by running my hand along the wall.

There has to be a light here *somewhere,* I thought, wondering why all those Nancy Drew mysteries I'd read hadn't taught me to carry a flashlight at all times.

Despite my growing frustration over not finding a switch, when my fingers finally brushed against one, my heart stopped. Horrifying images of what I might find locked away in Devon Barnett's basement flashed through my mind. Stacks of bodies, a windowless dungeon outfitted with iron shackles and chains...the climax from every horror movie I'd ever seen, from *Psycho* to *Silence of the Lambs,* replayed through my head.

You've come this far, I told myself firmly. You can't back down now.

I switched on the light, illuminating the entire space at the bottom of the stairs. I blinked over and over again, every muscle tensed as I struggled to adjust to the glaring brightness.

Instead of being shocked or horrified, I was overwhelmed with disappointment. So *this* was what Devon Barnett kept stashed away in his basement under lock and key. My overly active imagination had prepared me for anything except what I found: a photo lab. I scanned the room, taking in the developing tanks, enlargers, light boxes, shelves crammed with bottles of chemicals and boxes of photo paper, all neatly arranged and spanking clean. A dozen black-and-white photographs were clipped to a wire that was strung across the ceiling, looking like a row of handkerchiefs hanging on a clothesline.

Chess had been right. This really was Dev's studio, the place where he developed his photographs of celebrities. And, as far as I could see, that was *all* it was.

So much for the awe-inspiring investigative abilities of Jessica Popper, Girl Sleuth, I thought grimly. I scanned the string of photos the paparazzo had left to dry. Nothing here but a few shots of movie stars coming out of bars or lounging on the beach, looking like they've had a little too much to drink.

By this point, my eyes had completely adjusted to the light. I glanced around, still hoping to stumble across something that would give me a bit more insight into what made Devon Barnett tick—not to mention what made him tick people off. I spotted a wooden stool, more shelving, a two-drawer metal file cabinet, a large plastic bin filled with tongs and squeegees . . . and tucked into a corner, near the stairs, a plastic bowl of water and a rawhide chew stick.

So *this* is where Hilda locks up Zsa Zsa during her cleaning frenzies! I thought. When I stopped over on Tuesday on my way to the Sand Bar and heard the poor little Havanese's pitiful barks, she hadn't been stuffed into a breadbox. She'd been locked in the basement. Which probably explained why the sweet little dog was so alarmed by my suggestion that she accompany me down here.

At least I solved *one* mystery, I thought wryly.

But it wasn't much in the way of compensation. Sighing with disappointment, I turned around, planning to head back up the stairs. As I did, I nearly smashed my hip again Barnett's metal file cabinet. Just for the heck of it, I opened the top drawer.

The contents didn't surprise me. True, the three- or four-dozen manila file folders weren't labeled "Accounts Payable" or "Receipts," like most self-employed business people's. Instead, Devon Barnett had handwritten the names of his subjects on the tabs, the celebrities he stalked and photographed. They were filed alphabetically by their last names—and there were dozens.

My eyes traveled to the file labeled "Fontana, Hugo." I pulled it out and opened it, expecting to see copies of the photos of Hugo that Barnett had sold to the *Stargazer* and the *Gossip Gazette* over the years.

Sure enough, several photographs were stuck inside. I glanced at the first one, bracing myself for a shot of the Pulverizer doing something mildly embarrassing.

What I saw made my blood run cold.

The subject of the photograph was Hugo, all right. But he wasn't coming out of a nightclub with a starlet on his arm, or even brandishing his fist at an autograph hound.

This shot looked like it had been taken at a bar—a *gay* bar. Hoards of men in various states of undress were crowded together, some dancing, most with drinks in their hands. A few of the couples were groping each other or kissing or even engaged in much more intimate behavior.

But the focus of the photograph was the Pulverizer, who was vogueing for the camera, dressed in nothing but a leopard-skin thong. His sculpted torso gleamed as if it had been oiled, emphasizing his muscles so that he looked like a marble statue of a Greek god. Of course, unlike the man in this photo, Greek gods didn't wear false eyelashes.

I stared at the photograph for a long time, my mind racing as I tried to make sense of what I was seeing. A publicity stunt? I wondered. Maybe a photo taken on the set of a movie he was filming, one that had never made it to the big screen?

I moved on to the next photo. This one featured Hugo again, along with a young, handsome man I didn't recognize. He also had a well-toned body. It was certainly easy to tell, since both men were completely naked. These shots looked as if they had been taken by a Peeping Tom, since the windowframes and venetian blinds were clearly in view.

A Peeping Tom named Devon Barnett.

My head was spinning as I leafed through the rest of the photos. Each one featured Hugo, engaged in some behavior that was bound to have a detrimental effect on ticket sales. This was not the action hero audiences were used to seeing—the Pulverizer, capable of crumpling the trunks of cars with his bare hands as if they were made of aluminum foil. This was hardly the symbol of strength that men wanted to be—and women wanted to sleep with.

*No,* I thought, still struggling to comprehend what I was seeing. *This can't be what I think it is.*

With trembling hands, I skipped to the papers in back of the folder. There were several white sheets, clipped together neatly. They looked like some kind of bookkeeper's tally. Handwritten on top was Hugo's name. A straight line had been drawn down the middle of the page. On the left side, a series of dates had been recorded, some in different colors of ink, but all in the same handwriting. To the right of each date, on the other side of the page, was a corresponding dollar amount.

January 10—$10,000.
February 9—$10,000.
March 10—$15,000.

There it was, spelled out so clearly that there was no longer any question about what Devon Barnett's game had been.

*"Blackmail!"* I breathed.

I felt strangely light-headed as I slipped the stack of paper back into the manila folder. Even though I had seen it with my own eyes, I was having trouble processing the magnitude of what he had been involved in. Not only had the merciless paparazzo complicated celebri-

ties' lives by publishing photographs and making up stories that cast them in the worst possible light. What was
nearly impossible to comprehend was that he'd taken it a
step further, terrorizing them by threatening to expose
secrets that were guaranteed to ruin them—and collect-
ing regular payments for his silence. Even his "first love"
hadn't been immune to his greed.

I studied the contents of the file drawer more carefully,
perusing the folders labeled with some of the biggest
names in Hollywood. As far I knew, most of them
weren't spending the summer in the Bromptons.

Then again, some were.

With moist palms, I grabbed the file labeled "Elliot,
Shawn."

I took a deep breath before opening it. Bracing myself
turned out to be a wise move.

I was fairly certain the photograph on top was the one
Kara had mentioned, the shot of Shawn on the beach at
Cannes with another woman. Both were naked except
for thongs, and the two of them were clearly engaged in
something other than making sand castles. Her description had been accurate. Shawn did, indeed, have his
hands all over her, and the two were kissing in a way that
looked too real for Hollywood.

But Kara hadn't prepared me for the fact that the
woman in the picture was Emily's mother, Delilah
Raines.

No *wonder* Emily dislikes him so much! I thought.
For all I knew, Shawn could even have been the reason
for her parents' divorce.

But that photo had been published in the *Stargazer*. If
I was correct about Barnett being a blackmailer, there
had to be even more incriminating photographs of
Shawn.

There were.

The next photograph also featured Shawn. He was

lying down again, but this time in a bed. A very *large* bed. This time, he wasn't even wearing a thong. Delilah, who was also in the picture, was similarly naked. So was the third person in the shot.

Kara.

I stared at the photograph for what felt like a very long time, trying to reconstruct the scenario behind it. Perhaps Kara had learned about Shawn's dalliance with Delilah, then tried to hold onto him by pretending to be tolerant of his attraction to the "other woman." Or maybe she figured that half of Shawn was better than none.

Whatever the reason behind the star-studded *ménage à trois*, I hoped Emily would never learn anything about it.

Emily aside, the media would have pounced on a photo like this. This one shot had the power to severely damage or even destroy three careers in a single swoop. The pictures that followed were variations on the same theme: the three familiar faces, with increasingly familiar bodies, engaged in an astoundingly wide variety of acts.

A few of the photographs were marred by obstructions that had clearly separated the photographer from his subjects—the slat of a venetian blind, the hem of a curtain. As he'd clicked away, Barnett had most likely been standing on a balcony, or even balanced on a windowsill, no doubt having trouble seeing through the lens, for all the dollar signs that were dancing before his eyes.

Once again, I found a record of payments stuck in front of the file. Shawn was another victim of Devon Barnett's probing lens—and another victim of the paparazzo's blackmailing scheme.

Still feeling dazed, I pulled out the folder labeled "Liebling, Kara." I opened it to find a stack of photographs fastened together with a paper clip.

As soon as I focused on the photograph on top, I gasped. I recognized Kara right away, even though she was wearing oversized sunglasses and her hair was tucked beneath a French beret. But I also recognized the other people in the picture, even though all three subjects were cast in shadow.

Christopher Vale and Richard Strathe. The two men who'd been convicted of attacking Delilah Raines.

I studied the photograph more closely. It had been shot at a low angle, as if Barnett had taken it from a crouching position. Hiding behind a bush, maybe, or stooped behind a low wall. But it clearly showed Kara conferring with the two thugs in a dimly-lit alleyway.

My hands were trembling as I moved on to the next photograph. This one featured the same three figures, standing in the same place. But in this shot, Kara and Strathe had their hands extended toward each other. She was handing him something. I couldn't make out exactly what it was, but it looked like an ordinary business envelope.

The third photograph proved me right. In this one, Richard Strathe had moved closer to the streetlight. While the setting was still pretty dim, I could easily see the stack of bills he'd removed from the envelope, as if checking to make sure the correct amount was there. It was a pretty thick stack, and the expression on his face was one of satisfaction.

The fourth showed Kara and Strathe shaking hands. Strathe's eyes had shifted so they were now looking in the same direction as the camera's lens. He was wearing a startled look, as if he'd heard something or gotten some other clue that someone might be lurking there. The coldness in his eyes was chilling.

But it was the expression on Kara's face that literally sent a chill running down my spine. She was *smiling*. In fact, she looked as pleased as if she'd just won a prize.

There was one last photograph: Kara walking off in one direction, the two men heading in the other. So

Barnett hadn't been discovered, after all. The deal had been made, and as far as all three of them knew, no one was the wiser.

How wrong they had been! Taken together, the five photographs were solid evidence that Kara Liebling had hired Christopher Vale and Richard Strathe to attack Delilah Raines. While I didn't know what Kara's motivation had been, the most likely reason was their love triangle with Shawn.

I felt sick as I returned Kara's folder to the file cabinet. I was beginning to believe that *no one* was who I thought they were. Nearly every person I'd met since I'd come to the Bromptons turned out to have secrets—devastating secrets that could destroy them with the publication of a single photograph.

As I slid the manila folder into place, one more name caught my eye: "Bolger, Russell." I pulled it out of the drawer.

The first photograph in the file didn't look particularly incriminating. It showed Russell poised at the doorway of what looked like a private club. He was glancing around nervously, as if he was worried that someone might be watching.

The building was made entirely of brick, with no windows. A small sign hung on the door, and I noticed a street sign with lettering that was too tiny to make out. I searched around the studio until I spotted a magnifying glass, a vital tool in the photography business. When I held it over the photo, I understood what I was looking at.

The street sign said "Mulberry Street," the heart of Manhattan's Little Italy district. And the letters on the door spelled out "Friends of Sicily Society. Members Only."

There was only one other photograph in Russell Bolger's folder. It showed him standing with a man who looked familiar, but whom I couldn't quite place. The two beefy bodyguards standing on either side of him, both their faces and their physiques reminiscent of Rufus's, jogged my memory.

Of course! Vinny "The Finger" de Ponzo, a reputed mobster whose guilt had never been proven. Oddly enough, during each of his three highly publicized trials, the witnesses kept disappearing, either committing suicide, skipping the country, or turning up floating in a swimming pool.

In this shot, Russell and Vinny were shaking hands. And the corner of a white envelope protruded from Russell's jacket pocket, a white envelope that didn't appear in the first picture.

Is this how Russell Bolger has been financing his movies? I wondered. Or perhaps something else, like a drug habit or a gambling addiction? The reason he needed money wasn't even the point. What really mattered was that Russell's creditors weren't exactly his local savings bank.

And publicizing Russell Bolger's wheelings and dealings with well-known mobsters wasn't likely to go over well with either the general public or The Finger's cohorts. He clearly recognized that fact, as proven by the handwritten list of payments I found neatly filed away behind the photographs.

So Devon Barnett had something on just about everybody in Hollywood, I thought, my mind racing as I slid the folder back into place. He was blackmailing all of them. And any one of them could have murdered him: Hugo Fontana, Kara Liebling, Russell Bolger, Shawn Elliott, or any one of the other victims of his deviousness. I scanned the thick stack of files, reading one name after another, overwhelmed by the number of blackmailing victims—and possible suspects.

Of course, I still couldn't discount the possibility that Barnett's murderer had been someone other than the people he'd been blackmailing. Perhaps Sydney had been part of his evil scheme. The two of them could have embarked upon this little sideline together, back when they were still married. Maybe the female half of the husband-and-wife team had finally decided it was high time she became the sole beneficiary of their little blackmailing enterprise. After all, she was just as capable as Devon of extracting large amounts of money as payment for her continued secrecy.

Then there was Chess. I still couldn't figure out what his true relationship with Devon had been. Was he just a gold-digger, hoping to cash in on his good looks by living off his lover's wealth? And what about the schoolteacher who had been killed in his hometown? Was Chess really innocent, or were people like the town librarian correct in assuming that his alibi had been nothing more than a fabrication—and that he really had been responsible for Edmund Sylvester's murder?

I even wondered if Hilda had been involved. My mind reeled with possible scenarios. For all I knew, Hilda the Housekeeper was really Devon Barnett's mother, his partner in crime, who kept up appearances by pretending to be someone other than who she really was....

I snapped back to the moment, remembering that it wasn't wise for me to linger. Chess—or anyone else, for that matter—could show up and find me here at any time.

My heart pounded furiously. *Think!* I ordered myself, struggling to figure out what to do next. The safest thing, I knew, was not to let anyone know that I'd been here— and that I'd stumbled upon Devon Barnett's secret stash of files. Yet I needed proof that he'd been blackmailing celebrities, and that meant having copies of enough of the career-damaging photographs and the payment sheets he'd kept so meticulously to incriminate him.

Instinctively I reached down and patted the pockets of my jeans. My keys were right where I'd put them. And not only did my key ring include my own keys, but it also contained the key to Suzanne's office, where there was a copying machine.

I glanced around, looking for something to carry the massive stack of papers in. I realized immediately that I didn't have a lot of choice. Chess hadn't been exaggerating when he'd characterized his lover as a clean freak. Devon's studio contained only the bare necessities, without a single empty carton or even a discarded shopping bag in sight.

The best I could do was a cardboard box filled with plastic jars of chemicals. I grabbed it off a shelf, dumped out the contents, and began placing the files inside, keeping them in the exact same order in which I'd found them. The box wasn't really high enough, and the cardboard was on the flimsy side. But if I held onto it carefully, I was pretty sure I could use it to transport the files to my van.

Before leaving Dev's studio, I glanced around one more time, just to make sure I'd left everything exactly the way I'd found it. Then I headed up the stairs, moving as quickly as I dared while cradling the heavy box in my arms.

I snuck out the back door, wanting to stay out of sight as long as possible. As I passed the edge of the house, however, I had to cross a stretch of bare lawn at least fifty feet wide before reaching my van.

At least it's dark, I thought as I stepped onto the grass.

I'd barely formed the thought when a blinding light suddenly flashed on. I froze, a sick feeling coming over me as I assumed I'd been caught red-handed. Then I realized the light was one of those automatic jobs that come on whenever somebody passes by a sensor.

Still, it was as bright as a spotlight, and I was as exposed as if I were standing on a stage. The last thing I wanted was for someone to see me leaving Chess's house with Barnett's files—at least, if that someone knew the records were a possible link to the paparazzo's murderer. Frantically, I looked around, checking the street, the backyard, the driveway. From what I could see, no one was around.

"So far, so good," I breathed. I moved toward my van as quickly as I dared, given the awkward box I was carrying. The files were now jutting out of the top at haphazard angles, threatening to spill out if I jerked the box too hard. It wasn't until I reached for the door handle, balancing the box on my bent knee, that I realized I was biting my lower lip so hard that I could taste blood.

I'd just opened the van door when everything went dark. The light on the side of Devon's house only stayed on for a relatively short period. My time was up.

I figured I'd take advantage of the darkness. I backed out of the driveway without turning my headlights on. Of course, my red taillights helped me find the way. They also made me realize that if anyone *was* watching, that person would have no trouble keeping track of every move I made.

*No one is watching,* I told myself firmly. It was more than an attempt at keeping my heart from pounding as hard as if it were about to burst right out of my chest. I really was pretty certain that no one had seen me go into Devon Barnett's house . . . or sneak out of it, bearing his secret treasure that he could well have been on the verge of converting into a charming vacation *château* in the south of France.

• • •

I flicked on my headlights as soon as I hit the street. From that point on, I acted like just another driver who was heading toward some perfectly legitimate destination—someone who wouldn't be the least bit interesting to anyone else. Even so, the trip to Suzanne's office

seemed endless. I hit every red light. I also ended up behind every slow driver in Norfolk County.

"Come on, come on," I muttered. I checked my watch
and saw that it was getting late. I had to hurry if I was
going to return the files to the basement studio before
Chess got back.

When I reached Suzanne's office, I wasn't surprised to
find it dark. Fortunately, an overhead light hung above
the front door. It was fairly dim, but at least it cast
enough light over the parking lot to allow me to get in
through the back door without too much trouble.

Just to be cautious, I parked my van behind the building so no one could spot it from the street or the parking
lot in front. No need to advertise the fact that I was alone
in an office building, late at night. Not when someone
was so enraged by my investigation of Devon Barnett's
murder that they'd kidnapped my Maxie-Max.

Suzanne's office seemed strangely eerie. During the
day, the rooms had been noisy and bright, filled with
bustling activity. Now, they were deadly silent, except
for the humming of the refrigerator and the ticking of a
clock. I was actually relieved when one of the dogs
spending the weekend recuperating in back let out a few
questioning barks.

Fortunately, the room with the copying machine was
windowless, so even turning on the light didn't give
away the fact that I was in there.

Without hesitation, I turned on the copier. I realized
immediately that it was going to take a while to copy
Barnett's files. Not only did I have to make copies of all
the payment sheets, I also had to copy the photographs
that had made Devon Barnett's blackmailing scheme
possible in the first place.

Which presented another challenge. I didn't know

how well the glossy black-and-white photographs would reprint. I desperately hoped they would be clear.

I held my breath as I tried the first one. I deliberately chose the shot of Shawn with Delilah Raines and Kara Liebling, kind of a personal payback to myself for being foolish enough to flirt with him.

The photograph came out fine, and I let out a sigh of relief. I grabbed the entire contents of Shawn's folder and began copying each page, working as quickly and steadily as I could.

"So far, so good," I exhaled, as I tucked all the pages back into place and picked up the next file.

I froze at the sound of footsteps.

Oh, my God! I thought, my heartbeat immediately escalating to sickening speed. Someone *was* watching me. Someone saw me come out of Devon Barnett's house— *with his files!*

And that someone was outside. I could hear the person who had followed me here trying to get in through the main entrance, rattling the door gently as if trying not to make any noise.

I crept into the next room, Suzanne's office. Crouching beside the window, I peered out just in time to see a figure slink by right outside the window, heading toward the back door. I even got a glimpse of him. Still, it wasn't much of a glimpse. It was difficult to see, since the parking lot outside Suzanne's office was so poorly lit. All I could tell was that he was wearing pants, a baggy jacket, and a baseball cap.

And then I remembered.

The back door! I'd left it *unlocked.*

At least, I thought I had. Telling myself not to panic, I struggled to remember if I'd bothered to turn the lock as I came in.

The back door creaked open, giving me my answer.

Oh, my God! I thought, panicking. *He's in the building!*

I stepped behind an open door, the first hiding spot I noticed. My heart fluttered, and my mouth was coated with the metallic taste of fear. I glanced around for something I could use as a weapon. Nothing. I thought about escaping through the front door, climbing out a window, even letting out the caged animals in back in the hopes that they'd rush at the intruder and give me a chance to slip out....

None of them were very good ideas. As I listened to the footsteps growing closer, I realized I'd be easy to spot. The gap between the door and the wall I stood against was large enough that anyone passing by was bound to notice me.

Yet there wasn't enough time to dart anywhere else.

Suddenly I heard the most unexpected sound: Suzanne's loud, high-pitched laugh, right outside in the parking lot.

I blinked, wondering if fear was making me imagine I was hearing voices. Could she really be here? It wasn't possible, not at this hour....

"Marcus, you *stop* that!" It was Suzanne's voice, all right. "You can wait at least two seconds until we get inside, can't you?"

"I don't think I can," I heard Marcus reply. "You make me crazy, you fox. You're the most scrumptious, delicious, *foxy* thing, and you can't expect the Marc Man to wait...."

"*Stop,* Marcus!" More giggling. "I have to get my key out. How can I open the door when you've got your hands—watch that, you naughty boy! Seriously, I'm still not sure this is such a good idea...."

"Are you kidding?" Marcus countered. "It's inspired!"

I heard the front door swing open, then slam shut. Then more footsteps. Only this time, the sound was welcome.

"There's not really a lot of room in here...*Jessie?*" Suzanne cried, her hands flying to her heart. She stopped in her tracks and peered at me through the gap in the doorway. "You scared me! What on earth are you doing here?"

"I came to copy some photographs," I replied, as astonished as I was relieved. I stepped around the door, no longer afraid of being in plain sight. "But what are you two doing here on a Saturday night?"

"It was Marcus's idea," Suzanne said, grinning at him. "We had dinner again—this time, just the two of us. Afterward, he wanted to come back to my place. But I told him about my lawyer's warning that my divorce negotiations are at a very sensitive stage and how I should be careful not to let Robert get anything on me. I was instructed to keep my nose clean, so I was afraid to bring him to my house. That's when Marcus came up with the idea of us coming *here.*"

"The Marc Man is very good at thinking outside the box," he informed me proudly.

I felt like throwing my arms around him—something I never would have believed could happen. The man's overly active sex drive could well have saved my life.

But at the moment, I had something more important to do.

"Look, there's somebody in here. Somebody who followed me—"

"What are you talking about?" Marcus demanded.

We heard the back door slam. The person who had followed me had ducked out, scared off by Suzanne's and Marcus's arrival.

"Excuse me," I mumbled, dashing in that direction. I flung the door open just in time to see a car I didn't recognize, tear out of the parking lot. I squinted hard, trying to make out the license plate. But with practically no illumination besides the car's dim red taillights, I couldn't see a thing.

"Jessie, what's going on?" Suzanne asked as she and Marcus joined me in the doorway.

I was so frustrated I could have screamed. Devon Barnett's murderer had been right in front of me, but I hadn't been able to see who it was. I stared out at the street, watching the taillights fade—and watching the answer to the question I'd been agonizing over drive away.

"Let's go back inside," I said with a sigh. "I'll tell you the whole story."

I was about to close the door, when something lying on the floor caught my attention. I blinked, not sure my eyes weren't playing tricks on me.

I leaned over to pick it up. Even in the dim light, I was able to make out what it was.

"Oh, my God," I breathed, closing my eyes as understanding swept over me like a chill.

I opened my eyes and focused on what I'd found, something so tiny it could practically have gotten lost in the creases of my hand.

But it told me who had murdered Devon Barnett.

# Chapter 18

"He that lieth down with dogs shall rise up with fleas."

—Ben Franklin

Sunday morning I awoke with the same heavy feeling in my chest Napoleon must have faced whenever he woke up the morning of a battle. But there was no way I'd let this turn into my Waterloo. Not with Max's life at stake—and only a few hours left to do something about it.

Figuring out who had murdered Devon Barnett—and most likely kidnapped my Westie—had been critical. Now it was time to prove it to Lieutenant Anthony Falcone.

"All set?" Nick asked as he and I piled into his car with Lou. He was trying to keep his tone light, but I could tell he was worried.

To be perfectly honest, I was, too. "As ready as I'll ever be," I answered, wishing I sounded more convincing.

As he drove to Russell Bolger's house, I kept my fingers clutched tightly around the handle of the tote bag I'd brought with me. In it, I'd crammed the evidence I'd need to present my case—that is, assuming things went the way I hoped they would. Staring out the window in silence, I ran through the list I'd carefully constructed in my mind. Step one, step two, step three... Just thinking about the next hour sent a wave of anxiety ballooning through my chest. I had a lot to accomplish—in a very short time.

As soon as the three of us got out of the car at Russell Bolger's estate, Lou began acting agitated. He darted from place to place, sniffing the ground frantically and barking for no apparent reason. I had several theories about the odd behavior he'd begun to exhibit. He could have developed a phobia about new places. Or he simply could have begun to find being around other animals disconcerting.

There was a third possibility, however, one that seemed even more likely. I desperately hoped I was right.

I turned to Nick. "Would you please do me a favor and take Lou out for a run? He could probably use the exercise."

"Yeah, he does seem kind of freaked out," Nick agreed.

I immediately figured out a way to calm my Dalmatian down. Halfway across the Bolgers' property, I spotted Emily sitting at the edge of the pool. She was dangling her bare feet in the water and looking bored.

"Emily!" I called.

She rose to her feet, shielding her eyes from the sun and peering in our direction. The look of confusion on her face instantly melted into a grin, and she started waving furiously. I dropped Lou's leash, then watched him bound toward her gleefully.

"I don't blame him for wanting to hang out with Emily," I commented to Nick. "She's probably the most interesting person here."

"In that case, maybe I'll do the same."

Once my two charges had been taken care of, I made

my way toward Russell Bolger's house, following all the other well-dressed guests who were heading inside. I was glad to see a couple of local cops on site, uniformed officers from the Town of East Brompton Police Department, who stood around with walkie-talkies, looking as if they felt very important.

I was also pleased to see so many familiar faces. So many familiar dogs, too. Many of the people who'd participated in the dog show had brought their animals with them today to watch the home movies. I found that endearing. Even though these celebrities regularly saw their names in lights and their faces on magazine covers and billboards, at the end of the day, it still mattered to them that they had a loyal fan at home who, as Shawn had once put it, liked them for themselves.

But my appreciation of the human–canine bond only lasted a few seconds. I had more important things to attend to. I scanned the room, my heart thumping wildly as I searched for the one face that mattered most.

I let out a sigh of relief when I spotted it. Lieutenant Falcone stood in one corner of the lobby outside Russell's theater, flirting with a beautiful woman. I recognized her as the supermodel I'd spotted on the first day of the dog show, the one with her own cosmetics campaign and her own viszla. From the looks of things, she'd recently acquired something else desirable: the blue ribbon for Best of Show. Her rust-colored dog stood beside her, his chest puffed out and his head held high, as if he was as proud of the blue ribbon fastened to his collar as his mistress was.

Falcone and the supermodel made an interesting pair: the striking darked-haired beauty, as willowy as a palm frond, looking positively radiant in a pale green linen dress, and the Norfolk Country Chief of Homicide in his slightly shiny off-the-rack suit, barely skimming her shoulders even though his posture would have put a U.S. Marine to shame.

"Step one," I breathed, pleased that I'd managed to accomplish the first item on my mental checklist. I even let myself relax—at least, for a few seconds. Then I remembered that luring Falcone to this event was just one small step in a whole staircase of events that still needed to proceed according to plan.

I perked up when I noticed him squaring his shoulders, puffing out his chest as if he were in competition with the viszla. Almost immediately, I saw the reason: the approach of a man balancing a gigantic video camera on his shoulder. Marching alongside him was a pretty blonde woman in a tailored suit who had to have been a television reporter.

I watched from across the room as they chatted. Then, both Falcone and the model nodded their approval. A bright light from the video camera flashed on, and the two of them were suddenly being interviewed.

I'm glad Falcone got what he came for, I thought with grim satisfaction. I just hope he leaves here with something even more meaningful.

The next item on my mental "to do" list, step two, was much more technical. More than a decade had passed since I'd been part of the stage crew for the Junior Show at Bryn Mawr. Suzanne Fox played the role of an absentminded physics professor in our class's spoof on college life, but I'd preferred to stay behind the scenes. At the moment, I was grateful I'd opted to stay out of the spotlight—and instead, learn something about the way things worked backstage.

Doing my best to look casual, I sauntered down the short hallway that ran alongside the theater, pretending I was heading toward the ladies' room—or, in this case, the Actresses Room. Instead, I hesitated outside the unmarked door that came before it, just long enough to glance around and make sure no one was watching me. Then, I ducked into the backstage area and quickly closed the door behind me.

This time, I'd had the presence of mind to bring a flashlight. I'd picked it up that very morning at an old-fashioned hardware store in the heart of East Brompton, one that combined the old-fashioned smell of wooden floors and mustiness with an impressive inventory of nuts, bolts, and twelve-piece sets of Le Creuset cookware. Instead of turning on any lights that might call attention to the backstage area, I was able to focus the beam precisely where I needed it.

I worked with fast, steady movements, making a few critical adjustments in the way things were laid out. Miraculously, everything I'd learned at college about being a stagehand came back to me—something I suspected wouldn't have happened if I'd tried to recall the knowledge I'd once absorbed about the Lake Poets or the German Expressionist Art Movement.

It didn't take me long to complete step two. But instead of feeling heartened, I found myself even more overwhelmed.

What I'd done so far had been the easy stuff. Orchestrating the other events I needed to make happen was going to be a lot more difficult.

I sneaked out of the backstage area, trying to buoy up my spirits by pretending I was one of Charlie's Angels. After taking a few deep breaths and forcing my facial muscles to relax, I ambled back to the lobby and grabbed a crystal flute of champagne.

"Jessie!"

I turned and saw Chess heading in my direction with a carefully brushed and fluffed Zsa Zsa in his arms. Both were dressed in pale pink, he in an expensive-looking silk shirt the color of roses, she in a matching pink ribbon perched perkily on her head. He was beaming from ear to ear.

"Hi, Chess," I greeted him. "I—I didn't realize you'd be here today." I was finding it hard to look him in the eye. For the first time since I'd concocted this plan, I found myself experiencing some serious doubts about revealing Devon Barnett's murder in such a public arena.

"Just because I wasn't part of the dog show doesn't mean I can't be part of the cast party," he chirped. "But I'm *so* glad you're here, Jessie! Phyllis Beckwith called me early this morning. She said she could hardly sleep last night, she was so excited about my iced tea. In fact, she's absolutely convinced that it's going to be the hit of the summer season!"

"That's great, Chess," I told him, doing my best to sound enthusiastic, even though my stomach was in knots.

"And I owe it all to you, Jessie," he went on. "Like I told you last night, I never would have thought of approaching Phyllis. But you're one of those people whose mind knows no limits. You're a *genius*!"

I was barely listening. Instead, my eyes traveled around the room, taking in all the familiar faces. My heart fluttered when I spotted another key player in the scene I was about to stage.

The lights in the lobby flickered, a sign that the afternoon's entertainment was ready to begin.

"It's showtime," I thought, my heartbeat racing and my mouth so dry that I gulped down a few sips of champagne just so I'd be able to swallow.

It was time for step three. I fought the feeling of anxiety that rose inside me, just from thinking about it. For one thing, the timing was critical. For another thing, it was going to require some pretty skillful acting on my part.

"Let's sit together," Chess suggested.

"Sure," I replied vaguely. "But first, there's something I have to do." In response to his look of surprise, I added, "Ladies' room. Save me a seat."

Instead, I sidled up to Kara Liebling, who I'd just noticed strolling toward the theater with her dazzling white borzoi at her side. Kara was also a vision in white, looking particularly angelic in a 1950s-style chiffon party dress with a full skirt that resembled a cloud and a diaphanous shawl loosely draped around her bare shoulders. Her soft blonde hair was piled up on her head and tied with a satin ribbon the same pale blue as her eyes. A few fetching tendrils spilled around her face, flattering her perfect features and luminous skin.

I caught up with her just as she was about to enter the small auditorium. "Kara!" I cried breathlessly. "I'm glad I ran into you!"

"Hello, Jessie. How nice that you could make it." Smiling sweetly, she added, "I thought you were going back home today."

"I am, as soon as this is over. But first . . . Kara, do you have a minute?"

She glanced at the stream of people surrounding us, laughing and chatting as they filed into the theater. *"Now?"*

"It's important." Afraid I was losing her, I pulled out the ace up my sleeve. "I don't usually get involved in anyone's personal life, but I have something to tell you about Shawn."

An unmistakable glimmer of interest flickered in her eyes. "All right," she agreed.

"We need to find someplace private, where no one can overhear." I headed toward the hallway, then gestured toward the unmarked door. "Let's go in here."

"What is this, a closet?" Kara asked uncertainly.

"The area behind the stage. It's perfect. No one will overhear."

I held the door open for the actress and her sleek white dog, then followed. As soon as we were inside, Anastasia wandered off to sniff her new surroundings. Kara, meanwhile, turned to face me.

"What do you have to tell me about Shawn?" she asked anxiously. "Has he said something?"

"I think you'll understand in a minute, Kara," I replied. "First, I have something to show you."

I fumbled with the papers I'd pulled out of my tote bag, meanwhile reaching behind me quickly to flick on a switch I kept hidden with my body. Then I held up the copy of the photograph of Kara with Christopher Vale and Richard Strathe I'd made the night before. "Does this photograph mean anything to you?"

She gasped. "Where did you get that?"

"Let's just stay I stumbled across it while I was trying to find something else—like my dog."

"I—I don't know what you think that is, but it's not..."

"I know exactly what it is," I assured her calmly. "It's proof that you hired these two thugs to beat up Delilah Raines in a dark parking lot."

"I have no idea what you're talking about!"

"I think you do, Kara. You set the whole thing up, and Devon Barnett was the only person who knew about it. In fact, he was blackmailing you."

"You're crazy! That Xerox copy is probably some kind of composite or something. As for Devon Barnett blackmailing me, that's simply absurd. You have no way of proving these ridiculous accusations!"

"Actually, I do," I assured her in the same even tone. "Not only do I have the original photographs Barnett kept in his files, but I also have the payment records, written in his own handwriting." I hesitated. "I also have proof that you're the person who killed him."

Kara's eyes narrowed. "Okay, so you snooped around

and found some dirt. So what if Barnett was blackmailing me? He was blackmailing half the people in Hollywood! Every one of them would have liked to see him dead. What makes you think I'm the one who killed him?"

"Recognize this?" I held up a tiny rhinestone, its usual sheen dulled by the thin layer of dust covering it. "I found this on the floor of Suzanne Fox's veterinary clinic last night, right after you followed me to her office—no doubt with the intention of doing whatever you had to do to put an end to my investigation."

"I have no idea what you're talking about!"

"All the pieces have finally fit together, Kara," I went on, sounding much calmer than I felt. "You knew I was investigating Barnett's death from the get-go, didn't you? You've known all along that there was never any doubt in my mind that he'd been murdered. Chess probably told you on Monday, the day after Barnett was killed—the day you and I ran into each other in Chess and Devon's kitchen.

"So you tried to scare me away. First, you tried leaving dead animals on my front porch. When that didn't work, you kidnapped my Westie. And because you knew I was trying to find out who killed Barnett, you watched me. You saw me come out of his house last night, carrying his files. You could see for yourself that I'd discovered what was going on—and that I was taking his records so I'd be able to prove it. You followed me to Suzanne Fox's office in Poxabogue, hoping to stop me. And you almost did. I was all alone in that empty office building. You were about to come inside and kill me, too, weren't you? You'd probably even figured out a way to make it look like an accident. But Suzanne and her friend Marcus showed up unexpectedly, so you had no choice but to run off. Of course, you were in such a hurry that you never noticed that one of the rhinestones fell off your Emilio Fratelli shoes."

She just stared at me without speaking. But I could see by the look of horror in her eyes that I'd gotten everything right.

"You'd used an Emilio Fratelli shoebox to deliver your last cash payment to Barnett," I continued, "and he stored it in his closet. By the way, you're probably the only person in the Bromptons who's still wearing them. And as soon as I found this rhinestone in Suzanne's office last night, right after I was followed, I remembered you were wearing them the day you and I watched the Toy Group judging together at the dog show. You also had them on when I came to your beach house with Max and Lou. I remember studying your outfit, noticing how perfect everything was except for your shoes. They were decorated with sequins and geegaws, but some of them were missing. Since I'd never actually seen a pair of Emilio Fratelli shoes before, I didn't make the connection right away. In fact, it wasn't until I found this rhinestone that everything snapped into place."

By this point, Kara's face was twisted into an expression of absolute fury. It was funny, even though she was considered one of the most beautiful actresses in Hollywood, at the moment she looked positively ugly.

"But there's still one thing I don't know, Kara. Why did you do it?" I continued. "Why did you hire those thugs to beat up Delilah Raines—and why did you kill Devon Barnett?"

I held my breath, expecting her to continue to deny everything. Instead, she glanced around, as if wanting to make sure we were still alone—and that no one could hear us.

"Since it's just the two of us," Kara said coolly, "and since you seem to have figured the whole thing out, I'll tell you precisely why I did it, Jessie. No one would ever believe you, anyway. Not if the only 'evidence' you have is a silly rhinestone. After all, there are dozens of people who could have killed Barnett. That slimy blackmailer had lots of enemies. If I hadn't killed him, sooner or later somebody else would have. I just happened to get to him first. His greed started getting out of hand once he found out my career was about to skyrocket. Just a few weeks ago, he arranged for us to meet so he could tell me he was tripling my payments! I couldn't afford to risk him going public with what he had on me. It would have meant the end of my career. I couldn't let that happen, could I?"

Her tone was no longer matter-of-fact. Instead, it was ice cold.

"As for the incident with Delilah, that was nothing personal," Kara went on. "It was just business. She had something I wanted: the starring role in *Day of the Unicorn*. I simply had to have that part. I was meant to play Catherine the Great. It's exactly what I need at this point in my career." Shrugging, she said, "I knew from my agent that I was the studio's second choice. At that point, it was simply a question of getting their *first* choice out of the way."

"You've been quite a busy lady, haven't you?" I observed.

"I've always had to work my butt off for everything I ever got," she replied nastily. "You have no idea how competitive the movie industry is. Besides," she went on, her voice practically a growl, "I did everyone a favor by killing Barnett. That creep was as low as they come. I deserve a medal for what I did."

"Unfortunately, a jury might not agree."

The voice sounded muffled, since it came from the other side of the burgundy-colored velvet curtains. But I knew immediately who it belonged to: Lieutenant Anthony Falcone.

Kara gasped as he emerged from behind the thick folds and stepped toward her.

"What—what is this?" she sputtered. "Who are you?"

"Lieutenant Anthony Falcone, Norfolk County Homicide," he replied, holding up his badge. "And you are under arrest for the murder of Devon Barnett. Anything you do or say may be used against you in a court of law. You have the right to consult an attorney...."

"How could you hear us?" she demanded.

"Microphone," he answered matter-of-factly. "Somebody hooked up the sound system. The mike's probably hidden somewhere in these curtains."

Clipped right onto the fabric, I thought smugly.

"But—but you don't understand!" Kara insisted. "I was *acting*! Everything you just heard me say was from a script I've been considering! I was just trying it out to see if the dialogue sounded realistic!"

"It sounded realistic, all right," Lieutenant Falcone said. "Very realistic. Like I started to say, anything you do or say may be used against you in a court of law. You have the right to consult an attorney...."

Kara whirled around to face me. "Jessie, is this *your* doing?"

"No, Kara," I replied solemnly. "It's *yours*."

Falcone, still reciting the Miranda rights, took a step closer to Kara, holding out a pair of shiny silver handcuffs I figured he'd gotten from one of the local cops patrolling the estate.

It's over, I thought with satisfaction. Now all I have to do is find out where she stashed Max....

As if thinking about a furry white dog had been enough to bring it on, Anastasia suddenly lunged into our midst from out of nowhere. The giant borzoi leaped between Kara and Falcone, emitting a frightening snarling sound as she lunged toward the police lieutenant, raising herself up on her two back paws and thrusting eighty pounds of solid muscle against his shoulders.

Caught completely unaware, Falcone reeled backwards from the force. Still, it only took him a second to regain his composure. By then, Anastasia had positioned herself in front of her mistress, growling menacingly and daring her attacker to get even a single step closer.

Falcone aimed his gun in her direction. I could see by the hard look in his dark eyes that his instinctive reaction was to get rid of the dog—fast.

"No!" I cried. I stepped forward, my own instincts taking over.

But my interference wasn't necessary. Falcone was fast, but Kara was, too. Anastasia's protectiveness had bought her the few seconds she needed. The slender blond ducked behind the curtains, vanishing inside the fabric's thick folds.

"Is there another way out of here?" I demanded.

"Don't worry. She won't get very far," Falcone returned.

I wasn't so sure. I charged toward the burgundy-colored drapes, flailing around blindly in an attempt at grabbing hold of her before she got away.

Then let out a shriek of surprise when I felt hands grab me from behind. Before I could react, a pair of arms wrapped around my waist as tightly as one of Raffy's snakes. I gasped, feeling all the wind rush out of me.

"Since you got me into this," Kara hissed, her mouth close to my ear, "you can get me out."

She began dragging me away from the curtains. Even though I squirmed as hard as I could, trying to wriggle out of her grasp, she turned out to be much stronger than she looked.

Her iron grip only made me struggle harder. But my gasps turned to hoarse choking sounds as she crooked her arm around my neck and squeezed. I struggled desperately to catch my breath, snorting loudly and blinking hard to stop myself from seeing stars.

"You may recall that I played a prostitute who moon-lighted as an assassin in *Woman On The Brink*," she growled. "I trained with a Marine drill sergeant for six weeks!"

"Convincing movie audiences that you're tough and actually *being* tough are two different things!" I shot back in a rasping voice.

"Maybe you'll find this more convincing." I suddenly felt something cold and hard at my temple.

A wave of terror rippled through me. At the same time, I was vaguely aware of the sound of something large and heavy being dragged. Kara loosened her grip and I managed to focus on what was going on around me.

Once again, I saw stars. But this time, it was a different variety. Someone—Falcone, probably—had pulled open the curtain. Beyond the apron of the stage was an entire galaxy of stars, their eyes wide as they watched the scene that was unfolding before their eyes, their expressions reflecting a mixture of astonishment and horror. Behind them, I could see photographers and reporters from the Long Island and New York City television stations clustered together. The bright lights shining from the video cameras indicated they were getting every second of this drama on tape.

I felt Kara tense up again, tightening her grip on my throat and pushing the barrel of her gun harder against my temple.

"You all knew what a bastard Devon Barnett was!" she yelled, this time addressing her shocked audience. "How many of you was he blackmailing? We all have secrets! We've all done what we had to do to get to where we are! Deep down, do any of you really blame me for what I did? Can any of you honestly say that you haven't thought about doing the exact same thing?"

"All right, it's over," I heard a soothing voice behind me say. It was such a switch for Falcone that it took me a moment to realize who it belonged to. "Just put the gun down, Kara. You've had your say."

Instead, she pushed it more deeply into my flesh. "What's the penalty for killing two people, instead of one?" Kara demanded, her voice shrill. "How much worse could it be? If I have even a small chance of getting away, why shouldn't I take it?"

She started to shuffle toward the edge of the stage, dragging me with her. I noticed that a few of the men in the audience were rising to their feet, as if getting ready to take action.

"Let them go," Falcone instructed the audience coolly. "Nobody move. We're not going to mess with her when there's a hostage involved."

*Wait a minute!* I thought frantically. *That hostage is me!*

My mind racing, I told myself he didn't mean it. He *couldn't* mean it. He had to have a plan. Or at least he was buying himself time.

If Falcone did have a plan, I certainly didn't know what it was. With the entire room looking on, Kara began pulling me down the stairs, off to one side of the stage, one step at a time. By this point, many people had left their seats. They stood in clusters along the edge of the theater, watching with alarm as the two of us shuffled down the aisle toward the doors along the back wall.

"If I see one person try to leave," Kara called out, "or one person take out a cell phone, this nosy veterinarian is history! At this point, I've got nothing more to lose! I *mean* it!"

The room was perfectly still. No one spoke and no one moved. And then, a tiny flicker of motion caught my eye. I suspected that Kara was still focused on the crowd, watching to make sure no one tried anything. Not wanting to tip her off, I forced myself not to turn my head to get a better look. Then I noticed more movement out of the corner of my eye. . . .

All of a sudden, it was as if a giant bird swooped down from the sky, directly behind us. I realized that something was swinging in our direction, using one of the ropes I'd seen backstage. I couldn't see exactly what was happening, but I heard Kara let out a howl of surprise. I also heard deep-throated grunts that sounded vaguely familiar.

Most important, I felt Kara loosen her iron grip on me.

Without pausing to think, I wrenched myself out of her grasp, at the same time twisting my body around so that I faced her. I reached down and grabbed the gun. Holding onto it with both hands, I pointed it at her heart.

It was only then that I was able to figure out what had happened. Less than a foot away from me, Kara stood paralyzed by the pair of strong arms that gripped her—arms that belonged to Hugo Fontana. I realized he'd managed to sneak backstage, most likely before the curtain had opened and maybe even before Falcone had made his grand entrance. Then, at just the right moment, he'd swung across the theater like Erroll Flynn or some other swashbuckling movie star by grabbing onto one of the ropes hanging backstage. He'd used it to plow into Kara, feet first, surprising her and knocking the wind out of her—and giving me a chance to break away and grab her gun.

"It's *really* over now," I told her. I gripped the gun, holding my hand steady and trying to look menacing, even though I questioned whether I'd ever have the nerve to use it. Thanks to Hugo and his powerful biceps, I wouldn't be forced to find out—at least, not this time.

"Barnett deserved it!" Kara spat out her words, breathless as she twisted from side to side in a futile attempt at getting away from Hugo. He, meanwhile, looked as if he hadn't even broken a sweat.

Lieutenant Falcone looked just as calm as he stepped over to her, holding out the handcuffs once again. "For the *third* time, you're under arrest for the murder of Devon Barnett. Anything you do or say may be used against you in a court of law. You have the right— Dr. Popper, you can put that gun down. In fact, why don't you give it to me?"

"Let go of me, you stupid, macho brute!" Kara demanded through a clenched jaw.

"Yeah, right," Hugo muttered. *"In your dreams!"*

Somewhere behind me, I heard a woman sigh. "That Hugo Fontana," she cooed wistfully. "He's all man!"

I struggled to suppress a smile as I handed the gun to Falcone.

*"Jessie?* What the hell is going on here?"

I turned and saw Nick rushing down the aisle, his face tense with confusion and concern.

"I'm okay," I assured him. "Everything's fine—" And then I let out a whoop of joy. Emily had come rushing in behind him with a very squirmy and disheveled Westie in her arms.

"Jessie, look who we just found!" she exclaimed.

*"Max!"* I cried.

He immediately leaped out of her grasp and into my arms.

"Oh, my sweet little Maxie-Max!" I cried, tears of joy sliding down my cheeks. They disappeared almost immediately as my beloved Westie covered my face with kisses. I felt as if the giant clamp that had been gripping my heart for the past thirty-six hours had finally been released. "You're okay! You're *alive!"*

Emily looked puzzled. "What do you mean?" she asked, pushing her glasses up the bridge of her nose. "Why wouldn't he be?"

"How did you ever manage to find him?"

"I didn't. Lou did."

" 'Lou'?" I repeated.

Emily nodded. "Nick and I were taking a walk along the beach, back behind the house. When we got to the wildlife preserve, Lou started going nuts. At first, I figured he was excited about the birds or some of the other animals that live there. But he headed right toward that storage shed that's stuck out in the middle of nowhere. It's this funny little wooden building with a 'No Trespassing' sign on it. It's covered with weeds, and it looks like nobody's been in it for ages. Anyway, he really went crazy, barking and jumping around, and I finally opened the door to show him there was nothing inside—and there was Max, barking *his* head off!"

"Oh, Max," I cried, burying my face in his soft fur. As he covered my face with dog kisses, I murmured, "I *knew* you were all right. You *had* to be! I couldn't imagine things turning out any other way!"

I turned to Kara. "Thank you so much for leaving my dog unharmed. I'm glad that at least you had that much compassion—"

"Compassion had nothing to do with it," she replied icily. "That little beast was my last bargaining chip. I figured if you ever did manage to make a connection between Barnett's murder and me, I'd be able to use your dog's safety as leverage."

"So you were holding him hostage," I said through clenched teeth. "Of all the horrible, despicable—"

Kara let out a shrill, high-pitched laugh before the two uniformed cops on either side dragged her away, toward the door. Falcone followed a few paces behind, talking on a cell phone. Finally, he hung up, looked around, and headed back in my direction.

Hugo beat him to the punch.

"You did okay out there, Dr. Popper," he said admiringly.

"You weren't too bad yourself," I replied.

"Hey, Kara's not the only one who's trained with the pros," he replied. "Still, you got great instincts. Good thing you grabbed that gun. That crazy bitch coulda shot me!"

"I guess we make a pretty good team."

"Actually, I probably don't deserve that much credit. I was just acting out a scene from *Pulverizer 2: The Devastation*. Maybe you saw it? ..."

I shook my head apologetically.

"You should rent it sometime," he said casually. "Personally, I think it was one of my best."

"Yeah, you did good, Mr. Fontana," a male voice muttered. "You both did."

Lieutenant Falcone had sidled up to us. He stood beside Hugo, looking like his shadow—about ten minutes after high noon.

"Thanks," Hugo said, brightening.

Begrudgingly, Falcone added, "I guess I, uh, owe you an apology, Dr. Popper."

"Really?" I asked, offering up my sweetest smile. "An apology for? ..."

"Uh, for not paying attention to what you were trying to tell me," he said gruffly. "Especially since you turned out to be right about Barnett being murdered, after all."

"Apology accepted." Somehow, the words he had just said were among the sweetest in the English language—aside from "I love you" and "Your pet's going to be fine."

All of a sudden, a crowd gathered around me. People I'd never seen before were solicitously asking if I was all right, congratulating me on my bravery and my cleverness and asking if I had any plans for opening an office on the East End. My sea of admirers included some familiar faces, too—Shawn, Russell Bolger, and even Phyllis Beckwith, all the new friends and acquaintances I'd made in the Bromptons.

But I couldn't ignore the impatient tugging on the back of my shirt.

"With all the excitement, I didn't get a chance to tell you the good news," Emily cried. She pulled me a couple of feet away from the crowd. "Dr. Popper, I'm going to live in *Paris*!"

"Emily, that's great!"

"I'm so excited!" she said breathlessly. "Last night, my mom and dad and I had a long talk on the phone about what *they* think is best for me, compared to what *I* think is best for me. And they agreed that I'm old enough to start having some say in how I live my life—which means spending more time with my mom. She told me there's this really good American school in Paris, where the classes are taught in English. And it's right near her apartment, so I won't even have to take the metro." She giggled. "That's what they call the subway in Paris."

"I guess you'll be learning a lot of French," I said. "But I hope we can write to each other and keep in touch through E-mail—in English."

"Really? You want me to write to you?"

"Absolutely! And in about ten years or so, we'll have to talk about going into practice together."

"You mean it?" Emily's eyes were shining.

"You have a real way with animals," I told her. "To tell you the truth, I'd be honored."

My enthusiasm faded when I noticed Chess standing alone in the back corner of the theater with a distraught expression on his face. Zsa Zsa stood at his side, glancing up every few seconds to see why, for once, she wasn't being cradled in his arms.

"Excuse me," I told my entourage, realizing that all

the attention was starting to make me feel claustrophobic. With Max still cradled protectively in my arms, I edged my way over to him.

"Are you okay?" I asked, gently putting my hand on his arm.

"Blackmail!" Chess breathed. "Honestly, Jessie, I had *no* idea. I never would have thought Nettie was capable of such a thing! And to think that *Kara,* of all people ... I thought she was my friend!"

"I know. The whole thing is hard to believe."

"You know, I once lost a teacher who was close to me. He was also murdered. But in that case, they never found out who did it." Chess's eyes filled with tears. "I owe you a lot, Jess. I've had to live with my grief over Mr. Sylvester's death, as well as the unanswered question of who did such a terrible thing. At least now I know who's responsible for Nettie's murder."

The expression on his face told me he was sincere. Any last lingering doubts about Chess's involvement in his English teacher's death vanished. "Do you think you're going to be all right, all by yourself?" I asked him earnestly. "If you'd like, I could probably work something out and stay another day...."

"I'll be fine," Chess insisted. "Besides, I won't be alone. Someone's offered to see me home and keep me company until I'm feeling better." I realized he was looking over my shoulder at someone behind me. "Here he is, in fact. If you want to go now, we can. I really don't have the heart to stay here much longer...."

"We can leave, if you'd like," Hugo said, sweeping up behind me. "I'll drive. You're probably not feeling up to it."

Chess looked at me and shrugged. If he noticed I looked as if you could have knocked me over with a dog hair, he didn't let on.

"I guess this is good-bye, then, Jessie," he said, leaning over and kissing my cheek. "But I hope we'll keep in touch. You've done so much for me. Figuring out who killed Nettie and seeing that justice was done, helping me launch an entirely new chapter of my life as an iced tea entrepreneur..." His eyes filled with tears. "Zsa Zsa and I will miss you. Take care, okay?"

I was ready to leave, too. I scanned the room, looking for Nick, when I felt a warm hand on my shoulder.

"Hey, Jess," Shawn said. "Russell's still planning to show the documentary as soon as things quiet down. You're staying, aren't you?"

I shook my head. "I don't think so. All of a sudden, it feels like time to get going."

Shawn thrust his hands into his pockets. "Well," he said, without quite looking me in the eye, "as the old saying goes, it's been nice knowing you."

"Same here," I told him sincerely.

"I can honestly say I've never met anybody like you."

"I'm going to assume you mean that as a compliment," I teased.

"*Oh,* yeah."

"Well, if you're ever..." My eyes drifted past him. "*There's* Nick. I've been wondering where he'd gone!"

"So I guess you're on your way out?"

"Yup. We're all packed up and ready to go. By the way, thanks for letting us use the guesthouse—"

"Do me a favor?" Shawn interrupted, his voice strangely hoarse.

"Sure."

"Tell that boyfriend of yours—Nick—he's a pretty lucky guy."

I watched him walk away, meanwhile giving my Maxie-Max an extra squeeze. He sighed, then nestled against me comfortably with his chin on my shoulder. Nick came up to me, holding onto Lou's leash with one hand and slinging his free arm over my shoulder.

"I'm glad you got Max back, safe and sound," he said. In a tighter voice, he added, "And I'm glad I got *you* back, safe and sound."

"Me, too," I told him. "On both counts."

"So we're done?"

I nodded. I was suddenly longing to see Betty and Cat and Prometheus and Leilani, and to settle back into my cozy little cottage—with Nick.

"Let's get out of here," I told him, feeling more contented than I could remember having felt in a long, long time. "It's time to go home."

# About the Author

CYNTHIA BAXTER is a native of Long Island, New York. She currently resides on the North Shore, where she is at work on the next *Reigning Cats & Dogs* mystery, *Lead a Horse to Murder*, which Bantam will publish in summer 2005. Visit her on the web at www.cynthiabaxter.com.

# Need to satisfy your animal attraction?

Dear Reader,

One of the things I enjoy most about reading is being transported to a world that has always sparked my curiosity. The same holds true for writing. Both *Putting On the Dog* and the next book in the "Reigning Cats & Dogs" mystery series, *Lead a Horse to Murder*, give us the chance to live inside worlds that, from afar, always seem glamorous and filled with delicious intrigue.

*Lead a Horse to Murder* centers on Long Island's polo community. The people involved in polo are passionate about it, and their enthusiasm for the sport is contagious. Even if horses aren't part of your life, I think you'll enjoy Jessie's foray into this fascinating world as she encounters a murder victim with a long list of secrets, an eclectic and sometimes surprising group of suspects, and of course, the ever-enthralling mystery of "whodunit."

Have fun!

*Cynthia Baxter*

**Read on for an exclusive sneak peek at the next *Reigning Cats & Dogs* mystery,**

# Lead a Horse to Murder

**Coming in summer 2005 from Bantam Books . . .**

# Lead a Horse to Murder

## Cynthia Baxter

On sale summer 2005

"A horse is dangerous at both ends and uncomfortable in the middle."

—Ian Fleming

My jeans and chukka boots were splattered with mud, my neck and armpits were coated in sticky sweat, I was practically choking from the pungent smell of manure trapped in the warm, humid air. . . .

It doesn't get any better than this, I thought blissfully, closing my eyes and letting the early September sun bake a few more freckles onto my nose and cheeks. There's nothing like being around horses to make you feel grounded.

The ear-piercing sound of Max and Lou yapping their heads off snapped me out of my reverie. I turned to see what had sent my Westie and my Dalmatian, two whirling dervishes that masquerade as pets, into such a tizzy.

And then I spotted him. A few hundred yards away, a lone horseman had cantered onto one of the grassy fields that sprawled across Andrew MacKinnon's estate. The steed was a magnificent Arabian, pure white with a massive chest and long, sturdy legs. From where I stood, he looked more like something Walt Disney had conjured up than a real animal.

But it was the rider who captivated my attention. He was clearly in control of both his horse and the mallet he gripped in his hand, exhibiting a combination of power and grace that mesmerized me. His shoulders, so broad they stretched the fabric of his loose-fitting dark blue polo shirt, gave him incredible strength. I watched, fascinated, as he leaned forward to hit the ball, sending it flying across the field.

Even from a distance, I could see he was extraordinarily handsome. His strong jaw, shadowed with a coarse stubble that gave him a roguish look, was set with determination. His dark eyes blazed as they focused on the ball. Yet a few locks of thick black hair curled beneath his helmet, making him seem charmingly boyish.

Even though the sight of the accomplished horseman was enthralling, I reminded myself that it wasn't the joy of spectator sports that had brought me to Heatherfield this morning. The night before, I'd gotten a phone call from Skip Kelly, the manager of Atherton Farm, a horse farm a few miles from my home in Joshua's Hollow.

"A friend of mine's got a horse that needs seein' to," Skip had told me. "Guy name of Andrew MacKinnon. He's over in Old Brookbury, a mile or two from the Meadowlark Polo Club. Sounds like Braveheart's got a tendon problem. But Mac's usual veterinarian is in the hospital with a broken leg. Seems one of his patients wasn't too happy with the service he was getting."

"Occupational hazard," I commented.

"Mac said he wanted the best, so naturally I thought of you. I gave him your name and number, so I figured I'd let you know they might be givin' you a call."

"Thanks, Skip," I told him sincerely. That kind of praise means a lot when it comes from someone you respect. Skip has been working for Violet and Oliver Atherton since I first began making house calls with my clinic on wheels. But he's been involved with horses practically his entire life, growing up around them in Kentucky, then working on various horse farms and even a few racetracks.

"And, Jessie?" Skip's voice had grown thick. "I've known Mac for years. Braveheart is his favorite horse. In fact, from what I can see, that gelding is the only animal he's ever really cared about. Take good care of him, will you?"

"Always," I assured him, not certain whether "him" meant the man or the horse.

I took special care to check my supplies and equipment before making the drive halfway across Norfolk County early that morning, wanting to be certain I arrived fully ready to treat a highly valued horse. I had a feeling Andrew MacKinnon's estate wouldn't exactly turn out to be typical of the suburban homes at which I usually made house calls. But I was completely unprepared for what I found.

I'd gotten some sense of the world I was about to enter as I maneuvered my twenty-six-foot van along Turkey Hollow Road. This entire section of Long Island's North Shore was like something out of an F. Scott Fitzgerald novel. In fact, Fitzgerald had written *The Great Gatsby* while living just a few miles from this very spot during the 1920s, immortalizing the flamboyant and often decadent lifestyle of the area's ridiculously well-to-do inhabitants.

In the early 1900s, some of the wealthiest individuals in the nation constructed palaces on Long Island, earning the North Shore the nickname "the Gold Coast." Frank W. Woolworth, the five-and-dime-store magnate, had built a fantasy estate, Winfield, that shamelessly embraced his passion for the Egyptian occult. Teddy Roosevelt's rustic house in Oyster Bay, Sagamore Hill, became the Summer White House during his two terms as president.

J. P. Morgan, William K. Vanderbilt II, and other wealthy industrialists who were the Donald Trumps of their time, except with better hair, also built dream houses along the shores of Long Island Sound. Even the characters in the movie *Sabrina*—Audrey Hepburn and Humphrey Bogart in the original version, Julia Ormond and Harrison Ford in the remake—lived on Long Island's Gold Coast.

While the MacKinnon homestead, Heatherfield, wasn't on quite as grand a scale, it was definitely of the same ilk. Yet most people who drove along Turkey Hollow Road would never even have noticed its entrance, much less guessed that a sprawling estate lay beyond.

As I drove through the black wrought-iron gate flanked by two stone pillars, I wondered if I'd made a wrong turn. From the looks of things, I could easily have entered the grounds of a country club or even wandered into the Meadowlark Polo Club. But I'd noticed the name Heatherfield etched on a gold plaque set into one of the pillars.

"This must be da place," I muttered, glancing over at Max, my tailless Westie, and Lou, my one-eyed Dalmatian, who shared the seat beside me. Even they looked impressed. Or maybe it was just confronting the endless stretches of green grass that had them spellbound. I could almost hear Lou thinking, "Somewhere out there, there's a tennis ball with my name on it." Max, I suspected, was imagining all the squirrels and rabbits who were just waiting to be chased.

I had to keep my jaw from dropping to the ground as I drove along a paved road that curved through an amazing amount of land—especially given the outrageous property values on Long Island. Some of it was dense wooded areas, towering oaks and lush maples, their leaves already taking on a reddish tinge that warned that summer would soon be replaced by fall. But most of Andrew MacKinnon's estate had been divided into large, grassy paddocks. Most were empty, while a few housed a horse or two. In the distance, I noticed a brown-shingled building that looked like a stable. But on the phone, Heatherfield's barn manager had told me the stable was yellow, so I kept going.

After driving nearly a quarter of a mile, I spotted an elegant stone house. Or mansion, depending on how much of a stickler for using the correct word you happen to be. Given the fact that it had enough rooms to pass for a small hotel, I suppose anyone who referred to it as a house would be guilty of understatement.

I finally spotted the stable. The one-story yellow building was U-shaped, a main section with two wings. I suspected it had originally been built as a carriage house.

Speaking of carriages, I noticed that so many vehicles were parked on the property that it looked like a used-car lot. A very *fancy* used-car lot. A Cadillac and a Mercedes sat on the paved semicircle in front of the house. Another half dozen lined the long driveway. Most were parked at haphazard angles, as if they'd been discarded by drivers who didn't consider them important enough to deal with properly. I spotted two SUVs, a Hummer, and a dilapidated station wagon. There were also two horse trailers, at the moment not hitched up to anything.

But the shining star of the makeshift parking lot was definitely the red Porsche, so low to the ground that the driver could probably feel pebbles on his butt. I wasn't sure, but I thought it bore an awfully close resemblance to a snazzy model I'd recently seen in a car magazine. Nick had shown it to me while we were browsing in a bookstore, marveling over its six-figure price tag. That was considerably more than the cost of the van that served as my clinic on wheels, and the Porsche didn't even come equipped with its own X-ray machine and autoclave.

I pulled my van up and opened the door. Predictably, Max and Lou shot out, acting as if they'd just been released from two years under house arrest. They spotted a tough-looking barn cat and immediately set off in his direction, hellbent on checking out any living, breathing creature with the audacity to venture within a quarter of a mile of where they were.

I headed toward the stable, lugging a big black bag with most of the supplies and equipment I expected I'd need to treat Andrew MacKinnon's prized horse. As soon as I entered, I sensed someone else's presence. Actually, it wasn't as much an eerie, Stephen King kind of feeling as a distinctive smell. Cigarette smoke, stinging my nostrils and making my throat raw.

"Hello?" I called. "Anyone here?"

For a few seconds, nothing. And then a man stepped out of the shadows, planting himself a foot away from my face. His creepy entrance made me wonder if he'd orchestrated the whole scene for my benefit. Not a very promising beginning, I thought with annoyance.

He stood roughly six feet tall, lanky, with knobby fingers that curled around his cigarette butt. His fashion statement was Aging Cowboy: jeans and a T-shirt, worn underneath a red plaid flannel shirt. His face looked as scorched as the Arizona desert. Despite the reptilian skin, I estimated his age in the mid-forties. And he positively reeked of cigarette smoke, as if part of his daily grooming routine was dousing himself in Eau de Marlboro.

He studied me coldly, his eyes a pale shade of hazel that contributed to his lizard-like appearance. "Who the hell are you?" he rasped.

"I'm Dr. Popper," I replied. "I got a call this morning about a horse that needs tending to."

"So you're the vet."

"That's right."

He continued to stare at me, as if he was waiting for me to say, "Naw, only kidding!" Instead, I stared right back.

"C'mon," he finally said, turning and heading in the opposite direction. "I'll take you to Braveheart."

"And you are...?" I asked, counteracting his rudeness by being overly polite.

"Johnny Ray Cousins," he mumbled. "Mr. Mac's barn manager. I'm the one who called you."

I drew my breath in sharply when my charming host stopped in front of a stall labeled "Braveheart." Andrew MacKinnon's gelding truly was a beautiful animal. The sleek Arabian was a deep shade of chestnut with a flowing mane, intelligent brown eyes, and a proud demeanor.

"How're you doing, boy?" I asked him in a soft voice, stroking his nose gently. And then, even though I could feel Johnny Ray's eyes burning into me, I leaned forward and nuzzled Braveheart's nose with mine. It was something I'd seen horses do with each other, so I'd adopted it as my own greeting whenever I was getting acquainted with one I was about to treat. When in Rome, I figured.

I turned back to MacKinnon's barn manager. "What's going on?"

"Looks like his tendon pulled up a little bit sore, over there on his right back leg," Johnny Ray mumbled. "Happened yesterday. Braveheart probably took a bad step, maybe hit a divot. 'Course, he coulda been struck with a polo mallet, but I didn't see it happen. Anyway, he stumbled, but Scott, the guy who was riding him, picked up on his reins and kept playing. He told me afterward he felt a funny step, but Braveheart here is a real trooper. He went on to score the winning goal.

"After the game, we took a look at it. It was a little bit filled and there was some heat. I iced it and gave him a couple of Bute, but a few hours later, it was still sore to the touch. I talked to Mr. Mac about it this morning, and he insisted we give you a call."

Johnny Ray shot me a hostile look, no doubt making doubly sure I understood that it had been his boss's idea to summon me—not his.

"Let me take a look." I set down my bag, ready to work.

Tendon damage is a frequent occurrence in polo ponies, ranging from a simple strain or sprain to a fracture that could put the animal out of commission completely. Injuries of this sort are especially common among higher-goal polo ponies, horses that play the game at its most demanding level. Polo requires them to run fast, then make short stops and turns—moves horses simply aren't built for. Getting tired out on the polo field is another factor, along with irregularities like stones or divots, clumps of earth pulled from the ground by galloping hooves or mallets. Still, polo fields are generally well-maintained, and tendon injuries usually turn out to be mild.

"Okay, boy," I said in a soothing voice. "I'm going to take a look at you. We just want to figure out what happened."

Braveheart stood still in his stall, patiently allowing me to examine his right back leg. From what I could see, Johnny Ray's analysis was correct. It looked like the gelding's injury was a simple soft-tissue wound—no open wound, no major bone fractures. Still, I couldn't be sure.

"I'm going to do an ultrasound," I said. I opened the carrying case that contained the portable unit. The nifty device consisted of two pieces, an extension probe and a processing computer with a monitor, yet weighed barely two pounds.

As I ran the extension probe over Braveheart's bruised

tendon, I studied the screen. Sure enough, the image clearly showed a pocket of excess fluid within the superficial digital flexor tendon at the back of the horse's right leg, an indication of minor structural damage.

"Okay, I see a weak spot in the tendon," I told Johnny Ray, pointing to the screen. "I'm going to put Braveheart on an anti-inflammatory, Naquasone, for a few days. Give him half a pill in the morning and half at night. I'd also like you to keep up with the icing or cold-hosing during the day, but put on a mud poultice overnight to draw out the heat and get the swelling down. During the day, keep the bandage on and keep him in the stall. I'll reevaluate his condition in a few days."

"Now I suppose you want to be paid," Johnny Ray said gruffly. "I'll take you inside to meet Mr. Mac."

He tossed his cigarette butt onto the ground, snuffing it out halfheartedly with the sole of his boot—not the best idea around wooden stables and the horses that were confined in them. I immediately opened my mouth to protest, then reconsidered. Andrew MacKinnon's barn manager and I hadn't exactly started out on the best terms, even though I suspected the reason was simply that I had the nerve to be female, a veterinarian, or a combination of both. Since he and I were going to be working together over the next week or two to ensure that Braveheart made a complete recovery, the last thing I wanted was to create any more bad feelings.

As we walked toward the house, I caught another glimpse of the elegant horseman I'd noticed earlier. "Who is that?" I asked.

Johnny Ray glanced at the field. "Oh, him. Eduardo Garcia. One of the Argies. He plays on Mr. Mac's team."

"Argies?" I repeated, confused.

"Argentines."

"Oh. I don't know much about polo, but it looks like he's really good."

"One of the best. Sometimes I come out here just to stand by the fence and watch him stick-and-balling. That means practicing. Y'know, hitting the ball around with the mallet."

He turned so that his back was to the polo player, scowling. "Those Argies have a helluva life. I wonder if them spics even know how good they got it."

It was a good thing Lou and Max chose that moment to come bounding toward me, panting with glee as if thinking, "Isn't this place the greatest?" Their arrival provided just the distraction I needed to keep myself from giving Johnny Ray Cousins a piece of my mind.

Not that he hung around long enough to continue our fascinating conversation. He strode toward Andrew MacKinnon's mansion, walking fast enough to stay at least six feet ahead of me.

Fine with me, I thought, trailing after him. Even being treated like a second-class citizen by a man with a chip on his shoulder the size of that Hummer over there is better than attempting to converse with him.

I took a moment to appreciate the fact that, thanks to my career choice, I spent more time in the presence of animals than people. And to reflect on how ironic it was that animals, not people, were referred to as "dumb."

I followed Johnny Ray across a brick patio at the back of the house, but stopped short when we reached a pair of elegant French doors. Peering through the glass, I saw they led into the mansion's center hallway. I had a feeling that wet paws and damp noses wouldn't be particularly welcome inside, even though this was an estate on which animals were clearly a priority.

"Stay!" I instructed Max and Lou. They looked at me in disbelief, clearly indignant that they were being left behind. Reluctantly, Lou lowered his butt to the ground. Max, meanwhile, stared at me hard, as if thinking, "How *could* you?"

As Johnny Ray and I stepped into the elegant hallway with its smooth marble floor, a young woman appeared in one of the doorways and rushed over to us.

"Hey, Inez," he mumbled. "Mr. Mac around? Or has he gone into the city already?"

"Meester Mac is in his study," the pretty young woman answered, lowering her head shyly. "I will tell him you wish to speak with him."

"No need." The barn manager barged right past her—in the process, tracking dirt across what looked to me like a very expensive Oriental carpet.

"Meester Johnny!" she called. "*Per favor*, Meester Mac does not like—"

Johnny Ray ignored her, striding down the hallway. "Damn Port-o Rican," he muttered.

Horrified, I glanced at Inez, hoping she hadn't heard. If she had, she showed no sign of it. Instead, she kept her head down, making a point of not looking at either of us.

I trailed after Mr. Congeniality, hoping Andrew MacKinnon wouldn't hold his bad manners against me. Then again, I thought, Johnny Ray works for him, so chances are he already knows what a Neanderthal he's dealing with.

I decided to forget about Johnny Ray. Instead, I concentrated on my surroundings. My original assessment of Heatherfield, that it wasn't exactly in the same league as the thousands of ranch houses and split-levels that covered Long Island, hardly did the place justice. As if the size alone weren't enough to knock your socks off, it was outfitted with elegant furniture, paintings, and accessories that made it clear that this part of Long Island still deserved to be labeled the Gold Coast.

Mr. MacKinnon's study drove that point home. As I stepped inside, I was enveloped by a room that had the restful feeling of a hideaway, created by the skillful integration of rich textures and intense colors. The walls were painted the same dark green as a billiard table, with dark wooden wainscoting all around. The deep, masculine tones were echoed in the couches and chairs, upholstered in brown leather the color of creamy milk chocolate. I placed my hand on the back of a chair and found it was as thick as a saddle but as soft to the touch as a kitten's ear.

The walls were covered with pictures, hung at every possible height. Whether they were big or small, framed photographs or signed lithographs or huge oil paintings with gilt frames, they all featured horses. And most of those horses had polo players on their backs, their expressions grim and determined as they leaned forward to whack the ball.

I couldn't help being curious about the man who had amassed enough wealth to buy himself such an impressive playground. I pictured Andrew MacKinnon as a suave James Bond type, wearing a burgundy-colored silk bathrobe and carrying a brandy snifter. Then I shifted to a slick Mississippi riverboat gambler with a waxed mustache and a string tie and the distinctive gleam of greed in his dark, beady eyes. Next, I tried on a dignified Anthony Hopkins type in a gray morning coat, smoking a cigar and reading the *Financial Times*.

None of the personas I'd invented for Andrew MacKinnon came even close to the paunchy man in his early sixties who stood up as we barged in unannounced. Instead of the shiny, slicked back hair of my riverboat gambler, he hardly had any hair left at all. What there was of it was almost completely gray, barely hinting at the fact that a decade or two earlier, he had been a redhead. He had a ruddy complexion to match, along with pale blue eyes rimmed with nearly colorless lashes.

And forget the string tie. Ditto for the silk bathrobe. This particular captain of industry was dressed in wrinkled khaki pants that sagged in the back and a loose-fitting lemon yellow golf shirt marred by a small but distinct stain. His abundant stomach protruded like Santa Claus's, stretching the knit fabric more than I suspected its designer had ever intended.

It certainly wasn't easy picturing him riding the princely Braveheart, galloping across a polo field with a team of muscular young horsemen like the one I'd seen stick-and-balling earlier that morning. In fact, I had to remind myself that this undistinguished businessman actually owned the castlelike estate that surrounded us: the mansion, the cars and trucks and trailers, the stables, the polo fields, and of course the magnificent horses I knew were worth plenty.

"How's my horse?" he demanded, dropping the *Wall Street Journal* he'd been reading onto his chair.

"You'll have to ask Dr. Pepper," Johnny Ray replied sullenly.

I could feel my blood starting to boil. I've been called Dr. Pepper more times than I can count. But being mistaken for a rival to Coke and Pepsi was usually accidental. The sneer on Johnny Ray's face made it clear that his slip was completely intentional—and that he wanted me to know it.

I decided to ignore him. "Mr. MacKinnon, I'm Dr. Popper," I said, stepping forward and shaking his hand. "I checked out Braveheart, and it looks as if he's suffered some minor structural damage on the back of his right leg—"

The sound of screaming, accompanied by quick footsteps across the marble floor, stopped me mid-sentence.

"What the hell...?" Andrew MacKinnon muttered, stepping out into the hallway.

"Meester Mac! Meester Mac!" Inez cried. "Come quickly! It's Eduardo! He fell off his horse—and he's not moving!"

# BANTAM MYSTERY COLLECTION

\_\_\_\_57204-0 **KILLER PANCAKE** Davidson • • • • • • • • • • • • • • • • • **$7.50**

\_\_\_\_56859-0 **A FAR AND DEADLY CRY** Holbrook • • • • • • • • • **$5.99**

\_\_\_\_57235-0 **MURDER AT MONTICELLO** Brown • • • • • • • • • **$7.50**

\_\_\_\_58059-0 **CREATURE DISCOMFORTS** Conant • • • • • • • • • **$6.99**

\_\_\_\_29684-1 **FEMMES FATAL** Cannell • • • • • • • • • • • • • • • **$6.99**

\_\_\_\_58140-6 **A CLUE FOR THE PUZZLE LADY** Hall • • • • • • • • **$6.99**

\_\_\_\_57192-3 **BREAKHEART HILL** Cook • • • • • • • • • • • • • • **$6.50**

\_\_\_\_56020-4 **THE LESSON OF HER DEATH** Deaver • • • • • • • **$7.99**

\_\_\_\_56239-8 **REST IN PIECES** Brown • • • • • • • • • • • • • • **$7.50**

\_\_\_\_57456-6 **A MONSTROUS REGIMENT OF WOMEN** King • • • • • • **$6.99**

\_\_\_\_57458-2 **WITH CHILD** King • • • • • • • • • • • • • • • • • **$6.99**

\_\_\_\_57251-2 **PLAYING FOR THE ASHES** George • • • • • • • • • **$7.99**

\_\_\_\_57173-7 **UNDER THE BEETLE'S CELLAR** Walker • • • • • • **$6.50**

\_\_\_\_58172-4 **BURIED BONES** Haines • • • • • • • • • • • • • • **$6.50**

\_\_\_\_57205-9 **THE MUSIC OF WHAT HAPPENS** Straley • • • • • • • **$5.99**

\_\_\_\_57477-9 **DEATH AT SANDRINGHAM HOUSE** Benison • • • • • • • **$6.50**

\_\_\_\_56969-4 **THE KILLING OF MONDAY BROWN** Prowell • • • • • **$5.99**

\_\_\_\_57533-3 **REVISION OF JUSTICE** Wilson • • • • • • • • • • **$6.99**

\_\_\_\_57579-1 **SIMEON'S BRIDE** Taylor • • • • • • • • • • • • • **$5.99**

\_\_\_\_58225-9 **REPAIR TO HER GRAVE** Graves • • • • • • • • • • **$6.99**

---

Please enclose check or money order only, no cash or CODs. Shipping & handling costs: $5.50 U.S. mail, $7.50 UPS. New York and Tennessee residents must remit applicable sales tax. Canadian residents must remit applicable GST and provincial taxes. Please allow 4 – 6 weeks for delivery. All orders are subject to availability. This offer subject to change without notice. Please call 1–800–726–0600 for further information.

| Bantam Dell Publishing Group, Inc. | |
|---|---|
| Attn: Customer Service | TOTAL AMT $_____ |
| 400 Hahn Road | SHIPPING & HANDLING $_____ |
| Westminster, MD  21157 | SALES TAX (NY, TN) $_____ |
| | TOTAL ENCLOSED $_____ |

Name _____

Address _____

City/State/Zip _____

Daytime Phone ( _____ ) _____